feral

HOLLY SCHINDLER

An Imprint of HarperCollinsPublishers

HarperTeen is an imprint of HarperCollins Publishers.

Library of Congress Cataloging-in-Publication Data
Schindler, Holly.
    Feral / Holly Schindler.
        pages   cm
    Summary: "After Claire Cain survives a brutal attack in
Chicago, she and her father move to Peculiar, Missouri, where
she discovers the body of a high-school girl and realizes that she
cannot escape her past"— Provided by publisher.
    ISBN 978-0-06-222020-2 (hardback)
    [1. Investigative journalists—Fiction.   2. Reporters and
reporting—Fiction.   3. High schools—Fiction.   4. Schools—
Fiction.   5. Post-traumatic stress disorder—Fiction.   6. Single-
parent families—Fiction.   7. Cats—Fiction.   8. Mystery and
detective stories.]   I. Title.
PZ7.S34634Fer   2014   2014001884
[Fic]—dc23   CIP
                                                  AC

Typography by Kate Engbring
14 15 16 17 18   LP/RRDH   10 9 8 7 6 5 4 3 2 1
❖
First Edition

The mind is its own place, and in it self
Can make a Heav'n of Hell, a Hell of Heav'n.
—John Milton, *Paradise Lost*

feral

Serena

In the rugged, underbrush-riddled rural town of Peculiar, Missouri, at the beginning of a January sleet storm, and beneath the dimming orange hues of dusk, a body lay half out of the window that led to the high school basement.

The body belonged—or really, the body had *once* belonged—to Serena Sims, a B average junior who loved her best friend, the sound of the rain, writing for the school paper, and her mother's chocolate mayonnaise cake with homemade icing, a family specialty.

She'd been a sweet girl with old-fashioned, simple dreams—to stop biting her nails to the quick (for *good* this time); to be kissed, just once, by a boy who *truly* loved her; to get out of Peculiar; to get a job as a *real* journalist at a national paper. But there was nothing simple about her current state. Or maybe, it was the simplest state of all: a past tense. Dead.

More than an hour after her heart had stopped, she found herself staring at the blue tips of her fingers, the wavy ends of her long brown hair, the dusty top of an old wooden desk, and the fractured tile of the janitors' office. It was all she *could* stare at, with her stomach still smashed against the windowsill, her head and arms dangling down toward the basement floor. Outside the building, a pair of hands clutched her hips to keep her from falling back inside, tumbling to a heap on the office floor for the fourth time.

The hands gripped her tighter, fingers digging deeper into her cold flesh just beneath her school uniform blouse, which was still damp with the frantic sweat that had poured from her in her final moments. She listened to a deep intake of air and a grunt as the hands jerked her farther outside, so that only the section of her body from the armpits up remained inside the high school. The hands lightened as the figure outside paused, trying to work up the strength for another heave, while Serena's legs lay on the bitterly cold, snowy earth, stretching straight out from the ground-level window. With one more violent tug, the hands yanked the last of her body out, banging her nose against the sill so hard that it broke.

Serena tried to yelp, but her mouth, purple and swollen, only flopped, like a door with a busted hinge. No warm, copper-flavored blood trickled from a nostril to her lip, even though her nose had just been snapped, as easily as a drinking straw.

She lay motionless in the freezing rain.

Seventeen and dead: it was the worst kind of vulnerable. She felt utterly exposed, as though she were standing naked in the center of the school auditorium while the faculty and students filed by her, one at a time, taking a good look at all her flaws: the stretch marks on her sides and the cellulite dimples on her backside that had never gone away, even after she'd lost her fifty extra pounds in middle school.

The shock of knowing the day would end this way would have given her a full-on asthma attack—the kind that had made her lungs feel like they were packed with concrete—as she'd sat at the breakfast table that morning with her Cheerios. Or had she eaten oatmeal? It seemed so strange, now, not to have paid attention to the details of her next-to-last meal. But the sadness of her overlooked last breakfast was nothing compared to the fear-laden reality that Serena had no way to protect herself, not anymore. An hour and a half ago, she could still fight. Kick and scream. Now, her fight was gone.

Her killer could do whatever he wanted with her. But Serena hadn't yet stopped feeling. No—she felt *more*, now that she was dead. Everything was intense, to the point of being painful. Her ears, only an inch away from the ground, acted like amplifiers, magnifying the sleet-rain mix as it pummeled the earth with the sound of a whole package of BBs spilling out across a linoleum floor. Her skin was as sensitive as a sunburn, and the frozen droplets were sharp—like the pointed tips of manicure scissors stabbing her over and over.

How would it feel when her killer disposed of her? What if he dismembered her? Surely she would stop experiencing the pain of the world around her—but when? Would she have to endure the whack of an ax? Would she have to listen to the screech of a saw blade whizzing against her bones? Good God—what if he tried to light her on fire? How hot did a fire have to be to cremate a person? Would she have to bear the agony of it, with no ability to even scream?

First, though, her killer needed rest; dragging her up and out a window had exhausted him. He collapsed on the frozen ground beside her, huffing and coughing and struggling to catch his breath the same way Serena's classmates all huffed when the lone gym teacher herded them over to the gravel track on the side of the school and tested them on the mile run. His breath shuddered, and Serena was left to only imagine his exhalations coming out in clouds, as her face was pressed against the ground, her eyes taking in the close-up of a frozen, brown blade of dead grass.

Serena wondered why he was just sitting there, leaving her body in full view of anyone braving the weather. Sure, school had been closed a full two hours early because of the ice, the principal's voice insisting over the intercom that all after-school activities be rescheduled, urging everyone to head straight home, no hanging out in the parking lot, no gossiping in the hallway. (Serena, though, had stayed, determined to keep her own after-school appointment.) By now, the school had a long-empty feel to it, like it did over Christmas or summer break. And the gray, cloudy day was slowly leaning toward night, leaving the two of them partially hidden by a darkening sky. And the sprawling old farmlands that butted up against the ancient school meant that the closest home was more than a mile away. But wasn't he still being awfully brazen, letting her lie there, completely exposed? Most importantly, *where was he planning on taking her?*

In the distance, a lonely siren sliced through the evening quiet.

Her killer gasped as he scrambled to his feet. He grabbed her ankles, and jerked her body with each of his own steps, yanking her across the small field between the back of the school and the nearby woods.

He grunted as he pulled her, forcing Serena's jaw open, as wide as its hinges would allow. With the next heave, her teeth ripped at the dead grass like a lawn mower needing its blade sharpened. Her mouth filled with dead bugs and last autumn's Weed and Feed and decayed animal droppings.

Her tongue, she found, also felt just as alive as it ever had, and she wished she could gag against the rancid flavors that exploded through her mouth. With the next backward jerk, the tip of her broken nose pinged against the sharp jagged peak of a rock. *Where is that rigor mortis, anyway?* Serena wondered, unable to cringe against the pain dancing across her face.

As her killer dragged her body, her open cardigan flopped; her shirt inched up, bunching around her breasts, and her skirt flipped up, making her white panties the only thing that separated her backside from the late January air. Her necklace, which had already been tortured and weakened during the struggle she'd had with her killer, caught on the thick, gnarled remnants of an old tree root.

She was overwhelmed by the urge to protect the old cameo she'd worn on a short chain to take attention away from the scar on the base of her throat. God, she hated that scar—the spot where doctors had sliced into her in the midst of her worst asthma attack ever—an attack that had shortly followed a hobo spider bite. The poison from the bite and the lack of air and the fear had made her crazed, wild, unlike herself—and she'd fought the doctors so that they'd had no other choice but to intubate her, force some air down her swollen throat.

Funny to think it, now—a little over three years ago, the ER doctors had all talked about how strong she was. Earlier today, she'd been overtaken as quickly as an utter weakling.

How was that possible?

The chain on her necklace snapped; the gold cameo that had once belonged to her grandmother lay glittering in a smear of dying late afternoon sunlight. But her killer just kept tugging at her ankles, oblivious to the little scrap of a clue he'd left behind.

Right then, though, Serena didn't care about clues. She didn't care about revenge. She cared about the rocks and ice that scraped her face, making her feel like the earth was peeling her. She cared about the way her flesh still felt as though it belonged to her. She cared about her killer's plans.

The siren circled closer; her killer tried to increase his pace, succeeding only in losing his grip on her ankles. He growled angrily, then flipped her over, letting her face turn toward the sky. Allowing the needle-sharp rain to hit her eyes, some drops dancing against the whites and bouncing off again. Others stabbed her pupils, her irises, like stickpins on a bulletin board.

He gripped one arm and one leg and tugged again. His foot caught on the edge of her black Peculiar High cardigan, ripping the pocket. He staggered, swearing under his breath. But he quickly steadied himself, tightened his grip, and grunted as he heaved her another step.

A new terror grabbed hold of Serena. *The woods*, she thought, the words like venom in her skull. *He's going to dump me in the woods.*

Overgrown thickets dotted the entirety of Peculiar, Missouri. Undeveloped, unpaved patches, filled with underbrush, stood out behind the town's only gas station and to the side of the Peculiar cemetery; they lined the highways leading into and out of the city limits. Bigger wooded patches separated individual homes; rather than city-style neighborhoods with cul-de-sacs and swimming pools, Peculiar was filled instead with white two-story farmhouses, separated by the acres that had been passed down among generations. While some residents continued to use sections of their land as grazing fields, most had let old farmland grow wild and unruly.

The small patch of woods just behind Peculiar High offered the students a haven in which to disappear between classes to smoke. A shortcut, when students were afraid of being beaten by the morning's first tardy bell. The patch behind the school was a hangout, an escape, a secret-special place for everyone at Peculiar High. Except for Serena.

Just looking at a dense patch of trees had drawn goose bumps across her skin, ever since she'd gotten lost, barely four years old, in the woods behind her house. She'd spent a cold, lonely night there, her tiny body surrounded by the yellow eyes of the wild creatures she swore peered out at her from the underbrush. She'd thought, then, that she was going to die. That no one would ever find her.

Fortunately, rescue had come, shortly after daybreak the next morning. But in the years following, Serena had never quite been able to quit feeling like beasts with untamed hunger and claws and fangs were peering out from between the branches, just waiting for her to return. To get close enough to grab.

At the beginning of eighth grade, Becca, Serena's brand-shiny-new best friend, lost her bird dog, Jasper. Poor heartbroken Becca had called Jasper's name as the days bled into weeks, then months, her desperate tones clanging like an unanswered dinner bell against the sky. Early the next spring, Becca's older brother, Rhine, returned from a hike, Jasper's collar dangling from his fingers. A skull, Serena remembered. He'd found the skull in the woods behind their own farmhouse. Jasper'd been killed by some wild Missouri creature—a bobcat, maybe. A wolf. Killed and dismembered by the very creatures Serena had sworn she'd seen peering out at her, when she was four, from in between the overgrown branches. And carried off in pieces by other animals.

Now, Serena predicted, her killer would drag her through the small patch of trees behind the school, across the dirt road, and into the thick, wild woods behind the closest farmhouse. He would dump her there, in a patch of land that had been allowed to grow wild for nearly two generations, and let nature take its course.

"Come on," her killer grumbled, tugging on her limbs like an impatient dog owner with a leash.

The menacing trees arced dangerously, heavy with ice. The same brutal rain that pierced her eyes froze the instant it touched the leafless winter branches, completely encasing the oaks and the maples, turning them into Popsicles.

Unable to turn away, to shut her eyes, Serena stared at the limbs that loomed above her, slicing shiny black patterns through the late afternoon sky—until the limbs began to crack.

She listened, horrified, as the cracks grew louder, closer together; a branch sheathed in a thick skin of ice snapped, rattling like a tambourine as it tumbled. It struck another limb on its way down, instantly breaking it free, too. Her killer dropped her leg and arm, and darted out of the way, just as one of the limbs crashed and collapsed against Serena's chest, smashing her into the ice-coated ground.

The ice pellets had hurt. Breaking her nose had hurt. But that had been nothing—a mere paper cut—compared to the pain that exploded through her body now. The force with which the limb struck cracked her ribs, nearly split her heart in two, and turned drops of congealed blood into glass-sharp shards that ricocheted through her veins.

"Not here," her killer moaned. "Too close to the shortcut. Someone could still find you here."

He tried to push the limb off Serena, his sneakers slipping out from underneath him, his knees thunking against the earth. He whimpered, frantic, his eyes as wide as moons.

He grabbed Serena's hand and pulled hard enough to actually dislocate her shoulder, wrench it out of its socket. Had her muscle tissue and skin not still been attached, her arm would have flown off, like a plastic Barbie doll arm. She felt herself wailing inside against the pain—the kind of hurt that would have sent her straight into shock, if her heart had still been beating. He tried again, a look of sheer desperation smeared across his face. But Serena was going nowhere. She was trapped. And the rain was falling harder. The world was getting slicker.

When her killer angrily threw her hand down, it landed bent at the elbow in a gruesome angle, her palm facing up. The ballpoint letters she'd doodled above her life line in journalism class earlier that morning proclaimed, "CHEATING."

He growled and kicked her side. "Dumb bitch," he howled, clearly cursing her for being stuck, being dead, being leftovers that were too big to get tossed down a garbage disposal, chewed up, and swallowed by the drain.

A few smaller branches jingled, scraping against the ground as her killer tossed them across her legs. He bent down and turned her face so that it wasn't staring straight up, right at him, but to the side. It was an odd gesture, Serena caught herself thinking—it almost showed a slice of humanity, of guilt, of remorse. He dragged another fallen limb toward her, tossing it over her head and smashing her cheek into the sharp ice.

The siren edged out from the distance again, growing louder, ever closer.

He bolted up and ran away, his footsteps growing distant. He fell twice—two thuds, one heavier than the other. Serena imagined the lighter thud was his knee striking the ground, the heavier whack his hip. She ached to run away, too. But she could only lie beneath the limb, listening to the click of freezing rain dance on bark. Listening to the trees crack, threatening to snap beneath the growing weight of ice.

The worst part was that her eyes were still open. And there were still too many spaces between the branches that her killer had laid across her head. She'd see the next horrible thing that would come for her.

Her ears perked against the sharp, rhythmic clatter of freezing rain hitting the trees as she waited for it—a growl, a sniff, the crunch of footsteps. Here she was, as she'd long feared, in the woods, with all those wild animals, all those yellow eyes, all that danger.

She couldn't rid herself of the feeling that more hurt was still to come.

ONE

The university library table feels clammy under Claire's forearms as she waits, staring at the stacks of journals she's pulled from the shelves. She drums her fingers in time to the evening rain that taps gently against the window behind her. It's been raining for so long that everything—even the interior of the library—feels sort of limp and damp. Everything except for Claire's growing annoyance. That feels hard and dry and hot, like a driveway in August.

"Where are you?" she asks aloud, frowning at her phone. She's been asking it for twenty minutes, long enough for the pouring rain to ease to barely a trickle. Now, when she asks, her voice almost pleads.

The world feels funny, lopsided without Rachelle—Claire's sidekick, as her father is always calling her. The two girls are so close, their edges have blurred; it's nearly impossible to tell anymore where one leaves and the other picks up.

When Claire's phone finally vibrates, she lurches to get a look at the screen. Grnded ☹ Rachelle's texted.

Claire shakes her head. It's the senior—the one Rachelle has been sneaking around to see because her dad isn't wild about him.

Claire texts back, Do I need 2 save u again?

And she smiles, waiting for the response. Thinking of the way she had, in fact, just saved Rachelle from the freshman who had transferred to their school at the start of the second semester. He was a scrawny thing who bounced on the balls of his feet when he walked and wore a uniform two sizes too big—attempts, Claire suspected, to seem taller and more muscular than he really was.

Claire and Rachelle actually tried to be nice to him, the first day he'd shoved his winter coat into the locker next to Rachelle's—they'd introduced themselves, but he'd rolled his eyes. "Losers," he'd muttered before pushing past them, into the hallway traffic.

They would have ignored him after that, but he started watching Rachelle spin her lock every day between classes. Memorizing the stops.

"Go ahead and watch," Rachelle began to tell him. "It's not like I have anything to steal. You have a burning desire to get your hands on my civics textbook?"

He always tried to pretend it wasn't true, that he wasn't watching her at all. His peach-fuzz mustache wiggled nervously across his top lip as he passed a pencil box from his backpack to the top shelf of his locker and back again, like he was never quite sure of the best place to put it.

"Really?" Rachelle finally asked one day. "A pencil box? With comic-book-looking lightning bolts? What is this, the second grade?"

He flinched, his cheeks turning horrible shades of mortified.

Claire and Rachelle were not usually that type of girl—as pretty as they both were, they could have wielded their looks as weapons. But they weren't teasers, not bullies; they weren't into high school torture.

Still, though, the boy had been rude, and they felt justified, somehow, in tormenting him a little. The day Rachelle succeeded in turning his face red, she and Claire walked down the hall, arms linked at the elbows, in a flurry of laughter.

But on a snowy day late in February, the drug dogs came, parading the hallways, sniffing locker doors while everybody was in class. Slobbering over the faint but distinct aroma of a secret that a student was trying to hide.

When they barked, a lock was snipped free, and the cops found it: a pencil box covered in lightning bolts. Filled with white crystal meth. Packaged into neat little plastic jewelry bags. Maybe twenty of them. Intent to distribute. Only, they found it in Rachelle's locker.

Claire immediately swooped in to the rescue, as fearless as a superhero in a satin cape. Told their principal exactly what happened.

The boy disappeared as an investigation was launched. His desk sat empty in every one of his classes.

That might have been enough for anyone else, but not Claire Cain, high school winner of the Robert F. Kennedy Journalism Award—already, for an article she wrote her freshman year. She was destined for great things, every one of her teachers swore, and now, in her sophomore year, the journalism instructor eagerly approved when Claire wanted to write a piece on the incident with Rachelle—which appeared in the school's weekly paper and online. The story was picked up, too, by local news stations. Claire was on TV. And Rachelle was vindicated. Claire put a stop to any gossip surrounding Rachelle; it was her superpower. Awe trailed behind her in the hallways, because stopping gossip was a power all her classmates wished they had.

Claire and Rachelle went to the movies to celebrate their victory. They bought the extra-large tub of popcorn, and Claire whispered to Rachelle about her freshman "boyfriend," because they were that kind of close—Claire could tease Rachelle about anything, even something as serious as being framed for selling drugs, and know that Rachelle would never take it the wrong way.

Remembering it all, Claire keeps staring at her phone, until the response finally comes: Next time.

She laughs, because it's true. She'd rescue Rachelle anytime.

She decides to go ahead and photocopy the scholarly articles she's already found in the general science journals that she knows so well, thanks to her father, the professor. She hugs the journals to her chest as she skips downstairs. She hogs the best copier on the first floor, not that the librarian minds. She is Claire Cain, after all, daughter of Dr. Cain, who received the Romer Prize back when he was still a predoctoral student; he is destined, everyone swears, for the Romer-Simpson Medal, the highest award given by the Society of Vertebrate Paleontology. They are alike that way, both of them racking up awards; they are both the academic type, and when Claire wins her Pulitzer, she just might thank the libraries at the University of Chicago.

Claire chuckles at her silly fantasy as she shrugs on her coat and hoists her backpack onto her shoulder. Waves good-bye to the library assistant, a worn-thin college girl who smiles and waves back. Now that she's snagged a few sources, she and Rachelle can brainstorm ideas for their paper later. The assignment isn't due for two weeks, anyway.

She heads straight for the door.

And thinks nothing of the feet she hears on the tile, a student or a prof or a TA leaving right behind her. She even holds the door for him—the low "Thank you" says it's a man. She thinks nothing of the others, either, clustered around the base of the front steps, smoking.

Claire spends so much time at the university where her father teaches that it just seems natural for people to gather this way. College kids always linger around stairs and buildings, clustered, talking, laughing. Claire passes them, still feeling light about her *texts with Rachelle:* Next time. *Rachelle loves her, needs her, as best friends do. Claire is needed. Knowing it makes the night air smell clean.*

The group out in front of the library lets go of the stairs and follows. But even this doesn't seem odd. Not yet.

The night feels far too cold to belong to early spring; Claire's breath is visible—just as visible as the fog that's building, laying like a gauzy curtain over items no more than five feet away. Her knees are going pink beneath her uniform skirt. Her nose tingles.

The rain that had been dancing against the library windows is picking up again, but each drop feels sharp against her face. The rain is freezing. It's already early April, but winter seems to be insisting on one last good storm. The sidewalk beneath her is turning the kind of slippery that almost makes her feel as though the soles of her shoes have wheels.

Claire hates the unsteady sensation.

They laugh, the group behind her, as Claire walks down one street, rounds another corner. They shout big talk, egging each other on.

Claire's phone buzzes. Dad stuck in lab, *her dad's assistant has texted.* Rain 2 freeze. Go home now. Take R with u.

Claire slips her phone back in her pocket. When her father has his grad assistants text her, it means he's completely unreachable. He's locked the door of his lab and won't be out again until he's ready to die of starvation.

He doesn't know that Rachelle never showed. He doesn't know Claire's alone.

Sure, she could go back to the library and call campus security, and she could have someone walk her, now that night is falling, to the science building. She could hang out with the grad assistant until her dad is ready to go home. But she suspects that by the time Dr. Cain finally pries himself out from his lab, the streets will be too slick for driving or walking. They'll be stuck trying to figure out a way to sleep on his office furniture.

Claire would rather sleep in her own bed.

She passes block after block. The group behind her trails by only about six feet. Their shouts are getting louder. The ground slicker. Cars are sliding. Claire needs to get home, because soon cars will start skating right off the road, careening onto sidewalks, where they can knock her flat. In fact, she figures she'd be smart to go ahead and get away from the main thoroughfares, all those slippery roads and cars with no traction, not on ice.

She turns down an alley—in Chicago, alleys are as common as trees, after all; they've never been the sinister shadow to her that they might have been had she grown up in another city. Passing by an empty garage, though, the laughter behind her starts to have a different ring to it. Sharper. A little mean.

"Schoolgirl!" she hears one of them say, and the skin tightens on the back of her neck. Hairs turn into porcupine needles. She's still in her uniform. They're talking about her.

She eyes the pavement, where she can see their long shadows swagger beneath the streetlights. She can smell their cigarettes. And something else—something metallic—the vague smell of danger.

Her heart thumps hard enough that each beat makes her fingertips tingle.

Now she does want to turn around, run back to the library. But the alley is so narrow, she'll send herself straight into the arms of the group behind her if she pivots on her heel. The only thing she can do is walk straight ahead, searching for an escape to open up in front of her.

Her eyes bounce about, between nearby streetlights and distant tree limbs that are all beginning to sparkle in the moonlight that peeks through the clouds, now that the ice is growing thicker. Icicles are beginning to form, dangling like stalactites from the edges of buildings. Freezing fog is accompanying the drizzle; when it lands, it sticks to all the cold surfaces. Before it settles, though, it creeps along the sidewalks like a cat on the hunt.

It seems as though the entirety of Chicago has rushed inside, all of them shaking their heads in disbelief. "An ice storm in April," they're all saying, as they thunk saucepans onto stoves, heating milk for hot cocoa. "Who'd have ever thought?"

Claire speeds up, flexing the thighs that feel tight beneath the wintry chill. The footsteps behind her thunder in a way that makes Claire believe not only that the boys are trailing her, but that they know she's now aware of being followed.

They can smell her fear.

She keeps eyeing the shadows that the streetlights draw long and lean at her side, noting that one of the figures behind her bobs up and down, obviously walking on the balls of his feet. A skinny kid, she can tell from the tiny shadows his arms make beneath the hiked-up sleeves of a coat. Skinnier than the rest. But wearing enormous clothes.

"You like ratting us out?" one of them shouts. "You like ruining everything?"

At this point, she starts to run.

So do they.

Claire screams, her arms pumping. But they're so fast. She looks over her shoulder once, and she sees them, faceless silhouettes surrounded by the fog. They will catch her, she thinks, if she doesn't get out of this alley. Her only available option is a parking lot, behind an apartment building.

The lot is vacant, even though there are lights on in a few apartments. There are signs here: Closed for Repaving. A job delayed by the storm. No work crews, not a single car, not a single person to help her.

Claire runs across the cracked pavement, because even though the cars aren't parked here tonight, the edge of the apartment building is so close. She will race around the side of the building and be on a street with lights and the apartment building's front entrance and she will run inside and the boys will not hurt her, not there, not when she screams in the lobby, making the worker at the front desk reach immediately for the phone: 911.

But when she gets there, to the far edge that she expects to sprint around, finding her escape, there is no out. The brick building butts up against the next, without so much as an inch between.

Claire pants, staring at her dead end. Still determined to save herself, she pulls her phone from her pocket and she dials 911.

Before it connects, she can hear the feet behind her grow louder, closer. She knows that everyone inside the apartment building has closed their windows against the storm, and with their TVs on or their phones pressed against their heads or their earbuds in, they will never hear her, no matter how loud she screams.

The phone finally begins to ring. But the feet are so close. There will not be time to tell the operator where she is.

Claire tries, in that moment, to steel herself against what is about to come.

She is frozen; she is caught. She stares at the seam between the two buildings, barricaded. She does nothing, just stands, and as seconds pulse, she knows there is no preparing herself for what they are about to do to her. There is no predicting it. She can guess, but her mind doesn't work like theirs do; her imagination cannot come up with ways to hurt another human being.

"911, what is the nature of your emergency?" the operator finally asks.

"Please, God," Claire whispers. "Don't let me die."

The boys are here. They surround her; they kick her to the ground.

Claire's phone flies from her hand, strikes the brick wall, shatters.

Shouts explode as her parka is shredded, the downy lining hitting the air like the insides of a feather pillow.

She fights back, but there are so many hands, all of them punching and scratching and tearing her clothes. She claws against the pavement, trying to hoist herself onto her knees, trying to crawl. But they hit her, knocking her down. Her skin splits open. It doesn't even feel as though she's being cut—she feels as though their hands and their nails and their anger, it's all tearing her, like she's an old bedsheet being torn into rags. They rip an inch-thick section of hair from her scalp. They shred her shirt, until it hangs in tatters. Until she's in nothing more than her bra.

One of them picks up a metal trash can. He dumps it, scattering slimy, foul-smelling refuse across her body. He slams the can against the back of her head, turning her skull into a gong. They laugh, take turns picking it up and throwing it on her over and over. The force of every blow turns so hard, so vicious, she doesn't even know what they're hitting her with anymore. She only knows that it can't be their fists. And all the way through it, they're shouting with glee, enjoying it.

She presses her palm against the pavement, tries once more to pull herself forward. Even now, she's trying to crawl away. But they strike her arm—the pain is so agonizing, she's not sure if they hit her with something blunt—some sort of club—or something sharp, like an ax. She screams as their laughter and their cheers explode again.

The same pain hits her legs. They're crushing her, snapping her bones. She swears she can hear them break.

The fingers of her right hand crunch when the boys begin to take turns stomping on them. Smashing them beneath their boots like cockroaches.

Hands reach under her skirt. Fingers curl under the waistband of her underwear. And she knows. Beaten and broken and dizzy from so much pain and the loss of so much blood, she knows what's coming. There's no stopping it.

The siren sounds like another cheer, at first. She's still whimpering soft pleas to stop when the police jump from the car. And then, in that moment before the truly horrendous can happen, the hands disappear from under her skirt. Feet stomp about her—the gang and the police both. She listens to shouts and other bodies being thrown to the ground and cuffs rattling.

The girl cop is the one who comes to Claire's side. She has blond hair in a ponytail, Claire notices—it's yellow like sweet corn. But she's got kind of a thick body—like there are lots of hours at the gym under her uniform. She's got that look of a woman who knows how to kick any guy who wants to rough her up to the curb. There's a soft roundness about her face when she looks at Claire. She's worried.

The girl cop tries to push Claire's hair from her clammy face. But her long hair is tangled in the blood on her chest and her *arms. Her hair is smashed into her bleeding sores, and when the girl cop tries to push her hair away, she winds up tugging the strands from her wounds, and it's like being sliced into all over again. Claire wails as the girl cop picks up her hand, and as other voices shout about calling the paramedics.*

The scream startles the girl cop, and she reaches up to grab hold of a small gold charm hanging from her own neck. She slips it off her head, puts the necklace in Claire's hand. "It's St. Jude," she whispers. The patron saint of the Chicago police force—and lost causes.

She frowns as she wraps her fingers around Claire's wrist. Searching for a pulse. She shakes her head; her charm has failed. "It's too late for you," she tells Claire. "You're dead."

Claire jerked herself awake, her skin coated with slimy, panicked sweat. That wasn't really what the girl cop told her, that night: *you're dead.* The rest of the dream—she'd actually been having the same nightmare for months—was always brutally accurate, in horrifying, blinding clarity. But Claire never dreamed that the cop said what she really had, last April: "You'll be okay. Hang on, hang on. Stay with me." Instead, she always snapped awake after hearing the cop tell her the same thing Claire herself had thought, drenched in pain and blood. *It's too late for you. You're dead.*

She'd said it to herself as she'd hung in the sky, above her broken, bleeding body. Wasn't that what people always said happened during near-death experiences? They hung in the air, staring down at themselves. Claire had stared at herself, too, looking more like a pile of ground beef than Claire Cain, and she'd sighed at the blood—all that blood—and she'd waited for the sense of peace everyone also swore they felt. But there was no peace—not then, and not now, really.

It had been nine months since the beating. Her bones had healed. Every time she took a shower, she swore her skin looked like a patchwork quilt, pink scars crisscrossing through her creamy skin in every direction. But no one had to know about the scars, not if Claire didn't want them to. So she wouldn't be wearing many camisoles or sundresses. What did that matter, in the grand scheme of things?

The beating was behind her. Yes, it had been terrifying—yes, it had hurt. Yes, she had nearly died. But it was over. The truth was out: a gang had recruited a kid in a private school—a new student, who didn't fit in—to sell their drugs to his fellow students, those kids whose pockets were perpetually heavy with their weekly allowance. And Claire had ratted, to save her wrongly accused friend. And she'd paid a price.

It was over, as far as Claire was concerned. The boys who had hurt her had been arrested. Here in January—the beginning of a brand-new year—she was walking beautifully. She had excelled in her physical therapy, just as she had excelled at any course she'd ever taken. She moved now without so much as a hitch in her step. She was still

Claire Cain, still destined for great things.

The dream, though, had not yet gotten the hint. The dream had not yet learned that the beating was behind her. It had taunted her relentlessly, especially the past week, as she and her father had given away their houseplants and had their mail forwarded and their cable subscription suspended.

Now, on their way to their new home, the damp winter chill seeped into the interior of her dad's '72 Gremlin (the same car he'd been driving since his grad school days), making Claire's bones throb. She brought her feet up into her seat, almost as if she thought hugging her legs could make the ache go away.

"You all right?" Dr. Cain (it was all anyone had ever called Claire's dad—*Dr. Cain*—always with a stiff nod of respect, if not always intimacy) asked. He placed his hand on her forehead, as though checking for a fever, without lifting his eyes from the road.

"Just the weird weather," Claire said, shuddering, hoping that it was enough to excuse the clammy skin she was sure her father'd found beneath his fingertips. She hadn't told him about the recurring dream. Not once in the past nine months. It was just a dream, after all. What damage could a dream do to anyone who wasn't a character in a *Nightmare on Elm Street* installment?

The afternoon was growing late enough—and the skies stormy enough—that Claire's father flipped on the headlights.

In the stream of light that flowed out from the front of the car, a green highway sign popped into view: Welcome to Peculiar—Where the "odds" are with you.

She snorted a quiet chuckle as they passed the city limits sign, the side of her fist stinging against the cold, dewy glass of the passenger window. She pressed her face against the path she'd just cleared in the window's steam, only to find herself staring, in the twilight, at a kind of gnarled rural landscape. Leafless winter trees. Twisting, narrow farm roads. Empty grazing fields. Miles of barbed wire. A lonely, enormous, ancient building looming on a distant hill.

Already, Peculiar looked nothing like Chicago. No skyscrapers, no university libraries, no alleys. Instead—cows. Grain silos.

She smiled until her phone buzzed. Freeing it from her pocket, Claire found another text from Rachelle. A simple *Good luck* ☺ that made Claire's stomach drop, like her father had just driven too fast over a dip in the road.

At times, it had seemed Rachelle had been the one in the beating. Because *she* was different. She'd spoken in a quiet voice around Claire. She'd moved daintily through Claire's bedroom during her visits, like a ballerina on pointe. She didn't jab her elbow into Claire's ribs, teasing her. Not anymore. For nine months, she'd treated Claire like a tangled-up mass of black electrical cords, all knotted in a way that would make anyone who saw it wonder if it could ever get straightened out again.

But there was nothing to straighten out.

Claire shook her head, replied, *Thanks*, just to get Rachelle off her back, and tossed her cell in the glove compartment. She still missed Rachelle—the *old* Rachelle. She'd hated the way this new girl had shown up in her house to eye Claire as though she were still in need of a rescue.

Claire sighed, grateful she had agreed to spend her father's sabbatical semester in Peculiar, Missouri. It would be a sabbatical for her, too. Time away from Rachelle's overly polite, quiet visits. A chance to get a full, deep breath.

Her father checked the temperature gauge he'd installed in the Gremlin, and cleared his throat at the same time he pushed his glasses into his face.

"What is it?" Claire asked, frowning against his nervous tic.

"Temp's dropping awfully fast," Dr. Cain said. "And that rain's not letting up anytime soon—see those clouds?" He pointed at the tall puffs. "Cumulonimbus. Lots more rain in those."

"We're here, though," Claire said, pointing over her shoulder. "We made it. We're safe now. Don't tell me you missed the sign. That thing was priceless. 'Where the "odds"—' "

"We might be in for trouble tonight," her dad interrupted, leaning into the steering wheel and tilting his head toward the sky.

"What kind of trouble?" she asked, fear instantly spilling in waves down her arms. She'd had enough of trouble.

"Dad?" she prodded. "What kind of—" She grabbed the door handle, and clenched the muscles in her stomach to stay upright as Dr. Cain shot the Gremlin off the snaking road and veered into the gravel parking lot of a gas station, a slice of civilization in the overgrown brush that was attempting to pass as a town.

Claire squinted through the rain-drenched windshield, wondering how her dad could have actually seen the store from the road. Instead of glowing neon signs, the tiny wooden building was dotted with old-fashioned enameled signs for Nehi soda and Oxydol soap flakes and Burma-Shave, each marred with giant chips and dark brown rust spots.

Dr. Cain steered beneath the tin roof that sheltered the gas pumps. He cut the Gremlin's engine beside a relic with a glass Mobiloil globe for a head.

"You really think that thing could still work?" Claire teased, pointing at the rusty old pump. "You *really* think this place could actually still be open?"

She leaned forward to look around her father, through his driver-side window, at the empty parking lot. A sign whose skin had grown completely orange with rust hung crookedly across the top of the rustic building: 'Bout Out General Store.

"A general store?" she asked playfully. "Like in the Old West? They have saloons here, too?" She laughed.

Her father turned to her with a smile branching out beneath his beard. Laughter spilled from his lips, too, like a bass line from a radio. He looked so goofy, with his open mouth and his eyes swollen to the size of shooter marbles behind the strong lenses of his glasses that Claire's laughter intensified. She held her stomach again—this time to feel the vibrations. God—laughter. Like the face of a long-lost friend.

On the opposite side of the lot, a pickup truck missing its tailgate—and its passenger door—and its front bumper— rumbled across the gravel. Mud-tinted water droplets hit the air as the front tire splashed through a puddle. Brakes squealed; the bed actually slipped forward on the truck's frame, bumping into the cab as the driver finally managed a crooked stop just barely within reach of another gas pump's hose.

The door of the pickup let loose a vulture's squawk as a white-haired man in a plaid shirt and a padded vest stepped out. The face he turned toward the Cains' Gremlin was covered in skin as yellowed and brittled by time as the pages of a Civil War–era diary.

He frowned at them, grabbed the closest nozzle, and shoved it into his gas tank.

"Looks like it works," her dad said.

"I stand corrected," Claire replied quietly, her smile slowly disappearing.

Dr. Cain pointed skyward. "Perfect conditions for this to turn into quite the ice storm," he explained.

Claire's face flushed; her mouth drooped. The attack had happened during an ice storm, too. Suddenly, the rain against the tin roof above them sounded like hundreds of fingers drumming impatiently against a table. Just like Claire had drummed her fingers on the university library table while she'd waited for Rachelle.

She cringed, her ears filling with the awful, vicious laughter that had erupted in the Chicago alley.

"Claire?" Dr. Cain asked, leaning forward. "You got peaked all of a sudden. I just realized—if this turns out to be an ice storm, it will be the first one since—"

She waved her hand, swallowed hard, shook her head. She offered a weak smile. "Peculiar," she said, "where the odds are with me," and winked, wanting her father to laugh again. Wanting to be that father and daughter they'd been just a moment ago, no baggage, no history.

But her father's eyes were concerned.

"You think it's going to get icy, huh?" she pressed.

Turning his face back toward the windshield, he said, "It looks like it's already starting to freeze to the trees—overpasses are probably a mess, too. You fill us up; I'm going to stock up on supplies."

"Supplies?"

"Just some canned goods. Hopefully, a place like this'll have a few kerosene lamps—"

"Wait," she said, a frown smashing her eyebrows together.

"How bad do you really think this is going to be?"

"It'll be fine. Just taking some precautions," he said lightly, as he threw his door open.

Claire nodded and hoisted herself from the passenger seat, watching as her father raised his corduroy coat collar over his ears, shoved his hands in his pockets, and raced through the rain toward the front of the general store.

"Precautions," she grumbled, shutting the door to the Gremlin. She had the sinking feeling that her father knew more than he was actually letting on.

TWO

Claire slipped the nozzle into the Gremlin's gas tank just as a white Honda whipped into the lot, careening past the old pickup truck and steering straight toward the entrance of the general store. The passenger door popped while the car was still moving.

"Wait, Becca," the driver barked, hitting the brakes too roughly. The car skidded. The gravel offered some traction, though—a way for the tires to find a grip now that ice was beginning to firmly encase the entirety of Peculiar. The car came to a stop less than five feet from the Gremlin.

A girl in a long blond ponytail, a tight long-sleeved T-shirt, and yoga pants far too thin for the weather emerged from the passenger side while a boy pulled himself out from behind the wheel.

"Wait," the boy called again insistently. He took a step from his car, leaving the engine running and the driver door open.

Catching sight of Claire, he paused. The pause turned into an outright stare, as the boy began to absorb Claire in the same way she'd been taking in the surroundings of Peculiar just a moment ago.

Claire straightened her shoulders beneath his gaze—not a particularly easy task under the weight of her naval trench coat, which stretched all the way down to her ankles and was made of a treated, weatherproof wool so heavy that the coat had a tendency to make her shoulders ache. Claire had often told her father it was a bit like wearing a house with gold buttons.

She listened to the gas pour into the Gremlin's tank as she eyed the boy standing before her—surely, come tomorrow morning, a new classmate. For now, a stranger. A beautiful stranger, with the chiseled face of a TV star and blond hair gelled perfectly from a side part over the top of his head. He wore jeans so dark and crisp they almost seemed dressy, along with a dark turtleneck underneath a black wool coat—nothing at all like the puffy ski coats or the jackets emblazoned with team logos the boys wore back in Chicago.

The rustle of paper in the wind made Claire turn her eyes toward the still-running Honda. The inside of the car was a mess—the dash littered with what appeared to be school papers and fast-food wrappers skittering about in the winter breeze, the floorboards covered with soda cans and wadded clumps of who knew what. An old sneaker was wedged beneath the driver seat. The car had the appearance of having been messy for so long that the clutter seemed like it was part of the car—like it had grown wild right out of the upholstery.

The girl in the yoga pants realized what had caught the boy's attention, and eyed Claire with curiosity, too.

Claire quickly noticed that this girl—Becca—was the kind of beautiful that could inspire both lust and jealousy that bordered on hatred. And she carried herself with an assurance that warned she wielded her beauty like a sharpened sculptor's tool.

Cocky, Claire thought, zeroing in on the way the girl held herself.

She felt silly, suddenly, inside the secondhand military surplus coat and the mailman shoes—literally, big black mailman shoes, with extra insole supports for her damaged feet—that she'd purchased online. She'd told herself back in Chicago that the shoes and the coat looked funky. She had doubts now, as the girl's beautiful face narrowed into a frown.

The old man at the other gas pump let out a rough, chest-rattling cough, making them all quit their staring contest. The boy dipped back into the Honda to kill the engine, and Becca pointed at the front window of the general store.

"Look, Owen. Chas is inside," Becca announced.

"Serena and Chas *broke up*," Owen said, slamming the driver door shut. His tone was weary—tired, it seemed, of having to reiterate a well-known fact. "Why would he have any idea where she is?"

"Don't do that," Becca pleaded, as her cocky exterior melted. "Please don't," she said again, suddenly a girl sick of being pushed aside. "Don't act like I'm being a nag. Not about this."

The air around the two grew heavy. The kind of heavy that found couples who'd been together too long, who had too much history and too many disappointments between them to ever be happy with each other again.

Becca raised her hands and made a pushing motion, as though she felt the heaviness, too, and wanted to knock it aside. "Look," she said, "I can see him inside. And we're already here. Come on. Let's—" But she swallowed the last of her sentence as her sneaker slid across a particularly thick patch of ice and she started to fall.

Owen lunged forward to catch her, his fingers gripping her like a football.

Becca righted herself and pried his hands free, wearing a look on her face that Claire interpreted as surprise—surprise at being caught, maybe even surprise that Owen was actually there to catch her.

"He's inside," Becca repeated. "I see him. I'm *asking* him where Serena is. He'll know. Trust me. Breakups lead to makeups."

Owen sighed, shook his head, and followed her up the front steps of 'Bout Out.

Claire blinked into the bitter wind, watching the screen door swallow the two of them.

Behind Claire, wind attacked a metal trash can. The sound of it crashing against the ground made her jump, swivel with her arms up, ready to defend herself.

Empty, the can rolled in the wind.

"Stupid," she muttered to herself. "Get a grip, Cain."

She shoved her hands deep into her pockets, as her dirty-blond, wavy hair clung to the large lapels. She tucked her chin down, trying to use the coat to hide her cheeks from the vicious slap of wind. She closed her eyes, listening to the gusts torture loose pieces in the corrugated tin roof above the gas pumps and hiss through the nearby naked trees. In between the hisses, she heard a soft, pleading meow.

Claire opened her eyes. The meow hit her ears again, begging for attention. She turned as a sweet yellow tabby emerged from behind the pump, curling his tail into a question mark.

Her heart ached at the sight of the lonely cat out in the cold. "Hey, sweets," Claire cooed, squatting so that her coat made a deep blue puddle on the gravel around her.

"Ain't no house cat," the man at the side of the truck called out to her.

Claire bristled. "If you know he's a stray," she mumbled,

"then maybe you should take him home."

She extended her fingers toward the tabby, cooing for him to come closer, the stretch pulling against her scarred skin and making her back ache.

"That ain't no kitty that curls up with you at night and starts kneadin' your stomach like dough," he went on, his voice saturated with a Midwest twang. In between the twang, Claire detected the singsong notes of warning: *You'll be sorry* . . .

"Come here," Claire called sweetly as the wind picked up, sending a cold mist flying across her lips. She wiggled her fingers as she tried desperately to ignore the man. "Come here, babe."

"That ain't no cute little thing that licks dribbled drops a' cream off the kitchen floor," the man shouted, loud enough this time for his voice to bounce against the tin roof.

Claire glanced at the front of the general store, wishing her father would hurry up.

"Ain't no different than a sewer rat," the man cautioned her, nodding once at the cat.

When Claire didn't respond, he continued, "That's a barn cat. Which is just a nice way a' sayin' feral." He pointed at the yellow tabby, then dragged his finger toward the cats perched beneath an awning at the far end of the lot, rubbing at their whiskers and ears with their front paws—then toward the cats crouched under the front porch of the old general store, lying close together for warmth, front legs curled contentedly under their bodies—and finally toward the cats taking shelter under a half-rotten canoe that leaned up against the side of the building, one of them with his back leg pointed skyward as he cleaned himself.

"Same as any old squirrel or chipmunk or possum," he said. "Wild creatures, all of 'em," he added, smiling sickly. "Live under the store, most of 'em.

"Maxine feeds 'em all the food that's hit their expiration date," the man babbled, not caring how his unwanted conversation was making Claire begin to sweat, even in the frigid temperatures. "Got a soft spot for anything ain't got a home a' its own. How her place got its name, you know. 'Cause when she first inherited the place from her folks, she was givin' so much a' her good stuff away to folks needin' a hand—'on credit,' she said, but ain't no credit with Maxine, it's give. So by the time a payin' customer came in lookin' for milk or crackers or Band-Aids, she'd have to tell 'em, 'Honey, you better buy it quick, 'cause we're *'bout out*.'"

He opened his mouth, showing off black spots of missing teeth as he wheezed into a laugh. And started to walk toward her.

Claire stood, turning her hands into fists. Her heart beat so hard, her jaw ached. She ran her eyes across the parking lot as she searched for a rock or a piece of glass she could use, if the man were to grab her.

"Dad?" she called.

"'Course," the old man continued, "Maxine had to quit the credit business with any human—if she wanted to stay in business. But the cats? She never did quit givin' to the cats. Now, though—" He paused to point again, this time at the cats hissing from a nearby bush—then at the cats huddled together on a stone wall behind the church across the street, tails flicking behind them. He shook his head. "Whole thing's gotten a little outta hand."

"Dad!" Claire screamed, loud enough to make the back of her throat burn.

The fear in her voice made the man's head jut back with shock, his mouth droop sadly. "I didn't mean—"

Claire swiveled, racing straight for the store entrance.

"Hey! You left—" the man shouted, pointing toward the nozzle still in her gas tank.

But Claire couldn't stop. Her legs pumped, racing all the way up the soft wooden steps that bowed beneath the weight of her body. On the front porch of 'Bout Out, beneath the corrugated tin ceiling, she pressed against the Nehi sign on the screen door and glanced over her shoulder just in time to see the old man squat down to pick a quarter up off the pavement.

He flicked it into the air, caught it, smacked it against the back of his left hand. He lifted his right hand, and brought his face down to get a closer look at the coin. "Whaddaya know?" he called out to Claire. "It's *tails*!" He pointed once more at the strays huddling for warmth, let out another wheezy cackle, and turned toward his truck.

He was just coming after the quarter, Claire, she told herself. *He wasn't coming after you.*

She stepped inside the old general store, wiping her sweaty forehead and trying not to pant so hard.

THREE

"Why would Serena be walking anywhere in this mess?" Becca asked.

Still breathing deeply, silently asking her heart to slow down, Claire glanced up to find the two she'd encountered in the parking lot now standing at the checkout counter, along with another boy and a wide-eyed, petite cashier whose sweet, small-featured face looked barely old enough to belong to someone in high school. The voluptuous curves on her small frame, though, told a different story—and could have belonged to someone old enough to actually own the general store.

"I don't know—she doesn't have a car," the second boy said, leaning against a counter made of gray barn wood. "What else would she do but walk? I don't really care what she does. It's not my business anymore."

"Not your—*damn* it, Chas," Becca shouted, "this is a *person*. I don't care if she is your ex. She's also a *person* in a *storm*."

Chas took a step to the side, craning his neck to look over the cashier's shoulder, through the front window. As he straightened up, Claire could see he was far beefier than lanky Owen. And far sloppier in appearance, with unruly dark hair and baggy black pants that fell behind the tongues of high-top sneakers and a letterman's jacket with cracked black leather sleeves. Claire couldn't understand how he could bear to keep his coat on inside; she was already sticky with sweat inside her own trench. The general store was apparently heated by a wood stove that almost made the small room feel *too* hot— like a dry sauna.

"Is it really getting that bad out there?" Chas asked.

"*Yes*," Becca asserted.

"Why does something bad have to have happened to her?" Owen asked. "Why are you so freaked out?"

Still rooted into her spot by the entrance, Claire slipped a hand inside her coat to clutch her suddenly queasy stomach. She didn't completely understand the conversation, but she didn't like it, either.

"Because she didn't come home after school, because I can't get her on her cell, because this is totally unlike her,"

Becca claimed. "You *sure* you haven't talked to her?" she asked Chas.

"Been here all afternoon with Ruthie," he said, nodding once at the cashier, then pointing at the string of Dr Pepper cans lined up on the counter in front of her, as though it were evidence of how long he'd been in the general store.

When Becca turned an accusatory glare her way, Ruthie swiveled her eyes down, bit her thumbnail hard enough to chip the bright purple polish. She hugged her chest, forcing her cleavage to bulge out of the top of her tight sweater.

"All afternoon," Becca repeated. "Figures," she snarled.

Ruthie squirmed, shooting a pleading, doe-eyed look at Chas. When Chas caught her eye, he only shrugged, shook his head. Rolled his eyes.

So that's what this is about, Claire thought. Her father had homeschooled her throughout the rest of her sophomore year and the first semester of her junior year. It had apparently been just enough time to forget about this—the high school drama, the petty jealousies, the boyfriend-stealing, the gossip. Claire felt her wave of nausea subside.

"She's not at her house—even though she said she had to get to work on a story for the paper," Becca told Chas.

"The paper," Chas grumbled, rolling his eyes at Owen in a way that made him chuckle.

"So *what*?" Becca snapped. "She likes to write for the

paper." When the two boys continued to snicker nastily, Becca thundered, "Might be good if you two goons cared about something other than football and getting laid."

Ruthie squirmed, shooting her pleading eyes at Chas again. *Tell her*, she mouthed. Chas frowned and avoided Ruthie's eyes, pretending not to understand.

"Look, he doesn't know, okay, Beck?" Owen groaned.

"Serena has to be *somewhere*," Becca barked.

Owen sighed so loudly, the sigh was itself almost a word—a *Jeez*. "Let's go home," he said. "Please. This is crazy."

"And do what?" Becca screamed. "I can't just—"

"She'll turn up."

"She'll turn *up*? Owen, she's not some old set of keys, for God's sake."

"Do you see how bad it's getting out here?"

"If you had *answered* your *phone*, we could have started looking two hours ago. You owe me—"

"Becca, I already told you I was helping my mom carry groceries out of the car. It's not like I sit around doing nothing but staring at my phone. Besides, neither one of us can help anyone if we're in a ditch," Owen told her.

"Put your tire chains on," Becca said.

"That's sheer ice," Owen argued, pointing through the front window. "You want to die out there?"

"I should call my dad," Becca blurted.

"Whoa, Beck," Owen said, reaching out to snatch her

phone. "The sheriff? Are you serious?"

"Yes. I'm *serious*. This is so not like her."

"Fine," Owen grumbled. "Look. I'll take you by Serena's house again. See if her mom's heard anything. She's probably there right now. Probably just had to stop by the library before she went home or something."

"Dr. Sanders told everyone to go *straight home*," Becca argued.

"Yeah, and if Serena needed background info to work on a story, do you think a warning from Sanders could keep her from it?"

Becca slumped, her posture saying Owen was right.

"We're stopping by Serena's house *first*," Becca said, just as a door banged open in the back of the store.

"Ruthie!" a woman's voice thundered. "We got honest-to-goodness paying customers in here. Gossiping with your friends is fine when we don't have any shoppers, but I told you to knock it off now that the storm's closing in. We got to help people get ready."

A heavyset woman appeared with a metal cart loaded with boxes and shovels and bags of ice melt and kitty litter. "Come on, now," she urged, grunting as she reached forward to start unloading the supplies, "you got to help me get some of this out on display."

"Yes, Mom," Ruthie said quietly.

"Here, let me," Owen said, trying to relieve Ruthie's

mother of a large cardboard box of canned goods. But the box teetered in his arms.

"Watch out there, pretty boy," Chas said. "Oughtta leave that to the athlete."

"Whatever," Owen grunted, refusing to give up the box, even as he struggled for balance. "I'm on the football team, too."

But Chas reached out and plucked the box right out of Owen's arms. In Chas's hands, it seemed more like a box of matches than a box of heavy canned food. "What's with you?" he teased. "You act like you just ran about a hundred wind sprints. Your mom's groceries must've worn you *out*. You're even wussier than usual."

"Are you two done with your pissing contest now?" Becca interrupted, tugging on Owen's sleeve. "Can we go look?"

"I'm staying to help," Chas announced, wrapping his large hand around a couple of shovels and carrying them toward a display space by the door.

"Fine," Becca snapped. "Come on, Owen," she insisted, stomping right past Claire in a flurry.

"Claire!" Dr. Cain shouted, popping into her face. "Got some things for us. Maxine, the owner," he said, pointing at Ruthie's mother, "took me into the storeroom to give me the pick of her canned goods. Been a run on them in the last couple of hours."

Claire accepted her father's plastic shopping basket.

Cradling it in her arms, she peered inside to find canned meat, as well as Spam and chili, pork and beans, and vegetable soup.

"That kerosene lamp!" Dr. Cain shouted, pointing. Ruthie turned to pluck it from a shelf behind the counter. "Looks like the last one, too," he said, happily handing over his credit card. He hummed as Ruthie punched the buttons on a brass cash register that looked like it had been freed from the shelves of an antique store, not noticing the embarrassed flush that was still painted across her cheeks following her exchange with Becca.

Dr. Cain pushed Claire outside quickly, announcing, "It's getting dangerous. I think we can make it before the storm turns the roads completely impassable, if we hurry."

They'd moved so fast, in fact, that the couple who'd clustered about the counter were still piling into the white Honda as Claire and her father stepped through the door of 'Bout Out.

In her haste to get in the car, Becca knocked an empty NOS energy drink can into the lot. Her voice carried across the still parking lot as she urged, "Come on. Hurry."

Car doors slammed; the Honda revved and skidded across the lot.

Claire swore that the girl in the passenger seat was eyeing her through the windshield as the car swerved around the gas pumps toward the exit. Suddenly feeling self-conscious, Claire reached for the lapels of her coat, cinching them together.

"What's that all about?" Dr. Cain wondered, as the car screeched onto the street.

"Looking for their friend," Claire assured him. "Trying to beat the worst of the storm."

They walked down the front steps, into the lot, grocery sacks propped on their hips. Claire flicked her free hand, once, as though to toss off the way her fingers were inexplicably trembling.

She pulled the nozzle from the Gremlin's tank and lowered herself into the passenger seat, her paper bag crackling loudly into her lap.

As her father pulled out from the lot, steering toward the farmhouse they'd rented, Claire glanced through her window just in time to see a yellow tabby cat step into the gray sheet of icy rain and completely disappear.

FOUR

Claire felt as though night had taken her up in its fist by the time her father's car snaked its way off the main road and down a gravel path. A dark charcoal sky loomed just beyond the windshield; bare tree limbs etched an even deeper, darker black into the horizon, like a kind of deathly-looking fringe. Claire's ears filled with the sounds of deep-voiced dogs barking. Gravel popping against the tires. And the icy rain, of course. It pattered against the windshield, the roof, ceaselessly.

An animal skittered straight into the headlights, making Dr. Cain hit the brake. Claire wrapped her hand around the door handle, eyes wide, as the car slid in a diagonal line, the front tires skidding to a stop an inch from the ditch.

The cat they'd nearly hit pulled himself out of his defensive crouch and raced toward the opposite side of the road.

Dr. Cain let out a shuddery sigh as Claire shook her head at the creature who raced off into the darkness. *Just how many cats are there around here?* she wondered. Her eyes darted about, taking in the barbed wire fence in the headlights, the thick, winter-dead underbrush that seemed to have gone untouched for the better part of a century.

"Close one," Dr. Cain muttered, backing the car up to square it in the lane, then shifting back into drive again.

He turned a corner and crept down a road without a single streetlight to help cut into the darkness.

He finally pulled into a driveway, paused to let the headlights shine on a two-story white farmhouse. The house featured all the quaint details Claire had expected to find when her father announced he'd rented a home built at the turn of the twentieth century: a large covered porch complete with a swing, wooden shutters, and filmy white lace curtains hanging in old sash windows. A second-story balcony wrapped the entire home.

The years had bullied the house, though, giving it a sad, used-up look. The place was desperately in need of paint; the asphalt shingles were starting to curl; the clogged gutters coughed and sputtered in the rain like an old man with emphysema.

Tonight, the house was also wrapped in a thin sheet of ice, which caught the hazy moonlight in a break between the clouds, sparkling like a star against the black sky.

Claire took a step from the car, her shoe sliding underneath her. She gripped the door for balance, and glanced up to find a figure in the front window of the house across the street. A hulking figure, enormous, standing so close to the glass that he looked like a featureless silhouette as he stared at her, the light of his living room shining brightly behind him.

She narrowed her eyes, refusing to gasp. Turning back toward the car, she tugged her suitcase from the backseat and her phone from the glove compartment. She slammed the car door as she stared at the silhouette, hoping it sounded like a punch.

"Hey," her dad called, already halfway up the walk. "What are you doing just standing there? You'll catch your death."

The phrase kicked Claire. "Coming." She forced her feet to start moving up the ice-coated front walk, straight through the entrance, into a tiny sitting room with a fireplace and a wood floor and doilies on chairs and a couple of Norman Rockwell framed prints.

"How about the official tour?" Dr. Cain asked. They dragged their suitcases with them, going from one tiny room to the next, finding that each one featured a slightly different pattern of floral wallpaper. The out-of-date kitchen décor sported a linoleum-covered counter and a small sink with a dishpan, a round fridge from the fifties, and an old enamel stove.

"We can light that thing with a match when the power

goes out," her father said, pointing at the stove while the rain continued to patter against the drafty windows.

"Wait," Claire said. "*When* the power goes?"

But Dr. Cain had already moved on to the note in the center of the table: *Welcome!* their temporary landlords had written. *A casserole is in the fridge, a loaf of homemade bread on the counter. Make yourselves at home. —The Sims Family.*

The bathroom offered only an old-fashioned claw-foot tub with a free-standing porcelain sink and pink and aqua floor mats. Her father grunted at the tub. "No shower," he grumbled.

Together, they climbed the stairs, the threadbare green runner halfheartedly absorbing each blow from their shoes. "No second bathroom," he sighed, after having stuck his head through every doorway.

"Which one of these do you think is the master?" Claire asked with a chuckle. Because the three bedrooms—each barely big enough to hold a desk and a twin bed—seemed exactly the same size.

Her father laughed. "Beats me," he confessed. "Which one do you want?"

Claire pointed toward the closest room. "This is fine." She stepped inside, gently placing her suitcase on the floor, next to a small dresser adorned with glass knobs, its top decorated with a vintage pink dresser scarf. The scarf wasn't on straight, though—it was bunched up into a pile in the middle. Claire reached to straighten it. But her fingers had not yet even grazed the material when it came back to her in a chilling *whoosh*—the memory of the robe she'd worn her first night home from the hospital.

It had been pink, too, and kind of silky, just like the old scarf. Her father had bought it for her because the weather was growing too warm for Claire's old terry cloth robe. He'd wanted her to have something light and comfortable to wear. And pretty, too—the robe was pretty. Girls were always drawn to pretty things, after all.

She'd waited for the din of her homecoming to finally subside—for Rachelle to go back to her own house and her father to go to sleep and the dark of night to cover the Welcome Home! signs in her bedroom. Claire had grabbed her walker and forced her broken body out of the bed and into the bathroom. Unable to lift both hands from the walker at the same time, she'd flicked the light on with her elbow. And she'd rolled her shoulders backward, letting the silky robe fall open.

She'd cried, seeing herself in the mirror for the first time. Cried, and sworn angrily under her breath, because everyone had lied to her—it *was* bad, the way she looked. She would never be pretty again—not like she had been.

When she'd finally run out of tears, she'd advised the puffy-faced girl in the mirror, "Cut some bangs. Wear your hair down. Move on."

She'd avoided mirrors after that. It hurt to look at the truth in a mirror—like staring directly into the sun.

Claire snatched her fingers away from the dresser scarf without bothering to straighten it. She turned away, staring instead at the footboard of the antique iron bed that would be hers for the duration of her stay in Peculiar. But even that made her think of Chicago.

She'd been sitting cross-legged on her own bed little more than a week ago when her father'd knocked on her door and sheepishly eased into her room with a printed email in his hand.

"I don't know how you feel about it," he'd said of the last-minute opportunity for a sabbatical in Peculiar, Missouri. "It isn't what we planned on."

What they *had* planned on was Claire returning to her old school in Chicago for the spring semester. In all honesty, though, that email had lessened the tightening pressure of going back to her old life, like a clamp being released all at once. No Chicago alleys? No classmates looking at her with pity as she finally made her return, all of them knowing what had happened to her? No putting on the same uniform she'd been wearing the day of the attack? Not having to make incessant *I can't this afternoon, have to run* excuses to Rachelle, who would no doubt be letting her eyes roll across Claire like a woman in a supermarket turning a piece of fruit over in her hand, expecting to find bruises? It sounded like paradise.

She'd smiled at her father—the kind of honest smile that just had to be believed, no questions asked. "Let's *go*."

Dr. Cain had cocked his head to the side in pride. "You're so brave," he'd told her admiringly. *Brave.* He'd been using that word ever since the hospital, when she'd first cracked open her eyes and squeezed his hand. *A real fighter.*

Now, though, Claire's shoulders drooped as she glanced about her new room. Instead of feeling as though she'd found her escape, Claire felt no different—no lighter, no happier, not even relieved. She was the exact same person she'd been a state away—surrounded, now, by beat-up antique furniture and overgrown everything and freezing drizzle tapping against her window. When she peered through her gauzy curtains, the hulking silhouette was still in the window across the street.

She shook her head and muttered, "What have I gotten myself into?" as a draft poured in through the ill-fitting Dutch door that led to her balcony. Though she was still wearing her coat, the cold, wet night air trickled across her face, and she shivered.

She plopped down on the old bed, pulling her phone from her coat pocket. She opened her email account, chose Rachelle's contact, and typed, *You wouldn't BELIEVE this place! So creepy! Perfect start to a horror movie!* Then clicked "Save Draft."

Claire had been writing to Rachelle for the past nine months. No—she'd been writing to the *old* Rachelle, the friend she never would have avoided. The friend who never would have looked at her like she was about to fall apart. And clicking "Save Draft" instead of "Send," because the old Rachelle was gone. Claire didn't know how to talk to this new Rachelle, worried Rachelle, tiptoeing-on-eggshells Rachelle. She'd smiled when Rachelle visited. She'd sent her quick, single-syllable texts in response. But she had stopped talking to her—really *talking*—like they always had. Suddenly, instantly, that always-there understanding between them was gone. There was no going to the movies to celebrate anything. No jabbing each other in the ribs. No teasing. She scrolled down the contents of her "Drafts" folder, which contained more than two hundred unsent emails to Rachelle.

"Race you to that casserole!" Dr. Cain shouted from his room down the hall. Claire smiled at the excitement in his voice, tossed her phone and her coat on her bed, and hurried down the stairs to join him in the kitchen.

"What's the verdict?" Dr. Cain asked her as he peeled the aluminum foil back from a blue-and-white CorningWare dish and shut the refrigerator door with his foot.

"It's . . . different," she managed. "But no real adventure ever started out with the same old, same old, did it?"

Her father smiled at her again—a proud smile that warmed her.

They heated their dinners in a small convection oven on the counter beside the coffeepot, filled the floral plates they discovered in the cabinet, and carried them to the table just as sirens started wailing in the background.

Claire tightened her fist around her fork, her heart picking up pace.

"Wonder what that's about," her father said, turning his head in the direction of the wail.

Before Claire could think of anything to say, the overhead light flickered, buzzed, then died completely.

FIVE

Half an inch of freezing rain was all it had taken to yank the power line straight from the electric weatherhead on the roof of the Cains' rental . . . and from the other two houses sharing the winding road.

But the storm didn't stop there—it kept pummeling Peculiar, long after every light on the horizon died, enveloping the town in two full inches of sheer ice. Trees rustled in the wind, their smaller branches clinking together. Larger limbs groaned incessantly—and as the weight of the ice pressed harder, they began to pop, filling the air with sounds like shots from a firing range. Every once in a while, a limb would break free, jingle like a falling chandelier, then explode against the air with a furious *boom* the moment it struck the ground.

The relentless noise kept Claire awake that night as she lay on the living room couch by the fireplace, struggling to find even brief moments of sleep as her father snored in a nearby chair. There were other sounds, too—the kind of rural chatter that had never filtered in through her Chicago bedroom window: an owl, the lonesome wail of a distant coyote, and a soft hum that she recognized as the absence of any sound at all. It struck Claire that this was the first time she had ever been somewhere that she couldn't hear a single car—no engines, no tires splashing in puddles, no horns. *Even stillness has its own strange buzz*, she thought.

A wild growl and a scream made Claire rise up, toss off her blankets, and race across the living room to her father.

"Dad," she hissed. "Dad."

Dr. Cain bolted up, scrambling to find his glasses.

"What is it?" he asked as he pushed the wire frames up his nose. "What's the matter?"

"*Listen*," Claire whispered as the desperate wail filled the air again. "Someone's hurt," she insisted. "Someone's screaming. There it is again! I think it's a girl."

Dr. Cain put his hand on Claire's shoulder. "It's a bobcat," he told her. "Probably fighting with some other animal." He paused, looking at her. "Are you okay? Do you want to get up for a minute? Pretty sure I threw a deck of cards in my suitcase. Challenge you to a mean game of Go Fish till you're tired again."

Claire smiled. "No," she whispered. "That's okay. Go back to sleep."

She covered herself back up, but somehow, the popping of the trees seemed oddly familiar to Claire. Frightening. Especially when the air in between the popping was filled with that high-pitched scream.

Hours later, dawn finally broke to reveal that nature had only added to the misery being heaped upon the residents of Peculiar; a heavy layer of fog had persisted that night, hovering over the ground, twirling from the ice-covered branches, slinking through the air in clumps and swirls. The moisture-heavy fog added another coating of ice, weighing down the last of the still-attached tree limbs—and the main power line running down Claire's street, in between transformers.

She tried to busy herself, as the morning hours progressed. She flapped out the front door in her naval trench to beat at the ice on her front step with a hammer in an effort to make the entryway less slippery. She placed skillets of water on the front porch, and retrieved them when they were frozen, sliding them into the old refrigerator. The ice, she hoped, would turn their fridge into a kind of giant cooler, help preserve the few tidbits on the shelves. Dr. Cain had cautioned her against putting their perishables in the ice along their back porch, like she had first intended. "Might bring hungry animals to the door," he told her.

Which only made her remember the bobcat's scream.

As if all that wasn't enough, three additional inches of snow fell that afternoon. By the time night arrived—marking a full twenty-four hours without power—the whiteness of the new-fallen snow reflected both the light of the full moon and the weird blue glow emanating from the whining, busted transformer near Claire's house. The reflecting light made the world still feel dimly lit, even a full hour after sunset.

While Dr. Cain heated canned chili on their gas stove, Claire emerged from the house with a large piece of cardboard tucked under one arm—a sign made from one of their few moving boxes. She clutched a roll of duct tape and a box cutter—both of which she'd found in the garage.

The world around her looked as though it had been suspended in a chunk of Lucite as Claire stomped toward the curb, while the giant hulking silhouette from across the street stood in his window, staring. He'd been staring at her all day—every single time she'd stepped from the house. Claire tried to convince herself it didn't mean anything, that he was probably a combination of worried and bored, just like everyone else in town.

Still, though—he gave her the heebie-jeebies.

Claire frowned at him as she sliced off a piece of tape with her cutter. The blade, sharp and slender, raw and dangerous, flashed in the bluish glow from the transformer.

She finished taping her sign—in which she spoke directly

to Peculiar's power company—to the metal trash can at the edge of her yard: NO POWER—WEATHERHEAD UNDAMAGED. READY FOR HOOKUP written in thick black marker.

The sign was a bit overdramatic, maybe. But Claire didn't think she could stand another night lying in the living room listening to the sounds of snapping limbs. Their creaking and groaning drew goose bumps all over her skin. It made her heart beat like the world's fastest metronome. It forced fearful sweat to break out on her forehead. And though she had thought about it off and on as the hours had passed, she still could not figure out why.

Besides, the utility company's work trucks had circled in the distance all day. She had seen them from her bedroom window as she'd tried to fill her hours by unpacking. Workers in white buckets had been visible as they'd tried to reattach lines. For some reason, it felt as though they were avoiding her street.

Now, beneath the building pressure of glistening limbs, the road's main power line sagged even farther, threatening to completely pull free from the transformer.

With one more gust, the transformer sparked, spitting orange rain.

Claire shrieked, raising her arm over her head. When the sparks died, she lowered her arms and reached into her coat pocket. She dialed the number for Missouri Electric—which she'd memorized, by this point—with the box cutter still in one hand.

The same busy signal bleated into her ear. She growled in frustration, hung up, and dialed another number. *9-1—*

She paused. Staring at the numbers on her screen, her ears filled with the sound of stomping feet—a whole gang running.

She gritted her teeth as she closed her eyes, let her thumb land on the final "1," and held the phone to her ear.

"What is the nature of your emergency?" the 911 operator asked, as Claire hugged herself, still gripping the handle of her box cutter.

"I have a live line in the street," Claire said, telling herself that this would be the solution. "Three of them, actually. The lines to the houses on this street have all been ripped free. And the main line that runs down the road is about to get ripped from the transformer, too. I—"

"Ma'am," the tired voice answered, "that's a matter for the power company. If you are not in any immediate physical danger—if this is not a dire emergency—"

Claire's jaw chattered as she gestured toward her own house's line, illuminated by the transformer's glow that lay black and coiled in the ditch, like a snake ready to strike. "Three live lines," she repeated, as if she were surprised the operator couldn't see it herself. "Tomorrow, if we get any sun at all, they'll be laying in melting snow. That's an emergency, isn't it? Besides," she went on, "I've—I've tried the power company all day, but I keep getting a busy signal. And their trucks just keep circling around here without ever coming down our street."

"Ma'am, the power company is responding to priority issues."

Claire sighed loudly into the phone. The selfish side of her—the side that hated how afraid her dad was of burst water pipes, the side that wanted to stop wrapping her feet in Saran Wrap to hold warmth in her shoes, the side that could not stand the idea of another night without a TV or radio to cover up the awful, brutal popping of limbs (God, the noise was worse even than the bobcat's wail, somehow)—wanted to ask what could possibly be a bigger priority than heading into day two with no power in subzero weather.

"Ma'am," the operator barked, "Missouri Electric has been doing an admirable job of reattaching lines, considering the magnitude of this storm. I'm sure it's a long wait on your road, but you'll just have to be patient."

Another gust of wind forced the tiniest slivers of branches to jingle like charm bracelets. Behind Claire, the transformer threw sparks the size of golf balls.

In her attempt to get out of the way, Claire tripped over her own feet and fell from the street straight into the edge of her yard, her hip slamming painfully against the small curve of a shallow drainage ditch. She threw her left hand out to catch herself before her face hit the ground, too. Her cell flew out of her grip and her palm burned as it pressed through three inches of snow. Her coat had pulled back from her body as she'd spun downward; cold seeped straight through the side of her jeans. The fall sent echoes of pain through the once-broken and stitched-together bones that had already been aching since the start of the storm.

Across the street, a front door flopped open in a burst, and the faceless silhouette emerged wearing a leather jacket that only emphasized his girth. His enormous shoulders took up the sky like a billboard.

Claire shivered at the sight of the giant coming toward her. "No, no, no," she pleaded, struggling to find the cell phone she'd dropped. She gripped her box cutter even tighter as she slipped again, banging her tailbone against the road.

The figure clomped across the street, showing no sign of discomfort as brutal gusts sent tiny frozen pellets flying into his face.

Claire could see him clearly now as his boots thudded closer—see his face, not just the black outline of his head. The indentions of his scowl deepened in the glow from the transformer.

"Stop," she ordered, her voice the high pitch of panic. She raised her weapon, holding the point toward the towering hulk. "*Stop*," she tried again. God, the guy was big. He could be a full-blown psychopath, for all Claire knew. He sure as hell looked like one.

She could see her cell—or at least the small rectangle in the snow where it had fallen; she slipped once more as she tried to push herself forward. The tips of her fingers burned against the cold as she clawed through the snow and pawed at the solid layer of ice beneath, attempting to grab her phone. The man paused just behind her, looming over her in a way that made her feel like a June bug wiggling on its back, struggling to right itself.

When he squatted, reaching for her, Claire screamed, her voice slicing through the still night air.

"Oh, hush," he grumbled as she squirmed.

"Watch it—" Claire shouted. "I'm—talking to 911," she lied. "I'm—"

The man lunged forward and grabbed her wrist with one enormous hand, his tight grip making her relax her fingers. She whimpered as he snatched the box cutter away from her.

"Please," she begged as she scrambled, trying desperately to get to her feet.

"They teach you that move in some self-defense class in Chicago?" he asked.

The softness in his voice made Claire stop. "Say what?" she panted.

"It's a great move—sliding around on ice with a knife in your hand."

She flinched when he retracted the blade.

He was young, she realized, now that she was staring right

at him. The face beneath the black stocking cap was no older than her own.

He snorted, shaking his head. "The sheriff lives at the end of the road," he said, pointing. "It looks like favoritism if we get power first. But they'll be here," he said, nodding at her sign. "Believe me."

Now that he was standing close, Claire found something oddly calming about him. Maybe, she thought, it was because there were no expectations. No eyes staring out from his face pleading with her to be okay.

"How'd you know we came from Chicago?" she asked, still suspicious. "Or *did* you know? Was it a guess?" She pointed at the plates on the back of the Gremlin. "You assume everybody from Illinois lives in Chicago?"

"Claire Cain, junior," he recited. "Agreed to spend her dad's sabbatical semester in Missouri, while the geology professor-slash-paleontologist did his scientific thing in a just-discovered cave on the outskirts of Peculiar."

"How did you *know*?"

"Everybody knows," another voice rang out. When Claire turned, she found herself staring at the girl from 'Bout Out— the blonde who'd been looking for her friend. Her pretty face was engulfed by a black wool hat with earflaps. She stood securely, even on a section of road that dipped slightly, angling toward the ditch.

The girl was wearing cleats, Claire realized, tugged on over a pair of hiking boots. Claire felt a bit foolish from her spot on the ground, the chill of the ice biting through her jeans into her backside. She struggled to right herself; the boy from across the street reached out to help her.

"I guess it's true, the way word travels in a small town," Claire said.

"Even faster when your dad's the sheriff," the girl agreed. "I'm Becca Holman," she added, introducing herself. "My family's at the end of the road." She pointed toward the same house that the boy from across the street had already identified as the sheriff's place. A gust of wind made her butter-colored hair ripple out from under her hat like a sheet of silk. "Looks like you've met Rich."

"Rich Ray," the boy told her, gesturing toward a mailbox at his curb, the side hand-painted with his last name.

Becca craned her neck, squinting behind Claire's shoulder. "Jasper!" she shouted. "Jasper 2!"

A large brown dog trotted up to her side, and she reached out with a gloved hand to rub him behind his ears. "We've been up and down this street about twenty times," Becca confessed quietly.

"You need any help?" Rich asked. "I'm in that house by myself without anything to do. I'm the official portrait of stir-crazy."

"Where're your folks?" Becca asked through a slight frown.

"Running a warming center at the church." He turned to

Claire to explain. "It's got an in-ground generator, for anybody who doesn't have one of those small gas-powered things. And it's right across the street from 'Bout Out, so they've got their pick of stuff to eat. Dad wanted me to stay to keep an eye on our place."

"Preacher's kid," Becca told Claire, wagging a thumb at Rich.

"What about your dad? Still hasn't found anything? No tips?" Rich asked Becca.

"It's so slick out," Becca said, staring at the glistening road. "And it's night. Again," she added, her voice cracking. "What does she do at night? How can she get away from the cold?" She looked directly at Claire and asked, "Have you seen her? Has she been by here?"

"Who?" Claire asked, shaking her head, not understanding.

"Serena," Rich told her. "Serena Sims. Missing since the beginning of the ice storm."

Claire felt her stomach bottom out. Becca's friend had never come home. The conversation she'd overheard at the general store hadn't been mere high school pettiness. It had been serious. "Why would—"

"You're staying in her old house," Becca said softly, staring up at the second-story balcony. "Her great-great-grandparents built the place. When she was ten, the family built a new house and moved. Left the old furniture inside it and decided to use it as a rental." She chuckled, her eyes glistening with so many tears they suddenly looked as though they, too, had been coated by ice. "She hated the new place," Becca admitted. "*This* is the place with the wallpaper her grandmother hung. *This* is the place with hardwood floors her great-grandfather laid. She hated letting other people come stay here. Especially since it wasn't important to them. They all wound up breaking tiles in the front hall, or putting holes in that rose wallpaper her grandmother liked."

"Not that there have been many renters," Rich reminded her, stuffing his hands in his pockets. "What—maybe three in seven years? Who comes to Peculiar, right?" He rolled his eyes at Claire as he made his last point. "I'm sure Claire and her dad'll take care—"

"Has she been by?" Becca pressed, a tear threatening to tumble from her right eye as she stared at Claire. "I mean—if she knew someone was here, again, I thought, maybe—maybe she was trying to get out here, you know? Welcome you—or tell you about how it was her family home or something."

Claire shook her head as Rich eyed Becca with pity. "No. Sorry."

"I know," Becca said. "It's illogical to think she'd still be out here walking around, making visits. I just—I've been everywhere that *is* logical, and I can't find her. I'm so scared." She bit her lip as though it could act as a dam against her tears.

Glancing to the side, she let out a small snort. "Look," Becca said, pointing to the spot in the snow where Claire had reached for her phone. "Look at the track you made. It looks like an *S*." And she laughed again.

"Becca—" Rich tried.

"Serena writes her initials on everything," Becca went on, ignoring Rich. "She's—a—what do you call it—a doodler. She scribbles on everything. She draws silly pictures, writes notes to herself. Mostly, though, it's her initials—*SS, SS*. I actually started out looking for her hoping that the *SS* might show up somewhere—like some bread crumbs I could follow to where she was."

Rich shuffled his feet a little nervously. "Maybe you should check with your dad, Becca—"

"*You* haven't heard anything?" Becca asked, turning her pleading voice toward Rich.

He shook his head. "You would know better than I would," he said. "You took my place a long time ago."

His voice hadn't been accusatory, but the way Becca narrowed her eyes made it seem as though that was how she'd interpreted him. "Look," she said. "I just want to know when you saw her last."

"After journalism, when she told me she was going to stay for the story," Rich sighed.

"What do you mean, she stayed?"

"To work on the story," he repeated. "About the basement. That's what she'd planned, anyway."

"Wait. The basement? Of the school? She meant she was

going to be at *school* working on her story?"

"What else would she mean?"

"I thought she was going straight *home* to write. Maybe hit the library on the way. I didn't think she was at school. Why didn't you *tell* someone?"

"Because—she told me her plan in the morning. And when Sanders closed school early, I didn't actually think she'd stay—"

"You didn't think at *all*," Becca growled.

The harsh tone in her voice made Rich blurt, defensively, "I thought you always knew where your little shadow was, in case you had some job for her to do—like kiss your feet."

"Excuse me?" Becca snapped.

"Oh, don't act innocent," Rich told her, his voice staying even. He seemed almost immune to anger—but unapologetic at the same time. "You like having her around to worship you. You're probably going through withdrawal right now, not having your magic mirror to walk around with you, constantly reminding you with your every breath that you, Becca Holman, are the fairest of them all."

"That's *not true*," Becca insisted as Claire watched in shock. "I love her. She's my best friend."

Rich just stared.

"I've got to call my father," she said. "Someone needs to look at the school."

"Someone *has* looked at the school—"

"Not the basement, you jerk," she thundered. "I mean, for God's sake—she said she was staying to work on the story of the kid who died in the damn basement. And you didn't think that was *important*?"

"You don't think I'm not afraid for her, too, Becca?" Rich asked softly. "You think you're the only one who worries about her? Do *you* hear her when you sleep? I do. Like she's calling out to me—like when we were kids. Calling like she wants me to come get her. Don't act like you're the only one who cares. If you want to know the truth, you probably truly care the *least* about Serena. You just want to make sure you've still got a president of your fan club."

"That's not fair," Becca hissed, before turning her back to him. She took a step, whistled at Jasper 2 to follow her.

"You take care of Serena's *house*." Becca pointed toward Claire, before stomping off toward the other end of the street.

The conversation left Claire feeling weak and dizzy. She shivered as she watched Becca go, her cleats taking angry, crunchy bites out of the ice. Again, Claire wondered, *What the hell have I gotten myself into?*

"Everything all right out here? I heard some loud voices."

Claire pulled her head up, staring straight into Dr. Cain's concerned face.

"Rough start to your semester," Rich told Dr. Cain,

pointing at their ice-coated surroundings.

He nodded in agreement, dipping his bearded chin inside his corduroy coat collar. "It is," he agreed. "But you know," he added, flashing his professorly smile, "even when the earth is brutal, she's a beautiful thing."

Rich leaned forward, his hand extended to introduce himself. "Rich Ray," he said, shaking Dr. Cain's hand. "I've got a kitchen full of food and a garage full of tools if you guys need anything." He took a step backward as Dr. Cain smiled, seeming to be relieved, if only slightly, by Rich's offer.

"I'm going back inside," Rich told Claire as he turned toward his house. "It's cold out here. You guys should go in, too."

Before Claire could respond, another tree limb snapped in the distance. Something about the noise was so bloodcurdling, so familiar—she jumped like a frightened rabbit before she could stop herself.

"Yes," Dr. Cain agreed, reaching for Claire's arm. "Come inside."

"No," she said, pulling herself free. "I—I'm going to get some firewood." In truth, she needed a few minutes to collect herself.

"Claire, come on now, we've got a good fire going already. And besides, dinner's almost done," Dr. Cain said.

But Claire hoisted on such a picture-perfect brave face

that her father couldn't argue.

"Okay," he relented. "Be quick about it. It *is* cold out here."

Calm down, Claire, she scolded herself as she made her way toward the wood stacked under a tarp beside the porch.

But her hands shook anyway.

SIX

The back porch, Claire noticed, was riddled with tiny plastic bowls, the kind that people used to feed their pets. But there wasn't a single morsel of food in any of them—in fact, if it weren't for the sheet of ice lining their insides, the bowls would have all been completely empty.

But Claire couldn't bother to think much about those bowls; not with the words Becca and Rich had lobbed back and forth at each other still growling inside her head.

A missing girl, she thought, shuddering at the possibilities.

"Quit it, Cain," Claire grumbled out loud, reaching beneath the blue plastic tarp draped over the mound of wood at the edge of the back porch.

The moment that her hand touched one of the dry logs, a hiss of warning filled the air.

Claire froze, afraid to pull her hand back too quickly. The hiss gained strength, grew louder, like static on a radio.

Slowly, Claire lowered her head to look beneath the covering. In the moonlight that bounced off the backyard snow, she watched a cat lift her bloodstained jaws from the warm, half-eaten belly of a newly slaughtered rat. The cat's eyes flickered angrily against unwelcome company, and she snarled again, flashing teeth stained dark with rot.

The cat lowered her face back into the rat's belly one last time, pulling out one more good bite of bloody entrails. She chewed, as some of the still-steaming intestines spilled out from the rat's wound, drawing slimy, bloody splatters across its corpse. She purred, as though enjoying the sweetness of the warm ooze against her mouth. She swallowed the last savory bite, then swiped her face clean with her rough cat tongue.

As Claire stared in horror, she backed up, inching away slowly. She continued to move in slow motion, retreating as the cat inched forward, casting a sinister-looking shadow across the toes of her shoes. The cat emerged, flashing a pair of angry yellow-green eyes, marked with black vertical stripes. Tiny ears rose and fell with jagged edges that spoke of old fights. Her tail swelled fat with rage.

The calico glared wickedly as she crept out from under the tarp. This cat was nothing like the sweet yellow tabby Claire had seen at 'Bout Out. Her eyes were matted, and now that she was completely exposed, Claire could tell one ear had actually been torn in half, and her body was covered in the kind of filth it took more than a decade to collect. Joints swollen with arthritis, back crooked, face covered in raw, pink patches. And something was tangled in her tail—something shiny, almost like a string of tinsel from a Christmas tree.

Claire cringed at the cat's sickening appearance—but at the same time, she couldn't quite peel her eyes away, either. A gold charm dangling from the shiny string on the cat's tail had wound itself tight enough to actually look painful.

Wanting to help the poor thing out, Claire lunged forward.

The cat yowled.

"Shut up," Claire snapped. "I'm trying to help you. You need help." She lunged forward again.

But the cat arched her back, opening her mangled face to let out a squalling, hissing cacophony of tones. She leaned against her back feet, ready to race away.

"*No!* Wait! Let me help!" Claire shouted.

The cat took off, jumping over a nearby fallen limb and scurrying across the yard and into the darkness of the frigid night. Claire stared out across the yard, sorry she hadn't managed to free the poor cat's tail. But at the same time, she felt grateful that the awful thing had left, taking her parasites and filthy claws and half-rotten teeth with her.

She turned back toward the woodpile, hesitantly this time. Her eyes rested on a thin, shiny object hanging from one of the fallen, ice-laden branches nearby—the same long thread that had dangled from the old cat's tail. Only, it wasn't just a thread, she realized as she squinted. It was a cameo necklace. And it must have been pulled free as the cat raced away.

The necklace looked old—maybe even antique—with a broken clasp. As Claire held it up toward the moonlight, she saw it, like the flash of a camera: the St. Jude charm dangling above her head.

She brought the necklace down in a jerk, flinching against the vision. She still had the St. Jude charm the cop had given her. She had tucked it away in the bottom pocket of her suitcase—the first thing she'd packed, actually. Because maybe it *had* helped her through. Maybe it *had* been lucky. After all, Claire hadn't wasted away in the parking lot, not like she'd thought she would that night as she'd hung in the sky, hovering over her ground-beef-looking body, thinking, *It's too late for you. You're dead.*

"Time for a new good-luck charm," Claire decided. She twisted the last metal loop in the chain until it opened, and wrapped the necklace around her throat. She pinched the loop tight, the metal stinging against her cold fingertips.

But the memories of that night persisted. After all those months, it was as clear as ever: the boys circling all around her, beating her. The boys lifting metal cans and hitting her with garbage. An object coming down on her leg, crushing it.

Claire groaned, instantly understanding why the snapping limbs had sounded familiar.

My bones, she thought. *They'd sounded just like the snapping branches when they'd broken.*

And the screams Claire had let out had sounded exactly like the screech of the bobcat.

She grimaced and shook her head, trying desperately to push it all away.

Reaching beneath the tarp, though, her eyes focused on the slaughtered body of the rat.

It's too late for you, Claire heard ringing in her head all over again. *You're dead.*

Her hands shook as she used a smaller fallen limb to drag the body away from the woodpile and covered the poor thing with a few handfuls of snow. She straightened herself, finally grabbing a couple of logs for the fire, and rushed into the house before her father could ask if something was wrong.

SEVEN

Even Peculiar, Missouri, had the occasional blue sky, Claire was relieved to learn three mornings later, as her father drove through the puddles of melted ice between their house and the high school. Power had returned the day before as work crews had arrived to reattach their lines, just as Rich had predicted.

It might have even been hard to believe the storm had happened at all, if the casualties—snapped branches and downed trees, some of them surely big enough to be more than a hundred years old—weren't also being cleared, hauled toward the edges of properties. Piles of ice-coated trees lined the streets as Dr. Cain steered toward the high school, the growl of chain saws following them along the way.

"You didn't tell me Edgar Allan Poe went to school here,"

Claire quipped as they pulled into the lot, only partially joking. She leaned into the windshield, staring up at Peculiar High—the odd, solitary building she'd first seen at the top of a distant hill as she and her father had passed the city limits sign. Made of some sort of stone that might have once been white, the entire building was now wrapped in the gray, dirty hue of cigarette ash. Winter-scorched ivy, brown and brittle, swirled across the front, surely blocking the sun from entering classroom windows. More than just old and dingy, the place had a kind of forgotten air about it. The persistent fog, swirling about the base of the school, didn't exactly make it seem any less menacing, either.

"It's a little . . . rough," her dad conceded, rubbing his beard as he stared at the faded name above the entrance and the rusted bike rack.

"Oh!" he exclaimed, twisting to reach into the backseat. "I got you something."

When he pulled his gift into Claire's lap, her face fell. "A red backpack," she said, seeing a school supply aisle in a Target on a hot August afternoon. Summer before her sophomore year. Goofing around with Rachelle as they'd tossed their backpacks like basketballs into their shopping cart. Rachelle had chosen black, but Claire had decided on a tomato red, sure it would pick up on a thread in the plaid skirt of her school uniform.

The bag had looked so bright and new and ready for

the possibilities and even—almost—*happy* there under the fluorescent lights of Target. And it had looked so different lying on the ground in the cracked parking lot, the cloth black in places from being stomped, wet and shining from all the slimy garbage, glistening in a sad, wet, destroyed way under the streetlight. The police had picked it up and taken it with them. Evidence, they'd said. Claire had never seen the bag again.

"You don't like it," Dr. Cain said.

"Of course I do," Claire said.

She fumbled with the zipper, opening pockets as though to examine the bag in full. Really, though, Claire was stalling.

She liked the look of the parking lot right then—empty, except for the four old, banged-up economy cars in the faculty section and the puddles of melted ice that had mixed with oil stains so that they all shimmered with pink and yellow iridescent ripples. She could almost convince herself, staring at all the unused parking spaces, that she still had time to spare.

A pickup truck careened into the space next to them, its radio squawking and thumping with some indistinguishable heavy metal song, the guitars and drums muted by the truck's rolled-up windows.

It was starting—everyone was beginning to arrive. First day back to school after the storm—or, for Claire, just plain first day of school. Even though she wasn't having to face her old school back in Chicago, the words *first day* still stung.

"Ready to get registered?" her father asked, throwing open the driver door, its hinges crying out against the cold.

Claire stepped from the passenger side just as Rich slammed the door of his Ram. His eyes scanned her face, then landed on the gold necklace that dangled at the base of her throat and peeked out from in between the lapels of her coat.

Claire nervously tucked the cameo inside her sweater. She'd tried to take the necklace off as she'd dressed that morning. But as she'd leaned in toward the bathroom mirror and spun the necklace to get a good look at the back, to figure out how to pry open the last loop again, she realized she'd actually smashed the chain in on itself. And the necklace was far too short to slip back over her head. She'd attempted a halfhearted tug, but the chain burned against the scars on the back of her neck. She'd given up trying to take it off, and had decided to simply wear it to school—*What's the difference, anyway?* she'd asked herself. *Besides, it's your lucky charm, isn't it?* But there was something in the surprised way Rich stared at the necklace that quickly brought an embarrassed flush to her face.

"You coming?" Dr. Cain called from halfway across the parking lot.

Claire hurried forward, the front flaps of her coat flopping open in the harsh wind.

She'd just caught up with her father when Rich motioned

for them both to stop, nodding at a guard in a black uniform.

"Think you—need—a—visitor's pass?" the guard said, his voice cracking on the last note. He cleared his throat, one hand flying self-consciously to a large pimple on his chin before he crossed his arms over his chest.

Claire felt her legs weaken beneath her.

"She's a student, not a visitor," Rich said in a flat tone.

"Right. The girl in the old Sims place," the guard said, nodding uncomfortably. "Sanders said you'd be coming today." He was the kind of enormous that made Rich look average; he could have worn one of Claire's belts like a dog collar. His cheeks were without the trace of any stubble, dotted instead with a few haphazard splotches of acne. He wore his authority like shoes that had yet to be broken in. His eyes darted, and he glanced behind his shoulder as though he half expected someone else to take up the cause of turning away unapproved guests.

Claire swayed slightly. Peculiar High had a guard—just like her old school in Chicago. *A guard*, she kept thinking. *What does he need to protect us from?*

"Are you gonna let us in or not?" Rich moaned, rolling his eyes.

The guard tossed his weight onto one hip. He teetered, leaning toward Rich as he asked, "So what're they like?" as if Claire and her father couldn't hear him.

Rich shrugged. "Eat a lot of Spam; sacrifice goats after

midnight. Who doesn't?"

The guard chuckled, relaxing a little.

"We just need to get her registered," Dr. Cain said.

The guard nodded, pointed toward the door with the sureness of an eight-year-old hall monitor.

Rich reached around the guard to grab hold of the tarnished handle and swing the front entrance open.

Their shoes echoed against the marble floor as they stepped inside.

"Why do you need him?" Claire demanded, pointing back at the entrance.

"Rhine?" Rich asked, tugging a stocking cap from his head to expose a mop of wavy brown hair. "Just in case, I guess."

"But—a guard," she said, feeling sweat break across her forehead, wetting her bangs. "Has there been—is this—in case of what?" Her heart thudded as she waited for the answer, praying that it wouldn't have anything to do with the missing girl.

Rich glanced past Claire's shoulder at Dr. Cain's equally worried face. "Look," he said, "that's not even really a guard. That's Becca's brother. Rhine, short for Rhin-*o*, because it felt like you'd been trampled by one when you got hit with his tackle. According to last year's seniors, anyway. Construction jobs are scarce right now. He's not exactly college material. Call it a small-town favor. Let me show you to the office," he offered, hurrying ahead of Claire and her father.

Claire straightened, slathering on a brave face and priding herself on the way it relaxed Dr. Cain's shoulders. As her father turned away, Claire slipped her hand inside her coat, clutching her queasy stomach as she tried to take in her new school for the first time.

Peculiar High looked as if it hadn't been renovated once in the more than hundred years it had been in existence. Tarnished brass sconces lined the ugly beige walls, giving the place the appearance more of an old hotel than a school. It reeked of heavily waxed floors and old sets of encyclopedias and polished antique moldings. It made Claire think of the insides of a trunk that had been locked up for decades; when it was opened, the summer air of 1922 reached up to smack her nose.

Rounding the corner, they found a metal bucket in the middle of the tile floor, catching each drip that worked its way down as the ice continued to melt in the sun. The leak had created the appearance of a brown Rorschach test on the ceiling. Nearing the front office, Claire couldn't shake the feeling that one of those brown splotches looked exactly like the mottled face of the calico she'd seen out in her woodpile.

Rich paused, allowing Claire time to take in the contents of a nearby trophy case. A picture of a familiar face—messy dark hair, thick frame emphasized by football shoulder pads— had been propped on the top shelf. Chas Winters—This Year's MVP, the letters above his picture proclaimed. Claire stared at the face she had first seen Monday afternoon at 'Bout Out, at the start of the ice storm, while Rich tapped on the front office window, his knuckles echoing through the stillness.

"New student," Rich said, as the small office window slid open. The woman inside blinked to attention, slammed the front window shut, and raced to open the door that led to the suite of faculty offices.

"Of course! Dr. Sanders will see you," she said. "*Be* with you," she corrected herself.

"Catch you later, Claire," Rich said, touching her sleeve lightly before heading to his first-period class.

"Sure, thanks," Claire muttered, just before she and her father entered Sanders's office shyly, the soles of their shoes making *shh* noises as they dragged.

"Come in," Sanders urged, waving at them without turning his eyes away from the bulletin board cluttered with school announcements. The walls of his office were covered in athletic photos and award certificates and a Peculiar High banner. His ancient wooden desk drooped in the middle, sagging from the weight of office equipment and towers of files. A picture of an overweight, friendly-looking woman and two young boys was the only personal item in sight.

"Two of you?" Sanders asked, without pulling his eyes away from the bulletin board.

"I'm Dr. Cain and this is my daughter, Claire. A junior. We just moved into town for the semester," her father said, as Claire began to wonder if Sanders wasn't having a staring contest with a thumbtack. Not that she could really tell for sure where his eyes were pointed, behind the sickly brown tinted lenses of his glasses.

"Ah, yes, Claire Cain," Sanders said, turning his head stiffly toward the two chairs in front of his desk. As he shifted in his own seat, Claire noticed that his suit was about thirteen sizes too big—the brown jacket stood out from his shoulders like the pads in a football uniform, and his shirt was so roomy, the heaviness of his necktie tugged the striped collar down, so that a bouquet of white curly chest hairs poked out. Dressed the way he was, under the pea-green glow of fluorescent lights, Sanders looked like he'd been taken captive six months ago, chained to his desk, and fed only a couple of saltines every other week or so.

"Is the guard out front really necessary?" Claire persisted. "I could imagine it in Kansas City, maybe. St. Louis. But here?"

"We take the safety of our students very seriously," Sanders snapped, then repeated, softer this time, "*very* seriously. Especially during times such as these."

Claire flinched. *Times such as these?*

"I suppose—with the storm—and all—" her father said, in a tone of complete over-politeness. He shot Claire an uneasy look—the same kind of uneasy look that had preceded his announcement, nine months ago, that he'd made arrangements for a counselor to come see her at the house. Not just any counselor, though—a friend of his from the psychology department. Dr. Agee, with the balding head and the unending supply of blue plaid shirts. Healing was internal as much as external, Dr. Cain swore.

But Claire had been protective of her thoughts—especially with one of her father's friends. She was sure her father thought the opposite would be true, that it would be easier. But talking to the professor who had so often come to the Cains' summer barbecues just felt strange—like telling her own father all the details of a first date.

She'd shot that shrink all the right answers. In turn, he'd spoken to her father in another room, using satisfied tones. And her father had reappeared, smiling at her, his brave little girl.

You still know how to say all the right things, she assured herself. *Just calm down, calm down . . .*

"School-wide lockdown occurs at eight fifteen," Sanders was saying. "If you're not inside the building at that time, you will be sent away. No excuses. And there will be no bribing of the guard, either. As a recent PH grad, I'm certain he knows all the tricks for getting in and out of the building—his knowledge of the Peculiar High premises is exactly why I asked for him specifically."

"Lockdown?" Claire croaked, her pulse turning the insides of her ears into kick drums.

"That's a full fifteen minutes after the tardy bell rings," Sanders justified. "Surely you can be here—"

"We're just from a bigger town," her father said, immediately jumping in. "That's all. It's a bit of a surprise—"

"I assure you, we take education every bit as seriously in Peculiar as you did in Chicago, Dr. Cain. More so, I might wager."

The ceiling tile directly above Sanders's head dripped. A water droplet hit the top of his head, and he flinched as it trailed around the top curve of his forehead, racing through a wiry eyebrow.

Sanders scowled as the drop hurried toward an eye, quickly removing his glasses.

A gasp rippled through Claire's throat as Sanders pawed at his brow. Sanders's eyes were grotesque—a thick, milky skin covered the colored portions of his eyes, while the whites had turned the awful dusty green of bread mold. The eyeballs bugged and bulged, as though ready to tip and fall out of their sockets. Patches of skin near his temples and lids and around his brows were marred by deep, silvery scars, discolored pink spots of flesh.

Claire looked down, clutching her hands in her lap, refusing to react to the repulsion crawling up her arms. Judging by the fact that Sanders didn't have a white cane leaning in any of his office corners, and by the fact that the papers on his desk were written in black seventy-two-point-font letters, Sanders wasn't completely blind. And offending her new principal on day one wasn't exactly how she wanted to start off.

Besides, she reminded herself, she wore her own fair share of scars.

"Here," Sanders said, placing his hand on a large 9 x 12 envelope. "Inside, you will find the Peculiar High handbook, as well as information on the lockdown and uniforms."

"Uniforms?" Claire asked.

"New students are usually somewhat reluctant about the uniforms," Sanders conceded. "But I know that they really are grateful for them after a while. Saves everyone from having to figure out what they'll wear every day. You appreciate that, don't you, Ms. Cain?"

Without allowing her a chance to answer, Sanders continued, "We will provide you with a temporary uniform to wear until you purchase your own. I'm sure you'll feel much more comfortable looking like the rest of your classmates."

"I—uh—I—" Claire stammered.

Peculiar was supposed to have been a quiet rural town. If this school was exactly like Chicago—if this wasn't going to be a sabbatical for her, as it was for her father, then why had she agreed to it? *This can't be happening*, she kept thinking, feeling the room turning like a carousel.

Feet scurried about in the tiny hallway that snaked beyond Sanders's door, and the woman from the front office returned cradling some black-and-white garments. "Here you go—

until you get your own," she said, as though she were doing Claire a favor. "I think these should just about fit." She placed them in Claire's lap and left. Claire unfolded the articles: a white blouse, a black pleated skirt, kneesocks, and a black, much-worn cardigan with a school insignia on the pocket. Her stomach lurched.

This is no escape, no better, it's all the same—the guard, the uniform—just like my old school. The ice storm. The missing girl, who stayed to dig up research just like I did. And I'm in her house. . . .

"Only for today," her father promised, leafing through the papers in the 9 x 12 envelope. "Says here uniforms can be picked up at Cicily's, a clothing and fabric store just off the town square. I'll pick up your own uniforms when I stop for lunch."

Didn't her father see what was going on here? *Let's run,* she wanted to beg him. *Let's run, let's run . . .* But then again, she knew what happened to a person on the run. *They chase you and then they throw you to the ground and they rip you and break you . . .*

"Perhaps you'd like to go change," Sanders said. "The ladies' room is just outside the office."

Claire nodded absently and pushed herself out of her chair, sweat pooling inside her coat. She swayed on her feet.

"Are you all right?" her father asked her.

"Water," Claire croaked.

"There's a fountain in the hallway—" Sanders said. And as Claire darted for the door, she heard him ask her father, "Will she be all right? I saw in her file—"

"Yes, well, we'd appreciate it if that incident remained in her file," Dr. Cain said.

"Of course, of course," Sanders agreed. "I will request that the information be kept private . . ."

Claire staggered into the hallway, dizzy with the heat of pure fear, finding herself face-to-face with a bulletin board advertising Winter Formal! in glittering type.

She pushed herself away, toward the bathroom. She burst through the door, heading straight for a frosted-glass window on the far side of the room. She pushed it open, welcoming the cold January air that seeped in.

But as she looked out, she saw a number of feral cats sitting along the back edge of the parking lot, as if in wait.

Serena

Serena had spent the entirety of the ice storm in the woods behind the high school, underneath the crushing weight of the fallen limb, hoping for something to change.

A few things did—noises began to echo inside her head in a muffled, tinny way. And the woods she observed through the spaces in between the branches her killer had draped across her face began to seem a little blurry—as though her eyes were made of a scuffed-up glass.

Time was odd, without the old markers. She didn't get hungry or tired. She didn't need sleep. The branches took up so much of the sky above her that she was not quite sure how many times the sun had risen and fallen. But whole days had passed; she knew that much.

She was not *gone*—not as she'd expected to be. She had

not floated out of her body like a helium balloon whose string had slipped out of a child's hand. She had not drifted straight up to the heaven that waited on the other side of the clouds.

Serena was dead; she kept telling herself so. But *dead* wasn't a title she could accept, not if she was still here, still inside her body. *Dead*—she had hoped it would start to be a relief, at some point. After all, everything now was outside her control. There should be peace in that.

But there wasn't.

She wanted someone to find her. Not in the same way that she had wished to be found in the last moments of her life—not in a frantic, desperate way. But she was protective of her body—it still felt as though it belonged to her. Even though it didn't work anymore, it was *hers*, and she was still afraid of what could happen out here, in the woods.

Peace—what a joke, Serena thought.

She wished for certain things, as she lay in the woods: first, to talk to Becca one last time. Then she wished for grief. Because here, at the end, it would mean that someone had cared.

As time had pulsed on, though, some of Serena's wishes changed colors—they faded and slowly began to evaporate, without Serena having to decide to let them go.

Each time one of her earthly wishes (to taste her mother's chocolate mayonnaise cake once more, to finish that last story for journalism) faded away, she felt herself spread slowly outward. She felt both inside her body and bigger than her body. She saw out her eyes and down on the world, too. She still experienced the world through her body—she still felt the sting of ice, the crush of the limb—but at the same time, she could watch the world from afar. It was as though she were somehow able to see twice—once through her eyes and once perched from above, far enough away to see the entirety of the school grounds. It was *more* than odd—it didn't make sense. (But what about her death *did* make sense, so far?)

Earlier that morning, as her classmates had returned to school, she'd watched them pull their cars into the lot and stream through the doors. She'd watched Becca knot a yellow hair ribbon on the flagpole before she stepped inside the building.

The ribbon pleased Serena. Becca missed her. Missing someone—that was grief, wasn't it?

Though Serena's awareness was swelling, spilling outward, she was not exactly all-knowing. She could not see inside the school. So when the bell rang, she was left only with the woods, the ice. The parking lot . . . and the cats.

The ferals arrived after the eight-fifteen lockdown went into effect, after even Rhine slipped inside. A pack of twenty or so slowly began to emerge, to creep closer, edging through the lot, toward the back of the school.

Serena knew that hunting must have been hard the past few days for the wild creatures that had begun to overpopulate the town. Rodents had surely taken shelter under floors of barns and in old logs during the storm, hidden from the ravenous ferals.

Black cats, yellow cats, gray cats now edged cautiously toward the Dumpster at the back of the school, as though hoping for some pizza crusts or half-eaten hamburgers, maybe a ham and cheese on white missing only three bites. The hungry homeless cats jumped to the lip of the Dumpster, one after another. They dipped their heads toward the interior of the trash bin, all but empty because it was now Friday, and the students hadn't been at school to toss out their leftovers since Monday.

Serena easily zeroed in on a familiar animal—the calico cat she'd been feeding for months on the back porch of her old house. Sweet Pea—that's what she'd called her, every single time she'd brought a can of tuna or Fancy Feast, trying to convince the old cat to come close, to let her scratch her head.

Sweet Pea crouched low and moved toward a group of ice-covered bushes at the back of the school, trying not to be seen by the ferals who lined the edge of the Dumpster. She disappeared for a moment in the brown bushes, and emerged dragging a young bunny with a small but deadly puncture wound, a poor thing maybe even making its first outing since the storm. She scooped the creature into her jaws, squeezing until its juices overflowed from her mouth and trailed down her neck in a bright shade of pink. Lifeless long ears and back legs flopped from the old cat's jaws as she twisted her head this way and that, looking for a place to eat her kill in peace.

But she stopped short when she noticed a pair of pointed ears rounding the edge of the Dumpster. And another. Whiskers. Paws. Tails pointed skyward. All of them closing in on her.

Hunger buzzed from the pack of feral cats, making it clear that they all were willing to fight for the rabbit. Especially since the calico was old and not in the best shape.

Sweet Pea tightened her jaw and darted away from the school, through the small empty field that led straight into the woods.

The ferals followed as she raced in between piles of fallen limbs, her feet bouncing up with each step, making it appear that the ice was cold enough to burn the pads on her paws.

Sweet Pea stopped abruptly and opened her mouth, letting the slaughtered bunny fall to steam against the snow. She stuck her nose into the air, letting it twitch back and forth.

She smelled something far better than that bunny. She staggered forward, a delectable new scent dragging her like a rope.

Serena could smell it, too, suddenly—the overpowering scent of fresh meat.

Sweet Pea followed the scent, her mouth squirming with anticipation. Serena could practically read her mind, the wild creature she'd come to know on the back porch of her old house. *What just died out here in the field?* Sweet Pea seemed to be asking herself. An animal—far bigger than her rabbit. A soft, fleshy creature, judging by the smell. A possum? A coyote?

Twigs snapped. Ice crunched. Sweet Pea glanced behind her. The hungry ferals were still coming—following the same scent.

The cat raced forward a bit, attempting to lengthen her lead. Not too much, though—she didn't want to lose that mouthwatering scent.

Poor thing, Serena thought. Without those cans of cat food, that tuna, her empty stomach probably felt as shrunken as a deflated balloon.

But then, the cat stuck her head beneath a fallen limb, the explosion of her joyful purr indicating she had found it: the source of the smell.

It was a human.

It was *Serena*.

The shade from the trees—all those limbs, those hundreds of gnarled, intertwined branches—had protected the ground from the sun. The ice surrounding the trees in the woods had just begun to warm enough to form a watery skin—but hadn't yet melted enough to drip. The thaw here was still new.

Serena's body had been preserved by the ice, but now it was thawing. And sending out invitations for a feast.

Don't do it, Serena quietly pleaded, staring at Sweet Pea through eyes like shiny stones. *Please, Sweet Pea, don't do it. Don't you recognize me?*

The ferals—two calicos, several black and gray cats, and a large yellow cat—salivated as they moved in. The sandpapery surfaces of their tongues dripped.

Oh, Sweet Pea, Serena thought. *Please don't let them. Please.* Her body had been damaged enough by those brutal last moments right before her death, by being dragged into the woods and being hit by the fallen tree. She didn't want the cats to do this to her body, too. She was terrified that if they completely destroyed her body while she was still somehow tethered to it, they would also destroy her spirit—that strange, still thinking, still feeling *thing* that had not yet completely slipped away.

But even if Sweet Pea could have heard her, she would not have listened. She was too hungry. And the other cats' need was every bit as great. Sweet Pea edged her head deeper beneath the branch, hurrying, racing ahead of the other cats. Sweet Pea was so happy, her whiskers quivered—she was more than ready to be the first to sink her teeth into the flesh, ready to start feasting before any of the other cats had a chance to steal the choicest bite.

It didn't matter to Sweet Pea that Serena had been feeding her for months, taking pity on her, showing her kindness. Sweet Pea was a wild thing. And she was hungry.

Serena tried not to look through her eyes at the cat, but down on the woods from her strange spiritual perch high above. She tried to distract herself from what was about to happen by thinking about how much like wrists the tree trunks looked, how the smallest branches were fingers reaching for the sky.

She wished that she could reach her arm up, too. Wished that she could grab hold of some magical force that would rescue her from enduring this final horror, the very thing she had feared since she was little. The monsters—in the woods— salivating as they grew close. It was happening.

Their feet sped, crunching through the snow. They purred as they grew close. They ran their rough tongues over their teeth.

Serena *knew* what was about to happen. And she was powerless to stop it.

EIGHT

To be released from hours of rigmarole—changing clothes, registering, collecting textbooks, filling a locker, getting the official school tour—just in time to face the horrors of lunch as a complete and total outsider, Claire had decided, was truly its own special punishment. She'd missed her first four classes, including journalism. Of all things. The one class she'd truly been looking forward to. At least, that was what she told herself. She wanted it back, her love of stories. She wanted not to think of writing and remember what had followed the last story she'd cracked. It was maybe the worst thing that gang had done to her—soil the way she thought of journalism.

She filled her tray with soup and a soggy-looking grilled cheese, paid, and turned toward the buzzing cafeteria—tables upon tables of strange faces.

Claire glanced about nervously. Around her, chairs screeched across the tile floor; voices babbled on, as unstoppable as the gurgles of a river over rock.

And all of them—strangers.

She began to sweat nervously. Her body felt clunky. Her knees felt like they'd been wrapped with jogger's weights. Her tray grew as heavy as a concrete block.

"Hey there," a voice rang out beside her.

When Claire turned, she found herself staring into the prettiest thing she'd seen since she'd arrived in Peculiar. *Ms. Isles*, read her lunchroom monitor badge. *Isles*, the perfect name for a woman with eyes the kind of blue that could only exist somewhere tropical. A woman who even smelled like coconut, like a vacation breeze—and who had perfectly coiffed beach-blond hair and the kind of ridiculously perfect body that begged to be put in a bikini.

Isles stretched her hibiscus-red lips into a smile. "I think someone's trying to get your attention," she said, pointing across the cafeteria.

Claire followed Ms. Isles's pointed finger and saw Becca Holman at a table, waving.

She took a grateful step forward. Behind her, the cash register tallied up another lunch, and Owen veered around Claire, taking long strides toward Becca's table. Maybe Becca hadn't really been waving to her at all, Claire thought, her shoes squeaking against the tile floor as she came to an abrupt halt.

She watched as Owen strutted, his body ladder-straight, his shoulders thrown back. He carried himself like a peacock, throwing his colors about wildly.

With another ring of the cash register, a second boy stepped around Claire—Chas, still wearing his letterman's jacket with the leather sleeves. He carried his tray of food with one hand, easily sidestepping a girl who threw her chair backward without looking, right into Chas's path. His movements were so easy, sure. No wonder, Claire caught herself thinking, he was named last fall's most valuable member of the football team.

She stood, looking down at her tray, feeling dumber than ever as she continued to search for a place to sit. She wished she could melt straight into oblivion.

"Come on," a low, smooth voice murmured into her ear.

When Claire lifted her head, she found Rich smiling at her. And just as it had happened in her street during the ice storm, Claire felt her nerves unwind.

"Don't just stand there," Rich said, his hands full of both a lunch tray and a stack of yellow papers. "You don't want to miss a close-up view of the Bold and the Beautiful." He winked, threw his head forward once in a gesture that insisted she follow.

Claire walked behind Rich and Ruthie, the cashier from

'Bout Out, straight toward the table where Becca sat, Chas and Owen like bodyguards on either side of her.

The air filled with high-pitched scrapes as Rich and Ruthie pulled two chairs back on the side of the table opposite Becca and the two boys.

"Claire Cain, a junior, just like us," Becca told Owen and Chas, nodding once at Claire. "Her dad's the prof on sabbatical. Renting the—" She stopped repeating the story her own dad had surely told her, and clenched her teeth, making the muscles on both sides of her jaw bulge. She cleared her throat, tucked her blond hair behind both ears. "The old Sims place." She exhaled slowly, like the words had been hard to lift.

"Hi," Claire mumbled. Realizing she was still standing, she hurriedly dropped her tray onto the table, slopping her vegetable soup over the edge of her bowl and onto her cheese sandwich in the process. She screeched her chair backward, and sat down between Rich and Ruthie, her face hot and sweaty. She felt uncomfortable in her heavy black Peculiar High cardigan, but she couldn't take it off—it covered the scars on her arms, where the cuffs of her blouse rode up.

"Owen and Chas," Becca said, pointing.

Owen nodded once, but Chas barely looked up from the video game he'd begun to play on his phone.

"*Stop* it," Becca snapped at Owen, before dipping the tip of her fry into some ketchup.

"Stop what?" Owen asked.

"Staring at Isles."

"I wasn't staring at Isles," Owen argued.

"Who doesn't stare at Isles?" Rich muttered.

"*I* wasn't, *Wretch*," Owen snarled. "I was thinking."

Rich shook his head, rolling his eyes in a *should have known* manner as the nickname hit the air.

Before Claire could ask about the name, Chas snorted at Owen. "Since when do you think?"

Owen glared.

"Hey, give me your algebra homework, will you?" Chas asked. "Mine got lost in the ice storm."

Owen shook his head. "If you'd get off that thing for five minutes," he growled, pointing at the phone, "you'd get yours done, too."

"Ooooh," Chas said, laughing as he punched at his phone, seeming to enjoy the comeback.

Owen continued to stare at him in a way that said he hadn't meant it as a playful jab.

"You must be pretty bad off if you're asking *him* for his homework," Becca snorted.

"Whoa," Rich said, holding his hands up in a way that demanded their conversation be cut short. Rich, Claire realized, didn't usually run with this group. That much probably should have been obvious with his "Bold and the Beautiful" comment.

She eyed the faces surrounding her table, wondering why so many people insisted on being books that spent the entirety of their high school years in one genre section—mystery (the loners), romance (the jocks and cheerleaders), literary (the brains and nerds), sci-fi (the socially inept techies)—and never wandered anywhere else. But then again, she reminded herself, she had once felt perfectly content never to wander from her own space, permanently—and happily—reserved at Rachelle's side.

Suddenly, Rhine appeared, clomping his heavy shoes straight toward their table. "Rich," he said. "I saw the flyer. I want to help. Tell me what I can do."

"Help with what?" Becca asked. "What flyer?"

"That's what Ruthie and I came over to tell you guys. We're getting together a search party," Rich said. "Three o'clock."

"A search party," Becca repeated.

Chas sighed, shook his head while he tried to zero back in on the game on his phone. Owen raised his arms—his own uniform shirt had been immaculately ironed, Claire noticed—and covered his mouth, like he was trying to convince himself not to be sick.

"We're all going to meet up at 'Bout Out," Rich announced. "I think maybe we should start looking there, then fan out. Maybe she was trying to get there, during the storm. It would have been dry and safe. Dad's still got that warming center going, because we've got a couple of families with pretty bad damage to their houses, stuff that needs to be fixed by an electrician, and who don't have power yet. I'm sure they'll come help. I know Dad will—and I'm sure we can get Mom involved, too.

"I figure," he went on as Becca's face grew distant, "I'll go home to grab all the warm clothes I can find: long johns and Thinsulate socks and hiking boots and my weatherproof parka and extra sweatshirts and jackets. Nobody'll have to bow out because they're cold."

"I was right here," Rhine said. "At school. I mean, I keep thinking I should have maybe seen something. When Sanders cut the day short, it was like it shocked everybody. They all ran out, then started to come back for the papers and the books they'd accidentally left behind. I must have been here another hour, letting people back in, after the doors were locked. I never saw Serena. But if she never made it home from school—I just keep thinking I should have seen her at some point."

"You can hang some of these flyers," Rich said, handing him a chunk of his stack.

"We've hung flyers in the front window of the store, too," Ruthie added. She leaned over the table, her chest bulging over the top button of her too-tight blouse. She shook her dark hair from her eyes just before reaching around Claire to push one of Rich's yellow paper notices across the table. "We used her last yearbook photo. If you've got something more recent . . ." Her voice trailed, as Becca rubbed her forehead and pushed the flyer back toward her.

"Funny thing, isn't it?" Becca snapped at her. "*You* wanting to help?"

Ruthie shot another pleading look at Chas. But he was lost in his game.

"I *knew* it," Becca told Chas. "That first night, when she wasn't at her house, and she wasn't at yours, either. I knew something was wrong."

"For God's sake, Becca," Chas moaned.

Becca seemed to ignore his tone, preferring to gaze at her reflection on the back of her spoon. Her hand flew up to smooth her hair on the side of her head. The gesture seemed kind of thoughtless, though—it looked like a habit, like Becca was the kind of girl who spent a lot of time looking at her reflection: in the mirror taped to her locker door and the shiny sides of metal napkin dispensers and even windows, when the light hit them just right. She was obviously the kind of girl who cared a lot about the way she looked. But why wouldn't she? She was so ridiculously perfect, with that silky butter-colored hair and the face of a Cover Girl model, she was practically a cliché. She probably got stared at all the time, Claire figured. A girl who got stared at so much would just naturally spend a lot of time double-checking her appearance, making sure people would like what they saw.

But today, as pretty as she still was, she looked a bit unraveled. She only had eyeliner on one eye and her blouse was buttoned wrong.

"Why would Serena want to talk to *me*?" Chas asked.

"Because I *know* her," Becca said, leaning toward him, fire in her glare. "Maybe *you* don't, but *I* do. I know her; I can predict where she'll wind up—like Dad knows how to follow the dirt roads straight to every fishing hole in the county. I *know*. It doesn't matter that she found out about *you* two," Becca went on, dragging her pointing finger from Chas to Ruthie, who flinched. "She would have tried to end things on a good note."

"Becca!" Chas shouted. "Enough, okay? You were the one who built up some great romance in your mind. *You.* I'm telling you, it never happened. Serena and I just got smashed together, because *you* liked the idea of us being together. Just because you and pretty boy over there," he said, pointing at Owen, "are a couple, you thought it would be cute for the best friends to be a couple, too. *You* were the one who liked the idea of me and Serena. We didn't. Trust me."

Becca narrowed her eyes. "Serena would never want *anyone* for an enemy. Not even someone who had screwed around on her. She'd think of something—return a box of your stuff, maybe—ring the doorbell, and wind up talking to you on your front porch. You'd sit on the porch swing, like two people who had only just met, until your fingers were blue from the cold, and she'd finally stand to go, and you'd turn toward your house, not thinking anymore of how horrible you were, you ridiculous *cheater*, but realizing what a cool person Serena really was. And how much you were going to miss hanging out with her. It was Serena's gift. She could never let anger be the last note. She's just so *likable* . . ."

"Likable?" Chas repeated, scooting up in his seat. "Are you joking? She was dull. Seriously. She never had a damn thing to say."

"Has," Becca corrected.

"Whatever," Chas said. "You know what I mean." He rolled his eyes.

"What about you?" Chas said, nodding once at Owen. "You're not going to defend me? Going to let your girlfriend skewer me here, like I'm some horrible person, just because I didn't want to date her stupid friend?"

"Chas—" Owen sighed. His face was turning gray. "Not—now."

"Why *not* now?" Chas bellowed. "What is *with* you? What's with everybody? Why should it matter—*damn*," he swore, tossing his phone onto the table. "I don't care *what's* going on with Serena. It doesn't magically change the way things really were. *We didn't want to be together. I didn't want to be with her. Get it through your skull, Becca.*"

"If you didn't want to be together, you should have said so," Becca said. She pointed at Ruthie, saying, "It didn't give *you* two the right to . . ."

Ruthie tucked her long dark hair behind her ears, leaned forward, and started, "Listen, Becca—" But she didn't have the time to get it all out before Rich interrupted her.

"Come on, Becca," Rich moaned. "We're trying to help here. I know everybody's frazzled—the storm—not knowing where she is . . . We all want to find Serena. It's finally clear enough—safe enough—for us all to get out."

Becca shook her head. "No," she grumbled repeatedly. "No."

Claire tilted her head at Becca, confused by her response. "Don't you want a search party?" she asked quietly. Because the first thing she and her father had done when the power had gotten back up was turn on their TV. She'd heard the entire story, finally—the missing girl. The ice storm. *Fear the worst*—that was the phrase they'd used.

Claire knew all about the worst. She'd looked it square in the eye. Didn't Becca want to save Serena from it?

"Do I *want* a search party?" Becca repeated, her mouth dangling open. "Haven't you ever had a best friend?" she blurted, staring at Claire.

Claire drew her arms in toward her body, unable to answer.

"You don't even know what we're looking for," Becca told Rich, shaking her head. "My father told me, though."

"What?" Claire finally asked Becca. "What are they looking for?"

"A body," Becca said. "My dad said they're looking for a body. And what did *we* do that first day of the ice storm?" she asked, looking straight at Owen. "We went home."

Owen pushed his tray away from him, without touching so much as a single bite, obviously feeling guilty about the way he'd dismissed Becca's concerns at 'Bout Out.

"We got off the road to save our precious cars and our precious selves," Becca went on, "while *Serena*—" She shook her head, tossed her napkin onto her tray.

"Whatever," Chas mumbled. He grabbed his own tray and his phone, stood, and stormed out of the lunchroom.

"Becca," Rich said, leaning across the table. There was just something about him, Claire noted—he was as comforting as a cool rag on a fever. She wondered if he hadn't picked that ability up from his father, the preacher. "Everybody's worried, okay?" he said evenly. "It's making us all crazy. But there's going to be a search party, and I'm going to be there. And I hope you will be, too."

She nodded. "Thanks, Rich," she croaked, taking hold of her tray and standing.

"You can come out with us, too, Claire," Rich said.

"I can't," Claire muttered, "I just—can't." She grabbed her own tray and hurried away, before she had to explain that the word *body* was still ringing through her head—along with the knowledge that she had only barely escaped being a body, too.

NINE

One more hour, Claire chanted to herself that afternoon, ducking her head into her chest as she attempted to navigate the dark hallways of Peculiar High. *One more hour, and this nightmare of a day will finally be over.*

Checking her schedule for the fifth time, Claire turned into her history classroom only to find Ms. Isles, the lunch monitor, sitting behind the large desk at the front of the room and Becca Holman sitting at a desk beside the window. As Claire stood, dumbly, in the doorway, Becca lifted her head and offered a weary smile and half a wave. She tried to usher her toward the empty seat beside her.

But Claire sidestepped Becca's offer, lunging straight for a seat in the back. She didn't mean to be rude, but she was exhausted and she didn't have the energy for another encounter like she'd had at lunch. *Haven't you ever had a best friend?* The words had settled into her skin like bruises.

She hid her face behind her hand while Becca tried to get her attention, whispering her name all through seventh period history.

Not that Ms. Isles noticed. At least, she didn't act as though she did—she didn't snap at Becca, not like any other teacher would have, calling her out by name and embarrassing her into silence.

When the final bell rang, Claire bent forward to scoop up her backpack, the old cameo bouncing once against her chin and then falling back into her blouse, adhering to her sticky, nervous skin as she bolted from the classroom.

"Claire," Becca hissed.

Claire didn't answer. She raced into the hallway, which echoed now with the thudding of metal locker doors. All those combination locks, spinning open. Claire remembered the last time she'd visited her locker at the end of a school day. She remembered that when she'd slammed the metal door, Rachelle had been standing right there, leaning against the wall. *Haven't you ever had a best friend?* The question lingered in Claire's mind as she remembered the plans she and Rachelle had made. The library. *I'll meet you there*, Rachelle had said casually.

It was too much, all of it. Remembering Rachelle and feeling lonely and being in Peculiar during an ice storm and knowing a girl had disappeared and being surrounded by a sea of school uniforms—it made her feel as though danger had perched on her shoulder. And even though she tried not to, she still missed her best friend. She had never had another person in her life who fit beside her like Rachelle had. Being alone in a new school and apart from Rachelle made Claire feel like half a sentence missing its ending. She tried to remind herself that Rachelle had changed after the accident. That she had treated Claire like a damaged thing. She tried to remind herself how much she'd hated it. Still, she missed the old Rachelle so much, the ache nearly crushed her chest.

Claire darted into a bathroom, where she lurched into a back stall, slammed a silver slide lock into the door.

She closed her eyes and pressed her forehead against the cool stall door. She gritted her teeth, heart beating inside her like a club.

Her shoulders heaved with raw emotion as she cried silently. She cried for her friend and because she was lonely and because she already hated this place—this rotten, old, scary place. She cried because she was in a uniform and a guard was outside and her escape—Peculiar—felt exactly like Chicago, the very place she'd wanted to escape from. She cried because a semester felt like the longest stretch of time in the world.

She cried because all she wanted to do was run away. She cried until the stalls around her emptied and voices tapered off.

Claire wiped her eyes with the back of her hand, slid the lock free, and cracked the door of her stall. She splashed some cold water on her face and hurried to her locker, where she quickly shrugged herself into her coat.

The hallway echoed as she raced through the vacant corridors and down the stairwell, branded with a giant black panther—the Peculiar High mascot that stared at her, its fangs exposed as if it, too, were feral, and coming after her. She could almost hear it snarling.

She sucked in a breath at the base of the stairs, and pushed through the back door, into the frosty late-afternoon air. The ice-coated snow crunched and gave beneath Claire's shoes as she cut across a patch of grass and hurried toward the parking lot out front. In the stillness of the deserted school grounds, each step Claire took echoed inside her, the same way granola cereal echoed inside her ears as she chewed.

She stepped onto the gray sidewalk. Chunks of rock salt popped under her soles as she hunkered down inside her coat.

With an abrupt burst, a streetlight came to life above her. Claire flinched, staring straight up into the orange light glowing against the darkening overcast sky. Her mouth ran dry as she remembered the streetlights buzzing the last time she'd walked home alone, from her father's library. With her eyes tilted upward, her foot struck a patch of ice, and she skidded. She threw her arms out, saving herself from a fall. But she slammed headfirst into another awful sense of déjà vu.

She shook it off, shoved her hands deep into the pockets of her coat, and pressed forward. As she neared the corner, the doors opened on an old white Honda parked against the curb. Claire slowed, watching Becca step from the car, along with Owen and Chas.

Claire shivered as she glanced toward the school parking lot, finding that even the spaces reserved for faculty had emptied. Rich's truck was gone. No one was left—except for Rhine, who paced beside the front door in his big black uniform, thumbs hooked stupidly in his belt.

Rhine stopped pacing to eye Claire, at the same moment that the front passenger door of the Honda swung shut.

"Hey," Becca said, leaning against the front fender. "I'd started to think we'd missed you."

"Missed me?" Claire repeated.

"I thought if your dad's working, you'd probably like a ride. It's *freezing* out here." She shuddered to emphasize her point, but didn't need to. Beneath her short black parka, her bare knees were already beginning to turn a pinkish-coral hue in the cold.

Claire nodded in agreement to Becca's observation on the cold, ducking down deeper inside her own coat.

"Great," Becca said, taking Claire's nod as an agreement to let them drive her home. "Come on—if you want, we can drive you to 'Bout Out, too. So we can all go to the search party. I've got to get some jeans before I head out. We can wait while you change, too."

"Don't know how you girls can stand those schoolgirl uniforms in the winter," Chas said, eyeing Becca's pink knees.

Claire instantly felt all the blood pour straight down to pool at her ankles. The hair on her arms stood up like porcupine quills inside her coat. *Schoolgirl.* The word echoed inside her skull. The same word that had tipped her off, in the alley. That had first made her think those boys were following her.

Right then, she didn't want to go anywhere with anyone. She just wanted to be *home.*

"It's not that bad," Claire answered. "This coat is like wearing a brick house. Honestly. I'm going to walk."

"Walk?" Becca asked. "Don't be silly. We live on the same road. I'd feel weird leaving you out here."

"I appreciate it," Claire said. "I just really would like some time—to myself." To prove it, she turned and hurried down the sidewalk, in the direction of her house.

"Must be my winning personality," Chas snickered. He slipped into the backseat.

Claire relaxed a little as car doors slammed shut behind her. They would drive away now, she told herself. *It's okay,* she tried to assure her racing heart. *Uniforms, the ice, streetlights. A word. So what? It's coincidence. It doesn't mean anything. You know that. "Schoolgirl." Really. You're going to let some harmless word scare you? Please. Be logical.*

The car started just behind Claire's shoulder. But instead of the engine growing quieter and farther away, it grew louder.

"Claire!" Becca shouted, making Claire flinch. "Come on! This is silly."

Claire turned, frowning, toward the street. Instead of leaving, the Honda was crawling along beside her. The passenger-side windows were rolled down. From the backseat, Chas stuck his head out to call, "Hey there, new girl. Do me a favor and get in this car. Becca won't let us leave until she gets you in this car. Pretty please?"

"Nah, it's okay." Claire *could not* do it. Because when she looked at that car, she only saw a dead end. Just like the one she'd raced into in that Chicago parking lot.

"Come on," Owen's voice called from the front seat. When Claire looked, she saw him nearly lying in Becca's lap, looking out the open passenger window. "Becca's right. You shouldn't be out here on your own like this. Come on. If you don't want to sit with Chas, you can have the front seat."

"No," she said, her voice stronger, final this time. "I'm walking. Thank you."

"Hey, pretty girl," Chas called.

Claire's frown deepened and she hurried forward.

"Don't pay attention to him," Becca moaned, jabbing her thumb behind her shoulder, toward Chas. "He's an idiot. Come on."

"Pretty schoolgirl," Chas called, singsong. The word—*schoolgirl*—was like a hand grabbing her.

"*Buzz off,*" Claire shouted viciously.

Becca's head jutted backward in shock.

Claire picked up the pace, hurrying down the sidewalk, past Rhine, who still stood at the school's door.

The Honda's engine roared. She turned to find the grille sneering at her, inching closer. Claire shoved her hands back in her pockets and quickened her pace again. Her breath came faster, harder, turning the air around her head into a cloud.

"Is something wrong?" Becca shouted. "Come on. Don't be like this. Let us take you home."

"Not on your life," Claire snapped, and turned her face forward again, pretending to feel tougher and faster than Becca . . . and two male athletes . . . and a car.

Blood turned into a white-water rapid against her eardrums. *Not on your life? Buzz off?* Who talked like that? Surely they all knew exactly how rattled she felt.

The granola crunch of a second pair of feet made her look behind her shoulder; a black uniform, like a giant puddle of spilled ink against the white backdrop of the snow, started to trail after her, too.

"Hey," Rhine called. "Hey, you! What's going on? What's wrong?"

Claire tried to jog, but her backpack held the clothes she'd worn earlier that morning and just about every single book known to man, now that she would be expected to get caught up with the rest of the students in her classes. And with every step, the straps pulled against her shoulders, making her feel like a bicycle whose rider kept slamming the brakes.

And still, the car followed. Rhine followed. Why couldn't they just leave her alone?

Simply asking herself the question made the smell of a wet alley explode in her nose. Laughter—it clanged against her ears like a bully's taunt. Voices—big talk. Egging each other on.

Desperate, Claire reached down and grabbed a handful of snow. She quickly packed it into a ball and heaved it at the front of the Honda. It splattered across the windshield; brakes squealed. The car slid a little on a patch of black ice; a front tire edged up over the curb, toward Claire's sidewalk.

"Hey!" Owen shouted. His door squeaked open.

Claire bolted from the sidewalk. She raced straight into a thick patch of the fog that had continued to linger around the fringes of Peculiar High.

Breath like the rub of sandpaper inside her ears, Claire glanced up ahead, toward a patch of woods—the kind of thicket that she'd seen lining the highways coming into Peculiar and separating just about every house in town and cradling the general store.

"Don't!" Owen called, racing after her. "Hey! Don't go in there! You'll get lost!"

But *lost* was the goal—at least, losing *them* was the goal.

So Claire just kept running, her feet crunching through the snow as she thanked every lucky star in every sky she'd ever lived beneath that her clunky shoes had such good soles.

"Stop!" Becca called.

She tried to increase her pace, fighting the depths of the snow and the weight of her bag pulling her back. Her legs hurt, her joints hurt. Running on the bones she'd broken was like being hit with mallets.

A whole herd of shoes crunched in the snow behind her. Just as a herd had slammed against the pavement, in Chicago, the streets not yet slick enough that they couldn't get traction.

As she neared the fringes of the trees, Claire glanced over her shoulder to see four black silhouettes, stark against the white snow, wisps of fog dancing about the outlines of their bodies. Becca's and Rhine's unbuttoned black winter coats caught the wind and flapped like the wings of vultures.

"Don't!" Owen shouted.

Claire opened her arms as she entered the lines of trees, as though to hug the dense patch, grateful for the safety it promised. *This will be different*, she told herself; she would be hidden here, not like in that empty parking lot with nothing to duck behind, no concealment, just pavement—that rough, ragged pavement that ate the skin on her knees.

But the woods were a regular briar patch, filled with thick sections of ice that had only barely begun to melt. Broken tree limbs lay in a haphazard, random pattern on the ground. A few limbs that had only partially snapped still clung to trunks, hanging by little more than splintered threads of bark.

And the ice—piles of it lay undisturbed. Mountains of ice clumps—fragments that had broken off limbs as they'd tumbled to the ground.

And the piles were precarious, Claire learned as soon as she planted her foot into a mound. The outer crust cracked, broke, and gave way. Claire's foot sank; the ice swallowed her up to her shin. The cold chewed on her leg through her sock.

She groaned, trying to free herself. That damned crunching of footsteps in the snow was getting louder. Closer.

"Stop!" Owen shouted.

"Claire," Becca screamed. "Come on. Where're you going? Come back."

A frantic shriek filled the air as Claire freed her foot from the ice and began to run again, pumping her arms, sprinting. This time, she avoided shiny piles of ice, aiming for the inches of matte snow instead.

She was winning. Skittering on ahead of the herd behind her. Lengthening the gap between herself and those who were chasing her. She swore that the humming of a few gas-powered generators still running in the storm's aftermath and the buzz of chain saws were growing louder. She was making it— getting closer to other buildings, other homes. Civilization. *She was going to break free this time.*

The voices behind her turned into distant barking. Claire

felt a smile break across her face. And still, she kept pressing forward, occasionally making a misstep and sinking deep into piles of ice, but always wrenching herself free and pressing on, frantic. The fingers of fallen limbs reached for her, grabbing, tugging at her hair, clawing at her thighs. But they couldn't stop her.

No one could. Claire was going to do it. She was going to win.

Yes, yes, yes, she thought, her coat flying out behind her in the brutal wind, exposing her legs to the cold.

Claire pressed faster, using every drop of strength, until a shattered limb tripped her, and she went flying, landing on her knees. She screamed, her voice shredding the sky, as glass-like shards of ice sliced her cold skin as easily as a knife could slice a block of cheese.

Scrambling to free herself, Claire turned to see exactly how badly her feet were tangled in the fallen limb. But the shattered branch that had just tripped her was a strange shade of blue—purple—gray.

Claire twisted in the snow, turning herself onto one hip. Panting like a marathon runner, her eyes zeroed in on what appeared to be a cluster of five tiny, twig-sized branches, all attached to one larger limb. But the bark looked leathery, not really like wood at all.

She dragged herself closer. She squinted at the branches—which, now that she was close up, didn't look so much like branches, either. She reached out, touched the thick trunk of the limb to understand what it was. Touched it again. Lowered her face. Gasped. Jerked herself backward.

My God, she was staring at a human hand. Palm up. Fingers—those tiny branches were *fingers*—the tips painted red. No—not painted. Missing. The red meat beneath the skin was now exposed on each finger. The palm had been branded, "CHEATING."

"What the—?" Claire breathed.

Claire leaned down for a better view, lying flat against the ice-covered field, her thick wool coat protecting her chest from the inches of snow. As she looked beneath the fallen tree limb, a glassy blue eye stared back at her. A brunette curl. More blue skin. Cheeks raw with scrapes that had been filled with ice. A jagged black hole along the tip of the nose. A mouth open at a grotesque angle; a clump of mud, marred by brown blades of dead grass, spilling out from behind front teeth.

She threw herself backward as the whole picture came into focus—a girl. A dead girl lay pinned beneath the heavy, fallen limb. Her legs, her arms, all filled with pink pits.

Bite marks.

"No—*no*," Claire screamed, as she attempted to get away from the limb and the dead body, tripping on the hem of her coat in the process. She stumbled back to the earth, falling on her backpack. The blood on her sliced knees poured warm from her body, but instantly chilled in the winter air, making her cuts sting against the January wind.

An angry hiss pried Claire's eyes upward, away from the waxy, blue fingers.

A cat edged forward from his perch on top of the limb that pinned the body; a pair of yellow eyes with black stripes narrowed at Claire; pink fangs flashed. Nearby, another yellow set of eyes popped from the shadows, as a tail curled up onto a black curved back. More fangs. More eyes. More angry, fat tails.

Ferals. Black and gray and yellow. Their mouths all stained a frightening shade of pink.

Claire's mind spun as the hungry ferals hissed territorially. They lowered their chests toward the ice, elbows hugging their ribs. They crouched, inching toward Claire. They snarled, because her appearance had made them scatter, made them pull themselves from the glorious feast that had been taking place for hours.

Two hissing ferals beneath the limb danced, in the crowded space, like a couple of fencers. Fighting beside the girl's battered face. While they threatened each other, a third feral—this one the color of wet newspaper, with some sort of giant, fleshy tumor on his left shoulder—crept up on the arm trailing out from the limb, opened his mouth, and sank his teeth into the exposed flesh on the heel of the girl's hand. Gnawing on the flesh—moving into the center of her palm. Chewing up the ballpoint word: "CHEATING."

Claire tried to scream again but found no sound.

She gagged. They were fighting over her. Eating her. *It's too late for you*, she heard ringing in her ears. *You're dead.*

"Please come back," Becca screamed, as footsteps crunched still closer. "We live on the same road—it doesn't make sense for us to leave you here."

Claire felt the bile rising in the back of her throat as the cats continued to gnaw. A gang. Another wild gang. Devouring her.

"Come on," Becca called. "I'm sorry if Chas said something boneheaded. I'm sorry if I was weird at lunch. I'm just worried. Please. Get in the . . ." Becca's voice trailed, only to be replaced by a gasp, then a grunt of disgust as she watched Claire gag violently, her vomit burning the back of her throat before spilling onto the snow. The grunt became a wailing squeal as Becca saw first the hand, then the uniform skirt poking through tree branches, then the rest of her friend's remains.

"No—no, please, no," she begged, dropping to the ground, not caring that her knee fell into Claire's vomit. "Serena?"

"Ah, hell," Rhine moaned, catching up with his sister.

"Serena?" Becca cried again as she started to crawl beneath the limb. Owen wrapped his arms around her waist, hauled her backward even as her legs and arms moved wildly, like a kid trying to learn how to swim.

Claire's stomach crawled into her mouth again as Rhine started squawking into his cell.

She lifted her head, weakly, only to find herself staring into the face of the mangy old calico from her woodpile.

The cat tilted her head and eyed Claire curiously.

Rhine stomped his feet and threw his arms about, attempting to shoo all the ferals away. Most of the cats scattered, racing off. But the calico stayed at Claire's head, braver than the rest of the wild things whose claws clacked against the still-icy ground cover.

"Yeaaaa!" Rhine shouted, waving his arms to scare the last of the body eaters away.

"Go away," Claire begged the calico, while the hot, bitter remnants of her vomit clung to the insides of her mouth.

She panted, her breath and her vomit filling the cold air with white clouds. But the body under the limb was as cold as the ice itself. No steam—no breath—just stillness. Claire's world flashed, switching between two scenes: first the night sky, the Chicago parking lot, the April ice storm, the chase— then the afternoon sky, the empty high school parking lot, the ice crunching beneath her feet, the woods, another chase. The school uniforms, the guard—his dark clothing making him look like a police officer. The way she'd been stuck to that sky, in Chicago, staring down at her own pulverized body. And this body before her, filled with pink marks, bite marks, all that slashed flesh. She had looked just like that, she thought, staring at the strange girl's body. So torn up, so shredded, destroyed. When that girl cop saw her, that was what she found.

Her worlds alternated, back and forth, first like the flipping on and off of a light switch: Chicago, Peculiar, Chicago, Peculiar—then faster, faster, like the images in a flip book. Her mind was folding in on itself, one thought bleeding into the next with no boundaries. Chicago, Peculiar, Chicago, Peculiar—she was looking down on her body, that pile of ground beef. Chicago, Peculiar—she was the girl beneath the limb. She was staring at herself. *Claire* had been ravaged by those ferals. Chicago—the chase, the gang, the untamed rage. Peculiar—the ferals. Eating her body. Eating—hungry—screaming—tearing—flesh—ripping—cold—pleading—laughing.

It's too late for you. You're dead, she heard staring into her own lifeless face as her two worlds blurred together into the same wild smear.

TEN

The air swirled with screams. Pleading tones, cries that begged the scene not to be real. Phone—someone was on the phone. It was ringing. Claire could tell. "Hello?" she heard. It was Rhine's voice. "Hello?"

When did Rhine start working for 911? Claire wondered.

"Hello?" he asked again.

"Hello," Claire murmured. But it was too late. She was dead. It took him too long to answer the phone.

"Missing girl," she heard Rhine say. Had that much time gone by? Had Claire been lying here in this parking lot so long that someone had actually reported her missing? "Woods," Rhine said. "High school."

"No," Claire moaned. He had it wrong. All wrong. No one would ever find her now, not if he was telling them to look at the high school instead of the parking lot by the apartments.

A girl's voice screamed, wailed. "No, no, no," she cried out, as another voice begged, "Becca. Becca, don't. Becca, calm down."

Becca? Serena thought. *When did Becca come to Chicago?*

A hand wrapped itself around her wrist. It was her, Claire knew—the cop. That girl cop with the hair like sweet corn and that big tough body. It was about time for her to show up, Claire thought. It seemed like it was taking her a long time to get there.

Maybe, Claire thought, she could ask her when Becca came to Chicago. But first, the cop had to give Claire a charm. Her St. Jude medal. Claire opened up her fist, waiting for the charm, warm from the cop's chest, to hit her hand.

Instead, the hand around her wrist tugged her. Lifted her shoulders and her back off the ground, and just kept tugging, like that girl cop expected her to stand up. But how could Claire stand on broken legs? Couldn't the cop see how much blood she'd lost? Why was she acting this way? She never had before.

"Come on," a voice pleaded. A low soothing voice. Urging her forward. When had the girl cop gotten *this* tough—so tough she sounded like a man?

Claire was being led away from the scene. On her own feet. With broken legs? How could it be?

The hand continued to grip Claire's wrist, leading her

farther and farther away.

Maybe, she thought, *I'm being led straight to heaven.*

Instead, she heard a creak, felt herself being guided into some sort of padded seat. She didn't remember being put in a seat—where was the stretcher?

A door slammed and Claire glanced up, into a mirror.

It was a small mirror, a rectangle up high on a windshield. A rearview mirror. And Claire was staring straight into her own peaked face. She reached up to touch her cheek, surprised that there was no blood.

She put her hands on the seat, rising up to get a better look at her chest in the mirror. Her head jerked backward in surprise. Her blouse hadn't been destroyed. She was still wearing a shirt, her naval trench. Both of which reeked of vomit.

Still shaking with fear, she turned to look behind her. Through the back windshield of a truck, she saw only an empty street. Through the window beside her, a vine-covered, ancient school—its flag adorned with a panther's face.

She wasn't in Chicago—she was in Peculiar. For her father's sabbatical. And she had not just seen herself—she had seen another person. The missing girl.

Claire had just stumbled upon the dead body of Serena Sims. And she was now in the cab of a pickup truck filled with piles of clothes and boots. *A search party*, Claire remembered distantly. There'd been plans for a search party.

Her backpack was here, too. That new red backpack her father had bought her. *Who picked it up?*

The back bumper of Owen's car sat at a crooked angle just ahead of her. The Honda was right where he'd left it before running after Claire, into the woods—the passenger-side front tire bumped up onto the sidewalk, three doors open, the engine left running. The driver-side seat belt dangled out into the street. Smoke billowed from the tailpipe.

The passenger doors slammed, and Claire saw Rich. But where had he come from? He slid into the Honda's driver seat, and backed up, steering the front tire back down off the curb.

She stared straight ahead, as first the brake lights flashed and died, then as the roar of the engine sputtered into silence, then as the exhaust clouds trailed off and disappeared.

The driver-side door of the pickup flew open, and Rich jumped behind the wheel, his face frantic. "Claire?" he asked. "Claire, are you okay?"

She nodded limply. But she wasn't sure. She had often remembered the scene in the Chicago parking lot—she had dreamed of it in gory detail. Her memories had always been vivid. But she had never misinterpreted her surroundings so completely, like she had in the woods. *What had just happened to her?*

Rich reached for her coat pocket. He tugged her phone free, found her dad's contact, and dialed. Claire was surprised when he started talking—not like he was leaving a voice mail, but like he was actually speaking to her father. Her father was within reach? He wasn't down in a cave somewhere?

When Rich finished his call, he placed his hand on the gearshift and pulled away from the school. He drove quickly, as a siren screamed in the background. He ran the only red light between the school and their street.

As they coasted to a stop in the driveway of the old Sims place, the front door flew open. "Claire!" Dr. Cain screamed, barreling down the front walk.

"Dad," she whimpered as tears pricked at her eyes. She stepped from the truck, the cold wind reminding her of the open cuts on her knees just before she collapsed into her father's arms.

ELEVEN

Dr. Cain ushered Claire inside, sat her on the couch. "I don't—I don't know what happened," she mumbled, trembling. What she meant was that she didn't know what had happened to *her*. She knew what she had seen—the woods, the dead girl, the cats. But afterward—Claire had been in Chicago. She had felt the pavement beneath her, felt the girl cop's hand around her wrist. *How was that possible?*

Panting, she listened to Rich ask if there was anything he could do to help. She watched her father give him a shopping list and money, then disappear into their bathroom and emerge with their emergency first aid kit. After standing her back up and helping her out of her coat, he cleaned the cuts on Claire's knees. He blew on them when the antiseptic made her wince, and he put Band-Aids on the cuts, like he always had when she was a kindergartner with a playground injury.

When he glanced up at her, Claire felt herself wrapping her arms around her chest protectively.

"Are you cold?" he asked, tugging a blanket from the back of the couch, draping it across her.

She gratefully pulled the scratchy wool blanket up to her chin, acting as though he were right. In truth, she'd recognized that look on his face—it was the same look he wore in the lab. He was observing her, weighing her movements, her reactions. Waiting to decipher the just-right thing to say to her, so as not to make the whole situation worse. After all, *what do you say to your daughter when she has just discovered a dead body?*

Before Claire could really figure out what she wanted, the doorbell rang. Her father touched her wounded knee gently before rushing to answer. Rich's voice returned. He'd been to 'Bout Out already. They spoke for a while, their whispered voices like Ping-Pong balls flying back and forth.

Her father closed the front door and rushed past her, carrying the groceries straight to the kitchen. In the complete stillness of the house, she could hear a peeler whacking the skin off potatoes, smell onions searing in a pan. And she let out a quiet, breathy chuckle. Her father was making her favorite cream of potato soup. He was taking care of her.

At that moment, Claire knew—she wanted to bring that proud smile back to her father's face. *Brave*, he'd called her.

The word was like a drug; she wanted another hit. *Say it again, Dad. Say "Brave."*

They ate, and he tucked her into bed. "Rest," he whispered. "Just rest."

When she woke hours later, she found him sleeping in the desk chair next to her bed, a blanket crumpled into his lap. He hadn't even changed into nightclothes or taken off his glasses.

"Hey," she said. "Dad." Mostly because she wanted him to get out of that awful position, his chin resting against his collarbone at an uncomfortable angle.

He snapped his eyes open. "What is it?" he asked. "What's the matter?"

"Nothing," she insisted. And because he'd tried to fix her with food the night before, she stammered, "Why—why don't we go get some breakfast? Get out of the house for a little while."

Her dad nodded, giving her a small smile. They had to leave Peculiar, taking a freshly plowed on-ramp to the highway to find a restaurant that was open so early, where Claire sipped a glass of OJ and forced herself to down some over-easy eggs. She ate to prove to her father that she still had an appetite.

Brave, she thought. *Don't you see it in me, Dad? Don't you think I'm still brave? Why don't you say it if you see it?*

The road home took them straight past the high school. The walk surrounding the grounds had been covered in stuffed animals and balloons and handwritten signs that promised, We'll miss you, Serena.

The car slowed as Dr. Cain stared at Claire, searching her face. "Claire. Do you want me to call Dr. Agee?" he asked.

"What?" Claire asked.

"Dr. Agee. From Chicago. I'm here, too, Claire, you know that. You can talk to me anytime. But you talked to Dr. Agee last spring, when you got out of the hospital, so you two have a history. I thought maybe, with all this going on—"

Claire shook her head. "I feel bad for her. That's all. I didn't know her. It's not like I'm—mourning, or something."

"But what you *saw*—"

She frowned. "It was a shock, but—"

"It was gruesome, Claire. I know."

"How?"

"Rich."

"Rich?" she parroted.

"He brought you home. Remember? He was driving by the school, heading toward the search party at 'Bout Out. And he saw Owen's car up on the sidewalk. And he followed the footprints in the snow."

"Of course," Claire answered, though the memories of the previous afternoon were anything but clear.

"When Rich brought the groceries back. He told me—about the cats."

Claire cringed.

"I just thought maybe it brought up some other feelings—about what happened—"

"Two different things," Claire said simply.

"But it had to have been—"

"Horrific," Claire said. "It was horrific what happened to her. Yes. I won't stop seeing her face. But it's over. Just like the incident in Chicago is over. Dr. Agee said it's nothing I can't deal with. Remember? How he said the memories will always be with me, but that's okay? You don't have to forget in order to heal, right?" She had taken great care to say the words *incident in Chicago* smoothly, without a hitch in her voice.

As her father stared, she whacked his knee with an open hand. "Come on, now," she urged, changing the subject, "isn't it about time you got our Wi-Fi up and running? You'll need it for work, and I'll need it for school."

Dr. Cain paused—as though trying to convince himself to believe her—and steered toward the old Sims place.

When they pulled back into the drive, two figures were already standing on their porch.

"Who's that?" Claire wondered, opening the car door.

The sound of the Gremlin had pulled the visitors away from the front of the house. It was Becca, Claire realized. And Owen. Both of them in dark winter coats and jeans, Owen with his hair slicked away from his face, Becca's pink cheeks and lips shining out from underneath a bulky winter hat with fur trim. And they were walking across the front lawn, toward Claire and her father.

"Dr. Cain," Becca greeted as they all stopped on the front walk, not two feet from the porch. She stretched her hand out. "We're Claire's classmates. We came to see how Claire was doing. After yesterday . . ."

Her father smiled, obviously grateful that Claire had visitors—*two* someones to talk to. Dr. Cain shook Becca's hand and Owen's, pumping their arms in an exaggerated way. "Nice to meet you. Actually, I have to bow out. I'm sure the three of you don't need a dad around, anyway." When they all entered, Dr. Cain disappeared upstairs; Claire, Becca, and Owen dropped their coats on a chair just inside the living room.

Becca plopped down on the living room floor, while Owen pulled back the fireplace screen and picked up a box of matches from behind the poker.

Claire stood dumbfounded by the comfortable way they'd made themselves at home.

"We used to come here all the time," Becca revealed. "With Serena. It was her favorite place. She had a key."

"To do what?" Claire asked, squatting down on the floor beside Becca.

"Nothing," Owen muttered, picking up a newspaper from a stack on the hearthstone and curling it into a tight tube.

"*Everything*," Becca whispered, her eyes glittering.

Claire eyed the hiking boots Becca had on with her dark jeans and a midnight-blue sweater that offered the perfect contrast to her blond hair and ruddy complexion. Becca was drop-dead beautiful—even grief-stricken, even without makeup. She didn't need makeup, Claire thought with a slight twinge of jealousy. Bare, her lips were the shade of pink summer geraniums. It must have felt good, Claire thought, to leave the house uncovered.

"This house was just someplace we went when we didn't have enough money for Ramona's," Owen said with a shrug.

"What's Ramona's?" Claire asked.

"Ramona's Beer Joint," Becca said softly. "A country bar off the highway. Never carded the four of us when we went out to dance to their rockabilly band and get out of this town for a while."

"Us—Chas went, too?" Claire asked.

"Of course," Becca answered. She frowned, shaking her head. "I don't know why he keeps acting like it wasn't a big deal, him and Serena. She loved him. Her first big love."

Claire's gaze darted up toward the fireplace just as Owen rolled his eyes, struck a match, and lit the edge of the newspaper.

Becca's expression grew distant as she said, "Serena always liked coming here better than the bar. We'd just—stretch out on the living room floor, in front of the fire, passing some bottle we'd snagged with the help of an extra ten-dollar bill and some random stranger outside a liquor store. We'd talk while the fire crackled. Sometimes, we'd lie flat on the throw rug, our heads all together in a tiny circle, our feet stretched out in front of us so that we looked a little like a human starburst."

"What'd you talk about?" Claire asked, because she couldn't stand the tense atmosphere that filled the room when Becca stopped chattering.

"Our—dreams," Becca said. "All of them were sort of variations on the same dream, really: to get out of Peculiar. Life starts on the other side of the city limits sign, after all."

Owen leaned forward, holding the edge of his newspaper to a log, clenching his jaw. Becca cocked her head to the side, watching Owen. When he replaced the fireplace screen and plopped down on the hearth, she reached out to touch his knee.

"I just want her back," Becca murmured.

Owen's face turned as gray as it had during lunch the day before. He shook his head, pulled out of her grasp, and stood. In two smooth strides, he was on the opposite side of the living room, reaching for his black wool coat.

"Don't, Owen," Becca pleaded. "Not now, not with all this going on. I can't help feeling bad. Just give me a few more days. Until the funeral. Please."

"You don't know what you're talking about, Beck. For the eight hundredth time, it's not what you think."

"It is," Becca argued. "I just need a few more days. Sit here with me. With us."

But Owen slipped into his black wool coat and hurried out the door.

Becca's face twisted with pure agony as she stared into the fire.

"What was that all about?" Claire finally asked softly.

"He's different," Becca confided. "You don't know—you didn't know him before. But he's different."

"How's that?"

"He used to be—well, first," she said, as tears collected in her eyes, "he used to be a slob." She chuckled. "Everything about him was sloppy. He was cute, of course—I mean, he's gorgeous, right? He's always been that. But a slob, too. Now, suddenly, his hair's combed and his shirts are tucked in, like he's going to a job interview or something.

"He started acting different with me, too," Becca added, her voice thickening, lowering. She straightened her back, wiped her face. With her eyes still centered on the fire Owen had lit, she divulged, "When we started dating, he was after me all the time. Like you expect a guy to be, really. We'd make out for hours on the couch in my basement. But it wasn't just that—he'd tickle me in the hallways at school. Or play with my hair at the movies. He just—always had to *touch* me. He doesn't do that anymore.

"He started acting like somehow, he was sort of—better

than me. And Chas, too," Becca blurted. "It's so funny, because, you know, Chas is the one with a chance at a football scholarship. Owen's mostly on the varsity team because it's such a small school that *anybody* can play for whatever team they try out for." She snorted. "They call him the half-assed halfback."

Claire stared at Becca as she continued talking, almost to herself now.

"I mean, I've got grades, you know, and extracurriculars with cheerleading. I can get a scholarship. Serena—she was always going to get some money, too, I figured, for being a reporter on the paper. Some nice respectable state school. But *Owen* . . ." She shook her head. "He's pretty. And not much else. He's got crappy grades and he's a half-assed halfback, and I always figured he'd be the one who would stay, wind up married, living on his dad's farm—maybe driving to Kansas City for some dumb car sales job, showing off his glistening white teeth as he flirted with the customers.

"But the last time we were all here—just a couple of weeks ago—there was something faraway in his voice," Becca confessed. "Like he had somehow taken a step away from all of us. Like *he* was the one who was the closest to the city limits sign."

The fire snapped, spit as Becca shook her head, tears streaming down her cheeks. "I think he's cheating on me."

"Why would he do that?" Claire asked. "You're the

prettiest girl at Peculiar High."

"Please," Becca chortled. "I bet it's one of those cheerleaders from Kansas City. The ones we see during away games. It's not like I can be with him the *whole* time—sometimes, he's off with the team afterward, and—" She shook her head. "Well. I just bet it's one of those cheerleaders. I bet he feels like he's really pulled one over on me. That's why he's acting like he's so much better than me."

"That can't be right. You must just be misunderstanding him," Claire tried.

But Becca wasn't listening. "When it came out that Chas had screwed around on Serena with that *Ruthie girl*, Owen started giving Chas high fives and sharing these inside jokes about me," she said. "I could tell. The two of them were kind of . . . thick as thieves, for a while, after the rumor exploded. And I was just a nag. Now, with this thing with Serena, he's not *there*. Not for me. Serena's gone, and now he's going to break up with me. Can you believe it? In the middle of *this*, Owen's going to dump me." She gritted her teeth and raked her fingers through her hair.

"She was a good friend to you," Claire observed.

Becca flinched. "What? Why'd you say that?"

"I can just tell—the way you talk about her," Claire replied.

Becca fell silent a moment. She hugged her legs to her chest as the fire snapped before them. "Girls are so much different from boys," she said. "Ever notice that? Girls get to places inside each other that even a boyfriend can't. Girls remember, they pay attention—not because it's going to help them avoid a fight later on, but because they *want* to know everything about each other. Serena and I were so close—there were times that it was like we were trying on each other's personalities, like skirts from each other's closets. Over the past few weeks, looking back, I think that being with a boyfriend is like a one-way friendship. Because I did all the searching, all the learning, and instead of trying to get to know me, too, Owen just—he's found someone else. I know it."

Claire's pulse swam in her ears, revving against Becca's description of friendship. All she could think of was Rachelle, and their last celebration at the movies, and jabbing each other in the ribs. *God,* she missed that.

"I was a terrible friend to her," Becca wailed, putting her head on her arms.

"That can't be true," Claire told her. "The way you looked for her—the way you—"

"It *is* true," Becca insisted, raising her head. Her face was instantly puffy from her tears. "I loved her, but—she had a couple of scars," Becca said, her mouth racing forward, like an out-of-control train. "Both of them were because of a hobo spider bite she got at summer camp a few years back. And it made her have this awful asthma attack. They wound up having to intubate her. You know—a trach?" she asked, touching the base of her throat. "It left a scar. She used to cover it up with a necklace.

"The *other* scar, though," Becca went on, "the one on her leg? Where the bite actually was? By the time she got to the hospital, the skin around the bite on her leg was already dying. Turning black. Took almost a year for the wound to heal. That scar was so ugly. Looked almost like a bullet hole. She wore body makeup, in the summer, to try to cover it. But she never could, not completely."

Her face twisted in pain. "I loved that scar," she admitted, her shoulders heaving.

"You couldn't have loved a scar," Claire assured her. "That's not something you ever love about a friend."

"No," Becca said. "I did. I loved it. Because it was one more thing," she went on, swiping her runny nose with the back of her hand. "One more thing that made me better."

Claire cocked her head and stared at Becca. "What do you mean?"

"Rich was right about me," Becca consented. "What he said about how I treated Serena. I *did* like being better than her. Smarter. A cheerleader. Prettier, even—I actually used to think that. I used to like that I was prettier . . . I'm not really a very good person." She dropped her head again, cascading into a new round of tears.

Claire tried to comfort Becca, awkwardly placing a hand on her back.

Becca wiped her eyes, pressed her cheek against Claire's

shoulder. "I'm sorry about laying all that on you. It's just that I want to do it all over again," she blubbered. "I want to be the friend I should have been. I know you're not going to be here very long, but with you being in her house, it just seems like—it's like it was meant to be. A second chance to do it right. Besides," she added. "You were there, too. You know what I saw. We're in this together. You understand."

Claire didn't disagree, but all she could think of was Rachelle. The way Becca had talked of her friendship with Serena made Claire feel gutted and sorry and achingly lonely all at the same time.

Once Becca's tears wound down, she said sheepishly, "Anyway, I'd better go. Sorry I'm such a wreck," she added as she put on her coat and shoved her hat down over her forehead.

"Totally understandable," Claire said, smiling at her. "See you in school Monday."

Becca nodded; the door had barely shut when Dr. Cain's feet thundered down the stairs.

"Think we're up and running," he told her. When she stared blankly at him, he added, "The Wi-Fi? Why don't you go see if your laptop connects, just to be sure?"

"Oh, right. Sure." Claire raced up the stairs, her head still swarming with everything Becca had confessed, in her grief. Everything she had said about having a best friend.

When she flipped her laptop open on her bed, Claire

immediately clicked into her email account, chose Rachelle's address, and started typing. She described it in brutal detail, the entire scene in the woods behind the school—the smells, the sounds. The way Serena had looked. *Just like me*, she wrote. *She must have looked just like me, that night, out in the parking lot.*

When she finished, the cursor hovered over the "Send" button. She ached to click it—she craved the kind of closeness that Becca had just described. Claire missed Rachelle with a new intensity.

But so much had happened. So much still stood between Rachelle and Claire. With a deep breath and a quick blink to clear away the tears, she clicked "Save Draft."

She scrolled through the list of emails in her "Draft" folder. She picked one closer toward the bottom of the list—one of the older ones—pulling it up on her screen.

"Rachelle," it started,

do you really think I'm stupid? You must, because you are outside my window. Right NOW, Rachelle. You are outside my window, and here I am, still laid up in bed. Didn't you happen to notice the way Dad pushed my bed up to the window, you dumb, selfish bitch? So I could get some sunlight? Because it's been weeks—no, months, now, since the beating. Did you forget how bad it was? I'd be happy to remind you: three broken ribs, a shoulder fracture, a wrist fracture, a broken arm, broken thigh bone, splintered ankle, smashed feet, shattered fingers, two surgeries for internal injuries, hundreds of stitches, and nerve blocks to manage the pain of multiple lacerations. Yeah. That's what I've been doing. Healing up from all of that. And you just came to visit—all smiles and happy. God, your stupid visits. You and your damned hospital voice. That's what you use when you talk—not even TO me, but AT me: a hospital voice. And you don't even rattle on about anything I care about.

And you look at me like I'm not the same. Don't you think I KNOW I'm not the same? Don't you think I'm reminded of it every single time I look in the mirror? You're still every bit as pretty as you ever were, and I'm here in a body that looks like a wrecked car.

Now you're on the sidewalk, outside my window, talking to some guy. Some damned new guy. Because guys still look at you. Guys won't ever look at me the same way again, not me in this ugly body that I'm going to have to cover up the rest of my life.

You're with a brand-new guy, because you decided your senior wasn't worth your precious time. Isn't that what you said? And you're talking to him like YOU. Like the old Rachelle. And you're going on with your life and here I am you selfish bitch and I can hear you and YOU DON'T EVEN HAVE THE DECENCY TO PRETEND TO CARE. I HEAR YOU, YOU BITCH. I HEAR YOU.

Claire flinched, closed the email. She didn't remember her old emails being so nasty. So angry.

Really, Claire, she told herself. *You should be glad you never sent them.*

But another feeling had found her, the moment she'd reread that email. *Yes!* that feeling cried out. *Yes! Yes! That's right! It's all true! She was never sorry—not really. She only pretended to be sorry when she was around you. She didn't give a damn! She maybe even loved your scars, just like Becca.*

"Claire!" her dad called. "I'm assuming that long pause of yours means you're already online."

"Yes—everything's fine!" she called as she flipped her laptop shut.

But in reality, her own words, glowing right there on the screen, said differently.

TWELVE

"Unfortunately," Ms. Mavis boomed on Monday morning, shouting so that her Journalism II class could hear her over the incessant growl of chain saws and the rumble of chipper-shredders. Tree-trimming crews continued their task of chopping up the limbs that had fallen during the ice storm and turning them into mulch—and judging by the noises filling the air, had decided to spend the bulk of the morning right there beneath the journalism room window. "Unfortunately," she repeated, "we have lost one of our own."

She paused for a moment to stick a finger into her enormous bouffant hairdo, scratch her scalp.

"Serena Sims," she went on, throwing her blazer to the side in order to put her fist on her round hip. "I'm sure we will all choose to remember Serena in our own way. I will remember her as one of the most passionate students to have ever entered my room. Ms. Sims had a love of journalism that made me confident I would see her name in a byline of her own in a major paper someday.

"Now," she added, her eyes roving behind her wire frames as she observed her students, "as unfortunate as it is, Ms. Sims was not the first student we have lost at Peculiar High. Three of our boys died hilltopping the year before last. A case of accidental alcohol poisoning two years before that. It was a disastrous, heart-wrenching incident, losing Ms. Sims. Something we will never forget. But I guarantee you, she will not be the last student to ever meet such a sad end. And we as journalism students must learn to deal with tragedy—to report it with honesty and compassion."

She paced through the room, her heels clicking as the reek of cheap musk trailed behind her.

Claire gagged as the scent grew stronger. She swore it reminded her of the stench of cat urine that continuously floated from the bushes in front of her house. She raised her head only to find that Mavis was staring directly at her.

Claire's eyes roved over the thick powdery blush that had worked its way deep into the crevices of the woman's face. The opaque nude pantyhose and the blue inch-high pumps. Mavis had the look of something bargain-basement, out of fashion. Like something that she and Rachelle would have found at a vintage store in Chicago, so worn-out that they'd have hung it right back on the rack, even if it did cost less than a dollar.

The comparison made Claire feel as though her emotions were duking it out. The back and forth between hating Rachelle and missing Rachelle was exhausting her. She shifted uncomfortably in her seat, crossing and recrossing her legs.

Feeling eyes on her, Claire glanced up to find Rich staring. If he were any other boy, Claire might have assumed he was eyeing her rustling skirt. The boys at a school with uniforms spent so much time staring at girls' legs, Claire often figured they were all experts in pleated skirts by the time they graduated. They could all predict how a skirt would behave in a gust of wind, how it shifted when a girl climbed the stairs. Boys at Peculiar High, Claire figured, knew pleated skirts the way her father knew sedimentary rock.

But Rich was different. He wasn't staring at her legs, but waiting to catch her eye. When he did, he raised the fingers of his right hand in greeting.

Claire smiled and nodded. There it was again—that deliciously calm sensation she got anytime Rich was around.

"It is our duty, now, to continue on," Mavis announced, pointing at the class like she was getting a room full of real reporters riled up about their deadlines—an easy comparison, since they weren't even in a classroom, but the journalism lab, each of them sitting at long tables rather than student desks, their faces illuminated by the glow of computer screens.

". . . to regroup and move forward," Mavis said. "And I

think we'll be able to do that with the help of a new student on our team."

Claire shifted again, squirming as the entire class swiveled in their chairs to look her way.

"Claire Cain, recipient of the Robert F. Kennedy Journalism Award. Her *freshman* year. Her sophomore year, she did some work on a local story that gained significant media attention in the Chicago area," she went on.

Claire felt herself begin to sweat. Her face burned with embarrassment. The story from her sophomore year was about Rachelle's locker search. About the freshman. The pencil box with the lightning bolts. Intent to distribute.

Everyone was staring at her. Waiting for her to say something. For her to talk about her stories. But she didn't want to talk—not about Rachelle. She only raised herself in her seat, squared her shoulders. Put on the pose of a girl who could win awards for *any* story she chased—even some crummy cafeteria mystery meat exposé.

Slowly, they all began to turn their attention back to their instructor.

"Investigative journalism," Mavis went on. "I want us all to really think about what that means. We've covered this material. And yet, none of you have really challenged yourselves. Fluff pieces. That's all I seem to be getting—even from the news department. I do believe our news editor could be of more help where that is concerned," she went on, throwing a bitter look at Rich.

Rich offered a half nod that seemed to acknowledge she was right.

"I'm sure we would all like to show our impressive new class member what we're capable of," Mavis said. She pointed at a sign-up sheet on the wall. "I would like every one of you to revisit your old ideas. I've made a few notes next to your topics. Talk to each other, move about the room, the hour is yours."

Chairs scraped; feet stomped the tile. Claire doodled a bit in her notebook, trying to come up with some topics of her own.

But as she tried to focus, she found herself thinking again about how it had been to discover Serena. Her memory was muddled, confused, but it seemed to her that the air around the body had smelled kind of tinny and preserved—like foil-wrapped hamburger patties taken out of the freezer.

The newspaper article and the TV reporters didn't say anything about that—how Serena's body had been preserved by the ice, kept fresh for the ferals to eat. In fact, the paper and the TV reporters hadn't mentioned the ferals at all. Or how the air around Serena's body had tingled with the same kind of danger that had spewed out of the transformers during the ice storm. Or how the puddle of Claire's vomit had steamed in the snow beside Serena's body. How there had been screams for help and pleas to calm down and how one person's voice had only made others wail even louder. How guttural and wild the entire scene had been.

Until Rich had shown up, anyway. Until he'd dragged Claire away from the woods, put her safely in his truck and driven her home.

She wondered, fleetingly, what Mavis would think about that for a topic: "The Five Senses of a Death Scene," an investigation by Claire Cain. She could tag along with the Peculiar PD, recording the smells and sights of old ladies, frozen by rigor mortis in their beds, and compare it to Serena. She'd go to the coroner's office, record how a day-old, already autopsied body smelled, how the skin reacted when she pressed her thumb into it, and compare that to how the flesh reacted on the hilltoppers who were apparently always biting the dust in Peculiar, when she reached through their shattered windows and pinched their still-warm arms.

No matter how she tried to occupy her mind with real topics—decent topics—for the school paper, Serena Sims's death scene kept interrupting her thoughts. She gripped her pen tighter, as though it might somehow settle the dizzy spin in her head.

When she glanced up, Rich's eyes were on her again. He got up from his own chair, slipped into the plastic seat right beside her.

"How are you?" he asked. "The last time I saw you—" He pointed toward the window, in the general direction of the woods.

Claire nodded. "Pretty gruesome," she muttered.

"Yeah," Rich said. "Lucky your dad was already home when I called."

Claire grunted an agreement.

"I mean—I guess your mom—"

"No mom," Claire said.

"In—Chicago?" he asked hopefully.

"Died in childbirth," she said. "One of the rare modern-day cases." Somehow, though, mentioning her mother made her think about how horrible and vicious *that* scene must have been—hemorrhaging to death on Claire's birthday. It made it seem like Claire's entire life had been tainted by violence, right from the start. She wondered if violence didn't follow some people, the same way bad luck trailed after others.

Rich's stare was far too intense for Claire. She didn't want to continue their conversation. She patted his arm, pushed her seat back, and walked to the front of the room, where the sign-up sheet hung. Rich came along, too, right on her heels.

It had been crossed out, but Claire could still see it, near the top of the sheet—*Serena Sims: Basement.*

Clare stared at the subject, written in Serena's own neat handwriting—the *s*'s curling like ribbon on a Christmas present.

"What's that—'Basement'?"

"It's nothing," Rich mumbled. "That's what Mavis and I were trying to tell her, anyway."

"Oh, yeah?" She paused, intrigued, her mind tumbling over the possibilities. She grinned, feeling it again—faintly, but there just the same: that old spark, that fire. Her love of stories. "I want to finish Serena's piece. Pick up where her research left off," she blurted.

"Why?" Rich asked.

"Think about it," Claire said. "What would be a better tribute than to finish her work?"

"A bit ordinary," Mavis said, crossing her arms over her chest as she approached Rich and Claire. "Not quite what I expected, given your track record. And not exactly what I was hoping for, either." She leaned forward to add in a hushed voice, "I'd actually hoped you would kick these guys into gear. Hoped you'd really push them."

"Just for the first story," Claire vowed. "I'll ramp it up the second time around. I just feel it's really important to—honor her. Serena."

Mavis took a deep breath.

"Unless there's nothing there, of course," Claire continued. "If I get into it, and there's nothing, I'll drop it."

"All right," Mavis said, reluctantly agreeing. "You've got a short leash on this one, Cain. You're also doing the dance."

"The dance?" Claire repeated.

"The Winter Formal," Mavis explained. "I know—one dance is the same as another—but Dr. Sanders requires us to cover all school events. A week from this Friday. Take a photographer."

"I'll do it," Rich croaked.

"You're an editor, not a photographer," Mavis argued.

"To get her settled in. Give her the 411 on working for the paper," Rich offered.

Mavis sighed loudly through her nose. "You should take it as a compliment," she told Claire. "He usually refuses to cover the dances. Calls them—what was it again, Rich? Clichés on parade?" She grinned as Rich's face turned pink.

Claire pulled Rich aside. "I'd like to get started on Serena's basement story as soon as possible," she told him. "This afternoon."

"The library's the place to start," Rich said. "For background. I'll take you."

THIRTEEN

"I just need to do some research. For school," Claire said into her father's voice mail that afternoon, as Rich steered toward the public library.

They jiggled along in Rich's truck—the cab was so pristine, she'd actually thought, for a moment, that she should take her shoes off before getting inside. She hadn't had her wits about her enough to notice, the day she'd discovered Serena. But the truck gleamed—and it smelled like a Christmas tree. The smell actually complemented the snow that flew through the air—not exactly a blizzard, but instead, one of those quaint snowfalls in which flakes circled and never seemed to drop.

In the distance, though, the ice storm had given the landscape an odd, cracked, bitten-into look.

"So—I'll—see you for dinner," Claire promised. It

felt lonely talking to a machine that couldn't hear her, and knowing that her father was too far below the surface of the earth to get her message. He wouldn't hear her voice until he came up out of the ground, shucked off his coveralls, and checked his messages before starting home for dinner himself. It felt awful to be so removed from him, like she could scream and scream and never be heard.

Claire had just dropped her phone into her coat pocket when a new message came in. Hoping it was from her father, Claire hurried to read it, and felt her body revving up all over again: *Read article abt girl found. U ok? Pls answer.*

The text was from Rachelle. And if Rachelle had just sent it, that meant she was still within reach. Claire could text her right back, and get an immediate answer. The kind of answer that would spark a whole conversation. Rachelle would get tired of typing—as she always used to—and call Claire's number.

Claire envisioned it all—so real to her, she could almost hear Rachelle's voice. She knew how good it would feel to settle back into the shorthand that longtime friends always had. The kind of understanding in which a half-finished sentence could mean more than a thousand texts.

But that shorthand was dead. For the past nine months, Rachelle had treated her like an antique with a crack in it.

You're just feeling a little nostalgic because of the way Becca talked about Serena this past weekend, she assured herself.

And besides, she was with Rich. On the way to the library.

Claire turned off her phone and shoved it deep into her backpack as Rich parked. She climbed out of his truck, hoisted her backpack onto her shoulder, and took a step forward, toward the single concrete step that led to the door of the public library.

As she stared, her entire body felt as sturdy as a half-melted gummy bear. In that moment, the large snowflakes dancing in front of her face felt sharp, like sleet. Like one last ice storm before spring could settle in. The longer she stared, the more she remembered—voices, laughter. She could see them all, clustered on the steps, smoking. Waiting for her.

"Hey, you okay?" Rich called.

Claire glanced up, hating the look of concern that crinkled his face. Hating that she had cemented herself into place beside his truck. Hating the fear heating her veins.

"Of course," she said, but clenched her fists as she raised her foot to climb the solitary step. *It's not the same library*, she tried to convince her racing heart.

She trembled, sucked in a breath, and pushed through the doors—grateful that her coat hid the way her chest shook with each breath.

The library smelled like old paper and mold and earth. Claire wondered if every building in Peculiar reeked with age.

"Help you?" a voice rasped with authority from the research desk.

When Claire turned, she found herself facing a woman who—judging merely by her appearance—spent every workday behind this very desk and whose only taste of adventure surely came from the pages of a book. The librarian's back was bent at an arch, the fingers she'd placed on her desk red and knobby. Her entire body appeared as one twisted, inflamed knot of arthritis.

"Yes. Thank you. I'm looking for back issues of the Peculiar newspaper," Claire explained.

"Microfilm," the woman offered, her blue eyes rotating above red bags of skin as she pointed toward a gray cluster of metal cabinets.

Claire nodded a thank-you and raced forward. "Got it," she said, not wanting to make the librarian move. She knew firsthand how hard it was to steer a body that only wanted to rest until the pain subsided.

But Rich caught her arm. "Actually, we're looking for information on the incident with Dr. Sanders," he said.

"*Sanders?*" Claire asked. "What does he have to do—"

She stopped mid-sentence when she saw the woman's face lengthen, her features shift downward, as though the mere mention of the event had filled her with sadness.

"November 2007," she whispered.

"You know what he's asking for?" Claire asked. "You can remember the date off the top of your head?"

The woman's blue eyes darkened as she admitted,

"Something like that—you don't ever forget."

"Thanks," Rich said, turning and heading toward the metal cabinets of microfilm.

Claire followed, still jarred by what the librarian had said. Were there truly incidents so horrific that they never faded in time?

Rich tugged a drawer open, reached inside. "Pretty old-fashioned, compared to Chicago, I bet," he said as he ushered Claire toward a nearby chair and fed the microfilm into a reader.

"There he is," he said, pointing at the black-and-white image on the screen.

"There who is?" Claire asked.

"Casey Andrews," he said.

"Casey—"

"Andrews," Rich said. "For your story about the basement. Your urban legend."

"*That's* what Serena was researching? An urban legend?" Claire's eyes scanned the print glowing on the microfilm screen. She leaned forward, making the zipper on her backpack let out a little scream as she threw it open. She propped her computer into her lap.

"Yep. Serena was sure there was a story here."

"Okay, then talk," she instructed Rich. "The facts are good, but I need to know all the human interest stuff, too— the things that Serena would know about, because she'd lived here her entire life."

"What are you going to do, take notes?" Rich asked, eyeing her keyboard.

"I'm writing the backstory as *story*," Claire said. "I don't care how impartial a reporter's supposed to be, a story's not a story until it's got guts. And a story doesn't have guts until some emotion gets mixed in with the facts. So—talk."

She listened, and her eyes danced about the screen of the microfilm reader. She began to transcribe the events, her fingers tapping out details so horrendous and vibrantly real, she couldn't help but imagine it all from Casey's eyes— especially the last scene. The scene that had played itself out more than a month after Sanders was hurt . . .

Seven Years Ago

Casey Andrews slammed the door of his pickup, parked in the small field just behind Peculiar High. He stood on a soft muddy patch of earth, feeling the bite of the wintry night air as he watched his breath stream out the front of his face. He eyed the stars. He felt the weight of his father's shotgun in his hand.

His feet crunched against the dead leaves out behind the school. Summer had held on longer than usual; the trees had all turned brilliant shades of red and orange shortly before Thanksgiving. Even now, a week before Christmas, leaves were still tumbling onto sidewalks. Kids were still being told by parents that they could earn their allowance with a rake. It was one more thing he'd never do again, Casey thought as he approached the window. He'd never rake his parents' front yard, the smell of burning compost wafting about his face.

He crouched down low, toward the ground-level windows to the basement. It was easy to find the ones that led to the boys' locker room because they were tinted, so no one could see in. The girls' locker room didn't have windows at all.

He counted the dark glass squares, pressed his hand against the fourth from the right. When he pushed, it gave. Just like he expected it to.

He'd broken the window a month ago. Broken the latch, anyway, from the inside of the building. Busted it with the quick smack of a hammer swiped from shop class, while the rest of the guys in third period gym were in the showers.

He'd laughed when it had broken, then hidden his smile along with his hammer as he'd raced back to the showers before anyone could suspect anything.

It would have been easy, too, for any of them to think he was up to no good. Of course, "no good" with Casey had always been uttered through a grin. He was a prankster; that's what everyone had said ever since elementary school. An old-fashioned prankster, the kind that had always been able to escape any real punishment because his antics had even made his teachers smile. The tools of his trade had been whoopee cushions and confetti in buckets propped on the top of classroom doors. In middle school, he'd gone running buck naked through a soccer game. By freshman year, he was standing up in the middle of lunch and belting out "The Impossible Dream" in a fake-operatic voice, just for the fun of seeing people stare at him like he'd lost it.

He'd had a plan, a month ago. Another prank—the best prank of all, he'd thought, sneaking into the locker room through his broken window, a good two hours before the big goony jocks came strutting in to get ready for the championship game.

He was already giggling as he'd dropped to his knees in the midst of the lockers, placing his supplies on the floor: a two-liter soda bottle filled with paint and a small container of dry ice that he'd crushed into pieces small enough to fit through the bottle's neck. He'd slipped into his dad's heavy-duty work gloves and smiled as he'd shoved the dry ice into the container, quickly. He shook the bottle, threw it, and ran. He had enough paint in that bottle for a good thirty-plus seconds of spray. Of hot neon pink spray.

Casey's bomb was going to throw a cloud of pink over everything: the lockers, the towels, the toilet paper, the toilet seats, the mirrors, the urinals. Most importantly, pink paint would splash across the uniforms, all hanging in a row beside the lockers, like they always were before a game, because Peculiar High had a laundry service for the athletes. Small towns took care of their own.

Everything was going to be pink. And everyone would know— this has got to be another Casey prank, they'd laugh, hugging their blankets around their necks in the stands as the team appeared in hot pink splatter-painted uniforms.

It was so, so perfect.

Except for the fact that Dr. Sanders was still around. Casey hadn't planned on that. Nor had he planned on Sanders hearing noises coming from the boys' locker room.

The dry ice burned Sanders when it had flown into his face the moment he'd gone to check out the strange racket, spraying him right in the eyes. He'd let out a horrible, shrieking wail, like a man being set on fire.

Casey'd raced back inside the locker room, feet slipping on the sloppy pink paint that had sprayed across the tile. He'd dragged Sanders to the hall, and he'd pulled his cell out of the back pocket of his jeans to call 911. He'd tried to help flush Sanders's eyes clean in the water fountain, and he'd cried as the ambulance took off.

The damage was done, though. Sanders had all but completely lost his vision in one eye and the other was only marginally better.

Grief came to sit heavily in Casey's chest, torturing him. He'd blinded a man. All because he wanted some football numbskulls to wear pink jockstraps.

"For God's sake, Casey," his dad had said when the bills started arriving. "Didn't you ever think about how dangerous that dry ice was? Didn't you ever think that we would have to pay for your stupid nonsense?"

He hadn't, actually. He hadn't thought of anything but the laughter his prank would create. But his family was liable for the uniforms—and Sanders's medical costs. Casey's sister's college money had gone up in a giant black cloud.

And no one wanted to touch the horrible story themselves, not voluntarily, not even a little, which meant that no one was calling his father the plumber to unclog their drains, not anymore. The family business was teetering on the brink of nonexistence. No one talked to his sister at school. She ate alone in the bathroom. She didn't think he knew, but he did. And his mother—his poor mother—all the other moms around tried to pity her, tried to be overly nice to her, but that just made things worse. She behaved as though she'd been shunned, choosing to shop at a grocery store thirty miles down the highway. She cried while she did the dinner dishes.

Nothing was the same. Every day something else crumbled into black ash.

And it was all his fault.

Everyone who'd had anything to do with him—his childhood friends, his parents, his teachers, his old soccer coach—acted like they had screwed up, like they had helped create some kind of horrible, vicious person and they couldn't figure out just where, exactly, they'd gone wrong. Small towns took the blame for their own, after all. He had hurt a man, blinded him for the rest of his life. He had taken his sister's future away. He had surely stolen his father's business. All for a prank.

The horrible part, he'd come to realize, was that everyone was right. He was selfish, he was stupid, he was maybe even vicious. Something was wrong with him. He could not tell anyone how badly he felt about it. Because all anyone ever did if he tried was nod in a way that said, "You should feel bad."

He told himself that it was the low point, that he would

dig himself out, just like a rat climbing out from the sewer. But how could he help make things better when every day brought something new—another bill that they couldn't afford to pay, his sister's tears—and he knew that what he had done had ruined everything? They would go bankrupt. His sister would never have the life she wanted. So why should he have his? The world would be better off without him and his stupid ideas, all the things he'd destroyed that he couldn't bring back, the mistakes that he would never be able to make up for. Some stupid suspension from school and probation until he graduated would never atone for it all.

It would be his Christmas present to everyone, he thought, as he slipped in through the still-broken window, into the boys' locker room.

Quietly, slowly, he walked to the same spot where he'd squatted to assemble his paint bomb. The walls around him were marked with stains that would never come out—awful pink smears so wild, Casey almost swore they were screaming.

Happiness was a charred pile of ash, he thought.

He turned off his phone. He didn't want to be interrupted.

Closing his eyes, he took one last deep breath before putting the barrel of the gun in his mouth.

FOURTEEN

Claire stopped typing, collapsed back into her chair. "It just built upon itself," she murmured. "Until he felt like he had no choice. Until he—" She sighed, shaking her head sadly.

"They closed the basement after that," Rich said. "At the time, the school was being used as a middle *and* high school—that's why two gyms, one upstairs and one down. They moved the middle schoolers out, into an offshoot of the old elementary school. Moved the high school gym and classes upstairs. The idea was to keep the basement closed until they had enough money to completely renovate the place. One of the top priorities was to replace the old boiler, if I remember right. Everyone said it got too hot for the classes that were held down there. School board's tried a few bond issues, but nothing's really worked. They haven't hit the fund-raising goal."

"Under these circumstances, you'd think everyone would want to chip in to fix the place up," Claire said.

"They would if they could have. But times have been hard here. Nobody's had a lot of money to give. The Andrews family moved away a while back. The basement's been locked to the outside ever since the accident."

Rich's eyes grew distant as he clarified, "In a way, it kind of feels as though the basement's always been boarded up to the outside. That door that leads to the downstairs basement— the one next to the front office? I don't think it *is* locked— janitors sometimes toss stuff down there—but it might as well be. Everybody knows it's off-limits, and besides, nobody really wants anything to do with the place, any more than they really want anything to do with a cemetery at midnight."

Claire rubbed her chin, a long sigh filling the air around her head. Her eyes were gritty from staring so intently at her computer screen, and her throat was dry.

"But this isn't investigative," she said. "This is a finished story. With the exception of the pending renovations, anyway. What could Serena have possibly been looking into?"

"I'll be back in a minute." Rich hurried away, returning with a stack of microfilm nearly as long as his arm. "This is what she was researching." He fed reel after reel into the machine, showing Claire articles about odd incidents at

Peculiar High in the years following Casey's death: water fountains gone berserk, flooding the floors. Strange knocking noises. Janitors reporting bleachers had pulled themselves out in the old gymnasium.

Her chest heaved as she read. "*This* was it?" she asked.

"I don't know what any of it could have amounted to. I was calling it Serena's silly ghost-hunter piece, and you already know Mavis thinks it's weak. All of those incidents were explained shortly after they took place," Rich said softly. "Once the kids who'd been students with Casey had all graduated, it sort of—opened things up for everybody to start building on this story of a ghost haunting the basement. Nobody'd known him personally—they hadn't grown up with him—and it didn't really seem all that disrespectful. He was an urban legend, something that didn't seem real. Look at the dates, Claire. Every one of these incidents took place around Halloween. April Fools' Day. Senior Prank Day. Just kids—"

"Just kids being kids," Claire interrupted. "I know what happens to kids," she said gravely.

Rich leaned closer. "Yeah—I know you found Serena," he said. "I was there, too, remember? I saw her out there. Just like you did. I was with you."

Claire sighed, running her fingers through her wavy hair. He didn't have a clue.

"Why did Owen call you that?" Claire blurted. She'd wanted to ask ever since she'd heard it, during her first lunch period. "Wretch. Why did he say that?"

Rich flopped back into his own chair, shaking his head. "It's stupid, really. Serena and I were friends when we were little. She lived in your house until she was about ten, so we were neighbors. We were both sort of—on the fringe. She had asthma and braces, and we were both overweight. Not exactly the Bold and the Beautiful.

"But around middle school, she lost a lot of weight, and got really pretty. So she was suddenly acceptable for Becca to hang with. And I went through about four thousand growth spurts. Obviously," he said, pointing at his chest. "They took her braces off, and they gave her one of those retainers for a while, the plastic kind that fits on the roof of your mouth. She had a really hard time talking around the thing, and when she said my name, it sounded like—"

"Wretch," Claire finished.

"Right. And Becca started calling me that in this vicious way, like I was some awful person. Like I was some kind of hulking monster. I always thought it was her way of showing Serena I wasn't worth hanging with—that she needed to cut ties."

"And Serena just went along with it?" Claire asked.

Rich shrugged. "I didn't hold it against her. We were twelve. She wanted to be popular. So be it."

"But *you* didn't want to be inside the golden circle?" Claire asked.

Rich chuckled. "Don't you know that the people inside those circles aren't really gold? They're gold-*plated*."

"Do you miss her?" Claire whispered.

"Sometimes. The old Serena, anyway, the fat one who wore braces and shared her favorite banana Popsicles in the summer. But that Serena's been gone a long time. The old Serena was just a little kid—and so was I."

"The old Serena," Claire repeated. She had been thinking of Rachelle in that way, too—*the old Rachelle*, that was the person she missed. The use of such a similar phrase made her feel an instant kinship with Rich.

"Becca was right," Rich sighed. "I *should* have said something about her staying to work on her basement article. I think about it all the time—maybe it would have made a difference. Maybe someone would have found her—" He cut himself off, shaking his head.

Rich pushed himself away from the table and disappeared into the local history room. While he was gone, Claire went through all the articles a second time, typing notes and names and a few quotes into her laptop. When Rich returned, he slid an old yearbook under her nose.

"Here, look at this. Casey's last school picture."

Claire shuddered, staring into the face. The yearbook picture was far clearer than anything on microfilm. She could tell the boy had a thin frame. A peach-fuzz mustache. Déjà vu rippled down her arms as images slashed like painful light across her eyes. Uniforms. The ice. The dead rodent on her back porch, staring up at her with glassy, vacant eyes. *You like ratting us out?* And a boy, bobbing on his heels.

"Come on," Rich said, reaching in front of her to slam the yearbook shut.

Claire jumped in her seat.

"My dad just texted. Now that you've got your backstory, I've got to stop by the church."

FIFTEEN

The inside of the Peculiar First Baptist Church was sparse—simple white walls, old-fashioned wooden pews, an upright piano. It had a funny smell, too, Claire noted as she and Rich stepped inside—not exactly old in the musty sense, like the school or the library. More like a grandmother's house. Like generations of the same family had trampled through the rooms, grown up right there between the same set of walls. Like decades of holidays and gatherings and tears and triumphs.

"I haven't been—in years," she confessed, feeling self-conscious. In truth, Claire and her father had gone to church for weddings. The occasional funeral. Her father, the scientist, had never been regular-churchgoing material.

"Don't worry about it. I don't exactly live here, either," Rich admitted.

Claire raised an eyebrow. "Really?"

"It's by design. Dad figures if he lets me make my own decisions about going to church—about what I believe—there's nothing to rebel against. No preacher's kid gone wild. I'm here every once in a while, but not every weekend."

Claire nodded as Rich led her down the stairs, into a basement with a large open space filled with tiny kindergarten-sized chairs and construction paper drawings. They passed a kitchen, the counter lined with paper plates for Sunday school snacks, and slipped into a small office where bookshelves were crammed full of volumes stacked every which way, where padded chairs filled corners and an overgrown philodendron wrapped its vines like tentacles around four filing cabinets. Pictures of a chubby boy took up a cluster of frames on the desk.

"Dad," Rich called.

Pastor Ray glanced up from the screen of his laptop. He was every bit as big as Rich, his muscular arms tugging at the sleeves of a black sweatshirt. His balding head had been shaved clean, and he smiled at Rich as he pulled a pair of glasses from the tip of his nose and tossed them on his desktop.

"This is Claire. From the old Sims place," Rich said.

"Ah, yes." Pastor Ray stood, wrapping Claire's hand in both of his. The touch was warm, friendly, without being overly solicitous. "I've been meaning to come by and say hello," he informed her. "Rich, though, is sometimes protective of new friends." He winked, like he was sharing a secret with her, while Rich grumbled wordlessly under his breath.

"I was going to ask you to read this," Pastor Ray told Rich, as he gestured toward his computer. "What I've started to prepare for the Sims funeral."

Claire felt her stomach twist. The funeral. Somehow, she'd forgotten there would be a funeral.

"The school will shut down for the service, of course," Pastor Ray said. "And all businesses will be closed. No doubt the whole town will turn out. I need your help figuring out how we'll get them all upstairs—those pews surely won't—" He shook his head. "But I really wanted you to look at what I'm preparing to say. You knew her."

"When we were kids, Dad," Rich said. "I haven't known Serena for a long time."

Claire watched from her spot near the doorway. Even a disagreement with a father felt calm, when Rich was involved. No shouting, no gnashing of teeth.

"Well. I don't want to keep you two, but I'd appreciate it if you'd give this a look—"

"If you really want me to," Rich conceded with a shrug. "But I'm sure that whatever you have planned—"

Pastor Ray's eyes drifted behind Rich's shoulder, toward the flat-screen TV anchored to his wall. He picked up a remote off the corner of his desk, aimed, and made the screen pop to life.

". . . coming to you from the police station in Peculiar, where Sheriff Holman is preparing to address the community regarding the Sims case . . ."

"What's this?" Rich asked as voices continued to pour from the TV.

"Local Kansas City station. Been promising the results of Serena's autopsy all day," Pastor Ray said.

Claire turned her own eyes toward the screen. The man who stepped up to a small cluster of microphones, sporting bulldog jowls and a large paunch, shifted his weight awkwardly. He looked about as comfortable as a girl in her first pair of heels. "Thank you all for coming today," he grumbled into the mics. He shuffled a few papers nervously.

"My name is Sheriff Holman, and I would like to thank, first of all, the community of Peculiar for their outpouring of sympathy during this time. And on behalf of the Peculiar PD, I would also like to extend our condolences to the Sims family.

"The statement I will now read has been prepared by the coroner and the Peculiar Police Department." He shifted his weight again, cleared his throat, sucked in a shuddery breath.

"The autopsy on Ms. Serena Sims has been completed. The coroner's examination indicates that Ms. Sims died of suffocation. There is no sign of foul play. The results show that Ms. Sims's death was not caused by strangulation—no petechial hemorrhaging present in the eyes, no tissue under the nails to indicate a struggle.

"To further explain how we reached this conclusion, the body of Ms. Sims was discovered in the wooded area behind Peculiar High. She was found beneath an ice-coated limb, wearing only her school uniform. We believe that the cancellation of school early on the day of the ice storm startled Ms. Sims—as I can assure you it startled other students and faculty. In her rush to leave school, Ms. Sims forgot her coat. But the doors, as the security guard has assured us, locked behind the students, in an effort to ensure that all would go home before the roads deteriorated.

"With only her school cardigan to protect her from the elements, Ms. Sims would surely want to get home as soon as possible. In her rush, we believe she decided to cut through the woods behind the school—a common practice among the students. The injuries to Ms. Sims's face, combined with a dislocated shoulder, allowed us to conclude that she was struck by a falling limb and knocked unconscious. The weight of the immense branch would have made it impossible for her to breathe, leading to her suffocation. The official cause of Ms. Sims's death, therefore, is being classified as 'accidental.'

"While we are sure the town will continue to mourn for our lost loved one, we can all rest assured that there was no criminal intent. Ms. Sims was unfortunately in the wrong place at the wrong time."

Pastor Ray hit the remote again, pressing "mute" as

flashbulbs popped on the screen. "An accident," he said, as though trying on the word for the first time.

Rich grunted and nodded.

"You don't want to listen to him answer any questions?" Claire asked.

"He won't," Pastor Ray said.

Claire squinted at the screen, watching as Sheriff Holman nodded to the small crowd of reporters, waved, and disappeared inside the station.

"How did you know he wouldn't—" she started.

"Sheriff Holman," Pastor Ray said as he slid back behind his desk, "would never say anything that wasn't prepared down to the last word. He doesn't know how to handle himself during an incident like this one, because he's never been asked to before. He's patrolled these roads with nothing much to do, throughout the course of his entire career." Pastor Ray's eyes grew distant as he acknowledged, "He's always reminded me of a mean dog someone got to guard their house. But his owners spoiled him with table food, let him get fat and lazy, and now he doesn't even know how to handle basic commands. I've only known him to write maybe a half dozen speeding tickets in his entire career."

"I can only think of three arrests," Rich agreed. "And those were kids playing Halloween pranks. Come to think of it," he added, "he can't even be trusted with tomatoes. He's let hornworms destroy them the past four summers."

Pastor Ray chuckled along with Rich. "Hey!" he said suddenly. "He still has my barbecue tongs. From—"

"Two presidents ago?" Rich finished.

Pastor Ray laughed harder. "The portrait of hard work," he quipped. He started to gesture back toward his laptop when he caught sight of Claire's horrified face.

"Rich," he said. "Take your friend home. We can talk about the funeral later."

Claire allowed Rich to steer her out of his father's office. "Is the sheriff really that bad?" she whispered as they reached the stairs.

"Oh, he's more funny than bad," Rich said dismissively.

This time, though, when he smiled and put a hand on her arm, he didn't give Claire the same calm feeling. Not even close.

SIXTEEN

Claire unloaded the contents of her backpack across her bed—the printouts, the articles about strange events centering on an urban legend and the Peculiar High basement. She reread every one of them, as the daylight on the opposite side of her windows slid toward night.

"What was the draw?" Claire asked, sifting through the old news stories she'd printed from the microfilm reader. "Why did you want to write about this, Serena?"

Shivering in the constant stream of cold air that poured from her warped balcony door, Claire glanced up at the scarf lying in a heap in the middle of the dresser. She still hadn't straightened the material out—it was every bit as bunched and crooked as it had been the moment of her arrival. But maybe, Claire had started to think, some things really were like that—they never did get straightened out. Sometimes, bruises never got a chance to heal. Serena's didn't, anyway.

Accidental, Sheriff Holman had said. But the word didn't sit right. Especially now that Claire had a better idea of who Sheriff Holman really was.

Claire rubbed her eyes. "There has to be more to it. Did you see something? Were you running scared through those woods?"

She sighed. "You had to have stayed pretty late. Otherwise, Rhine would have let you back in. Wouldn't he? But why, Serena? Why did you need to stay after school? You could have drafted your story anywhere. Why would you risk staying? Why—?" She felt the blood race out of her face as she remembered the angry words Becca had shouted at Rich in the street during the ice storm: *Someone needed to look in the basement.* That's why Becca'd been so angry.

Claire picked up a printout, staring at a news photo of the front hall of Peculiar High, crime scene tape stretched in front of the basement door. "Someone needs to look in the basement," she said aloud.

"Maybe I do, too," Claire added, gathering her papers together just as her father began to call her down to dinner.

She arrived at school twenty minutes early the next morning, only to find the front hallway had been invaded by the marching band—most likely an attempt to escape the persistent, bitter cold.

Claire eyed the door beside the front office marked Faculty Only. She wanted to see the basement for herself in peace. But the band director was a tall man who shouted at the tuba section, "Pep! More pep!" in a gravelly voice and stared at Claire with what she interpreted to be suspicious eyes. She didn't need him reporting her curiosity to the main office, so that a secretary would come out jingling a set of master keys to lock the basement up, eliminating the possibility of the new kid getting a chance to look around.

Feigning complete disinterest in the basement door, she took her time sauntering down the front hall. Turning the corner, she found the cheerleaders in the midst of their own early rehearsal, filling the side corridor with the sounds of their clapping hands and their voices shouting cheers in unison.

Becca was in the middle of the group, wearing a Peculiar High sweatshirt and black sweatpants. Her eyes settled on Claire's face as she rustled her pom-poms just before sliding into the splits.

Claire nodded a polite hello and quickly veered around the cheerleaders, heading upstairs to her own locker. She hung her trench on the hook inside, working to cram the shoulders and tuck the tail into the tiny space, and slowly began to make her way back, hoping the band had left the front hall.

Back in the side corridor, though, the cheerleaders had apparently just wrapped up; the squad was breaking apart when Claire rounded the corner, the girls all sprinting for the bathroom to change for class. Becca waved, an awkward smile on her face.

Claire waved back and tried to scoot past her, but Becca jumped in front of her path.

"So," Becca began. "You're going to the dance with Rich."

Claire forced a smile. "I don't think I'll ever get used to the speed of small-town news," she admitted.

"Do you know what you're going to wear?" Becca asked excitedly.

Claire flinched against Becca's enthusiasm.

"I'd be happy to take you shopping this weekend," Becca offered quickly. "In Kansas City. Where we—where I—got my own dress. I know some good places."

"I have something," Claire blurted. She hadn't expected Becca to pounce so quickly on her promise to be a better friend the second time around. And she didn't want to endure the horrors of a dress shop changing room with someone who would have to be told the entire gruesome story of the pink scars that made Claire's skin look like a road map.

Becca tilted her head. "Probably way better than anything you could buy around here, anyway," she said. "I'm sure you're going to look really beautiful."

Judging by the syrupy tones in her voice, it was exactly the kind of thing Becca felt she should have said to Serena.

The word made Claire flinch, though. *Beautiful.* It made her feel unbalanced. She cleared her throat, straightened herself. "Gotta get to journalism," she lied. "Talk to you later," she promised.

As she edged away, disappearing into the gathering throng, Claire realized the only way to slip into the basement unseen was if she were surrounded by a crowd. She needed the bustle of classes changing. A distraction.

The dismissal to lunch would be perfect.

That afternoon, as the talking, shouting, laughing hordes made their way toward the cafeteria, Claire drifted toward the cool wall along the front hall, gripped the Faculty Only door handle, and twisted. While the crowds were paying attention only to each other—to their friends and their plans and their small-town gossip, Claire slipped behind the door.

Mind spinning, Claire hurried down the stairs. The hallway bleeding out from the bottom step was dimly lit. The basement had been closed up so long, it smelled empty—sour, like the inside of an unused refrigerator.

Claire poked her head through the first open doorway. To her left, she found shelves packed with half-opened containers of soaps and bleaches, stained squeegees and sponges, and racks of paper products for the bathrooms. Mops leaned against the sides of old buckets. An abused red tool chest slumped in a corner. A large, battered, wooden teacher's desk stood near a small group of metal lockers; here, heat trailed from the boiler, as uncomfortable as a thick wool blanket on a summer night. As she glanced about, she noticed a faded Janitor sign glued to the door.

One of the lockers by the desk looked tortured; its warped door stood open a few inches. It hung funny, promising never to shut completely again—or to never open if the door ever happened to be forced shut.

A cold breeze circled the room, pushing the heat aside and hitting Claire's sweaty skin in a way that made her shiver. She jumped against a sudden thud; her breath became ragged as she began to raise her arms, as though to guard her face. With another brutally cold gust, a crooked venetian blind bowed out, then slammed against an open window near the ceiling.

"Stop it," she scolded her racing heart. "Just stop it," she said as she walked across the floor, feeling a need to push the window shut. But the ground-level window was up near the ceiling of the office. She had to climb up onto the old wooden desk in order to reach it. She grabbed hold of the latch, pushed it down.

Turning back around, she noticed the desk beneath her feet was covered in dust, with strange swipes through it—like someone had hurriedly knocked some of the dust off with their hand. She swore she could see long slender stripes—swirling marks from four fingers.

There was something so weird about the room—an off-kilter feeling that made her back out quickly. She raced into the hallway, turned one corner, then another, hurrying past classroom doors, not even sure, at this point, what she was really looking for.

She paused in the center of a corridor, listening to the muffled sounds of Peculiar High above her. Foot traffic, metallic thuds of locker doors, voices calling to friends, laughter, teachers barking at students, "Come on, hurry up. No dawdling in the hallway. Get to the cafeteria"—all of it seemed miles away. She felt buried deep beneath the earth's surface.

Claire glanced over her shoulder once, then again. But she felt so bare—unprotected—vulnerable as she stood in the corridor. All the open classroom doors began to seem like eyes, staring.

She darted through one of the doors, pulse pounding out a prayer that the room would feel safer, like a hiding spot. *Just for a minute*, she promised herself. *Just until I get rid of this odd feeling of being watched.* She found herself inside a sprawling old gymnasium being used as some sort of storage facility. Wooden bleachers had been pushed back against the far wall, and the gym was crammed with broken desks and tables. Buckets of half-used roofing tar, brooms, moldy mops, and even an old push mower drew her attention. Spiderwebs caught the light near the windows along the ceiling. At the back of the gym, a metal bar had been fed through the door handles of the exit, then chained into place, giving the room a prison-like feel.

All the scooting in and out of furniture and floor waxers had destroyed the court, now missing so much paint that it looked like an eraser had been taken to the floor. A scraggly-looking net dangled from a gray, faded basketball backboard. Along the ceiling hung dirty remnants of state championship banners.

Claire frowned at the school history that seemed to be rotting away, instead of on display, proudly. Pictures of girls' basketball teams hung in a line near the entrance, as did blowups of one particular athlete—a gorgeous girl, blond hair—number 21, Jennifer Isles. Top scorer.

"Isles," Claire repeated, taking a step closer. She squinted at the picture of her history teacher. A former Peculiar High student herself. Today, Isles looked exactly like she had in high school—maybe a bit more polished. But not any older. Those photos, Claire told herself, couldn't have been taken that long ago. Somehow, though, in the midst of the dusty gym, those pictures, those basketball wins seemed like ancient history.

Glancing at the piles of discarded equipment, Claire began to think the gym looked untamed, overgrown—like all the scrub brush that surrounded the town. It did look like an enormous hiding place. But not for her. For someone else. Someone lying in wait.

Last time, they waited right out in the open, on the stairs, but wouldn't it be more fun for them if this time they could jump out at me, like kids playing a twisted game of hide-and-seek, before grabbing me, throwing me to the ground?

The distance between Claire and the memory of her attack began to shrink. There it was, this thing that Claire had shoved into a rearview mirror, only to finally glance at the printing along the bottom of the glass: *Objects closer than they appear . . .*

Hurrying out into the hallway, she paused by a sign labeled Boys' Locker Room.

"Casey," she mumbled. Remembering the story of Sanders's injuries and Casey's own sad, brutal death, she sucked in a breath and took a hesitant step forward. "Come on, Cain," she told herself. "You want to know what Serena was investigating, right? This is it—the boy in the basement. The urban legend. You wanted to see for yourself, so *go see for yourself.*"

The locker room was as still as death. The lockers stood empty. The benches had grown a thick layer of dust. The showers on the opposite side of the room had not dripped, she thought, in years.

Evidence of Casey's paint bomb was still everywhere, nearly a decade after his prank. Wild, pink sprays of paint were splashed across the walls; splatter marks trailed across the lockers, the benches.

The longer Claire stood, though, the more those splotches began to look like a spray of blood—began to look more like evidence and stains left by Casey's suicide.

Her head swam; glancing about, Claire found a bright pink handprint on the wall just behind her, under the light switch, looking desperate and afraid. That handprint looked so fresh, Claire swore it was pleading with her to come closer, to help.

Claire ducked back out of the locker room and into the hallway. This was a bad idea, she scolded herself. Incredibly bad.

Her eyes immediately landed on the door to the gym, and she remembered the piles of discarded junk, the hiding places—and her ears filled with taunting laughter coming toward her, all of it male. Tinged with the anticipation of an attack. They were back. They were after her again. She needed to get out of there, out of the basement. *Now.*

She walked faster, trying to find her way back to the stairs. But Claire was turned around. She was alone, in a labyrinth. Her chest felt suddenly too small for her heart. She was lost.

"Wrong turn," she grumbled, panic starting to swell. But she suddenly felt as though *all* her turns had been wrong.

Pipes along the ceiling began to unleash a strange vapor, filling the entirety of the corridor with a kind of mist that was not unlike the fog that had surrounded the old Sims place— or the edges of the Peculiar High parking lot—for days. The same kind of fog that had filled the alleyway back in Chicago, during last spring's final icing.

Her breath, now quick, streamed out in frozen clouds. Her

cheeks burned against a sudden bitter wind. Her ears popped with the sound of ice-laden branches striking each other.

Claire turned once more—and found herself not in another hallway, but an alley with cracked pavement and a dark sky. Stars glittered above. She gasped as she inched forward, the soles of her shoes sliding against the thin skin of ice beneath her. Shadows lengthened, spilling out from streetlights and bare trees. Freezing rain crackled against buildings and tree limbs. When Claire lifted her face, she felt the prickle of sleet against her cheeks.

She wasn't inside Peculiar High anymore—she was outside. At night. During an ice storm.

Footsteps thundered behind her—hurried, forceful, angry. She sped up. So did they.

She glanced nervously over her shoulder. Behind her—a man's silhouette. "Hello?" she said, her head still pointed behind her, feet still moving. If she talked to him, she thought—if she showed him that she knew he was there, maybe that might discourage him. Maybe, if she just kept walking, but didn't run like she really wanted to, maybe that was a little like standing her ground while trying to get away all at the same time. It was a flimsy plan, she knew—but all she had.

"Can you help me?" she asked, her voice sounding too high and too pitiful. "I was looking for the stairs." She cringed. It was a stupid thing to say. Stairs—who could care about stairs? Why didn't she ask them where they *were*? But then again, would not knowing where she was walking show how confused and vulnerable she really was?

The silhouette moved toward her in slow motion, each of his movements creating an intensification of emotion and sound. Claire could hear his feet cracking through the half-frozen puddles in the pavement. He walked strangely, bouncing on the balls of his feet. He stepped into and out of a streetlight—so quickly, like a blink—but Claire swore he had a peach-fuzz mustache.

"*Schoolgirl!*" he boomed.

Claire opened her mouth to scream, but only whimpered. Tried to run, but fear had weakened her legs—or maybe it was that she couldn't count on her legs to respond any longer to a threat, not after they'd been shattered. She cringed, closing her eyes as tightly as she could.

He's found you, he's here again, he's probably brought all his friends, maybe hundreds of them this time, hundreds, and the next time you open your eyes, you'll see them: fangs. Because they're wild they're here to tear you apart this is it the end the end the end . . .

When she finally cracked her eyes open, she saw it for sure this time, only inches in front of her face: a peach-fuzz mustache. But this wasn't the face of the freshman that had turned horrible shades of mortified when Rachelle had teased him. This was someone else—his features flashing before her in black and white.

"Casey," Claire whispered.

"You shouldn't be here," he told her. "Bad things happen to people who aren't where they're supposed to be. Don't you know that?"

When she didn't answer, he gripped her arms, shook her. "I paid the price. Because Sanders wasn't where I thought he'd be. Because he was in the locker room when he shouldn't have been. I tried to tell Serena, too. People should stay where they're supposed to be. Do you hear me? You *shouldn't be down here.*"

Claire screamed, struggled to push herself away from Casey. As she fought, a sliver of light pierced her eyes. She grimaced, trying to wiggle away from it. But the hands on her arms refused to let go.

"Please—" she muttered. As she opened her eyes again, she realized the light was bouncing off a pane of glass in a nearby classroom window. She could see herself there in the reflection—standing in the basement of Peculiar High. Not an alley. There was no ice storm. Claire was in a hallway. And the hands gripping her arms belonged to Rich.

"Did you hear me?" Rich was asking.

Claire shook her head. "What?"

"You shouldn't be here. I was at the other end of the hallway when I saw you slip through that door upstairs. You're lucky no one else saw you. Good way to get suspended for the rest of the semester."

Claire panted, fear returning to her in waves, even though Rich was here, even though Casey and the alley and the ice had disappeared.

Because she knew what she had seen. Those articles were wrong—those odd instances weren't pranks. Casey was real. *That* was why Serena had come down to the basement. That was maybe even why she'd died.

We're in it together. Isn't that what Becca had said? She and Claire were connected by what they'd seen: Serena, torn to shreds, ravaged by a wild pack. Feral.

Serena and Claire were connected, too. They'd both stayed to work on an assignment. At the beginning of an ice storm. And look what happened. *Just look.* Claire's ears filled with the sounds of snapping limbs. Breaking bones. But she was not just remembering it. Those sounds were back, crackling in her ears. Taunting her.

Wild creatures that had torn them both to shreds—they had that in common, too.

It was all connected. Claire could feel it. Serena had stayed to work on a story about a boy up to no good and had turned up dead. Claire had written a story about a boy up to his own kind of no good, and had turned up beaten to a pulp in the middle of a Chicago parking lot. The kind of beaten that had very nearly resulted in her own death.

It was too similar. Too, too similar. There were no mere coincidences this strong.

Serena needed Claire. Because no one else saw Peculiar the way Claire did—with fresh eyes. Something was going on here, in this town. Something that Claire would understand, because of what she'd been through.

It's okay, Serena, she thought. *We're in this together. . . .*

"Claire?" Rich asked. "Claire? Are you okay?"

Limply, Claire nodded.

"Come on. Let's go back upstairs."

Claire fought to gain control of her legs, weakened by fear, as Rich led her around the corner and toward the exit of the out-of-bounds basement.

SEVENTEEN

Claire wondered, as she sat beside Rich at their lunch table, if she should tell him about what she'd seen in the basement. If anyone would entertain the possibility of a spirit being real, wouldn't it be the son of the preacher? He would be, she felt, the last to look at her like she was crazy if she were to come right out with it: Casey was no urban legend—he was real. And Casey obviously knew things—he knew about the alley Claire had been in during the Chicago ice storm. He had shown that alley to her, down in the basement. But what had he shown Serena? Had something happened to her—something other than an accident? Was Casey somehow responsible?

"What's your dress like? The one you brought with you from Chicago?" Becca asked from the opposite side of their table.

When Claire stared back blankly, Becca went on, "The one you told me about this morning. For the dance."

"Oh," Claire said, trying to remember what it was, exactly, that she had packed. Certainly not a formal. "Just—it's black and—kind of—basic."

"*Classic*," Becca corrected. "Sounds pretty," she chirped. "You know, I was thinking—we all could go together. Me, you, Rich—"

Rich snorted. "You and me?" he blurted. The question wasn't antagonistic—instead, showed a genuine surprise.

"Sure," Becca said. "And Owen, and Chas."

"I'm not going," Chas announced, plopping his phone down on the table as he picked up his sandwich.

Becca frowned. "But you'd planned all along—"

"I don't want to go, all right?" Chas snapped. "I never did."

"The next thing you know," Becca told Owen, "you'll say we aren't going anymore, either."

"*Becca*," Owen sighed, wiping his face in exasperation. "I'm so sick of this. You've got it in your head that something's going on with me, that I've got some girl on the side. What girl, Becca? Huh? You really think in a town this small that nobody would have said anything by now?"

"Chas kept his secret," Becca challenged.

"Yeah, for two seconds," Owen reminded her.

"You're different than you used to be," Becca said, twisting her paper napkin with the force of a woman wringing the neck of a man who'd wronged her.

"She's right about that one, pretty boy," Chas agreed.

"So what? You're not supposed to change in your life? Ever?" Owen thundered.

"Change is good," Chas told him. "Becoming an asshole generally is not."

"I'm an asshole now because—why? I changed my hair?"

"Because you built yourself a pedestal and sat on it," Becca said.

Owen frowned, holding his hands palms up, as if to show his innocence. "Jesus. You know what—forget this," he said. "If you want to go to the dance, Becca, that's fine. I'm happy to take you. But I don't want to go just to be told all night how much I suck." He grabbed his tray and stomped off, leaving the table quiet and the air around it tense.

Claire felt bad for Owen as he hurried away—she didn't care how he'd been acting lately, it didn't seem right for Chas and Becca to gang up on him that way.

She glanced to the side, at Rich, her mind instantly drifting back toward his rescuing her in that basement. She wanted so badly to tell him what had happened. But her questions returned—about Casey, about what she'd seen, about what had happened to Serena—piling up until she felt like someone who had just inherited an antique heirloom she knew nothing about. She needed to find out more before she said anything to Rich, she decided—otherwise, she just might end up accidentally giving away something incredibly valuable.

"No need to remind you guys, I'm sure," Isles said that afternoon, picking a stack of paper up off the corner of her desk, "but our chapter test was scheduled for today."

No, no, no, Claire thought as Isles began to make her way toward the closest row of desks, distributing the papers. Isles, her bright hibiscus-red lips glowing against the moldy backdrop of the school. Isles, who trailed the warm smell of coconut everywhere she went.

"Is that really the best idea?" Claire blurted. "In light of everything that's happened the past few days?"

Isles flinched. "We've been preparing for this test for quite some time," she said. "I think that you'll find this exam to be no problem, based on your grades from your previous school." And she winked.

Claire frowned; she wasn't ready—since arriving in Peculiar little more than a week ago, she hadn't so much as cracked a book. She was still trying to come up with a reason to ask to be excused—an F wasn't exactly the best way to start off any class—when the test paper hit her desk.

A matching test. Claire felt the nervous knot inside her begin to unwind. She could fake a matching test.

But the moment before she could scribble her name on her test paper, she caught Becca staring at her from the opposite side of the room. Becca's wounded look bounced Claire's words right back at her—*Is that really the best idea in light of everything that's happened*—and asked, at the same time, *What do you really know about it?*

Claire's question had obviously upset Becca. Her stare said to Claire that it didn't really matter that she'd seen Serena dead. True horror was reserved for Becca, who'd known the way the face beneath the pile of limbs had looked smiling in the July sun. Becca, who'd once felt those half-eaten arms around her neck, hugging a friendly hello. Becca was the one who was suffering—not Claire. *If I can take this test, you can,* Becca's eyes seemed to insinuate.

Claire watched Becca swivel to face forward again, a sad slump settling into her shoulders.

What if I had died? Claire asked herself. *How would Rachelle have acted then? What if she had seen me lying out there in the lot? What would it have done to her?*

Claire noticed the way Becca's hands trembled as she smoothed her test sheet and pressed too hard against her paper, snapping her pencil lead violently—and she wondered, *Did Rachelle look just as frazzled and upset when she'd come to visit me at the hospital?* Yes, she had—but didn't she almost gag, too, seeing Claire the first time? For a split second, just before telling her that it wasn't nearly as bad as she'd expected? *Yes!* She had—Claire remembered it now, clearly—there Claire was, hopped up on the kind of painkillers that could have knocked out the Hulk, and mostly, Rachelle was just disgusted.

Rachelle had just *kept* looking at her like that. Like some horrible, nasty bloodstain that was not the same, even when the bandages and the casts were removed. Oh, she'd smiled. She'd pretended. But while Claire was being homeschooled the entire fall semester of her junior year, while she was going through excruciating physical therapy and while the nurses and her therapist and her father had all busied themselves with cheering her on, there was Rachelle, scooting herself into Claire's bedroom for after-school visits, looking at Claire like she was never, ever going to be the same.

No wonder Claire'd written those awful things in her unsent emails. All that pain—for what? For a friend who grimaced, wearing her disgust out in the open when she looked at Claire. *It was for you*, Claire heard the voice in her head cry out, as her hand tightened around her pencil. *I got that way because I swooped in to save you!*

Her pencil began to pop beneath the pressure of her hand, threatening to snap in half.

"Time," Isles called. "Pencils down."

What? Time already? Claire thought, panicked. She pushed her hair behind her ears and curled herself over her test paper.

But the letters running down the side of the page only seemed to swim, like leaves on top of a river. *Write anything, Claire*, she told herself. *For God's sake, anything.*

She'd just begun to make her first mark when Isles slid Claire's paper off the top of her desk.

Claire scrambled after it, trying to snatch it out of Isles's hand. But Isles was already snaking up the aisle, leaving the faint scent of coconut behind her.

EIGHTEEN

"I want to go—"

"Claire," her father interrupted, his tone putting a pall over their dinner. He cleared his throat as he pushed his glasses up into his face.

"What?" Claire asked, frowning against her father's nervous tic. "There's nothing weird about wanting to express your condolences by attending a funeral."

"But *this* funeral, Claire," he pointed out, shaking his head. "I just worry. . . . Besides, you didn't know the Sims girl."

Claire sucked in a breath, pushed her creamed spinach about on her plate.

"I want to do this," she told her father, in an *I'm in control here* tone. The same tone she'd used months ago, when her story about Rachelle had been picked up, going from a piece Claire had written for the school paper to a bit on the evening news.

Dr. Cain simply nodded. "All right. Then I'll go with you," he said.

Claire nodded. She could live with that.

The Cains' Gremlin was quite literally the only car on the road that Thursday, as Claire and her father drove to the church. They passed by dark houses, deserted sidewalks. Wadded-up newspapers danced through the desolate high school parking lot like tumbleweeds as the car edged past 'Bout Out, where a Closed sign had been turned outward.

The parking lot at the Peculiar First Baptist, though, was crammed with cars and trucks; parked vehicles spilled into the nearby streets and grassy areas.

"Looks like we're just about the last two people in the entire town to arrive," her father observed, steering their car into one of the seemingly endless rows of pickups in the muddy field behind the church and to the side of the walled-in cemetery.

Inside the church, a sickeningly sweet smell exploded. It traveled halfway down Claire's throat, tugging out a gag. And as she and her father eased down the aisle—forcing an entire pew of mourners to press their sides together, pursing their lips disapprovingly—the smell only grew stronger.

Claire struggled to keep the contents of her stomach down.

Lilies, she realized, glancing about the church. They'd never bothered her before. Today, though, there were just so *many* of them. Sprays of them blanketing the casket and lining the walls. All of them radiating nauseatingly strong perfume. Her father eyed her nervously as she wiped sweat from her forehead and put her sweater sleeve over her mouth, attempting not to have to breathe in the scent. All crammed together, the lilies began to smell foul—as though they were radiating the strong stench of decay.

She coughed as the scent invaded her nose again, crawled into her brain, burned like fumes.

Her raspy cough turned heads. At the front of the church, in the first pew, Rich angled his head to toss an expression at her that Claire interpreted to mean, *Everything okay?*

She offered a slight nod as Becca turned around in the pew just in front of Claire and her father.

Becca sighed, glanced about the church. "Where *is* he?" she asked Chas, who was slouching uncomfortably beside her. At her left, she'd propped her purse into the wooden seat, as though to reserve a spot.

Chas shrugged. "Dunno," he mumbled.

Becca shook her head, clenching her jaw in annoyance.

At the piano up front, a woman struck the full, warm-sounding chords of a hymn; as the song died down, Pastor Ray turned to thank his wife for the musical accompaniment.

While Pastor Ray gathered his thoughts, an arm flew in

front of Claire's face, plucking Becca's purse out of the seat. Owen placed it on the floor and slid into place at her side.

Becca's eyes widened as she stared at him.

"Did it already start? Am I late?" Owen asked, staring into Becca's shocked face.

"For what—your meeting with all the rest of the accountants?" Chas asked.

Owen shot him a glare. "Shut up."

Becca's look of utter bewilderment intensified as her mouth drooped open and creases appeared between her eyebrows. "A three-piece suit?" she whispered. "With a tie?"

"So what?" he asked. "You dressed up, too," he added, pointing at her long-sleeved black jersey dress.

"So—you wouldn't even wear a tie to homecoming," Becca hissed. "And wingtip shoes? Dress socks?"

Chas snickered.

Owen simply shook his head and ran his hand across his immaculately combed hair, parted on the side and gelled over his crown. He straightened his back, took a deep breath, and gave his full attention to Pastor Ray, in a way that suggested Becca and Chas should follow his lead.

Less than ten minutes into the service, Chas's head dropped forward. Claire eyed him, expecting his shoulders to start heaving with sobs. For a sniff to erupt. For him to wipe his nose or his eyes. But as Claire took in his slow, deep breaths, she slowly began to realize he was asleep.

Asleep! Claire could hardly believe it. Even if he had wanted out of their relationship at the end, Serena had still been his girlfriend. And now he was nodding off at her funeral like it was no skin off his teeth?

Claire coughed again, her cheeks turning shades of red, even as she tried to calm herself, to hide her face beneath the curtain of her hair. She was sick; the smell of flowers had become the smell of a body. Throughout the service, she could not stop thinking of the way Serena had stared back at her from underneath the fallen limb. She could not stop thinking of the biting, yowling ferals. Even sitting in a church, at her father's side, she couldn't lose the odd sensation of being chased by vulture-like figures screaming her name. The memory of the woods was magnified; it buzzed in her ears. It became too close, with no escape (*Escape from what, though?* Claire wondered). She was terrified—and the soothing tones of Pastor Ray's voice offered no relief.

Claire eyed the enlarged portrait of Serena positioned on an easel next to the casket, taking deep breaths and trying to calm herself.

As she stared, the portrait slowly began to bulge forward— to ripple, almost like the picture had been caught by a gust of wind.

There was no wind in the church, though. Not even a draft.

She glanced about at the faces surrounding her. Was she

the only one seeing this?

As she stared, Claire began to realize that it wasn't the picture that was moving—the image was. Serena's face was spreading outward, into a smile. And she was staring right at Claire. Gradually, Serena's chest began to turn. The light streaming through a nearby window bounced across a necklace at the base of Serena's throat: a gold cameo.

Claire gasped, letting her fingers trace the cool, bumpy surface of the cameo that she still wore. The necklace she'd found on the cat's tail, that had refused to snap, that she'd decided to leave on, thinking it wasn't doing any harm. *A new good-luck charm*, she'd thought. Now she knew it was Serena's necklace. Knowing made the necklace feel more like a noose.

The moment the service ended, Claire raced out onto the front step, as January decided to spit on her all over again, unleashing a fresh round of sleet that instantly began to tangle in her eyelashes.

Mourners poured out of the doors, their black coats flowing around her like a polluted stream. She knew she should get out of the way, but somehow, simply moving to the side seemed as far to her as walking back to Chicago. Rich paused on the step beside her, his girth like a dam that kept the stream of people behind him from flowing as it wanted.

"You okay?" he asked, in a way that implied she didn't look okay. Claire already knew she didn't, though—her forehead was damp with anxious sweat and she felt the kind of clammy that had no doubt turned her peaked cheeks into white sheets.

"If you want to talk to my dad—" he offered.

She shook her head, as the stream of mourners trickled off, and as the entire town marched around the church, toward the cemetery. They followed the pallbearers, straight to Serena's grave.

"Remains," everyone called a body—the word bounced through Claire's head. "Remains," implying it was just the leftovers. What got shucked once the soul left. As though the physical aspects were the least important, not the most.

But those words, she suddenly realized, didn't match up with the mourners' actions. What they were truly honoring, it seemed, with the flowers and the glistening casket, *were* the remains. The body.

The body was nothing, Claire knew now—a container. Because of what she'd seen in the basement—the way that Casey's spirit had outlived his physical being. His spirit was the strongest part of him.

So where, exactly, she wondered, *is Serena?*

Rich was still standing beside her as she raised her eyes toward the winter sky—the kind of sky in which the clouds looked like cupped hands cradling tiny mounds of snow. Clouds whose fingers could part at any minute, send flakes tumbling toward the earth.

"I'm—fine," Claire finally mumbled, trudging forward, her shoes sinking into the sloppy mud. All around her, half-melted snow pooled in the footprints left by the hundreds of residents who had marched across the same cemetery that held their grandparents, their ancestors. That would someday be their own resting ground. Claire wondered what it must feel like to know the smell of the earth that would someday cover your own face like a winter blanket.

She stuck her hands inside her coat, hugging herself as the wavy ends of her long hair began to coat with ice, to harden like tree branches.

". . . tragedy . . . ," Pastor Ray was saying. ". . . love that endures . . ." He went on, babbling, it seemed to Claire. Her mind wandered so much, she felt he wasn't speaking in full sentences, but just tossing out words, the same way people in a parade tossed out candy as their float drove by. All of the tidbits sweet, light, and easy to forget as soon as they melted.

"The soul," Pastor Ray preached. "The soul never dies. 'For whosoever liveth and believeth in me shall never die.'"

It was so true, Claire thought. The soul never died. The soul was the strongest part. Far stronger than the body.

Pastor Ray's voice grew distant as Claire's ears filled with an icy crunch and crackle. Mist danced on brittle limbs, half-frozen droplets making clicking sounds as they danced against the shoulders of wool dress coats.

In the spaces between the snapping sounds of the world freezing over, the sounds of heartache hit the air: sniffing—murmurs—half-squelched wails—sobs.

Claire glanced toward the entrance of the Peculiar cemetery, its wrought-iron gates curving like a witch's arthritic fingers.

". . . youth . . . ," Pastor Ray went on, his last few words beginning to feel like the ache caused by a cavity.

". . . ashes to ashes . . ."

Claire glanced out at the rest of the town's mourners, noting the way that the droplets had begun to glitter across everyone's shoulders.

". . . dust to dust."

This last phrase thunked against the air. Serena's "In Memoriam" was over.

The crowd began to snake again, and to split—half the mourners inching closer to the grave, the other half turning and making their way back toward the cemetery gate.

Claire trudged toward Owen and Becca, watching as Owen wrapped an arm around Becca's shoulder and kissed the side of her head. Claire edged past Mrs. Sims, who was getting no apparent comfort from her husband's embrace. Mrs. Sims wailed like something that had spent its whole life in the wild—like something that had never learned a single word of any language in the human world.

Claire hiked the large collar of her naval trench around her ears, as though the material could somehow block the sounds of Mrs. Sims's grief.

As she walked, she watched Rich step into place in between

his parents. Dr. Cain stopped to speak to Dr. Sanders.

Halfway to the gate, Ms. Isles pulled her heels from the mud and inched her way back toward the coffin, her red lipstick throbbing like a sore just above the black collar of her coat.

The last in the line of mourners, Claire arrived at the casket just as Isles stepped in behind Owen and Becca, draping her arms around their shoulders. Becca buried her face in her hands, and Owen dropped his chin on his chest, shaking suddenly. Death was a trembling rattlesnake's tail, Claire thought with sympathy. It was both frightening and powerful. And seeing it up close did strange things to people.

Becca and Owen broke away from Isles, heading back toward the gate. Isles stared at the coffin a moment; she reached out to touch its edge in a gentle way. And then she turned back toward the gate herself.

While Dr. Cain continued to talk to Sanders, Claire took another step closer to the casket.

Trembling inside her coat, Claire stood staring at the mound of lilies on the coffin's rounded mahogany top—until a flicker of movement stole her attention. She glanced up just as a cat with black-and-white speckled fur jumped onto the stone wall surrounding the entire cemetery. Her gaze slid down the wall. All four sides were lined with cats. Every single feral in town. Some were cleaning their whiskers—others staring right at her.

She was surrounded. Cornered. She tried to call out to her father, but her voice failed her.

What are they doing here? Claire wondered about the cats perched along the cemetery wall. *Do they smell her? Do they smell Serena, there in her casket? Do they think she smells like raw meat, like a meal? Are they back for more?*

"They're *cats*," she muttered. "Just cats." And took a step backward.

Unexpectedly, Claire bumped into a figure just behind her. "Ooh!" she blurted in surprise. Wasn't she the last one to reach Serena's grave?

"Sorry, I—" she started as she turned on her heel. But her apology ended abruptly as she found herself staring into the weather-worn face of the old man she'd first seen in the parking lot of 'Bout Out, moments after arriving in town.

"Told you those ain't no house cats," he said, stretching his wrinkled face into a satisfied grin.

"Musta followed Maxine," he went on. "Since she and Ruthie came to the service. Those little critters follow her everywhere—she's like the Pied Piper of Peculiar, that Maxine!" He opened his mouth and wheezed into a laugh.

A cemetery worker appeared, squatted next to Serena's grave, and reached for the crank handle on the casket-lowering device. Metal pieces thunked against the winter air as the worker grunted and heaved. He waved for another to join him. "Frozen," Claire heard one of them say, as they groaned in another attempt to move the handle.

The worker called out a name—"Get over here," he shouted.

The old man turned, nodded in compliance, and joined the first worker, squatting beside the lowering device.

The old man works here, Claire told her thundering heart. *It's okay. Just calm down.*

More cemetery workers joined them, the group growing rougher with the device, rattling tools. "Take it off," the old man said. "We gotta take that casket off so we can fix it. Never did see that happen before."

The workers raised the casket, took a step to the side, and put it back down on the fake green grass surrounding the grave.

In the distance, car engines revved to life as they began to pull out of the parking lot. The ground fog thickened.

Cemetery workers grumbled in disagreement about whether the crank was stuck or broken. They continued to argue as they disassembled the device completely.

The ground fog swelled, swirled, clumped.

Claire took another step backward, deep into the thick fog. The sounds of the cemetery—the muffled voices, the clank of tools and the grunts of the cemetery workers—grew instantly distant, as though Claire had actually stepped inside a vault with a thick door and four walls that separated her from the rest of the graveyard.

"Hello?" she called out. "Hello?"

But no one answered. No one could hear her. She was somehow in the cemetery and *not* in the cemetery, all at the same time.

The fog completely encased her, wrapping her up in its arms.

NINETEEN

The fog surrounding Claire didn't drift or float. It *marched*, with the purpose of a line of soldiers heading into battle. A dense patch paused atop a gravesite, drawing out what was unmistakably a pair of arms, a torso, legs. The spirit was absorbed by the thickening mist, before the swirling white collective mass marched to the next closest grave.

Claire shuddered, her breath growing ever quicker, more shallow, as the fog continued to recruit another pair of arms. Elbows. Shoulders. Heads. Each time it absorbed a spirit, it only grew larger, more menacing.

Good God, Claire thought, *that fog isn't just fog. It's filled with the town dead. Their souls. They're all still here.*

"Sereeeena," the fog called. "Sereeeeenaaaaahhh." The spirits of the town dead continued to climb from their graves, to become part of the fog, and to call out with a single collective voice as it marched closer to Serena's burial site.

The fog whirled, the spirits mixing to form one single branch. *No*, Claire told herself. *Not a branch. An arm. They've all formed a single arm. And it's reaching for something.*

Claire flinched, raising her hand over her face protectively as a fiery streak popped like a bottle rocket straight out of the casket. Through her fingers, she watched it explode in the sky. Sparks formed a ball that zipped about frantically between the tiniest, highest branches of the tree closest to the open grave. Slowly, the sparks began to settle down, to cluster in a single spot in the sky, forming the portrait of a girl's face.

Claire trembled; she'd just seen that face on the easel near the pulpit. It was Serena. And she was smiling at Claire, as she had inside the church.

Claire lowered her arm completely, too shocked to dislodge her feet from the mud. She was staring at Serena's spirit.

"Sereeeeenah," the fog called out again, in its own unified voice.

Serena's face shifted to an expression of pure fear as she struggled to move, trying to pull herself from her spot near the top of the trees. But it seemed Serena's spirit was stuck to the sky, like a butterfly pinned to a scrapbook.

"Come," the fog urged. "Come, Serena. Come home."

The arm reached up higher, its misty grasp rising toward Serena.

Serena frowned and shook her head. Wherever the fog was going wasn't home. Not for Serena. Her home was still here, in Peculiar.

It's heaven, Claire thought. *That's where the fog wants to take her.* But what kind of place was that, really? Already, death appeared nothing at all like the peaceful state Pastor Ray had just described. He'd said nothing during Serena's funeral about fog and spirits rising up from graves. Heaven might not be the same kind of place they were all promised, either. Heaven just might not suit everyone, the same way not everybody liked Toledo or New Jersey.

Claire's chest heaved with frightened breath as a familiar old calico jumped from the cemetery wall. The cat bearing the gnarled, brittle look of age, with her knotted spine and legs as stiff as crutches—the cat from the Simses' woodpile. She blinked her matted, gummy eyes against the frozen mist, and shook her head, sending droplets flying from her whiskers and the torn tip of a partially missing ear. The calico edged toward Serena's grave, as though wanting to get close enough to pay her respects to the girl.

The hand of fog continued to climb higher into the sky, to inch closer to Serena, the fingers curling, readying to grasp her soul. To pluck her—like a wayward strand of hair. A wave of renewed terror flashed over Serena's face—and at the very moment the fog touched her, her terror fired, shooting her spirit high into the sky—high enough to surely see the top of the Peculiar water tower below her.

Serena paused at the top of her ascent, her face tipped forward, and she fell in a lurch—while the fog struggled to catch up, to grab her.

The calico at the side of the casket turned her face to the sky only to see Serena speeding toward her—only to fear being crushed by Serena's fall, with no time to dart out of the way.

Serena fell through the fingers of the fog, nose-diving into the earth.

The fall made a noise like a sonic boom that left Claire's ears ringing and silver sparks of light traveling across her eyes.

Claire could hear no distant screams of shock coming from anyone left in the cemetery. No stampeding feet. Nothing. Were they all too far away? How was it that no one saw or heard this—only Claire?

She blinked against the January mist, the savage winter air, letting the scene she'd just witnessed sink in.

Serena had fallen on top of that awful old calico, knocking the poor creature off her feet. The cat lay, looking every bit as lifeless as Serena had when Claire had first seen her, buried beneath the fallen limb.

The persistent fog peeled back, like a curtain.

The cat raised her head, slowly arched her back, and pushed herself from the ground. She raised a paw, peeked down at it, as if seeing it for the first time.

Claire was rooted as she watched wisps of color float

across the surface of the cat's face. The cat's face grew hazy, disappearing just long enough to let the image of a girl's face peek through.

Serena, Claire thought, the realization hitting her with the brutal force of a club. *She didn't just fall* on *the cat—she fell* inside *her*.

The persistent fog continued to swirl above the old calico, like a funnel cloud—as if it, too, knew that Serena had fallen so hard, her spirit was now inside the cat.

"Come," the fog demanded. "You need to come home."

The old calico took a step forward. The fog swirled back and forth above her, bouncing against her body. Without the speed and force that had fueled Serena's fall, the fog couldn't break through the calico's skin. The cat's living body was keeping the fog out.

Blue eyes replaced the cat's feline yellow eyes. A happy purr trickled out from behind her mangy fur.

Claire reeled, arms forward, trying to find a way through the mist that cascaded, that swelled, that pushed itself in front of her face, as thick as velvet curtains.

Muffled voices cried out behind her, calling her name. "Claire!" she heard. "Claire, wait!" But she was trying—couldn't they all see she was trying to get away from the cat, Serena, the fog—the horrible visions of what happened here in Peculiar? She was trying to get to them, but she was all turned around. Which way was the gate? The fog was too dense, suddenly, to make sense of everything.

Serena's in the old cat, she wanted to shout. It sounded crazy—she knew that. But she also knew what she had just seen.

She staggered, until a hiss made her stop moving completely.

Claire glanced down, only to look straight into the calico's mangled face. Claire balled her hands into fists.

The cat yowled. A bit of hazy light bouncing off the gold cameo at the base of Claire's throat reflected back onto the pink, raw spots on the cat's face. The cat rose up onto her back legs, and pawed at the air, attempting, it seemed, to get closer to her. Or, more likely, closer to something that Claire had on her body.

Claire gasped. Serena wanted her necklace back. The necklace that was stuck hanging from Claire's throat. *Why wouldn't she?* Claire asked herself. *It belongs to her.*

Claire threw her foot forward, stomping to scare the old cat away.

The cat spread her mouth, hissed again, and pounced. She took a swipe at Claire's ankle, exposed now beneath the hem of her black slacks. She scratched Claire, cutting into her skin with her dirty, disease-laden claws.

Claire squealed in pain. The squeal turned to a groan of disgust as she stared at a pair of swiveling, jagged, bleeding scratches that burned, tingled, pinched, all at the same time.

She swung her arms, hoping to frighten the old cat while at the same time moving in the direction of the muffled voices.

But in her attempt to get away, Claire felt herself tumbling—falling, just as Serena had fallen. Her mind spun until her back struck the earth, the blow ricocheting inside her like a hundred tiny pieces of shrapnel. She moaned, wanting to push herself up, but finding that her hands didn't even feel attached anymore.

"Claire," a faint voice cried out—the tone so soft, it had to belong to someone standing a mile away.

"Claire," the voice called again, louder this time.

As she opened her eyes, Rich's face emerged—he was calling her name, his expression riddled with worry. "Can you hear me?" he asked.

Claire realized her father was there, too. And the old man from 'Bout Out. And Pastor Ray. All of them staring down on her in fear, through thick billows of fog.

She raised her head, slowly dislodging it from the earth, which felt soft, slightly muddy beneath her. She put her hand out, feeling a cool wall of earth beside her. Another wall of earth on her other side. Walls at her head and feet.

She was in Serena's grave.

Claire opened her mouth and began to scream.

TWENTY

"Just raise your arms over your head," Rich said, his knees pressed into the cold mud at the edge of Serena's grave.

"No!" Claire shook her head adamantly. Her throat still burned from her scream. Her arms would burn, too, she knew, if she let him grab on to her recently healed wrists and yank her out.

Besides, she was weak from what she had seen and from her fall—she'd never get a solid hold on Rich's hands, not if she could only barely stand. "You're just as likely to fall in here with me," she argued, even though it was impossible, given Rich's size, his undeniable strength. But she could not stop shaking. She didn't want anyone to see her like this, so shaken and confused by what had just played out in front of her eyes.

"Use your feet," Rich said. "When I pull you up, just use

your feet to help me. You climb, I pull. Okay?"

"But—"

"Claire, you can't stay in there. Please," Rich begged.

Claire relented, only because everyone up top continued to stare at her, and no one else seemed willing to offer another option. She raised her arms, letting Rich wrap his hands around her wrists as she wrapped her own trembling fingers around his. "Okay," she called, when she felt their hands were locked around each other. She bit down on her lip as he started to tug.

It hurt every bit as much as she'd expected it to—her fingers throbbed, her arms pulsed as her newly mended fractures were tugged in two different directions: up to the edge of the grave by Rich, and back down to the depths of the earth by the weight of Claire's body. Her knees banged against the soil, reinjuring the cuts she got in the icy woods the day she found Serena. Her feet scrambled to get a toehold in the smooth wall of Serena's grave, and she suppressed another scream, even as she swore her breaks were being ripped back apart.

Mercifully, the tugging ended as Claire's hips hit the top of the grave. Rich let go. Claire pressed the palms of her hands on something cold and hard at the head of Serena's burial place as she struggled to hoist her legs out on her own.

She panted, moving her hands to find out that a rather elaborate temporary marker had already been placed at the grave—whoever had purchased all those lilies had also provided for a metal sign, pressed flat against the earth, bearing Serena's name.

Claire could see herself in the marker—her terror-stricken face seeming to plead for help.

"Claire," her father said, rushing to her side. "Claire," he repeated, helping her to her feet when all she wanted to do was just rest a minute, let the awful torturous ringing in her body settle down.

"You didn't hit your head on any rocks down there, did you?" he asked, looking into her eyes.

But it wasn't the fall that bothered Claire—it was what had preceded it. "The crazy fog," she grumbled, scrambling for any explanation. "I just—I couldn't see where I was going."

"The fog?" her dad asked, the pitch of his voice climbing up the scale.

She glanced out at the cemetery, finding the fog far lighter now than it had ever been since their arrival in Peculiar. Barely a wisp at all, she realized, glancing out among the broken limbs, piled on the opposite side of the cemetery. Tombstones shone out clearly—as did the old general store across the street. The world around her glistened brightly in the mid-morning sun, obscured by nothing. Even the stone wall—Claire swore she could see its most minute details, every different particle of color in the rocks. The world dripped, wet, melting. Muddy. As clear as Dr. Cain always swore the world looked behind a new pair of eyeglasses.

The pack of ferals was still there, still at the cemetery. But the cats weren't snarling, weren't menacing. *Drawn by the crowd, Claire*, she told herself. *That's all. And by the smell of the garbage.* In fact, their faces were all pointed in the same direction: toward the overflowing Dumpster near the church. Garbage still left from the warming center. They meowed, the hungry strays innocently racing each other, trying to be the first to get there, to scavenge.

But how could the cemetery have changed so drastically— so quickly?

A hiss poured at her from the wall. When Claire turned, she saw her—the old calico—*No*, she thought, *not the cat. Serena.*

She had something in her mouth—a small gray lump. She lowered her head, dropping it beside her. The mouse began to scurry, racing to make a getaway. But the old cat swooped, dropping down onto her front elbows and covering the mouse with both paws.

She turned her head to the side and hissed at Claire as if to taunt her.

The town wasn't just peculiar—it was sinister. And no one saw it but Claire. But after everything she'd been through, it only made sense that Claire would see the world differently. Didn't it?

Casey's ghost was in the basement. It was clear, too, that no one in Peculiar was dead—their spirits were alive in the fog. And now, Serena's spirit was staring out at Claire through the eyes of the cat. She freed her mouse once more, only to catch and torture it all over again.

She smiled wickedly at Claire, the victim she had clearly chosen to play her next game of cat and mouse.

TWENTY-ONE

Claire slept fitfully, tossing her sweaty body about beneath the blankets as she dreamed repeatedly of the terrifying events of the Sims funeral.

Mid-morning on Friday, she rolled to her side, hugging her blankets, glad that school had been canceled once more, this time for a "day of reflection." She wasn't sure if Becca and Owen had actually seen her fall into the grave—but she did know that small-town word of mouth would have informed them both by now. She also knew that she'd never be able to stand the look Becca would surely flash her, the girl who had been inside Serena's grave: concern and grief mixed with an unmistakable splash of horror.

It was almost like cheating death, actually—the idea of being inside a grave and then fished back out. Then again,

Claire had cheated death once before. She was good at it.

The more Claire thought about it, the more it seemed as though Casey and Serena had cheated death, too. Here they both were, two spirits who had somehow outlived their own bodies *and* somehow escaped the fog, the spirits of the town dead whose job seemed to be ushering the newly dead to the afterlife—whatever that consisted of.

She knew it—she knew what she'd seen in the cemetery and the basement of Peculiar High. She knew that Casey was talking to her. *People get hurt when they're not where they're supposed to be*, he'd told her, all while showing her the alley that had led to the parking lot where *she'd* been hurt—the alley that Dr. Cain had no idea Claire would try to use as a shortcut. Serena was talking, too—the way she'd shown herself to Claire at the funeral, and even when Claire had found her body. The way the world had switched up on Claire back in the woods, the way she'd felt certain she was staring into her own brutalized face and not Serena's—Claire felt absolutely certain that Serena was behind that, every bit as much as Casey was responsible for the Peculiar basement turning into a Chicago alley. Casey and Serena were manipulating the surroundings in order to get Claire's attention, to tell her something. At least, that was what she hoped. But that awful look on the cat's face back at the cemetery hadn't begged for help. It had threatened.

Claire knew, too, that if she told anyone any of this, they'd back away from her slowly, the same way she would have backed away from an injured tiger that had escaped from the zoo.

Sure, it sounded crazy. If Claire hadn't seen it with her own eyes, *she* would have thought it was crazy. But it wasn't her—it was the town—this awful town. She also knew she had to keep the real Serena story to herself until she figured it out—until she saw the full picture. She'd learned that after she'd spread the story of what happened to Rachelle on the Chicago evening news. You kept your mouth shut until you made sure no one was on your tail. You kept your mouth shut until you knew *everything*.

She pulled herself from her bed, headed downstairs, and found Dr. Cain curled over his computer at the kitchen table.

"You didn't go to work?" she asked.

Dr. Cain smiled at her. "I had a bunch of paperwork to get done. Notes to be transcribed."

Claire touched her queasy stomach. She could smell a lie on her father, every bit as clearly as soured milk. He was worried. He'd stayed to keep an eye on her.

"I planned to meet Rich this morning," she lied.

"After yesterday?" he said, his face drooping. "Don't you think you should stay and rest?"

"I'm fine," she said hastily. Why didn't anyone seem to realize that there was nothing restful about being stared at as though you were about to crack and shatter? She hadn't liked

Rachelle looking at her that way, and she didn't like her father looking at her that way now.

"How's that bump?" Dr. Cain asked, standing and reaching for the back of Claire's head.

Claire fought the urge to let out an exasperated sigh. She bristled against being babied.

"Oh, please," Claire said, rolling her eyes. "It's just a bruise." She hugged her dad tightly, grabbed a banana off the counter for breakfast, and scooted out of the kitchen, up the stairs.

She dressed quickly, tossing on a pair of jeans that rubbed like sandpaper against her ankle. The scratches that cat had given her were more tender than she'd expected them to be.

No, she corrected herself, *the scratches* Serena *gave me.* She paused, eyeing herself in her bedroom mirror as she prepared to tug a baggy black sweater on over her head. The cameo still dangled from her throat. Knowing the necklace had belonged to Serena gave Claire an undeniable urge to get to the bottom of whatever Serena had been investigating in the days leading up to her death. Had Serena seen Casey? Had she known about the town dead when something happened to her? Was that why she didn't want to go with the fog? Or was she unwilling to go because she had unfinished business here on earth?

Maybe, Claire thought, Serena's business had something to do with her.

She shuddered, remembering again the fiendish look Serena had flashed her, shining through the cat's ancient face as she sat atop the cemetery wall. *Cat and mouse* . . .

"Can't be," Claire said, dismissing the thought as she tugged her sweater on the rest of the way. "What could she possibly have against me? I haven't done anything to her."

She finished dressing and thundered back down the stairs. "See you later, Dad!" Claire called out, sliding into her naval trench and hurrying through the front door before her father could say anything else.

When Rich appeared in his own doorway, Claire felt any remaining queasiness lift from her gut. She felt the urge to talk to him, really *talk*, blurt out all those thoughts that had just been racing through her head. He would help her—without judgment.

Not yet, she reminded herself. *You don't have the whole story yet.*

What she did wind up blurting was, "My scratches are really sore. And we don't have anything to put on them. Thought you might."

"What scratches?" he asked through a frown.

"On my ankle. That cat—one of the ferals—scratched me yesterday, at the cemetery. That's why I fell in that grave. I was trying to avoid her. I don't want them getting infected."

"Let's take a look," he said, stepping out on the front porch and squatting down toward her, ankle level.

Claire hiked the leg of her jeans. A sense of relief flooded her—a kind of peace that she had not known, not since that awful day last spring. All because she'd shown Rich a silly little wound.

"They're a little red," he assessed, staring at her scratches. "That can actually be dangerous—you could get cat scratch fever."

"That's not a real disease," Claire said. "That's some old song."

He chuckled, turning his eyes up toward her. "Actually, it is a real disease."

"Maybe 'Bout Out has something," Claire suggested. "One of those great old-fashioned remedies."

"Prid salve, maybe," Rich offered.

"Prid what?"

He grinned, grabbing his coat from a hook just inside the door. "Salve. Prid salve. It's an old-school first aid remedy. People here swear by it. Ought to help draw out any infection that might be in there."

As they walked, Rich tugged his stocking cap out of his pocket and stuck it over his head, letting the wavy ends of his brown hair stick out like unruly weeds.

They trudged toward the general store, their breath floating hazily through the cold morning air, their feet making a path through the fresh two inches of snow that had fallen the night before.

She and Rich walked in a kind of uneasy quiet as they approached the little wooden building. Today, the rusted signs looked like faded tattoos on old skin—tattoos that advertised Mobiloil and Campbell's Soup and Coca-Cola "In Bottles." Claire felt she could come to 'Bout Out every day and never be completely finished reading all the signs.

Claire turned a hesitant eye toward the church and cemetery on the opposite side of the street—afraid to find the fog swirling about, but more afraid of turning a blind eye toward the churchyard just long enough to be snuck up on.

For the first time, she noticed that the white steeple of the church pointed toward the sky at an angle, as though the building had begun to lean because of a rotting foundation. Smoke seeped from a roof vent, swirling and curling toward the cemetery. The oldest headstones appeared crooked, too, like teeth growing every which way. The mound of exposed earth on Serena's grave, visible from the street, looked like a fresh wound on the earth.

And the fog slithered between the rows, swirled among the trees.

Claire shivered, the church suddenly seeming to lean under the sheer weight of Peculiar's history—its sadness, its unending misery. Its dead that could rise back out of their graves.

A clank closer to the stone wall that surrounded the cemetery drew Claire's attention toward the church Dumpster, overflowing with the trash that had accumulated during the ice storm, services that had grown in popularity since Serena's disappearance, and the funeral. Hordes of hungry ferals had jumped to the lip of the Dumpster, following the unmistakably sour smell of garbage, as they had at Serena's memorial. They edged their feet into the center, where the trash was packed tight enough to support their weight. They nosed their way about the containers, picking their way through.

A lone cat stood atop the stone wall, watching the others scrounge. The same scraggly old feral that had been under the tarp on Claire's woodpile—*The dirty feral that scratched my leg. The same mangy calico I saw Serena fall into*, she thought, as her skin grew uncomfortably tight beneath her goose bumps.

None of the cats paid much attention when a lone gray tomcat hoisted himself onto the lip, then edged his way across the overflowing Dumpster. Or when another calico jumped and began to forage.

But when the calico that had scratched Claire launched herself toward the open Dumpster, the ferals turned to face her, crouching low. They flashed their teeth. Snarled and wailed. They hissed, tails swollen. They opened their mouths, the afternoon sun reflecting against their teeth as though they were knife blades.

The ancient cat teetered precariously on the lip of the Dumpster, fighting to hold her ground.

A black feral narrowed his green eyes, snarled, and threw

his paw out, taking a swipe at her. The calico skirted away, not quite fast enough to miss his claws completely. Blood poured from her aging skin, a bright vibrant red against the white and tan fur on her leg.

She fell from the Dumpster, her body swiveling and twisting in midair as she tumbled toward the ground. When she hit, she staggered in a way that made Claire remember her own disorienting fall into Serena's grave, how hitting the ground had made her body vibrate, turning her bones into the keys of a xylophone.

The calico hoisted herself over the stone wall and scurried across the street, right across the path that Claire and Rich were taking to 'Bout Out.

"*Sereeeennnnnaaahhhh*," Claire heard, the hiss like a hundred whispers exploding all at once. When she turned toward the cemetery, the fog thickened. It swirled, heads pulling out of the white clump, their mouths moving in unison. "You will not win," the fog warned.

As the old cat scampered to get away, more ferals perched in the 'Bout Out lot yowled at her, flashing their teeth.

"The cats don't like you, Serena," the fog warned. "You're not natural; they'll stop you, they'll kill you, destroy the body you've stolen. And we'll take you. You cannot stay here forever."

"Claire," Rich called, the sound of her own name interrupting the horror playing out around her.

She followed his voice to find him standing on the weather-worn front porch of the general store, icicles clinging to the corrugated tin roof above his head. "Are you coming?" he asked, in a tone that said he'd already asked her more than once. He pointed at the entrance. "It's warm in there."

"Yes, coming," she agreed, but what she really wanted was another look at the cemetery—at the fog and the cats and Serena. When she glanced across the street, it was as though a spell had been broken. She heard no voices, saw no faces in the fog. The cats ate peacefully from the Dumpster.

"Don't worry about those cats over there," Rich said in a reassuring tone. "I know you had bad luck with one of them, but for the most part, they really are harmless. Especially that old calico—she followed Serena everywhere—probably because Serena left food out for her at her old house. Sweet Pea."

"Sweet Pea?" Claire repeated, her mind a pinwheel.

"That's what Serena called her, anyway. I used to hear her calling her to dinner."

"If she's so sweet, why did she scratch me? Why do the rest of the cats react to her like that?" she blurted. She already knew the answer to the last part—she'd just heard it, straight from the fog. But she wanted to hear what Rich had seen, what he'd heard.

"*Sweet Pea* scratched you?" Rich asked, obviously surprised. He shrugged. "It might be that the other cats are turning on her 'cause she's old, she might even be dying. Sometimes animals sense those things."

When his words did nothing to dislodge Claire's feet, Rich called, "Come on—Prid salve, remember?"

"Right. Prid salve." Hesitantly, she climbed up the creaky, soft front steps. As Rich opened the door, Claire paused at the side of an old cracker barrel, the wooden staves gray from weather, the metal hoops rusted.

"Got it?" Rich called, his fingers slipping from the screen as he stepped inside.

Claire pressed her hand against the door, holding it open herself, forcing a smile at Rich.

Just before entering 'Bout Out, Claire's eyes landed on a white cooler, branded Ice, sitting to the side of the patched-up screen door.

She shuddered, sucking in her breath. The cooler was covered in ferals. The yellow tabby she'd seen when she and her dad had first rolled into town. More calicos. A solid black cat with electric green eyes. A gray-and-white tomcat whose stripes looked more like alternating patterns of caked-in filth. They bared their teeth, tails swelling as they crept toward her, in a pack, drawing closer to the edge of the cooler. Bile burned the back of Claire's throat, just as it had out in the field behind Peculiar High when she'd discovered Serena's body.

All of them, hissing.

"Just cats," Claire reminded herself. But the instant she

said it, Serena's face flashed in front of her eyes—Serena's face as it had looked in the woods, beneath the branch. Filled with bite marks left by the feral cats' feast.

As Claire stood in the open doorway, Sweet Pea scurried ahead of her, straight into the store.

"Hey," Claire barked. "You shouldn't be in there."

The cat paused momentarily at the sound of Claire's voice. Blood from the Dumpster altercation trickled down the old calico's front leg. She disappeared, scurrying deep into the store.

Claire sighed, glancing back at the cooler. But the cats were no longer threatening. In a blink, the same animals that had seemed so menacing only moments before were now perfectly tranquil. They nuzzled each other, cleaned each other's faces with their rough tongues. They behaved exactly like the kind of sweet little kitties that the old man in the lot had tried to warn Claire, on her arrival, that they were not. And maybe he was right, in part—maybe they did have some wild tendencies. She'd *seen* their wild tendencies up close. But they were, in fact, just cats. Feral was another word for stray, wasn't it?

Claire finally stepped inside the store, which smelled comforting, like hot coffee and Maxine's warm muffins. But the comfort disappeared as soon as a stack of newspapers beside the front counter greeted Claire with a bold headline from the *Kansas City Star*: BODY OF MISSING TEEN FOUND BY CLASSMATES.

She frowned, turning prickly inside. Now that the funeral was over, she'd expected the story to have died down. Maybe, she thought, it was the circumstances in which Serena's body had been found that reporters were still finding newsworthy. *Found by classmates*, Claire thought. *Found covered in cats, being eaten, being ravaged . . .*

As she stared, the school picture below the headline began to change, flipping back and forth as quickly as strobe lights flicking on and off: Claire, Serena, Claire, Serena—*Claire*. Her own school picture was now centered under the words BODY OF MISSING TEEN FOUND.

It was *her* body that had been found—that's what the headline proclaimed. Claire's body.

No, not yours, she told herself. *It can't be. You were* almost *a body. But you survived, remember?*

"First aid's this way," Rich called. Claire glanced up to find him pointing toward the back of the store.

When she glanced back down again, the front page bore only Serena's image.

Stop it, Claire. Get ahold of yourself.

But she was not entirely sure that she had simply envisioned her own picture on the front page of the *Star*. Where was the fog? Where was Sweet Pea? Was Serena playing mind games? Claire was on edge. She felt as though the atmosphere inside 'Bout Out was pressing down on her skull, like a vise. A headache began to pound behind her eyes.

She staggered forward, clutching the side of her head. The quicker she found that salve stuff, she figured, the quicker she could get back outside and away from the searing heat spewing from an old wood stove in the corner of the store. Away from the frightening headline and the awful ferals.

But before she could catch up to Rich, the front door flapped open again, and Sheriff Holman entered, along with Chas and Owen.

TWENTY-TWO

"What's the matter with you?" Chas asked Owen as the two boys stepped closer to Maxine's display of hot coffee, and Sheriff Holman hurried down an aisle, pausing in front of a sign proclaiming, Fresh Sugar Donuts!

"Nothing," Owen grumbled, as Chas reached for a Styrofoam cup and started to squirt hot coffee from one of the thermoses situated on a small wooden table near the front door. Steam danced above the black pool of liquid.

"Something is," Chas muttered.

Owen shook his head, clenching his jaw.

"Sugar?" Chas asked.

"I don't care."

"What's your *deal*?" Chas pressed angrily. "We're all suddenly beneath you, Mr. *GQ*?"

"I just don't want—" Owen started. He stared through the front window, in the direction of the cemetery. "Doesn't this seem weird, this morning? After everything?"

Chas rolled his eyes. "You'll change your mind when we get to the range. Come on. Two sugars and a shot of Hershey's syrup. Just the way I like it."

He moved with such enthusiasm that Owen chuckled despite himself.

"The range?" Claire blurted.

The boys turned, startled to find her standing less than five feet away.

"Didn't really expect to see anybody out," Owen offered as a way to brush away their obvious surprise. "After."

"Aw, come on—the funeral's over. Can't we just move on? Even Becca was up and out early this morning," Chas justified. "I saw her leaving her house on the way here."

"What's the range?" Claire pressed.

"The shooting range," Chas said, sipping his coffee. "We go every weekend, me and Owen—with Becca's dad. Usually on Sundays. Becca's dad's on call today, but with the whole town sort of still . . ." Chas's voice faded as he struggled to find the right words. "*Shut down*," he finally said. "While the town's basically shut down, he thought we'd be free to get our practice in."

Claire still felt off balance from having imagined her own picture on the front page of the paper, and now, this talk of a

252

firing range made her scalp constrict and the hairs rise on her arms. Something about the idea of those two particular boys firing pistols caused the air to smell metallic, like danger.

"Why are you out this morning?" Chas asked, giving Claire a friendly once-over as Owen turned his face back toward the plate-glass window. His expression grew distant as he eyed the cemetery.

Claire nodded, pointed over her shoulder. "Just came—needed some first aid stuff," she said nonchalantly, hoping to conceal her fear.

"I think I want you guys to take me home," Owen said. "I don't think I want to go today."

"What're you going to *do*?" Chas asked.

"I've got plenty to do," Owen challenged.

"Yeah, that's what Becca says," Chas barked.

As an argument flicked to life, the boys seemed to forget Claire completely.

Good, Claire thought. *Get the medicine and get out*. But where had Rich gone? The store was small—an eighth of the size of the supermarket she and her father had frequented in Chicago—and she wasn't quite sure how he could have disappeared so easily.

"Rich?" Claire asked. "Where's that Prid salve stuff? What aisle?"

She began to make her way down the center of the store, eyeballing the contents of each aisle before passing it by. She turned from the bologna and American cheese in the deli counter, hurried past the row of Tangee lipstick and Coty face powder, glanced down an aisle with Wonder Bread and Shredded Wheat, and paused.

Having abandoned their squabble, Owen and Chas walked past her, toward the counter.

As Claire searched the store for a sign of Rich, she saw it: a drizzle of red blood on the wood floor. She gasped, wondering when the source of the stain—Sweet Pea—would jump out from her hiding spot. She backed up, her shoes smearing the blood, as a hiss exploded into her ears. She swiveled, the blood beneath her feet making the floor slippery. She stared, yet again, into the eyes of the old calico.

Sweet Pea hissed a second time, her tail swelling fat. She raised her injured leg, waving it like a cat playing with a toy. She pawed at the air as light from the front window settled on the gold charm at the base of Claire's throat and reflected back on the cat's face. Serena was trying to get at the old cameo necklace—just as she'd tried in the cemetery, after the funeral. Wisps of Serena's spirit floated just behind the surface of the cat's face—the way a figure inside a bedroom could still be seen behind a pair of filmy curtains.

As Claire prepared to defend herself yet again against the old cat, she was also aware that Officer Holman was paying for coffee and some Little Debbie Donut Sticks. The last of two boxes. *Better hurry*, Maxine was saying, her voice sounding garbled and distorted. *We're 'bout out. Ruthie, ring these boys up.* Normal, everyday action serving as the backdrop of terror.

A delivery truck was arriving, lumbering up to the back door, coming to replace the stock Maxine had lost during the storm. And Ruthie was letting out a giggle—flirty. *She's talking to Chas*, Claire tried to assure herself. But—no—had that giggle sounded sort of sharp, too—a little mean? Claire didn't like mean laughter. Her body ached as she remembered what followed it.

Maxine plunked something down on top of the wood stove and rushed toward the back door and the delivery truck.

It was so hot in that store. Everyone was staring at her. No—they weren't. She only saw backs of heads, backs of shoulders. Still, though, she felt eyes.

Claire turned her attention to the floor, expecting to see the old cat, but only finding the bloodstain. She was gone again, back in hiding.

And those flashing yellow *eyes*—Claire could feel them staring out at her from the shadows. A cat body crouched, ears pointed, whiskers twitching happily as she waited to sneak up on Claire, prepared for the attack.

"Rich?" Claire asked again.

God, it was so hot, the air rippled. Claire's skin poured out a sickly sweat beneath her coat. The cat was following her. She knew it.

Claire was so woozy. All she wanted to do was lie down

right there on the floor. Her eyelids drooped. Her mind spun like the insides of a blender.

Suddenly, a loud pop hit the air like a fist—with it, the interior of 'Bout Out disappeared completely.

Claire was transported; she clung helplessly to a night sky, hovering in the cold darkness, staring down at the parking lot below. The noise she'd heard—that pop—it had been a car door. The girl cop with the round, worried face had just slammed the passenger door of the black-and-white, and she was racing for Claire's body. The rest of the cops were wrangling the grunting, cursing boys to the ground, slapping on cuffs.

Claire watched from her spot high above them all. Stuck to the sky, just as she had been that night in April. She hung, not yet dead, but not really alive anymore, either. Waiting for her life to flash before her—waiting, too, for the sense of peace that refused to show its face. And she thought again, *It's too late for you.* Her body looked like a pile of ground beef down there. Bloody, broken.

As she comforted the shattered Claire, the girl cop slipped her own necklace over her head and put the charm in Claire's bloodstained hand. "St. Jude. Stay with me," she pleaded.

But Claire was soaring, flying through the sky, landing this time on the old back porch of the Sims rental, staring at the rat the calico had mutilated. Staring down at its ripped-open guts, listening to the distant taunts: *You like ratting us out?* But there was no time to answer. She was flying again—this time, into the woods behind the high school. She was looking down on the mangled corpse that the cats had found. They were eating her flesh. That was *her* flesh, Claire thought. She was the one under that limb.

Cats could smell rats. Just like those boys in Chicago had smelled her. Had followed her, hunted her. They were all connected: Claire, and Serena, and that poor gutted rat. They all knew what it was like to lay beaten and cornered and on the verge of death. *Yes!* They were connected, Claire and Serena. Serena could smell her. Because Claire was a rat. Serena was following her everywhere. Hunting her, following her into 'Bout Out. Serena needed her. She needed a rat.

Claire'd ratted those boys out in Chicago. Now Serena needed her to rat out someone else. Because girls did not just wind up mutilated all on their own. Someone else did that to girls. That's what happened to Claire and that's what happened to Serena—it was the truth, as bright and hard to ignore as a searchlight.

This was it! Claire's body thundered with certainty. Serena needed help. She was asking for Claire to listen to her. *She's trying to show me what happened. Because I know things about what can happen to a girl who's all alone during an ice storm.*

But what else did Serena know? Did she know something about Casey? Was that threatening look the cat had flashed her at the cemetery an attempt to show Claire the dangers she was standing in the midst of? Is that why Serena just showed Claire her own face on the front page of the *Kansas City Star*? Was Serena trying to warn her? She'd suspected it that morning, but now she knew for sure. Serena had just told her so. This was it, the reason Serena was following Claire, talking to Claire—there was more to Serena's story than an accident.

"Claire, please," she heard. "Come on. Wake up now, Claire."

"I'm listening," she whispered. "Tell me. Tell me what happened. Tell me everything." She would let the others know—Sheriff Holman and the Sims family. Everyone. "Just tell me," she begged Serena.

"You fainted," she heard, the words coming to her from a much lower voice than she'd expected.

When she blinked her eyes open, she found herself staring into her own face—or her face as it was reflected on the back of a small medallion hanging from Rich's neck. She wasn't in the sky at all; she was lying on the floor; her head was in Rich's lap, and as she pulled her eyes from the medallion, she realized Rich was staring down at her with a wide-eyed, frightened look.

As her eyes spanned outward, she found an entire cluster of worried faces staring down on her—Ruthie's, Maxine's, Owen's, and Chas's.

"You all right?" Sheriff Holman asked, his bulldog jowls also dangling down over her.

"You fainted," Ruthie said, confirming what Rich had just told her. "I told Mom she keeps that wood stove too hot in here."

"It was the difference in temperature," Rich agreed. "We walked in the cold long enough that the sudden change to hot knocked you out."

"It was the darn can that exploded!" Maxine shouted, hovering over Claire's face. "I put that soda can right on top of the stove. I hadn't opened it yet. I didn't even think about it. I was just so happy to hear that ol' delivery truck. Musta scared you to death . . ."

"Don't worry about it. I'll be fine," Claire breathed. She closed her eyes again, still feeling weak. Her head pounded, and her body was too heavy to lift.

"I'm gonna go get you somethin' cool for your face," Maxine shouted, racing off, disappearing.

Claire opened her eyes and nodded gratefully. But it was wrong, all wrong. Everything they were saying. They didn't understand. The world had changed in front of Claire. Serena had made it happen.

From the top shelf of the nearest aisle, Claire saw her—the face of the cat, partially hidden behind boxes of soap.

Something more, Claire mouthed to herself. *For me to find.*

Serena hunkered deep into her hiding spot, her eyes lowering into a squint as she began to purr in agreement.

TWENTY-THREE

Claire let Maxine hold a cool, damp rag against the back of her neck. And at Rich's suggestion, she put her head between her knees. Seemingly relieved, Chas, Owen, and Sheriff Holman left the store, their voices rattling off promises to drop Owen off at home before Chas and the sheriff drove out to the shooting range.

"You want me to call your dad for you?" Maxine offered. "Don't like sending you back out to walk in the cold, if the change in temp's what bothered you to begin with."

Claire shook her head. "That's really not necessary," she insisted.

"I'll take her to the church," Rich offered. "Dad's there. He can drive us back."

"Thanks, Maxine," Claire said, pulling the now-lukewarm

rag from her neck and pressing it into the woman's hand.

Maxine nodded reluctantly. "Feel better," she called out as they made their way toward the door. She kept her face pressed to the front window, watching as Claire let Rich lead her across the street.

Claire had expected to find the church empty. It was Friday, after all—and the entire town had been there only the day before. But the sanctuary echoed with the sounds of someone crying loudly and without any restraint, as though they believed they were completely alone.

"I couldn't stand it," the voice wailed. "I couldn't stand the fact that Dad was just going to take Chas and Owen to their stupid shooting range, like nothing had changed."

As Claire slowly edged forward, she could see Becca in one of the pews, Pastor Ray at her side. He was angled crookedly in the pew, turned toward her with his hands cupped slightly, almost as though to catch her confessions as they all poured out.

"Lying in bed this morning," Becca went on, her voice thick with emotion, "I heard Rhine head downstairs with Jasper 2. They were going outside to exercise, just like they always do when school's not in session. I could hear him yelling, 'Get it! Get it, boy!' like he always does when they play catch. I started to think about how it seemed like our family mourned the death of our old Jasper longer than they mourned Serena.

"I listened to cars, too," Becca went on, "whizzing down the roads, toward chores and shopping runs and errands as usual. It's like everyone fell right back into their old routines," she said. "People with the day off are treating it like any old weekend. Yesterday, we were all in the cemetery burying Serena. *Yesterday!*

"Everybody's acting like burying Serena was a chore—like cleaning out the garage—and now that everything's in place, now that it's tidy, they can dust their hands off and be done with it."

"Don't you think everyone else has a right to be happy, even without Serena?" Pastor Ray asked.

"I don't think we should move on yet."

"Why? You almost make it sound like there's some penance to be paid."

"There *is*."

"By whom?"

"By *me*. I—wasn't a good friend. Not to Serena." Her shoulders lurched violently with her sobs.

"Oh, Becca," Pastor Ray said, putting his hand on her shoulder. "We can't torture ourselves about the past. We mourn, and in so doing, we learn about ourselves. We let our grief teach us about who we want to be."

As Pastor Ray continued to comfort Becca, Rich motioned for Claire to follow him down the stairs, into the basement's kitchen area. He hung their coats on a nearby hook and pointed at a chair, silently telling her to sit.

"Becca's taking this hard," Claire said.

"Yeah," Rich agreed, dipping into the fridge and pulling out a container of orange juice—probably, Claire thought, left over from Sunday school. He sniffed it, found a glass, and filled it.

"Here," he said. "Some sugar ought to help."

"Thanks." Claire sipped—the cold sweetness of the drink was welcome against the dry, fevered insides of her mouth.

"Kind of almost over the top," she said. "The way she's mourning."

"How do you mean?" Rich asked, leaning against the kitchen counter.

"It's almost—guilty, the way she talks about Serena."

"A lot of people talk to my dad that way, when there's a death in the family," Rich pointed out. "Nobody ever has a perfect relationship. People feel bad sometimes when the opportunity to make up to someone's gone."

"Yeah, but she was at my house right after we found Serena, saying some of the same things to me—especially that part about not being a good friend.

"And Chas—he doesn't seem to care at all," Claire rattled on. "At least Owen's shown some sign of feeling bad. Chas just—it's like he never knew her at all. And according to

Becca, they really were into each other. She said she didn't know why Chas was playing the whole thing down."

Rich's face registered anguish and his cheeks turned ghostly white.

"What?" Claire pressed.

Rich's voice jerked and sputtered as he struggled to explain. "Ever since—I ran out into the woods to see what was going on—and saw her—" He shook his head.

"*Tell* me."

"We had this game, when we were little—Serena would hide and pretend to be in the woods. She got lost once, when she was really small. And we'd always play pretend like she was lost in the woods again. She'd call my name, and I'd find her. I remember, she used to call out to me, *Olly, olly, oxen free!* And I'd be this knight swooping in to rescue her.

"But the thing was, she *hated* the woods. I mean, she was terrified of them. Once, when we were still playing that game, I tried to get her to go—for real. Told her to call me and I'd rescue her from the *actual* woods. But she wouldn't do it. Told me there was no way I was ever going to make her go in."

"But that's where I found her. Sheriff Holman said in his press conference that she took the shortcut through the woods," Claire said.

"Yeah—weird. I mean, we haven't been close since we were kids, though, so I thought—maybe she got over it. Still—it's hard for me to believe she wasn't scared at all anymore of the woods. It was really like a phobia."

As Claire stared at him, he mumbled, "I hear her. Ever since—when I first saw Rhine lifting that limb off her—"

"Wait," Claire said. "When was this?"

"When I found you out there," Rich said, his words gaining strength, "Rhine was lifting the limb off Serena's body, and everyone was going berserk, and I could remember her, with that little kid's voice, calling out to me: *Rich! Olly, olly, oxen free!*"

This admission brought Claire to her feet. She paced a bit, finishing off the last of her juice and plopping the glass down on the counter.

Rich hadn't simply imagined her voice. He had *heard* Serena. Claire knew it. Serena was begging for help. Rich just wasn't willing to believe he'd heard her—he wasn't connected to Serena. Not like they'd been as kids. Not in the same way Claire was now.

But Claire knew—he'd *heard* her. Literally. Serena was calling out for help.

Rich frowned as Claire leaned against the counter beside him. "What is that?" he asked, pointing at her throat.

Claire started to tuck Serena's necklace back down into her sweater, embarrassed. Rich stopped her, wrapping her fingers in his warm hand and pulling her arm aside.

"It seemed familiar when I saw you with it the day you enrolled," he said. "It's Serena's. I'd bet anything it is. Where'd you get it?"

"It was tangled in Sweet Pea's tail," Claire said, feeling exposed beneath his hard stare. "When I first saw her—by the woodpile behind our house."

"Tangled? Did it always look like this?" he asked as he squinted to examine the chain. "Did something happen to it once you got hold of it?"

Claire shook her head no. "It was in pretty bad shape after it got yanked from Sweet Pea's tail. The clasp was broken. I smashed the chain together when I put it on, and now it won't come off."

"But did you tug on it? Hard? Trying to get it off? Did you really try to break it?"

"No. Why?"

"Because someone else did. This chain's all pulled out of shape. Some of the links are longer than others—misshapen, twisted, smashed. I bet the same person who tugged on it also broke the clasp."

"Maybe Sweet Pea was near Serena when she died," Claire said. "Maybe she saw everything." *And maybe*, she thought, *that's why Serena fell inside Sweet Pea. Maybe that's why she's still inside her. Maybe they're connected, too—by more than just Serena feeding her . . .*

"Sheriff Holman isn't much of a policeman," Claire reminded him. "That's what you and your dad both said. So did he miss something? Did Rhine disturb something out there, when he lifted that limb off Serena's body? What's really going on?"

In the fearful quiet that swelled between them, Claire said, "Do you feel like there's something else here—something more to the story? Something we're supposed to go find?"

Rich shuddered. "I do," he whispered. "I don't want to, but I do."

TWENTY-FOUR

"What do you mean, you fainted?" Dr. Cain asked, worry discoloring his entire face as Claire and Rich both stepped inside the old Sims house less than an hour later.

"It was nothing," Claire promised, as she watched her father clear his throat and push his glasses deeper into his face.

"No, it was a faint. A faint isn't nothing," he informed her, peeling her coat off and sitting her down on the living room couch. He sat beside her, placing a hand on her forehead.

"You should have felt that place," Claire insisted. "There's an old wood stove in there, and Maxine had it set to Tropical Swelter. Ask Rich," she added, pointing at him as he stood at the edge of the room, staring at her with his own troubled expression. "He even said it was the change in temp."

"I've seen it happen before," Rich said with a shrug.

"And you walked all the way back after that?" her father asked.

"We went across the street to the church. My dad dropped us off," Rich assured him.

"Are you okay now?" Dr. Cain pressed, his voice sounding tight. "Not woozy? Dizzy at all? How do you feel?"

"Dad, I'm fine," Claire grumbled. She glanced up again at Rich, who was staring at her father in surprise. "Really." She tried to push her dad away, but he continued to tug on her lower eyelid, look into her pupils, pet the hair on the top of her head. Her dad's reaction was over the top, even considering what had happened to Claire at the funeral the day before. The way Dr. Cain hovered was going to tip Rich off to the fact that he had other reasons to worry about her—reasons bigger than a fall into a grave, bigger even than the discovery of a body.

Claire reminded herself of the relief that had washed over her simply by showing Rich the scratches on her ankle—but she wasn't ready to show him her scars. She wasn't ready for word to get out in Peculiar about what had happened to her in Chicago. Sanders had kept his promise; the details of Claire's permanent record—the fact that she had been absent from school during the last two months of her sophomore year and the entire fall semester of her junior year—had been kept quiet, in her file. She wanted it to stay that way.

"Maybe you should skip school on Monday," her father said.

"No, Dad. Really? I'll be fine. I *am* fine," Claire asserted, wishing her words could work like an off valve for her father's fears. "I'm going to school, and you're going to work. Rich'll drive me. Both ways. No walking."

"I think a day off from all of this would be good for you," Dr. Cain reasoned, trying to wrap Claire into a protective hug.

Claire struggled against him, trying to push his hands away, but that only made him reach for her again, wrapping his arms around her neck. "Dad," she complained. "Seriously, okay? Enough. Dad—"

Glancing up at Rich's confused expression—and remembering the words he'd used at the church, the game he'd described playing with Serena, she echoed, "Olly, olly, oxen free!"

The odd saying made her father pull away. "What—?" he started.

"I'll drive her to school, Dr. Cain," Rich promised, cutting off Dr. Cain's words.

"Monday," Rich told Claire, "and every day for the rest of the semester."

"That's nice of you, Rich," Dr. Cain said through a startled frown, "but—"

"Don't worry, Dr. Cain," Rich said in a soothing voice. "I'll look out for her. My word is good."

That last bit made Claire shudder a bit. It almost felt like code—like he was referencing the words Claire had just used, the simple phrase that no longer felt like a game.

Claire felt torn between regretting using Serena's words to inform Rich that she was a girl in need of rescue, and feeling grateful that she now had a phrase she knew she could rely on—a way to get Rich's attention if danger ever crept uncomfortably close.

TWENTY-FIVE

That weekend, Claire treated her scratches with the Prid salve that Rich had apparently bought just before she'd fainted at 'Bout Out. She smeared the strange, black tarry substance on her tender cuts, wincing against the pressure of her own finger. On Sunday, when the wounds refused to show any real sign of improvement, she decided to just cover them completely with gauze, tape them up against the outside air and her own steady gaze. After all, if a watched pot never boiled, maybe a watched cut never healed.

Monday afternoon, in history class, Claire accepted the seat that Becca had saved for her. She'd been accepting seats from Becca all day long: one next to her in the student convocation center before the morning's first bell, as Becca prattled on about a pair of earrings she had that would look lovely on Claire, and didn't she want them for the dance? Another at lunch—beside Becca, instead of across the table—leaving Owen to sit in the seat Claire had been claiming for her own, across the table, next to Rich.

Claire had only just opened her history book when Isles began to hand out their test papers. Her shoulders slumped as she stared into the giant red F at the top of her test. Claire had never seen a flat-out F at the top of one of her tests before.

Becca leaned forward, saw it, and made a face that said, "Ouch." *Sorry,* she mouthed.

Claire eyed it, tracing the letter with her finger throughout the entirety of the class period. When the bell rang, she delayed putting the test in her bag—somehow, it seemed that once it mingled with her folders and pencils, it would suddenly become real.

As she finally stood, hoisting her backpack onto her shoulder, Ms. Isles called, "Claire."

Isles pointed to an empty desk in the front row.

"I'll wait for you?" Becca asked.

Claire shook her head. "Thanks, but I have a ride with Rich," she said, which was true. Rich was serious about the whole ride to and from school bit. He was serious about it lasting the entire semester. But it wasn't same kind of help that Claire had hated receiving back in Chicago—not the *just lie back in bed and rest while I fluff your pillows* kind of help. He wasn't treating her like someone who needed to sit still and wait for her next visitor, who, judging by the way things had been going, might very well be the Grim Reaper himself. So she found herself welcoming his help, his simple promise of a ride to and from school.

Claire dragged herself to the front of the room and slid into the chair Isles had chosen, the tops of her thighs squeaking on the glossy wooden surface.

Isles leaned on the edge of her desk, a beautiful flower surrounded by ugly walls. Claire couldn't believe how youthful Isles looked. Take away the heels and the red lipstick and the perfectly curled blond hair, and Isles was a sorority sister. Give her a ponytail, a white shirt, and some kneesocks, and she'd look like she was still a student at Peculiar High.

"I know these past few days have been really hard on you," she started. "First you move into town in the midst of an ice storm, then you see—well—and then, that fall you took at the cemetery. When I was grading your test, I had to stop and think about how *hard* this all must be on you. I can't tell you how sorry I am."

She plucked a sheet of paper off her large wooden desk and sat down in the seat beside Claire. She actually looked more at home in the student desk than in the teacher variety.

"It only seems fair that you should get a second chance.

A do-over," Isles said. "I'd like to offer you a chance to retake our test."

Claire sighed as relief washed over her. "I thought I was going down in flames," she admitted.

"No—I don't want you to do that. None of your teachers want that, Claire." She nudged Claire with her elbow and winked.

Claire flinched against the elbow jab; that was how Rachelle had teased her. It didn't seem right, somehow, for anyone else to do that. She eked out a crooked smile as she reminded herself that finally, something good was actually happening in Peculiar. "When do I—"

"Right now," Isles said.

"Wait, what? No—I'm—not ready," Claire pleaded.

"Oh, please," Isles said, rolling her eyes. "You're feeling better by now. In fact, this time around, I'll bet you'll ace it. I'm going to head to the restroom for a minute, but I'll be right back. 'Kay?"

She slid a new test paper in front of Claire and hurried out of the room, her heels clicking. On her way out, her right arm flew to the side, smacking a pull-down map. The map snapped, winding back onto itself along the roller above the blackboard. Claire frowned, realizing that the board was numbered one through twenty, with a single letter next to each number. Claire glanced back at her multiple-choice test. Twenty blanks.

Isles had given her the answers. Did she honestly feel *that* sorry for her? Never, in her seventeen years, had Claire ever heard of a teacher risking her own reputation—or her job— by allowing—no, *helping*—her student to cheat.

That's what it said on Serena's hand. It said that when I tripped and the snow was chewing on my skin and the fall through the ice was like jackhammers on my body. When I turned and I saw her eaten fingers, that's what it said right there in her palm: "CHEATING."

The realization traveled through Claire like sparks of electricity.

She got a sinking feeling that this was part of it, too. This test—and that word on Serena's hand. It was somehow all intertwined.

Claire sat immobile until Isles returned, pulling the map back down over the answers.

"Finished?" she asked cheerfully, holding her hand out.

Claire snatched her blank test paper, balling it into a tight fist. "Forget it," she said, "I'll take the F."

"You can't want an F." Isles looked like she'd been punched as Claire threw the test into the trash and bolted from the classroom.

"Claire. *Claire*," Isles called. "I'm just trying to help."

But why should she care? Claire wondered. *It's my grade.*

Looking back over her shoulder as she raced toward her locker, Claire crashed into a thick wool sleeve. "Whoa! Watch out!" a voice warned her. Rough hands steadied her to keep her from collapsing onto the floor. When she untangled herself, she realized that the hands on her shoulders belonged to Owen.

"This test—" Isles said, emerging from her classroom. She flapped the blank page emphatically as Claire pushed herself away from Owen and scurried down the hall.

TWENTY-SIX

laire sprinted to her locker, shrugged herself into her
coat, and raced down the steps, into the parking lot
where Rich waited for her.

"Cheating," Claire shouted, slapping her open palm on
the hood of Rich's Ram as she rounded the truck. She felt her
cheeks flushing pink with cold and the rush of having maybe
just uncovered a new puzzle piece regarding Serena's death.

"I know what it's about," Claire announced.

"Cheating, huh," Rich repeated, his voice muffled by the
rolled-up windows. His face drooped with disappointment.
"Get in," he said, leaning across the bench seat and popping
the lock on the passenger-side door.

"Isles," he said as Claire climbed inside. "You have Isles for
history, don't you?"

Claire's shoulders collapsed. "Yes. How'd you know?"

"Everyone knows," Rich said. "At least, all the students do."

"But—cheating? *Cheating?*" she asked, slamming the door shut beside her.

"Look, Isles just wants out of here," Rich said. "She was kind of a star when she was a student at Peculiar High. After college, though, the only place she could get work was Peculiar. You know what a blow that was to her ego? Instead of teaching someplace like St. Louis or Kansas City, she's *here*." He said it—*here*—with his lip raised, to emphasize his disgust. "In some respects, she's no better off than Rhine. We had to give her a small-town favor, too. She's been bumping up her grades ever since she got the job last fall, just so she can transfer."

"And everyone's okay with that?" Claire asked.

"Not everyone. The faculty doesn't know about it. And as far as the students are concerned, it just *is*. It's not about being okay or not okay. It's kind of like—you know the kid next to you is cheating on his test. Do you rat him out, or do you just leave him alone, figure his business is his business, and take your own test, worry about yourself?"

Claire flinched at his word: *rat.* "I thought a small town was all about knowing everyone else's business," she muttered.

"Knowing and acting on it are two different things." He sighed, stuck his key in the ignition.

"But it was on her hand," Claire insisted.

Rich pulled his fingers from the key, frowned at Claire. "Whose hand?"

"Serena's," Claire said. "Just before—when I found her, she had it written on the palm of her hand. 'Cheating,' all caps. Like somehow it was important. But the cat—while I was in the woods, I saw a cat—take a bite . . ." She paused to shake off the revulsion creeping into her gut as she remembered the scene. "The cat destroyed the word, while I was there watching. Sheriff Holman never would have seen that word on her hand."

Rich leaned back into the bench seat. "She doodled," he said. "On everything. When we were little, she used to even write words or draw things on her canvas sneakers. Her initials. She doodled those a lot, too."

"But 'cheating.' On her hand. The day she went missing. Why?"

"There was a lot of cheating going on in Serena's life, though. Chas, for example. You don't know for sure what that one word referred to."

"I don't," Claire agreed. "I wish there were some way to get in her head. If only there were something—even some draft of the story she was working on. About the basement. Anything. The tone of it, the words she used—it might give us some glimpse into what she was thinking about, in those last days of her life."

"Her laptop, maybe," Rich mused. "I think I might know where to find it."

Rich pulled into the drive at the Simses' house and sat in silence as Claire fumbled with the buttons on her coat. "Come on, let's go inside," he finally said, but the way he took a breath, as though trying to summon the courage to kill the engine and ring the Simses' bell, seemed to indicate he was talking to himself more than Claire.

The front door groaned its way open, and Mrs. Sims appeared, her face reflecting the shock she felt to find the two of them on her step. "Rich? It's—nice to see you." She hugged her ratty brown cardigan around herself, her eyes wide.

Rich hesitated. "Mrs. Sims," he started, but stopped, the right words obviously evading him.

"Mrs. Sims," Claire piped up, feeling her blood surge with urgency as she spoke. "You may not remember me, but my father and I are renting your old house. I apologize for not coming by earlier to express my condolences. To tell you how truly sorry I am for your loss."

Mrs. Sims hugged her cardigan tighter, as though it could somehow protect her from the reality of her daughter being dead.

"We know you weren't expecting us," Claire went on. "We're both working on the school newspaper—Rich and

I—and—we were thinking that maybe the best way to pay tribute to Serena would be to publish her last piece. Rich said that she had something she was working on. We were hoping you'd let us check out her computer, find her pages, and email them to my account."

Mrs. Sims squirmed, pushing a few wiry gray hairs away from her temples. "Well—I'm actually in the midst of—"

"I'm sorry—I should have asked—have the police brought the computer back yet?" Claire said.

Mrs. Sims's face crinkled into a blend of both confusion and pain. She looked at Claire as though she'd just driven an ice pick straight through her hand. "Her *computer* is in her *room*. Where it's always been. My daughter had an accident."

"No—" Claire jumped in. "I didn't mean—I wasn't implying that the police ever suspected she was involved in anything. I just—I assumed—" She couldn't understand it. A seventeen-year-old girl had gone missing—why *hadn't* the police swooped in and grabbed her computer, ten minutes after her parents had reported the disappearance? Wasn't that step one in any missing-persons investigation?

"I'll do it, Mrs. Sims," Rich offered. "I'll get the file. You can come with me to her room, if that makes you more comfortable."

But Mrs. Sims only shook her head no fiercely. "I can't go in there," she whispered. "I haven't been inside yet. Neither has her father . . ."

She was building up a protective wall—Claire could feel it. Mrs. Sims wasn't going to let them in; she was backing away; the door creaked shut an inch.

But Claire stepped forward, because she had a taste in her mouth, now—just as the ferals around Serena's head had once had a taste for blood, their jaws stained pink. "I'll sit with you," she offered. "Mrs. Sims, I'd be happy to sit with you while Rich looks." Because she needed answers. *That* was the taste in her mouth now. Answers about Serena. The fog. What, exactly, was going on in this town.

Mrs. Sims led Claire to the kitchen, while Rich climbed the stairs. Claire could tell from the slump in his shoulders, his slow shuffle, just how much he hated the idea of being the first person inside Serena's room after her death.

"I have—some coffee on," Mrs. Sims said. "Do you drink coffee?"

"Yes," Claire said, nodding. "That'd be great, actually." She shivered a bit inside her coat, to illustrate how chilled she'd gotten.

The Simses' current house was obviously one of the newer homes in Peculiar. The kitchen was quaint, with gauzy yellow checkerboard curtains, a gray stone countertop, and spotless white cabinets. It was bright and airy—a stark contrast to the expression on Mrs. Sims's face.

"How do you and your father like the old place?" Mrs. Sims asked, carrying two mugs of coffee to her table on a small tray, along with a sugar bowl and a spoon.

"It's very homey," Claire said appreciatively. She didn't mention anything about how the water had a tendency to get stone-cold if the tub ran longer than four minutes, or how much she hated lighting that old granite stove with a match. Or how the inside of the refrigerator smelled to her like a brick-hard, ancient box of baking soda—and how the smell somehow kept invading their milk carton to make it taste funny.

"Lot of history in that house," Mrs. Sims said, her eyes growing far away.

Claire fought for the right words. "You all lived there together," she finally offered.

Mrs. Sims's upper lip wavered. "Yeah," she said, tracing the yellow plaid on her tablecloth. "My mom grew up there. I grew up there. My daughter reached middle age there," she said, her voice turning to a whisper. "I was thinking that, the other day. You know? How eight for her was actually middle-aged." She shook her head. "I didn't have grandiose dreams for her," Mrs. Sims blurted. "I didn't dream that she would change the world. I just dreamed she'd get a chance to enjoy it."

Claire shifted, the weight of Mrs. Sims's grief making her uncomfortable. Her eyes landed on a pair of scratches in the wainscoting.

Mrs. Sims pulled a Kleenex out of her sweater pocket,

wiped her nose, then turned, following Claire's stare. She chuckled. "She used to write her initials on everything," Mrs. Sims said. Over and over: *SS, SS*."

"Must be a comfort," Claire babbled awkwardly. "To see something she did. Each time you come down for your coffee."

"Comfort?" Mrs. Sims asked. "Do you know what I see when I look at those scratches?"

Claire tensed, shook her head no.

"I see a little girl who knew—hardly more than ten years old—that the clock was winding down. Like she had some sort of premonition." Mrs. Sims was visibly agitated now. She trembled as she leaned over the top of the table, snarling at Claire. "I see a girl who just wanted to make her mark on the world, while there was still time. I see a little girl who desperately wanted the world to know she was *here*."

Before Claire could respond, a knock rattled the back door. A black faceless silhouette filled the yellow curtain covering the small window.

TWENTY-SEVEN

"Mom made you a new one," Owen said when Mrs. Sims answered the door. "Still feels warm," he added as she accepted his foil-wrapped casserole dish.

"Your mother is so kind," she cooed, no trace of her previous distress in her voice as she peeled the foil back to take a peek. Owen followed her inside as she carried the casserole to the counter, then flipped open a cabinet door and rummaged through the contents. "I washed the bowl you brought yesterday. If only I could remember where I put it," she said, pausing to wipe the tears off her cheek.

"I just—I—can't believe that she's still thinking of us," Mrs. Sims babbled. "Making us those lovely dinners. Serena's father and I—we both—it's so *nice*."

Owen shuffled his feet, leaning uncomfortably against the sink.

Claire watched, thinking that this must have been the daily exchange: a full meal for last night's empty bowl, and Mrs. Sims using her gratitude to try to cover up the fact that she hadn't gotten herself together enough to make dinner yet.

Claire's phone cut through the air in the kitchen, thick with awkward tension. She fished it from her coat, glanced at the screen to find another text from Rachelle: *Storm + girl found + no text from u = I'm worried. U OK???* Claire had actually lost count of the number of texts she'd received in the last few days, all of them relaying the same message.

Claire didn't have time—or the patience, right then—to placate Rachelle. She sighed, turned her phone off.

She glanced up, straight into the heat of Owen's glare. She wondered, for a moment, if he was going to say something about the test that he'd seen her running from.

Above them, Rich's large feet clomped about Serena's bedroom.

Mrs. Sims flinched, clutched her cardigan around her throat, and took a step toward the kitchen door, her eyes turned toward the ceiling.

Claire began to ramble, trying to cover up the forceful bangs and distracting Mrs. Sims from her obvious intention to kick Rich out of Serena's room. "I think this is the perfect way to memorialize your daughter," she told Mrs. Sims. "With her own words."

Claire gulped down the rest of her bitter coffee, just so she could ask, "Mrs. Sims, could you pour me another?" She exhaled deeply, with relief, as Mrs. Sims turned her back to her, toward the coffeepot. It was painful to see her so upset at the idea of someone being up there, in her daughter's room—yet, in Claire's mind, the chore was also completely necessary.

"I guess—I should—" Owen started, pointing for the door.

"Before you go," Mrs. Sims said, holding up a finger, "I wanted to ask you a favor."

Owen offered a half nod as Mrs. Sims took a deep breath, preparing herself.

"I need someone—to clean out her locker," she admitted.

Claire frowned against the weight of Mrs. Sims's request. "Why didn't law enforcement do that?" she blurted. When Owen and Mrs. Sims turned shocked eyes her way, she clarified, "When Serena went missing? Why wouldn't they have searched her locker?"

"They did," Mrs. Sims whispered. "But there was nothing there. Nothing that would help them, anyway. Serena was so fastidious. She—there was nothing there," she repeated.

"I see," Claire mumbled. But in her mind's eye, she pictured Sheriff Holman's lazy bulldog jowls. And she wondered what he'd missed.

Mrs. Sims left the room, coming back with an old cardboard storage container, *Serena* scrawled across the side in black marker. "I need someone to return her textbooks to the office, and to bring back anything that might be personal. I can't do it. See—see if Becca will—"

"No," Owen urged. "Don't bother Becca with it. She's been—" He shook his head. "I'll do it, Mrs. Sims."

It was a kind gesture, Claire thought. Saving Becca from having to empty out her friend's locker showed a level of compassion that Claire wasn't sure that Becca really deserved, in light of the way she'd been attacking Owen verbally, accusing him repeatedly of running around on her, of not caring.

As he stepped through the back door, a brief moment of quiet settled through the kitchen. Another round of shuffling and a loud bang from upstairs made Mrs. Sims frown, ball her hands into fists, and lunge for the doorway.

"Mrs. Sims, wait!" Claire shouted.

Serena's mother had only just swiveled on her heel when a soft rumble filtered through the kitchen.

"Wait for what?" Mrs. Sims asked.

"Did you hear that?" Claire asked, her eyes circling the kitchen for the source of the noise.

But Mrs. Sims continued to stare at the ceiling. "I hear a lot of things," she muttered.

Claire picked up on the rumble again—it sounded so content. Like a purr.

"Do you have a cat?" Claire asked.

Mrs. Sims shook her head—as if to indicate she hadn't heard anything or to say she didn't have a cat, Claire wasn't sure which. Maybe both.

Claire's scalp constricted. "There it is again," she said.

Suddenly, in a violent pop, Mrs. Sims's coffeepot burst. Mrs. Sims shrieked as glass shards scattered across the kitchen; they sparkled in the air, catching the light before raining against the cabinetry and dancing into the porcelain sink. Hot coffee gushed, pouring across the countertop and the laminate floor.

Before Claire had time to react, a frightened whelp exploded throughout the kitchen.

Sweet Pea jumped from her hiding spot on the top of the refrigerator. She landed on the floor and scurried straight for Claire.

She opened her mouth and hissed.

Claire screamed, drawing her legs up into her seat as Mrs. Sims quickly grabbed a broom and shouted, "Out! Scoot!"

The cat snarled, threw her front feet forward, and exposed her claws, trying to clutch on to the floor, to fight against the force of Mrs. Sims's broom.

Claire screamed again—because she knew what she'd seen at the funeral. She didn't have to see Serena's blue eyes or her smile floating about on the cat's face, like she had at the cemetery. She knew the truth about that cat. She knew that Serena was inside.

"I'm trying to help you," Claire whispered. "Why are you so mad?"

But the cat only yowled again.

"Out! Get out!" Mrs. Sims shouted, opening the back door.

Sweet Pea hissed, her swollen tail standing up angrily.

Mrs. Sims pushed the cat outside, slammed the door shut behind her. She propped the broom against the wall, and turned to look at the mess in her kitchen—the shattered glass, the coffee dripping from the countertop. Brown drops had sprayed everywhere, dotting the walls, the cabinetry, the pretty yellow curtains.

"That pot's been on day and night lately," she said apologetically, pushing her hair from her face in an exhausted manner. "I've had it for years. Guess it overheated."

"Where'd the cat come from?" Claire asked. Fear rooted her in her seat as Mrs. Sims reached for a rag.

"Strays get in through the garage sometimes," Mrs. Sims said, wiping the last few flyaway strands of hair from her forehead. "Warmer in here. Besides, *that* cat," she went on, her eyes growing wet and her voice quiet, "she followed Serena everywhere. Here to this house, and to our old house, too. Serena fed her at both places, but mostly at the old house, I think. Sometimes, it seemed my girl spent most of her time there—because she liked it better. She didn't think I knew that, but I did. I think she even tried to make a bed for the cat, inside our old house. Sweet Pea. Serena used to call her that."

Sweet—the word rang out sarcastically in Claire's mind.

Her eyes landed on the wainscoting again. *SS. Serena Sims.*

Claire trembled. *That cat's not looking for Serena,* she thought. *That cat is Serena. Even her mother doesn't hear her, doesn't recognize her. No one in this town can see her. They're all blind! Everyone just dismisses her, like they dismiss Casey. Pranks, they say. Coincidences. They don't know. But I do. I know it's real. I'm the only one. Getting to the truth about Serena is all on me.*

TWENTY-EIGHT

Claire removed her coat and reached for the dishrag hanging from the handle of the half-open silverware drawer. She turned her back to Mrs. Sims and fastened the top button on her blouse to keep the cameo hidden. If Serena was after her necklace, Claire didn't want to give it away—not even to a grieving Mrs. Sims. She wanted that cat to keep coming to her. *The cat knows the truth*, she thought. *No— Serena knows the truth. About this horrible town. And Casey and the crazy things that happen here. I have to fix this. I have to make it right. Serena wants me to make it right. I can't do anything that would send her away, or make her think I'm not invested in her story.*

She was on her hands and knees, wiping up coffee, and

Mrs. Sims was sweeping wet glass shards into tiny dangerous-looking mounds, when Rich entered the kitchen.

"What happened?"

"Coffeepot exploded," Mrs. Sims explained.

Still looking bewildered, Rich grabbed a towel and squatted beside Claire. "There's no story on her laptop," he muttered. "I looked for notes—handwritten notes—through all her desk drawers. Nothing."

"What about her phone?" Claire whispered.

Rich shook his head. "I can't find it."

"Mrs. Sims?" Claire asked. "Would you have any idea where Claire's phone is?"

Wrinkles deepened around the corners of Mrs. Sims's lips. Claire thought for a moment that the lines around her mouth were deep enough to cast shadows. "I don't care about things like that," she confessed. "Maybe those things mean something to you two, but—that didn't have anything to do with my life with Serena. Of all the things I'll miss, that's—" She leaned her broom against the counter, placed a glass-filled dustpan on the cold stovetop. "Excuse me," she said, and hurried from the kitchen, her face twisted as she attempted to mask the new round of tears beginning to stream down her cheeks.

"Mrs. Sims," Claire called, as she started after her. "I didn't want—"

Rich grabbed Claire's elbow. "Just clean the kitchen," he advised. "I'll help. We can let ourselves out."

The next morning, two days shy of the one-week anniversary of Serena Sims's funeral, life had returned to normal. At least, that was how it appeared to Claire as Rich drove her to school. Tree-trimming crews had officially finished gnawing away the remnants of the broken limbs. Parents, it seemed, as Claire visited her locker and listened to the chatter of voices making after-school plans, had already let go of the tight holds they'd placed on their daughters during the days when they hadn't known for sure what had happened to the Sims girl—when they'd feared foul play. It was a bad thing, what happened to Serena. But it had also been an accident—and sometimes, the word "accident" made it easier to fall back into old rhythms, the pulse of life as it had been before.

The tardy bell rang, allowing the journalism room to settle into a routine as comfortable as a down pillow as students turned on computers and moved freely about the room. Claire glanced up toward the door just as Owen passed by with a large box tucked under his arm, the side branded *Serena*.

She pushed her chair back and darted into the hallway.

"Claire!" Rich hissed. "Where are you going? You need a pass. Claire!"

Claire motioned with her hand for Rich to keep quiet. She

hurried forward, out of sight of the journalism door. She trailed Owen around one corner, down a deserted hallway. She slowed as he dropped his box to the floor. He consulted a wrinkled piece of paper—surely, Claire thought, the combination for Serena's locker, provided by one of the secretaries in the main office. Tucking the paper into his pants pocket, he spun the lock, tugged it free.

Owen glanced up. "Shouldn't you be in class?" he asked Claire, swinging the locker door open.

"Shouldn't you?" Claire countered.

Owen shrugged. "I have a good excuse. Nobody's going to give me detention when they find out I got stuck with this chore."

"You could do it after school," Claire challenged.

Owen eyed her. "I can't stand art class. I'm not going to waste my great excuse. If I time it right, I can miss most of it."

Claire took another step closer to the locker. It was, as Mrs. Sims had said, immaculate. No pictures or mirrors on the door, no wadded-up homework assignments on the bottom. No Snickers wrappers. Her textbooks stood up on the top shelf, looking like books in a library, spines facing outward. A fleece sweatshirt hung on the hook.

"After you left, Mrs. Sims told me—she didn't know where Serena's phone was. She wanted me to tell you," Claire started. She hadn't known what she would say to Owen when she started talking; her lie only began to knit itself together as she rambled on. "She wanted me to bring her phone back, because—"

"Why would *Mrs. Sims* care about Serena's *phone*?" Owen argued.

Claire blushed. "She—I—"

Owen sighed. "Does it look like there's a phone *here*?" he asked, pointing toward the top shelf.

It wasn't the shelf Claire was interested in. It was the pockets of the sweatshirt. She started to reach for it, when Owen stepped in between her and the locker, blocking her.

"Actually, I've been wanting to talk to you," Owen asserted.

Something in his tone gave her goose bumps. "Really?"

"Yeah. Really. You passed up a good thing, you know."

Claire's mind whirled. "What're you talking about?"

"The history test. The one you wouldn't retake."

"What do you care about my test?"

"Somebody gives you a free pass, you take it. Period."

"I'm not into free passes," she spat back.

"Bullshit. Everybody's into free passes," Owen said. "You know the only thing that counts in life?" he murmured. "The bottom line. That's it. Not how you got there. The right answer. The number of As. Transcripts."

Claire wasn't sure what to say—or if her tongue still worked. All she could manage was a surprised stare.

"Some of us aren't brain trusts. Some of us *need* a little help. So what? Seems to me, we've got a good thing going, with Isles offering just that—a little extra help."

"What do you want me to do about it?" she asked, her nerves sparking like the power lines during the ice storm.

"I figured you were the type to rat us all out," he said, reaching into the top shelf of the locker. As he pulled his arm back, Claire swore she heard it: laughter, hers and Rachelle's. And she saw a pencil box in his hand. Covered in lightning bolts.

"You—heard—I—what?" Claire asked, stepping backward, into a stream of sunlight pouring through a nearby window.

Only, when she stepped into it, it wasn't sun at all. It was a thin sheet of ice. A fragile one, that shattered the minute she touched it. Ice shards flew, hitting the air and falling like a sleet storm, clattering against the tile floor. Claire pressed her palm flat against the closest wall, finding that it was now covered in a thicker, two-inch coating of ice.

The entire hallway glistened. The floor. The walls. The ceiling. Icicles, fat as tetherball poles, clung from the lights. The windows glazed, so that the sunlight bleeding into the hallway had the same eerie glow as snow beneath moonlight.

When she tried to get a better look at the entire hallway, her feet slipped.

Owen reached back into the locker, freed the fleece

sweatshirt. An object tumbled from its pocket. *The phone,* Claire thought. *Get it before he can. Find out what's on it.*

She slid across the floor, nearly squealing with joy when she beat Owen, snatching it up before he had a chance.

But when her fist closed around it, her fragile bubble of victory burst. She wasn't yet sure what was in her hand—but she did know with certainty that it wasn't a phone.

Before she could get a look at it, her feet slid out from beneath her. Claire struggled like a passenger on a fitful boat, fighting to stay upright, searching for something solid. Her hands flew, but she slammed into the wall, finding herself mere inches from a window, her face reflected in the glass. She blinked at herself, at the sunlight, at the window now instantly and completely devoid of ice.

Claire panted, confused, as Owen snatched the item out of her hand. "What's with you?" he asked. "It's just her inhaler. So what?" He tossed it into his box.

"There's no phone here," he declared, shaking the sweatshirt. He draped the sweatshirt over the side of the box, then dropped Serena's textbooks into the box, too, letting the books thud like a gunshot.

Claire stared down the empty hallway. The tile beneath her shoes was dry. The ice hadn't melted—it had simply disappeared.

"What do you say?" Owen asked, as Claire's head

continued to spin. "Truce? About the history test? You get where I'm coming from?"

Claire nodded limply. What had she just agreed to?

Owen slammed the locker door and left her standing in the glow from the nearby sconces.

As his footsteps grew faint, Claire collapsed onto the floor and waited for her body to stop shaking.

TWENTY-NINE

Claire tried to slip back into the room unnoticed; she slid into a seat next to Rich, attempting to pretend she'd been right there, in class, all morning.

Glancing up, Claire was hit full force with their instructor's disgust. Mavis tightened her mouth as she deepened her glare, tucking her chin down to eye Claire over the top of her wire frames.

"Leaving my class without a pass gets you a warning this time, Ms. Cain," she said. "If it happens again, you get nonpaid leave. If you don't know what that is, ask Rich."

Claire turned toward him, eyebrow raised.

"It's a pass to go talk to Sanders," Rich explained.

Claire nodded. She ached to blurt it all out to Rich— how the hallway had just changed. How she could have sworn she was right back in the midst of the last winter storm. How the entire school had been encased in ice, for a moment. How Sweet Pea had followed her to the Sims house the day before. How Serena needed Claire, because no one—not even Mrs. Sims herself—was willing to believe that Serena could still be here, be part of the earth, be a creature who needed help.

I hear her; I can help her, she ached to say.

But she couldn't. The words stuck in her throat. Her mind flooded with the images of the hallway ice appearing and shattering with her discovery of Serena's inhaler. *Serena's telling me something*, Claire thought.

"How bad *was* Serena's asthma?" she asked.

"Pretty bad, actually," Rich said. "Even worse when the weather got hot. Why?"

"I just saw Owen cleaning out her locker. Her inhaler fell out of the pocket of a heavy sweatshirt."

"Fleece. Dark green."

"Yeah. How'd you know?"

Rich sucked in a breath. "She used it as her winter coat. It was big on her—she wore it over her cardigan. Maybe, when Sheriff Holman checked her locker, he thought it was just some extra sweatshirt—it's not the normal bulky winter coat—but I can't imagine her leaving school without it. Especially if it was already getting bad outside. Even if canceling school did startle her—it's just hard to believe."

"What about the inhaler? Would she have chosen to leave that behind, too?"

Rich thought a moment, shook his head slowly. "There's no *way* she'd be without an inhaler. Even if she had another one at home, I don't think she'd chance walking home without it, actually," he said.

"There's no phone. Not in her locker. Not in her room. And apparently, she wasn't carrying it on her when she died—I mean, Mrs. Sims didn't seem to know anything about a phone. The sheriff would have returned it if it was found on her, wouldn't he?"

He nodded somewhat reluctantly.

Claire's eyes grew large as she asked, "Seriously—don't you think it's weird that the police never searched through Serena's laptop?"

"Maybe," Rich said. "But it's a small town, too, Claire. I mean, yeah, they should have looked. But Holman's been the sheriff here longer than Serena was alive. She was best friends with his daughter. That girl spent too many weekends in his house to count. He probably felt like he didn't need to look at her computer because he *knew* her. There'd be school notes in it. No nasty pictures—no talking to perverts. He knew what kind of girl she was."

"*Did* he?" Claire asked. "Really? Or did he just assume? A girl in an ice storm, without her books, her coat, or her inhaler. In the woods that she was terrified of. It doesn't make sense.

We couldn't find her story, so we've got to get her phone. We need to know what led up to Serena's last moments."

Rich nodded. "I have a horrible feeling about this whole thing," he admitted.

Claire glanced up, toward the classroom window. The black threatening fringes of the woods loomed in the distance.

THIRTY

That afternoon, Claire swooped up her bag at the moment of the final bell, ready to bolt from her history class, down the stairs, and out of the school. Ready to get back to Rich, back to the truth just waiting to be uncovered. But Ms. Isles laid her hand on Claire's desk and stepped into the aisle, blocking her exit.

"Dr. Sanders and I would like a word with you," she said. She wasn't cocking her head to the side anymore, wasn't talking in a syrupy tone or promising second chances. She clenched her jaw until she gave herself creases in the flawless skin around her mouth. She tilted her head down, casting shadows that stretched from her eyes halfway down both cheeks.

Wordlessly, Claire followed Isles through the crowded hallways, straight into the front office.

"Two of you?" Sanders asked, at the sounds of two pairs of feet approaching his desk.

"It's me," Isles said. "And Claire. You're expecting us."

"Yes," Sanders agreed, leaning back in his chair. He frowned above the collar of a striped shirt and the jacket of a gray suit that fit him every bit as poorly as the brown suit he'd worn on Claire's first day. "Ms. Isles brought a matter to my attention this morning. Regarding a test retake."

"She did?" Claire asked, her mind reeling. Why would Isles tell him about the test? About the answers she tried to provide?

"Like I told you this morning," Isles said, her sweetness returning as she leaned forward to address Sanders directly, "Claire obviously misunderstood the entire situation. I give all of my students a retake opportunity. *All* of them. Like you and I discussed at the beginning of the year, I want my students to learn the material. Period. I'm in the business of educating. Not punishing with bad grades. So it's very, *very* important to me to give my students retake opportunities.

"It was also very important to me," she continued, "to give Claire a special opportunity to retake the exam in light of her recent experiences. I'm sure that scene in the woods would have impacted *any* student at Peculiar High. But Claire—why, the information in her file that you shared with me—"

"Wait," Claire said, her insides feeling unsteady, shaky. "You told her? She knows—?"

"Ms. Cain," Sanders said. "I cleared it with your father, the day of your arrival. You must have already left to change into a uniform when he gave me permission to share your history with faculty on a need-to-know basis. I would not have had to discuss that situation with Ms. Isles had there not been a problem in her classroom. I felt she needed to know your background. Just as she felt it was important to share the retake problem with me. We want to do what's best for you."

Claire fumed as she stared into Ms. Isles's porcelain skin. She was apparently an expert on manipulation—coming to Sanders before Claire had a chance to report her cheating scam meant that Claire had no recourse, not now, sitting in this office with no one else to corroborate her side of things. Her first inclination was to go get Rich, to insist he tell them the truth. But would that mean they would tell him about her, too? Tell him everything that had happened in Chicago? Would Rich then start looking at her like Sanders and Ms. Isles were right now—like she was damaged goods?

Anger was starting to burn a hole straight through Claire's rib cage. She hadn't misunderstood Ms. Isles's intentions. No more than she misunderstood the facts surrounding Serena's death. Peculiar, Claire swore, was a horrible place—filled with lies that people gulped down whole, even when the truth was staring them right in the face.

Isles and Sanders were ganging up on her, making her feel utterly powerless. The same kind of powerless she once felt standing in a Chicago parking lot, listening to feet stomping closer.

Without a word, she grabbed her backpack and rushed from Sanders's office.

She was halfway down the hall when the front door swung open and Rich stepped inside.

"Hey," he said, waving her down. "I was coming to look for you. I didn't know where you'd gone."

"Forget it," Claire barked. "Let's go."

"Aren't we going to try to look for—the phone—didn't you say in journalism—?"

"Forget it, I said," Claire thundered. "I need to get home."

THIRTY-ONE

Claire regretted being so short with Rich. She started to dial his cell a few times that night, her antique iron bed squeaking beneath her as she squirmed nervously, but felt in the end that it was better to act as though she'd never snapped at him at all. To shrug if he brought it up the next time she saw him, act as though she had no idea what he was talking about.

"Snapped?" she'd say, pretending to be shocked it had come across that way. "Guess Dad was right—I did need some rest." Because she remembered the way he'd talked about Isles—*He doesn't want to get involved in it*, she thought. Even if there was a way to get him to tell Sanders about Isles without learning the truth of what happened to Claire, he might very well resent being drawn into a situation he had purposefully decided to keep out of. She didn't want him to wind up resenting her so much that he pulled away from the rest of it, too. He was the one who knew the town—maybe not in the same way she did—but he knew the history of it. The urban legends. She needed him.

When her doorbell rang early the next morning, she raced down the stairs, her smile already shined up and glowing before she even tugged on the knob.

"Hey, Rich," she said, all singsong and happy.

But instead of seeing Rich, she found Becca standing in front of her, flashing her own smile beneath her large black winter hat with the earflaps.

"Thought you could use a ride," she said, pointing at the Honda in the drive. Owen sat in the driver seat, impatiently drumming the side of his hand against the top of the wheel.

Feet crunched halfway through the yard, forcing Becca to turn and see Rich making his way toward the front door.

"Rich drives me," Claire said apologetically, pointing at the figure that stood less than two feet from her porch.

"I just thought we could start making some plans for Friday," Becca said cheerfully.

Rich eyed Becca a moment—maybe, Claire thought as she took in his serious expression, he was even remembering that scene in the church, and Becca's tears. Maybe he was thinking, as Claire was, about how odd Becca's guilt was. How the only real way to find out more about her guilt was to talk to her.

"Go ahead," Rich said. "I'll follow you guys."

Claire nodded, even as she and Rich passed a questioning look between them. The kind of look that reminded each other of all the answers they had yet to find. She turned toward the Honda, where Becca was already opening her own door. Rich tugged a hat on his head and stepped toward his Ram.

They locked eyes again, just for a moment, before Claire reached for the handle on the back door of Owen's car. As she began to slip inside, a hand flew out to knock some empty soda cans off the seat, onto the floorboard. She hesitated, surprised to find someone else already in the back.

As if they were in the midst of some daily ritual, Chas motioned for Claire to slide in. She paused once more before lowering herself into the car and slamming the door shut behind her.

Claire kept her fingers gripped around the door handle until she heard the Ram roar to life across the street.

Owen backed his Honda out of the driveway, while Becca tugged at her hair, glancing over her shoulder at Claire.

"I just thought maybe you'd like a ride," Becca repeated. "I thought maybe you'd even like to come over, after school. Seeing as how the dance is the day after tomorrow. Maybe you'd like to see those earrings."

"Earrings?" Claire shifted inside her coat, feeling flushed and hot. Every time she moved, she disrupted another city dump pile of garbage—old class papers, fast-food containers.

Balled-up paper napkins. The seats themselves had a funny stickiness about them—almost like movie theater seats that had been coated in half-melted Skittles.

Becca frowned at her, her eyes like wounds. "I told you I had some earrings that would look nice on you. Remember?"

Claire glanced through the back windshield at the Ram on their tail.

"Earrings. Right." When she faced forward again, she caught Owen staring at her in the rearview. She straightened her back, pretending nothing was wrong and that she was not covered in nervous sweat. As she glanced down at her feet, she saw that her shoe had adhered itself to a napkin smeared with lipstick—old-fashioned red. The red bothered her. She'd only known Becca's lips to look nude, light pink. Maybe, she thought, Becca was right about Owen. Maybe there was someone else. An out-of-town cheerleader. But why would Owen be so brazen, if that were true? Maybe Becca wore red on special occasions, or when she went out at night. She dismissed the lipstick, kicking the napkin under the passenger seat in front of her.

Her leg brushed up against the car door, though, and she winced. Her ankle was getting awfully tender beneath her bandage. She'd actually bathed that morning with her leg hanging out of the tub. If the bandage didn't get wet, she figured, she wouldn't have to change it. She didn't want to look—she was afraid to know what was going on under the gauze.

"I thought maybe we could all do something together afterward—you and Rich and the three of us," Becca finally said.

Chas grumbled wordlessly and rolled his eyes.

"It won't be the same for you, though. Without Serena," Claire said, and watched in the car's side mirror as pain tightened Becca's face like a screw.

"No," Becca agreed. "It won't." Her eyes glittered as she added, "I hope you don't think I'm treating you like a stand-in for Serena. I hope I'm not—well. I guess I've been missing Serena so much . . . Serena was so sweet."

Owen snorted.

Claire fought a fidget, trying to look solid beneath Owen's continued glare in the rearview. But inside her coat, she was sweating so profusely that she was now completely drenched, soaked, as though she were wading in a pool. Even the growl of the Ram behind her could no longer make her feel safe.

"She wasn't perfect, Becca," Owen reminded her. "You used to get annoyed with her all the time. Did you already forget? How she got on your nerves? How you made fun of her? Sometimes, with all that crap about the paper—she could get kind of bitchy about her dumb stories. Don't you remember?"

Becca flinched. "I shouldn't have been that way. I regret it. I'll always regret it. . . ."

Claire blinked, rubbing salty sweat from her eyes. Becca's voice sounded strange—softer, almost far away. She tugged her hat off, as a dry, brutal scorch filled the entirety of the space around her. She could see ripples of heat in the car, the way an August swelter could make ripples above the highway.

As Claire coughed, struggling to force the heat from her chest, Owen removed his own stocking cap, the fringes of his hair dark and wet. Chas unlocked his seat belt and peeled his arms out of his coat.

Owen fiddled with the dials on the dash as a silver stripe of sweat trickled down his flushed cheek.

It's not just me, Claire thought. *They all see this, feel this. They can't ignore it.* But her cough grew raspy, hoarse, painful against her raw throat.

Becca began to cough, too, fighting for air as she reached for the vents, flicking them closed.

But the vents popped open again on their own, like jack-in-the-boxes that didn't need any cranking.

And still, the heat grew, swelled, as if someone had turned an oven to broil. The windows steamed. Becca tugged the collar of her coat away from her flushed throat. She tried to press the power control for her window, but nothing happened.

"What's wrong with this stupid thing?" Becca asked anxiously.

Owen tried the control on his own window, slamming his finger against the button repeatedly, to no avail. "I dunno."

He reached forward to clear a path through the moisture on his windshield with one hand, and tried to steer with the other, through the streets close to Peculiar High.

"What's going on?" Becca shouted.

"I really don't know," Owen said nervously, trying his own hand at shutting the vents.

They only popped open again.

He flicked the air conditioner on, but the dials no longer seemed to have any effect on the temperature control.

The heat swelled, built, bloomed.

Claire held her scarf to her mouth, gagging against the heat. The heat built walls, a lid. Heat was a grave she had fallen into. Even as the searing blast of air fell across her eyes, forcing them to droop like a saggy clothesline, she raised her arm, banged against her own steam-coated window. "Open this thing."

"I can't," Owen said as he careened into the Peculiar High lot, squealing his tires.

Through the swirls of heat, Claire could faintly see Becca and Owen. She heard them screaming and tugging on door handles. Their voices grew louder as they banged against windows. Beside Claire, Chas removed his coat and tried to signal for help.

"Help," Becca pleaded. "Help us."

Owen stopped abruptly, right in the middle of the lot.

Brakes squealed behind them. When Claire turned, she found the front bumper of Rich's Ram close enough to kiss the back of the Honda. She began to write in the steam on the back windshield: HELP!

Rich lunged for the job box propped on the bed of his truck.

"Please, Rich!" Claire called. "Get me out of here!" She was drowning in the heat. She had to use every shred of strength she could muster to keep raising her fist, knocking on her window.

No air left, Claire thought repeatedly, as her lungs struggled to pull in a single breath.

"Get back!" Rich shouted. "Turn around." A sound hit the air like a bomb detonating, and the back windshield shattered, sending glass scattering over the insides of the car. Shards flew with enough force to strike the dashboard, the backs of the front seats.

Claire turned, glass chips sparkling in her hair like New Year's glitter.

Rich stood framed by the jagged hole of the back windshield, a tire iron in his hand. "Is everybody okay?" he shouted. "Claire?"

Rhine raced across the lot, screaming at Rich, "Put it down. What are you doing? Put it *down*!"

Rich tossed the tire iron into the parking lot. "Something's wrong with Owen's car," Rich yelled, pointing.

Owen finally wrenched his door free, and burst from the car, gasping. "Everything," he said, pointing a wavering finger at his car. "Everything stuck. We were stuck in there, with the heat going up. And the air—it was like we were—we were *suffocating in there!*"

Chas let out a hoot as he threw open his own door, pointed at the busted back windshield. "Man, Owen's dad's going to skin you alive," he told Rich, wheezing out a laugh. "But thanks. Seriously. I thought we were goners." He stuck out his hand to shake Rich's.

Claire crawled across the back bench seat, trying not to put her hands on any of the glass that had sprayed through the inside of the car.

Owen shoved Chas as Claire pulled herself out. "You're so stupid. It's not a joke!" he screamed, still panicked.

"Me! *I'm* stupid? What about *you?*" Chas shouted back. "You're the one always messing around under the hood. And what happens? Complete and total electrical meltdown. Nice job, genius."

"Leave him alone," Becca shouted. "Isn't it natural to be afraid of something like that right now? Huh?" She shoved his chest, adding, "Why don't you ask *Serena* about how scary it is to suffocate?"

"Oh, get *off it!*" Chas screamed. "Enough with this Serena crap. She died. It's too bad. But it's over now. And *this guy,*" he went on, wagging a thumb at Owen, "has been acting weird for *weeks*. Months, even. Way before Serena.

"What the hell's changed?" he asked Owen. "Whatever's in your head, you're still Owen Martin—a guy with a solid 2.0 average, who's a half-assed halfback, who drives a now-banged-up car. You want to know why I went to Ruthie's? Because *you* sure as hell weren't around to hang out with. You stick your nose up at everything—even the shooting range last weekend. Nothing's good enough for you anymore. Not even your best friend. There's no *reason* for you to act better than anybody, you asshole. Because you're *not*."

"You get your own ride to school from now on," Owen said. "And the dance. And—"

"Screw you, Owen!" Chas shouted. "I'm not going to the dance, remember? How many times do I have to tell you and your girlfriend? *I'm not going to the dance.* Why would I *want* to ride in that thing, anyway?" he asked, pointing at the shattered back windshield. "Have fun freezing your ass off, buddy." He grabbed his backpack and stormed off, while Becca watched, wide-eyed.

She reached out, put her arm on Owen's shoulder, but he lurched out of her reach. "Knock it off, all right?" he said. "Just—quit it. For God's sake."

"Hey," Rhine said, stepping in between Owen and his sister. "I think we all need to cool it. Had a little scare. Now Becca and Claire need to make sure they get all that glass off.

They need to get to class. We need to get this thing out of the way so everybody else can park," he told Owen. "I'll help you find some plastic bags in the kitchen. We'll cover that hole, till you can get the car out of here this afternoon. All right?"

Owen nodded, his eyes still wild.

"I'll go with you," Rich told Claire, but Rhine caught his arm.

"Oh, no," Rhine insisted. "I'm gonna get stuck having to write up an incident report, thanks to you. Which means you're going to help me. I've got to do this by the book."

Claire and Becca headed for the entrance together. Claire tried to use the streams of students as an opportunity to slip away from Becca and any possibility of her hauling out an overly concerned hospital voice, after what had just happened. But Becca was having none of it. She grabbed Claire's wrist, forcing her to follow.

The glass brushed out easily enough, straight into the trash can in the women's bathroom. Becca's fingers felt soothing as she ran her hands through Claire's mane, helping her check one last time for anything sharp. But the feeling that had exploded into Claire's chest, right along with the flying glass, wasn't so easy to brush away.

Suddenly, as she went through her morning classes, it wasn't just the school basement that felt dangerous—not just the woods, not just the unfolding stories of Serena's and Casey's deaths. After what had happened in the parking lot, it felt as though everything had the power to inflict serious damage—even things that had previously seemed utterly harmless: the sharp corners of test papers, the electricity buzzing through wall sconces in Peculiar High, the tiny serrated edges of the butter knives in the cafeteria.

As she sat down at what had become her usual lunch table, Claire hoped she would pick up on something—some vibe that indicated everyone else fought the same fears. But no one spoke, not even Rich. They all kept their heads turned down, toward their plates.

Claire ached for someone to mention what had happened that morning—thought about trying to offer a "Jeez. Wasn't that insane?" But the mood was far too serious. And not serious enough at the same time.

They just think his car went haywire. They don't know the truth. They don't know how Serena is talking, trying to get my attention. Well, she's got it now. Why doesn't she just tell me what she wants? She shivered; being the only person who knew that car had not simply malfunctioned made her feel exposed and vulnerable.

A chair scratched against the floor beside Chas, and Ruthie sat down. "I heard," she announced, leaning forward, forcing the material of her blouse to tug against the buttons. "About what happened this morning. Are you guys okay?"

She stared with wide eyes at Chas, who only shook his

head at her and angled his body so that the back of his shoulder turned toward her. "What? I can ask if you're okay, can't I?"

Chas slammed a fist against the table and thundered, "Don't start with that clutchy crap. I can't stand it."

"Chas," Ruthie protested.

But Chas ignored the wounded look on her face, grabbed his tray, and stomped off.

Claire's mind flooded with the memory of Chas at 'Bout Out during the ice storm. *Tell her,* Ruthie had mouthed. Claire's palms grew clammy as she wondered, *Tell Becca what?*

In the wake of Chas's outburst, Owen shook his head, picked up his own tray, and hurried off as Becca lowered her forehead into her hands.

Claire glanced up at Rich, fearfully. *Temper,* she mouthed as she raised her eyebrows.

Rich clenched his jaw and nodded reluctantly.

THIRTY-TWO

Dr. Cain texted Claire, requesting that she come directly home after school that day. Sanders had called to inform him of the mishap in the parking lot—and assured him of his daughter's safety—but the father in him needed to see her for himself. When she arrived, he hugged her like a parent who had just been reunited with his toddler after being separated from her in a shopping mall.

Claire honored his wishes to stick close by, even though it felt to her that the clock was ticking increasingly louder. The time for finding the answers to Serena's death was passing quickly. Clues were disappearing by the minute—and were certainly not to be found on the Simses' old couch, beneath cushions loaded with long-lost spare change and ancient potato chip crumbs.

The next morning, shortly after the tardy bell announced that Thursday was officially in full swing, Mavis waved Claire to her desk. "I need a blurb on the incident in the parking lot," she told Claire. "What happened yesterday. With Owen Martin's car."

Claire bristled. "Why?"

"For our 'Goings-On' section," Mavis informed her. "It's a little column, highlighting stories too small to be features. We all take turns with it. And frankly, I need to see something from you. A reputation can only carry you so far."

"But why *that* story?" Claire asked. The tone in her voice caused Rich to pull himself from his own seat and weave through the students all bustling about the classroom, working on their own projects, calling about ad space.

"I'm sorry—I thought you were there," Mavis said, frowning at Claire behind her glasses. "Don't you know Owen? I'd thought it would be easy for you to get a quote. If I've got it wrong—"

Claire shook her head, took a step away. She couldn't write it, not even a little blurb—because she didn't have the whole story about the car. It was a sign, a clue—someone with an agenda had *made* the heat go haywire. She had assumed it was Serena, but couldn't it have also been Casey? One of—or worse yet, *all of*—the spirits in the town fog?

Claire knew firsthand that bad things happened to a girl who turned in a story without knowing exactly who was gaining on her from behind. . . .

As Claire stared, Mavis reached toward a pile of papers on the corner of her desk. "Here," she said, holding a previous edition of the paper toward Claire. "Here's an example."

To Claire's dismay, the example was written by Serena Sims. A hundred words on the exploding feral cat population that dominated the fields surrounding Peculiar High. The photo she'd included in the story was of Sweet Pea, the cat's tricolored, mangled face staring out from the tiny column. As Claire stared back, wisps of color began to shift behind the cat's face.

Wild creatures, all of 'em, she heard, rattling around in her skull. Suddenly dizzy, she staggered on her heels, tossing the paper back on Mavis's desk.

"We'll work on it together," Rich offered, putting his hand under Claire's arm. She took a deep breath, letting Rich steady her. But when she glanced up at him to smile appreciatively, the way he eyed her made her flinch. She didn't like the heavy concern tugging the corners of his mouth down.

"I can do it," Claire insisted, finally hoisting a smile on her face just before she returned to her computer. But the blurb proved to be an exercise in little more than staring into a blank screen. She really did try—to get Rich's alarmed stare off her, to appease Mavis—but getting words on a page felt more like trying to get three hundred winged insects to all stay put on the same sheet of paper.

"Did you ever finish it?" Rich asked that afternoon, after the final bell, as they headed for his truck.

"I never actually *started* it," Claire grumbled, never anticipating he would take her arm and steer her straight back toward the journalism classroom.

"Come on. You can do this. Just don't overthink it," he said as they moved like salmon against the stream, deeper into the school from which the rest of their classmates only wanted to escape.

Don't overthink it, Claire thought sarcastically as she sat back at her computer. *Everything here needs to be overthought. Literally. Everything. Nothing is as it seems, not even the car, not even a heater. The truth of what is going on in this town is closing in, and no one recognizes it, and now even Rich is looking at me with concern. Will anyone listen when I uncover the full truth?*

As her computer booted, her phone went off. Claire glanced at the screen: *U ok? PLS ANSWER* from Rachelle. She turned the phone off, tossed it into her backpack.

"All right. Let's do this," Rich announced, cracking his knuckles and raising his eyebrows in a way that made her laugh. He talked her through a hundred words, and a little over an hour later, he printed the finished article and placed it in the center of Mavis's desk. "She'll be impressed if it's waiting for her here first thing," he promised.

But Claire only wanted to snatch that blurb right back, race away with it, tear it up. That story was full of lies. *An*

electrical malfunction caused quite the stir Wednesday morning
in the Peculiar High parking lot, as . . .

Before Claire quite knew what was happening, the journalism door fell shut behind them and their feet were echoing through the stairwell.

Winter's early twilight had already begun to settle over Peculiar by the time Rich and Claire made their way through the parking lot.

Claire hoisted herself into Rich's truck, hugging her backpack against her chest as he cranked the ignition. But the dashboard lights only flashed dimly, and the engine coughed twice before sputtering to silence.

"Come on," he growled, cranking the engine again. He cranked a third time, slamming his foot against the gas pedal. But the truck refused to start.

"Damn," Rich cursed, slapping the palm of his hand against the steering wheel.

He glanced about the lot, but everyone had gone—even Rhine. "Wouldn't you know? Dad's at church."

"It's Thursday, though," Claire protested.

"There's always something going on at the church. Tonight is grief counseling—an idea inspired by Becca's last visit, no doubt. Tomorrow, the quilting bee meets downstairs. What about your dad?"

"He was going to have to work late today," Claire said, remembering the conversation she'd only half listened to during breakfast. "He didn't really want to, but . . . I think he's been cutting it short to make sure he's home when I am—I think he's probably way behind. I bet I'm going to wind up screwing up his entire sabbatical," she admitted.

"Not your fault what's been happening," Rich said quietly.

Claire nodded slightly. "So now what?" she asked.

"Now, we walk," Rich told her, pointing toward the cluster of trees in the distance.

Claire felt as though the entire contents of her stomach had frozen, right along with Rich's engine. "Are you sure— maybe we—"

"Our street is less than ten minutes away going through the woods. We stick to the roads, it's forty-five minutes. You pick."

"Some choice," Claire muttered as she and Rich both climbed from the truck.

Rich pulled a couple of emergency flashlights from his job box. "You need a hat or gloves?" he asked. "Got plenty back here."

Claire accepted a pair of camouflaged gloves and a stocking cap, offering what she hoped looked like a grateful smile as they began to make their way toward the woods. Their shoes crunched through the remaining thin layer of ice as they closed in on the leafless limbs and barren brush. The last few patches of snow seemed to absorb the hues of the setting sun only to spit them back out, casting a glow across the schoolyard.

They entered the dense line of trees; Rich started to steer her toward the path worn flat from decades of student shortcuts. Claire paused as she remembered in painful clarity the sensations of the afternoon she'd found Serena: the frantic burst of breath in her ears, the way her feet had sunk to mid-shin in piles of ice—the way Rhine's and Becca's black coats had flapped like vultures' wings as they'd gained on her. Breaking the silence, she remarked offhandedly, "The crews have cleaned away a bunch of broken limbs. Whole place looks completely different now."

Rich turned his eyes upward, at the broken limbs, jagged against a winter's sky. Claire found herself turning around, glancing down the path they'd taken from Peculiar High. She scanned the ground, her eyes stopping to rest on a long indentation. A black scrap of fabric lay poking out of the mud and half-melted snow.

"Rich," Claire called, squatting to pick it up. It was thick—made of woven yarn. Like a piece of a sweater. She turned it over in her hand. A red PH had been embroidered across the top edge.

"It's a pocket," Rich said. "From one of our school cardigans."

Claire pointed at long ruts in the earth, sections in which the dead winter grass had been pulled up. "Something was dragged," she said.

"Could have been the limbs," Rich said.

"But don't those ruts point straight at the school?" Claire asked.

"I'm not sure that means anything, Claire. It's been nearly two weeks since Serena's body was found," he said, as though reading her mind. "That's a lot of time for a lot of coming and going through the woods, you know."

She nodded reluctantly, tucking the piece of the sweater into her coat pocket. Rich led the way, the tongue of light from his flashlight showing the path ahead of him.

Claire's footsteps slowed. The gap between herself and Rich lengthened as he raced forward, determined to get out of the woods as quickly as possible. Claire swiveled her own flashlight through the trees, the light brutal and stark against the winter evening's growing blackness.

Claire paused, watching as the persistent fog began to grow in the evening chill, to thicken like steam from a hot shower.

Her phone went off; fishing it out from her pocket, a text glowed out at her: *Rain 2 freeze. Go home now. Take R with u.*

She flinched. How was it possible? It was the very same text she'd gotten from her dad's grad assistant nine months ago. The warning that had flashed on her phone before she'd decided to walk anyway.

A sudden flap—like the wings of some gigantic bird—exploded into Claire's ears. She swiveled cautiously. The sound had come from the two flags on the Peculiar High pole: one the red, white, and blue of the US flag, the other, the PH flag, adorned with a giant black panther.

The flag stretched out flat in the wind, allowing the menacing mascot to bare its teeth and flash its green eyes at Claire.

Cars whizzed down nearby roads, their headlights shining like beacons, creating moving shadows. As Claire took another step forward, a headlight washed across the tree in front of her, illuminating a familiar face: Sweet Pea. Perched on a branch above Claire's head.

The old cat hissed, baring her discolored teeth. She stood, holding her swollen tail as straight as the school's flagpole. Threatening Claire.

Claire gasped. "Don't you hurt me," she scolded, her hair rippling about her face.

Claire wanted to run, but she forced herself to stay rooted. *Find out*, she scolded herself. *Find out what this whole thing is about.*

It wasn't easy to stay, though—her urge to run only grew stronger, as the same face that had smiled at Claire from her funeral portrait, who had stared down at Claire from the air above the cemetery, began to flicker across the head of the old cat.

As Claire stared, Serena's face grew clearer, gained dimension. She shivered when she realized Serena's head was actually pushing its way *out* of the cat's skull. Serena's spirit was emerging.

"The clock is ticking down for me," Serena explained as she wrenched her face free. "Not much time left for me in this old body." She had not completely left the old cat yet; her shoulders, her arms were out, but the rest of her figure was still inside.

"Sweet Pea's life is ending. She's old—so old. Time's running out for me again," she said. "I don't want to leave—not the world, not like the fog wants me to. I want my old life back. I want to be seventeen, and I want to do seventeen-year-old things—I want to write for the paper and laugh with my friend, my best friend. Where is she tonight, huh? Getting ready for a *dance*. Trying to decide on the perfect hairdo. Hanging her pretty new dress out on the closet door. Like everything is the same as always. And where am *I*?"

Claire trembled against what Serena had just said, but stood firm, locking her jaw and making fists. "That's not true," she tried to protest. "She feels terrible. If you only knew—"

"Terrible! I'm the one in this awful *body*," Serena shouted. "This broken-down, nasty *body*. I don't want to be in here. I don't want to be some old cat. I want to be a girl. I want to go to school. I want to live in my old house. I want my best friend. I want my life. But I don't have my life. *You* have my life," she shouted, stretching one arm toward

Claire. "You have it," she repeated.

She moved closer to Claire, yowling and snarling.

Please, God, Claire thought, the words echoing inside her head. *Don't let me die.*

"Rich!" she screamed. "Rich! Where are you?"

Serena's image pressed against Claire's chest, her spirit so cold it burned. Claire fought against the truth of the moment. But there was no escaping it. This was *happening*. Serena was trying to get inside *her*.

The world before Claire began to flip, back and forth: Chicago, Peculiar, Chicago, Peculiar. She could hear the rattle of trash cans, the thunk of their metal sides crashing against the back of her skull. She could hear laughter. Cheering. It pulsed rhythmically—something like, *more, more, more, more . . . hurt her more, give her more . . .*

Chicago, Peculiar, Chicago, Peculiar—Serena's face grew still clearer, the wind catching her brown hair as her smile curled. Her cold hand pressed forcefully against Claire's chest. Chicago, Peculiar, Chicago—the cold gusts blew up her skirt as a hand reached around the waist of her underwear. Broken and bloody, she knew what was about to happen.

Panic completely enveloped Claire. "*Olly, olly, oxen free!*" she bellowed, utter desperation saturating her words. "*Olly, olly—*"

Serena laughed. "You think this is some sort of game, Claire? It's not. It's life and death—literally. My life for your death. They can have *you*," Serena snarled. "The fog. They need a soul to take? They can have yours. I'm going to get my old life back. It'll be beautiful. My favorite house. My best friend. My old school. Writing for the paper. If I get rid of *you*, I'll get myself back."

Claire screamed as Serena's fingers slipped through her skin, entering her chest. Seeping through the tiniest fissures in Claire's broken places, like water through a crack in glass. And though Claire fought desperately against her, Serena still managed to plunge her hand in yet another inch deeper—all the way up to her wrist.

The already charged atmosphere sparked as another figure appeared—a boy, bouncing about on the balls of his feet. A peach-fuzz mustache. A face in black and white.

Serena watched warily as he approached. "Leave me alone, Casey," she snarled. Frantically, she tried one more time to press herself deeper into Claire's body. But there wasn't enough time. Casey was closing in.

The burn in Claire's chest disappeared as Serena quickly wrenched away. She dipped back into the cat's body, which had begun to slump limply against the ground. Once inside, Serena righted the old calico and shook her head, trying to steady herself on her feet. She blinked, her blue human eyes shining out clearly.

Casey stooped, grabbing Sweet Pea by the scruff of the neck.

What's he doing here? Claire thought, panting, holding her hand over the aching spot in her chest where Serena had just tried to get inside her. *Why now? What does he want?*

"Come out," Casey demanded.

Sweet Pea squealed, swinging her legs, flapping her tail. But Casey held her at arm's length—far enough that she couldn't scratch him.

Claire remained a mere spectator, frozen.

"Come out," Casey screamed again, shaking her.

The old calico yowled, her face flickering like a TV picture about to go out. Images flashed back and forth, alternating between Sweet Pea's gnarled, scabby, gory face and the blue, frozen face of the girl that Claire had found right there in the woods.

"They can't take you, not when you're in there," Casey said, as the fog continued to thicken. The same arms and legs that Claire had seen rising in the cemetery appeared in the folds of fog. They reached for the cat, but jerked back each time they touched her fur, as though they'd hit a hard, impenetrable surface.

Terrified, Claire hugged her chest, in a flimsy attempt at protecting herself. Her own body was not so impenetrable. Not anymore. Not after what happened in Chicago. Serena had just proved that.

"You need to come out of there, Serena," Casey shouted.

The wind continued to shift, to swirl, to increase in strength, as the translucent faces of fog danced about Claire, the figures of the town dead packed tightly together, like bodies in an elevator.

Fear rendered Claire mute.

"Get out of that cat's body," Casey growled. "Serena. You don't belong in there. Let them take you home."

The calico wiggled violently, wrenching herself from Casey's grip. She dropped onto the snow and began to race through the woods.

"Serena!" Casey screamed. But she was gone.

Claire stood trembling. The fog slipped across the field, leaving Casey behind. As he stood, staring at the retreating wisps of mist, his face grew long, sad, and his image turned hazy.

But before he could disappear completely, Casey turned, wrapping his icy fingers around Claire's shoulders. "You've got to stay away," he growled at Claire. "You aren't supposed to be here—not after school, not when it's getting so dark. Terrible things happen to people who are not where they're supposed to be. You hear me?"

"That was her, wasn't it?" Claire asked, a shot of bravery filling her body. "You were holding her. Serena. I know you were. I know you're real. She's in the cat—that's real, too. Tell me," she begged. "Tell me what happened to her. Tell—"

The stream of a flashlight exploded through the darkness, bouncing off the icy side of a tree. In the harsh reflection, Casey's fog-drenched form disappeared.

"Wait!" Claire screamed. "Don't go! Wait!"

A figure lurched out of the darkness, grabbing Claire up in his arms.

THIRTY-THREE

Claire screamed, fighting against the arms circling her waist. She didn't know who had hold of her, but she did know now what Serena wanted. Why she'd looked at her in such a sinister way at the funeral. She didn't want Claire to know what happened. She wanted *Claire*. The world felt tiny. Claire felt cornered, trapped; she wrenched herself away and screamed again.

"Stop!" Rich shouted. "Claire! It's me! Why were you shouting back there? What happened?"

Panting, Claire pushed her hair from her face. "You came at the wrong time," she moaned.

"Why wouldn't I come? 'Olly, olly'—that's what you said. In the *woods*, Claire. When I hear those words, it means you need help. What'd you *expect* me to think? You *terrified* me."

"I was going to find everything out," Claire protested. Casey would have told her—about Serena and the fog and even why he had stayed, why he hadn't gone with the town dead, either. Claire felt sure of that. And if she'd known everything, she would have been better able to protect herself from Serena. Now, though, she knew that Serena had a vicious plan, and she had no idea how to defend herself against it.

"Find out what?" Rich asked. "What did you see out there? And why were you holding Sweet Pea? I thought you'd already been scratched once. You'd think you'd leave the poor thing alone."

Claire balked, shaking her head. "I didn't pick up Sweet Pea."

"You did," Rich insisted. "You picked her up."

"Where were you? Behind a tree? How can you be sure?"

Rich eyed her the same way some of the nurses had, back in her Chicago hospital. "How can I be sure you were holding a cat?" he asked.

A passing headlight swam through the trees, washing across icicles. Rich squinted against the glare as it hit the side of his head and the lenses of a pair of sunglasses hooked to a pocket on the front of his coat. Claire saw her own face for a brief moment in those lenses—her terrorized eyes, her drawn face, her mussed hair.

He took a step toward her, but Claire pushed him away. The woods had calmed; still she knew what she'd seen—souls of the town dead who wanted to take Serena's spirit where it belonged, but couldn't because Serena was inside a new body. The cat's body protected the soul from the fog, from the other spirits. Claire *knew* it. She'd seen it. Her eyes didn't lie—not hers.

She was Claire Cain, after all, the recipient of the Robert F. Kennedy Journalism Award her freshman year. Claire Cain didn't invent stories; she told the truth—even about what had happened with Rachelle's locker, back in Chicago. *That* had been true. Claire hadn't even needed to actually see the boy plant the drugs. She'd watched him enough to put the pieces together on her own. She'd been right, too. She wasn't an embellisher, a gossiper.

What Claire had always said had been *true*. And this time was no different, she told herself, her pulse thudding about like a stampede.

She had discovered a new truth: Serena wanted her old life back. She was going to succeed by destroying Claire. She wanted Claire's body.

But Serena wasn't going to get it.

THIRTY-FOUR

Claire and Rich walked the rest of the way through the shortcut in silence, while Rich shot her uncomfortable glances of concern every couple of steps. When they slipped out from the brush, edged around the back of the Ray house, and stepped onto their gravel street, they found red and blue lights swirling, washing against the night sky.

The sight of the sheriff's car parked in her driveway made Claire take off running, with Rich at her heels.

"Dad?" she shouted, sprinting up the front walk. "Dad?" she tried again, stomping through the front door.

"Oh, thank goodness," Dr. Cain exhaled, racing across the living room to scoop her up in his arms.

"What is going *on*?" she asked.

"I was going to ask you the same thing," he said. "I've been trying to call you since I got off work, and all I got was voice mail."

"So you called the police?" Claire asked. "I was with Rich."

"But why the voice mail?" he demanded.

He was so over-the-top upset, she felt ashamed to tell him that she'd been turning her phone off to avoid Rachelle's texts.

Wait a minute, the voice in her head shouted. *How'd you get that text in the woods, that same text you got the night of the Chicago ice storm, if your phone was off?*

Because Serena's getting stronger, she answered right back, a chill dancing up her spine.

"My stupid phone hasn't been working right," she lied.

"And you didn't *tell* me?" Dr. Cain shouted.

"Why are you so angry?" Claire asked. "Rich and I were together. Like he promised we'd be. Working on my story for the paper."

Dr. Cain glanced up at Rich. "Why didn't *you* call me, if her phone wasn't working?"

"I'm sorry, Dr. Cain," Rich said, his calm demeanor instantly diffusing the anger in her father's voice. "I honestly didn't know you needed to hear from Claire."

But the face Rich turned toward Claire was round, pale. It had the look of someone who had shifted from playing a game to knowing dangers were real—and that the burden of a rescue was on his shoulders.

"I'll get you a new phone," Dr. Cain told Claire softly.

"Rich will see you tomorrow."

Sheriff Holman tipped his hat, his services obviously no longer needed.

Rich followed, pausing in the open doorway, as if somehow expecting to hear those words one more time: *Olly, olly, oxen free!* "Claire, is everything okay? Why do I feel like something is going on, something other than Serena—"

"Everything's fine." Claire smiled wanly. "I'll see you tomorrow."

Rich nodded reluctantly and stepped onto the porch as Claire shut the door behind him.

THIRTY-FIVE

That night, Claire tossed about in her bed, nightmares stealing the restful sleep she so badly needed. Nightmares of the gang. The ice storm. The snapping of her bones, the shredding of her skin.

Blue and red lights reflected across the ice-coated surface of the bricks. Claire stared down from her spot in the sky, and she watched the girl cop reach for her arm. "It's too late for you," the cop announced with certainty. "You're dead."

"Of course I am," Claire agreed as she stared down on her mangled body, cut up like meat displayed in a supermarket counter. She was lying on a blanket, instead of in the parking lot. It was as though the girl cop had taken such pity on her that she had placed a quilt out beneath Claire. *A soft place to die . . .*

But Claire had a tail, too, in this dream. A long slender tail. And gray fur.

Claire snapped herself fully awake, blinking rapidly against the first streaks of sunlight that trickled into her room.

A soft rumble hit her ears—a rattling sigh of contentment that swirled, wrapping its way around a high-pitched caterwaul.

She lifted her head slightly from her pillow to look toward her legs. A calico sat in her lap, purring.

"Sweet Pea," Claire whispered. Repulsion replaced horror as the old cat lowered her face into the open belly of a large rodent, and pulled out a string of intestines. Sweet Pea raised herself up, dragging blood-engorged pieces of entrails across Claire's quilt.

Claire gagged. Too afraid to bolt from her bed, she simply let her eyes rove across her room. Ferals. Everywhere. Stretched out on the windowsill, sunning themselves in the early morning light. Watching from her hope chest. A rumble poured from the throat of a nearby gray cat's mouth—only to be answered by another cat at Claire's feet, and the cats on her dresser, the cats playing in front of the cracked-open balcony door.

She's brought a gang, Claire thought. *A whole gang.*

Sweet Pea clamped the rat in her jaws and started to move toward the end of the bed, dragging the entrails along with her, leaving a red pool on Claire's quilt.

The rest of the ferals all began to hiss, flashing their sharp front teeth. Tails swelled. Wails became threats.

A fight—the cats were gearing up for a fight.

"Why would you do that?" Claire asked. "The cats don't like you—out by the Dumpster, by the church—they fought you. Why would you lead them here, when they don't like you?"

"I'm not trying to take their food. I'm showing them food, this time," Serena said, her whispery voice rising out from the old cat. "They can have you when I'm done with you."

The scene in the woods flashed through Claire's mind. Serena's goal was to get inside Claire's body. Make it her own. Why would Serena want the cats to destroy it? "If you let them eat me, there won't be any left for you," Claire told the cat.

Sweet Pea spread her face wide, hissing, showing off her decayed, brown teeth. She blinked, letting Serena's blue eyes flash. Serena's face wafted about along the surface of the old cat's skull.

"It's your *soul* they're hungry for." Serena's voice rose above the angry sounds of the ferals. "Your soul, buried deep inside your body, will be tastier than flesh. They'll pull it out, pull it apart, gorge on it," Serena promised, as she began to knead her paws, pushing and pulling on the intestines of the rodent she'd just gutted. "And when you have no more soul, your body will be free for *me*."

Claire shuddered as she dipped deep beneath her blankets, Serena's words pounding against her ears as the cats crouched low and began to stalk, surrounding her, growing closer.

"You could have let me in back in the woods," Serena scolded. "You could have gone along with the fog. You've forced me to do this instead. To take your body and leave your *soul* for the cats to feast upon.

"If there's no soul for the fog to take," Serena asked, "if the cats destroy your very *soul*, isn't that really the worst kind of hell?" She snarled, her tail waving as she inched closer to Claire's face.

Claire snapped up into a sitting position, throwing her chest forward and letting the blankets bunch in her lap. She screamed, her mounting fear reflected in the antique bedroom mirror on the opposite side of the room. Some cats raced for her bedroom door and the stairs, while others—the braver sort—continued to flash their filthy fangs at her.

Claire screamed again. This time, her dad came running, still dressed in his flannel pajama bottoms and his long-sleeved T-shirt, his hair messed from sleep and his glasses not quite straight on his nose.

"Hold on, Claire," he shouted. He waved his arms, momentarily leaving to retrieve a broom. "Shoo! Shoo!" he bellowed, throwing open the door to the balcony. The cats snarled and hissed as he pushed them outside, like dust balls that needed to be cleaned away.

The old calico stayed. She crouched near the bed, as though she assumed that Dr. Cain would only want the others out. As though she felt she belonged. As though she had a right to be there. As though the house were hers.

She licked her pink-stained jaw, cleaning her whiskers.

"You get *out, too*!" Dr. Cain screamed, raising the broom one more time.

Serena yowled and skittered out the balcony door before Dr. Cain could see blue eyes shining, her spirit wafting across the face of the cat she inhabited. She raced away—but only, her hiss promised, temporarily.

THIRTY-SIX

"That door to your balcony doesn't fit right, Claire," her dad reminded her, propping his broom against the wall. He leaned into the Dutch door, forcing both halves to lock. "When I went to open the thing, it was already cracked—not far, but enough to let the cats slip inside. They obviously felt warm air coming from your room. I'm surprised they didn't get in before now. You go get yourself cleaned up. I'll take care of this mess."

Claire stood before the bathroom mirror, wrapped in a towel, tears streaming while the water ran in the tub. She could hear her father moving about overhead, gathering the bloody quilt off her bed and bagging the dead rat, sweeping the cat hair off the floor.

To add to her current misery, the scratches on her ankle were throbbing and burning. She had to know what was going on under the bandage she hadn't been able to look beneath. She leaned down, forced a thumbnail under a corner of the tape, held her breath, and yanked the bandage off.

She nearly collapsed against the cold edge of the sink, a groan of agonizing pain trailing from her lips. Sweat beads popped instantly across her forehead as she waited for the pain to lessen. She dropped the gauze into the sink, the bandage soaked with blood and pus, the hues of orange and red and yellow caked, stiffly, along the edges. A sickly green slime had piled like a diseased blood clot in the center of the gauze square.

She sucked in a string of shallow breaths as she looked down, into the black swirls across her ankle, the green lesions. But the cut on her knees, reopened on the same day her ankle had been scratched, had nearly healed.

She hoisted her foot into the sink, opened a bottle of peroxide, held her breath, and poured it over her ankle wound. The scratches began to foam, crackling like oil in a hot skillet. Another round of tears welled in Claire's eyes, and she forced a washrag into her mouth to swallow her wail. She watched as the peroxide foamed directly over two curving cuts: *SS*. Though it seemed utterly impossible, the scratches on her ankle were the same shape as the squiggles on the kitchen wainscoting in the Simses' kitchen.

SS. Serena Sims.

Claire shook in fear. She turned the hot faucet knob, groaning as the warm water washed the white bubbles of peroxide down the drain.

She's finding new ways to threaten me, to weaken me, to tear me down, Claire thought. *She's getting closer. Messing with my head. Playing her game—cat and mouse . . .*

She killed the faucet stream. The skin across her entire ankle turned black.

"All clear!" her father shouted.

"Gut me," Claire whispered, staring at her wound. "She's going to gut me. Just like she gutted that rat in my room. And then she can have what she wants—her old life."

She pulled her foot from the sink and dressed the wound again, leaving the bathroom without another glance into the mirror. She couldn't bear to look at herself, see the evidence of what Serena was doing to her reflected in the terror she knew would be shining out from her eyes.

Claire staggered into her bedroom. She couldn't tell her dad about the scratches—what would she say? "Excuse me, Dad, but the cat who scratched my ankle during the funeral is actually possessed by the spirit of a girl who may not have died quite as accidentally as everyone thinks, and does not want to go off with the fog filled with the spirits of the town dead. She wants in *my* body, so she can get her old life back. And I'm a little afraid, now, that these scratches—black as they are—are also part of her plan to wear me down."

She dressed, stuffed her still-wet hair under a hat, and hurried downstairs. She had plenty to do before Rich got there.

THIRTY-SEVEN

"Claire," Rich said as he drove her to school, "I think maybe you should talk to my dad."

She chortled. "Does he have some sort of cat repellant I can use to keep them all out of my room?"

"No—it's just—I think maybe some of this is starting to bother you, more than you realize."

Claire shook her head as she hugged her red backpack. "But something's off here. You see it. All those things Sheriff Holman missed. Why would I need to talk to your dad?" She swallowed her swelling anger, telling herself, *He doesn't know. If he only knew that I was being hunted, he wouldn't talk to me this way.*

They pulled into the school parking lot, and Claire bolted from the truck as soon as Rich parked.

"Claire," Rich continued, turning off the ignition and following after her. "There are too many weird things happening here and I think it's affecting you. My dad—he has experience talking these things out. He can help you make sense of it. Of how you *feel* about all this, anyway. It might be good for you."

"I'll be fine as soon as we figure this Serena thing out," Claire promised. She picked up her pace, hurrying through the hallways to drop her coat off at her locker. She monopolized Mavis's time in journalism, first discussing her blurb, then brainstorming ideas for her coverage of the dance, managing to avoid Rich.

There's nothing wrong with me, nothing. Serena's got the rest of you fooled. But not me. I know things. No one can see like I do, Claire thought, grabbing her bag when the bell rang and tossing a "See you tonight for the dance!" at Rich before scurrying out of the room.

"Wait!" he said. "Won't I see you at lunch? What about after school?"

"I'll get a ride with Becca," Claire said, before being swallowed by the crowds. All it would take would be a simple word to Becca, asking her to wait for her after the final bell. Becca wanted to be Claire's new BFF, after all.

When her fourth period class broke for lunch, Claire slipped her backpack over her shoulders and crept down the hallway, sliding behind the Faculty Only door that led to the basement.

"You want to play, Serena?" she asked as she stomped straight into the first room, marked Janitors on the door. "That was a sneaky trick you pulled this morning. Now you're going to play by *my* rules, on *my* turf. I'm in control of the next round. Which," she added through a grin, "is going to be your last."

She climbed onto the dusty wooden desktop to reach the ground-level window—the same window that she had pushed shut during her first visit downstairs. She forced the window open, unzipped her backpack, and pulled out a can of tuna. She retrieved a can opener from the front pocket of her bag and ran it around the lip of the can before setting it on the sill.

She jumped from the desk, pulling out all the cans she'd tugged from the cabinets at home—leftovers, remnants of the ice storm. Cans of tuna, ham, roast beef, Vienna sausages. Her hand grew tired as she worked the can opener, placing the smell-laden contents all over the dusty wooden desktop. She opened the final can of Spam and let the blob slide straight onto the desk. She unwrapped a small block of cheese and crumbled it across the desktop for good measure. *Cat and mouse, Serena.*

Heat pouring from the boiler made the room uncomfortably hot—nearly as hot as 'Bout Out had felt when Claire had fainted.

"Can't stop," Claire told herself as sweat trickled down her face and around the edge of her jaw, dripping down the front of her white blouse. "Food," she said. "Eating—that's all these cats want to do. Just eat and eat. Even Serena. She wants to swallow me whole. Well, here's your food, Serena. Come and get it. Come straight to me. Me and Casey. Because Casey's down here," she reminded herself, running the can opener around canned white chicken. "And Casey's on my side. He wants you to go with the fog, Serena. Casey will help me. Maybe no one else will. Maybe," she went on, thinking of Rich, "everyone just wants to tell me things are bothering me. Bothering me! Of course having someone on my tail bothers me. But not like anyone around here knows. No one living, anyway. Casey knows, though—he knows all about you. And he'll help me. I'm going to get you down here. And me and Casey, we'll make sure you lose."

She smiled with satisfaction at the small metal circles full of food—her tasty little trap. She eased out of the room and up the stairs, opening the door a crack to make sure no one was looking before slipping into the hallway.

THIRTY-EIGHT

Claire waved good-bye to Becca that afternoon as Owen's car pulled back out of her driveway. She eyed the plastic still stretched across the back windshield of the Honda, grateful the ride home was finally over. She'd hoped Owen and Becca would offer a welcome reprieve from Rich's concerned stare, but she'd only found a new pressure riding with Becca—the pressure to be a friend. Clutching Becca's small gold earrings, she breathed a sigh of relief as the Honda disappeared up the street and she slipped into the house.

She raced into the kitchen, hung her coat on the hook beside the back door, and found a note that Dr. Cain had left pinned to the front of the fridge:

Claire, his crooked handwriting proclaimed. *Left new phone in your room. Be home before you leave for dance.—Dad.*

She bolted upstairs and tossed her backpack onto her dresser, knocking the pale pink scarf onto the wood floor. It landed with an unexpected clatter. Claire frowned as she picked up the silky scarf, finding her new phone tangled up inside.

She tossed it onto her bed and plugged it into her charger. *Good*, she thought. *I didn't bang it up. And with a new phone, I won't have to worry about any more texts from Rachelle.*

She attacked her closet, going through the just-in-case clothes she'd brought along with her—the dressier variety. The kind of thing she was always having to pull out so that she could accompany her father to some university event—an awards ceremony, a tea.

She tugged out a long black chiffon skirt covered in red roses, a sleeveless red silk turtleneck, and a black drape-front gossamer cardigan to cover her arms and tie at the waist. Dressy enough to pass for formal attire, long enough to cover her ugly scars.

As she laid her outfit across her bed, a soft knock danced against her bedroom door. She turned to find her father standing in her doorway, nervously clearing his throat as he pushed his glasses deeper into his face.

"Just getting everything ready for tonight," she said through a fake smile.

"Sweetheart, are you sure you want to?" he asked her. "Maybe it's not such a good idea. You've been at school all day—you ought to rest, take care of yourself."

Claire flinched against the *sweetheart*. Her father never called her that. The two of them weren't pet name kind of people. It was a sign, she thought—a sign he thought she was—what was that word Rich had used? *Bothered*.

"It's an assignment, Dad," Claire reminded him. "It's not like I'm going to be out until the break of dawn. I'll go with Rich, get what we need for an article, then be back in time to watch something good and mindless on TV. Okay?" She walked over and hugged him, smiled. She hated lying to him. But she couldn't miss the dance. She had plans.

"Okay," he relented. "But call me if you have any trouble. And—stay near Rich."

Claire nodded. As Dr. Cain retreated down the stairs, Claire took a deep breath and flipped her laptop open, clicked into her email account. Heart pounding out a syncopated rhythm, she typed hurriedly:

Rachelle—I'm going to tell you this, and I know you won't believe me right off. But I know this—the same way I knew about the boy and the pencil box. You knew it, too, then, but I was the one with the power to talk. Because if you'd said it wasn't you, if you'd pointed the finger, it just would have been he said, she said. Right? I had the power.

I've got the power now. Because there's a cat here, in town—Sweet Pea. She's old, and she's following me. Because

I found the girl. Serena. I found her, when she was dead and eaten. I SAW her being eaten—and I saw her spirit. It fell in the cat. And the cat is following me.

Weird things happen in this town, Rachelle. The kind of things that shouldn't happen anywhere. Things like boys shooting themselves in basements and then haunting the school. So I KNOW this thing with the cat is real. Casey is proof that ghosts are real. Things like that happen in this place. It's Peculiar, after all.

So I'm going to a dance tonight. And I'm going to confront the girl in the cat. I'm going to fight it out with her. Because I can't just wait for her to corner me. Not like last time. I have to stay in control of this thing. I have to, because then I won't get hurt. Last time, I let my guard down, and I wasn't in control, and I got hurt.

This time, I'M going on the hunt. I'm going to hunt a little kitty and I'm going to make sure that everyone knows the truth about the girl inside. I'm going to show that she was killed, because it's all too weird—her inhaler, the pocket, the woods. It's wrong. And I know it's wrong, and this time I'm going to fix everything. I'll be in the paper again, but it will be because I fixed everything.

Claire sighed. It felt good to get it all out—it didn't matter that it was all in a crazed, confused rush. She just needed to write it. To *say* it somehow. Typing it on her computer, in an email with Rachelle's name at the top, was almost like talking.

Still, though—she ached to say it—actually *say it*, all of it, to the old Rachelle. The Rachelle who would understand. Who would believe her. Her eyes glistened with tears, blurring the screen a moment before she saved the draft as usual and signed out of the account.

She dressed, eyeing her outfit a moment before turning from the bedroom mirror and racing straight toward the bathroom. She rifled through a drawer, picked up a pair of nail clippers, and leaned in toward the bathroom mirror. She grabbed the cameo and snipped the weakened chain free, finally.

She returned to her room, and attacked the suitcase she'd packed in Chicago. She clicked it open and slipped her hand into the pocket, pulling out the St. Jude charm. She smiled as she slipped it around her neck, behind the gossamer cardigan. Her old good-luck charm—just in case.

She grabbed an assortment of brushes, began to work on her hair and makeup while she stood before her bedroom mirror. A couple of hours later, she slid her newly charged phone into her small clutch purse and the old cameo necklace into the deep side pocket of her skirt.

She was ready.

THIRTY-NINE

Rich and Claire paused at the entrance, underneath the glittering Welcome to the Winter Formal! sign.

"I didn't think you were coming," he told Chas, who only rolled his eyes.

"I wasn't. Coach made me come. To show school spirit. Especially since I was named the MVP for this season, and am in the running for athlete of the year." He shook his head.

"Football's over, though. You could have blown it off," Claire challenged.

"Not for next year, it's not," Chas reminded her. "Your ticket, please, ma'am."

Claire glanced at Rich. "We're working. This is an assignment, not a date. Do we need tickets?"

Rich slipped his hand into the pocket of his blue suit,

pulled out two tickets. Chas tore them, handed the stubs to Rich, and dropped the rest of the two tickets into a cardboard box. "You know, if word gets out that you're *only working*, you're going to have your hands full," Chas told Rich.

"How do you mean?" Rich asked.

"Because *that one's* the prettiest thing to walk through the doors tonight," Chas said simply. "Everybody's going to want to slow dance with her. Going to have to beat them back with a stick."

Claire squirmed. Was he hitting on her? Her father had said something similar when she'd come downstairs—something about Claire *looking absolutely beautiful tonight*—the kind of thing that Claire had dismissed as fatherly kindness instead of truth. Now, though, coming from Chas, the compliments made Claire pull her gossamer sleeves down below her wrists, clutch the neck of the cardigan around her throat. She didn't want to be gawked at. Especially not by someone as suspicious as Chas. Chas who had cheated on Serena. Chas with the temper. His eyes rolled over her in an uncomfortable way.

"You two have a lovely time," Chas said acidly, and returned to pacing back and forth in front of the door.

Rich led Claire into the decorated gym, where black silhouettes of trees clung to the walls, each limb adorned with silver foil icicles. Ceiling fans spun, their wintery breeze making aluminum foil stars dance, sparkle. Crepe paper streamers slapped together in response, while casting long, black nighttime shadows on the gym floor. Strobe lights beat against the winter-pale arms of girls in formals, making them shimmer like yet to be trampled on snow.

The gym had been dressed up to mimic the beauty of an ice storm. Claire grabbed hold of Rich's arm for balance. She couldn't take another storm. Not even a pretend one.

"It's all right with you if I get the shots out of the way, isn't it?" he asked. "I'll be back in a flash."

"Shots?" she repeated, overlooking Rich's lame attempt at a joke. A sudden headache made her skull feel as though it'd been caught in a vise.

Rich raised his camera. "For Mavis. All right?"

Reluctantly, Claire nodded and forced herself to pry her fingers from his arm, plastering on a plastic smile.

Something's going to happen. I'm going to make it happen. Right here, tonight . . . she thought, watching Rich as he aimed his camera, letting the flash shoot out at the crowd. She took a step backward and bumped into someone standing just behind her.

"Hey, Claire," Becca greeted, too wrapped up in the festivities to notice Claire had left her earrings behind on the lip of her own bathroom sink. She was dressed in a beautiful violet shimmery halter gown, looking less like a high school knockout and more like a movie star. She yammered on, but her words were intermittent, staccato-sounding, as the music kept drowning her out in spurts. Owen stood beside her, appearing disinterested and far calmer than he'd been a couple of days before, when the heater in his car had gone berserk.

"I can't believe her," Becca blurted, glaring at Ruthie, dressed in a black satin dress with a full flirty skirt that danced about her knees. Her voice climbed above the thump of the music, obviously not caring that Ruthie was well within earshot. "You know she didn't even come with Chas? I mean, she ruins Serena's relationship, and then she just *moves on*, like it was nothing."

Claire's head swam as she watched Ruthie's expression harden. She seemed to swallow the floor in two large steps, coming to roost with her hands on her hips less than a foot from Becca's face.

"Stop it, okay? Just *stop it*, Becca. I didn't do anything to Serena."

"You totally did—"

"You ever stop to consider that a rumor might not be true? Huh? You want to know what Chas was doing in my basement? Watching ESPN. Yeah. He wasn't after *me*, he was after my *cable*."

Becca snorted. "If you expect me to believe—"

"Believe what you want, Becca. But I'm telling you, he came over to hang out. Period. Because Owen wasn't around. We watched games and ate Doritos, and he complained all the time about the fact that you'd forced Serena on him. When the rumor about us first broke, he asked me not to tell the truth, because it got him out of that Serena thing, once and for all. He didn't care that it made him into a bad guy. It got him out of it. He didn't like Serena. And now, no one else *will* go out with him, because they all think he's a cheater."

The image exploded into Claire's face: Serena's palm, that ballpoint word. The cat lowering her face to take a bite of her flesh . . . Chas didn't cheat. Was this a piece of Claire's puzzle? If so, how did it fit in?

"Give him a break, Becca," Ruthie said, and stomped away.

Becca shook her head, not yet ready to believe Ruthie or to forgive Chas.

She just keeps hanging on to her hatred for Ruthie, like it tastes good to her. Like it's a juicy gutted mouse, Claire caught herself thinking.

The sides of Claire's neck felt as tight as a coiled rope. Screws were twisting into her temples. Her headache was getting worse. She needed to get away from Becca for a moment.

"Excuse me. I have—to do a story—about the dance," Claire muttered, and scooted away toward the opposite side of the gym. She leaned against the wall, its coldness almost soothing against the back of her shoulders, through the filmy material of her gossamer cardigan.

Her thoughts were piling one on top of the other. She had answers to find. *If I know what happened to Serena, if I tell everyone, maybe then she can rest; she won't need more time, won't need my body; I'll be safe.*

She also needed to figure out a way to get into the basement without anyone seeing her. To find out if the lure of canned food had done the trick. *Where are you, Serena?*

Across the room, Rich was watching her. He placed the camera on a chair and hurried across the gym floor, while crepe paper streamers rippled above his head.

"Why don't we take a break?" Rich asked.

A break, Claire thought with spite. *Five minutes after we get here. He must really think I have problems. He's right—I do. But I'm going to fix them. Tonight.*

Claire plastered on her very best *I'm fine* expression. "Let's just dance," she suggested, making her voice sound light. She thought if she could lean against Rich for a minute, she could catch her breath and prepare herself for whatever was coming.

She smelled it again—that faint metallic scent dancing through the air. Danger.

In spite of the whirling fans, the gym began to heat up.

Rich took her hand, seeming both surprised and flattered by her invitation. Together, they passed the line of chaperones; no one paid attention to the two of them—not even Isles, who stared listlessly across the gym. Isles, in her stunning red dress, looking like a tropical flower in the midst of an otherwise dead bouquet as she stood in a cluster of stodgy, bland old teachers.

Claire straightened her back and slapped another smile

across her face, trying desperately to seem solid and steady on her feet. But the moment she and Rich hit the center of the dance floor, the walls of the gym began to close in, shrinking the room to the size of an elevator. The entirety of the Peculiar High student body appeared to crowd on top of her. Girls who had only moments before put their heads on the shoulders of their dates as a slow song began now had black shadows where their eyes had sparkled; their grotesquely smiling mouths cracked and bled; their cheeks turned leathery and blue. Every couple in the gym waltzed together, all of them making identical moves in the same direction. The faces of death opened their mouths and began, collectively, to scream.

Claire pulled away from Rich and wandered across the dance floor.

Serena's messing with my mind, Claire thought. *She's got to be close. She's got to be here somewhere. I need to get to the basement.*

"Claire?" Rich called out, but the music all but completely swallowed her name.

Claire trembled as she looked about the gym for the old cat—or the fog—or Casey. She took a deep breath, as if preparing to do battle.

They'll never get me, Claire promised, one hand in her pocket and the other on the St. Jude charm around her neck. *Not this time.*

FORTY

Claire stumbled toward the refreshment table near the windows. She reached for the punch bowl ladle. *A drink*, she thought. *I just need a cool drink.* She disturbed a few ice cubes swimming in the red liquid; when they crashed together, they exploded like firecrackers in her ears.

Fighting to gain control over her surroundings, Claire dropped the ladle and turned from the red punch—*like a pool of blood*, she caught herself thinking—to watch the nearby couples dance. But the couples were spinning too fast—more like ice-skaters than dancers—and she grew dizzy. Claire couldn't stare at any one of them and stand up straight at the same time.

She turned her eyes instead toward the fringes of the dance floor, deciding she was better off focusing her attention on someone solid, stationary, unmoving. But at the same time, Rich was trying to scoot around Mavis, who kept raising her arm to point out still more shots she wanted him to take. And even in the line of chaperones, it seemed that Isles was restless, peeling herself away from her spot near the wall and slipping out of the gym. She passed by Becca, pacing alone near the exit.

Everyone, everything was moving—even the floor beneath her felt unsteady.

"What's up?" a man's voice thundered at Claire.

Claire looked up to see Rhine hovering over her, radiating the same kind of heat that Claire had found herself choking on in Owen's car.

"Something's going on with you," Rhine said, leaning still closer to Claire. "I know it. Somebody messing with you, Claire? Huh? Somebody in here need some straightening out?"

Claire stared into the thin scruff of whiskers trying desperately to grow across his cheek, suppressing a laugh. What good was he, really—little more than a door greeter. He couldn't save so much as a fly.

She attempted to calm him by patting his arm and shaking her head no. "It's just a little warm in here. I think I need something to drink," she said, reaching for the ladle again as she rocked on her unsteady high heels.

Rhine leaned forward, gazing into Claire's pupils, dilated with utter fear. "You didn't take something before you got here, did you, Cain?" he asked quietly. "I mean, not that I care, but it's my job, you know?"

Claire groaned. *He thinks I'm stoned. How funny—of all people to come to a dance loaded. Why would I? Doesn't he know I squealed on a drug dealer at my old school? Claire Cain, the rat, the whistle-blower.*

She shook her head again, the slight movement making her feel as if her brain were a Ping-Pong ball bouncing about inside her skull. "I'm just thirsty," she finally managed, but her tongue was thick. Rough.

Like a cat's tongue . . .

Claire dropped the plastic ladle back into the punch bowl, unable to stomach the bloody look of the punch, the bang of ice cubes crackling against each other. "Actually, I think I need some water. Just—plain water."

She excused herself, breaking away from Rhine to weave through the edges of the crowd, out of the gym, staggering down the eerily quiet hallway. The music from the dance trickled behind her, sounding increasingly farther away as Claire made her way toward the closest water fountain.

The water was cold against her fevered lips. The shock of it felt good—a welcome change from the internal heat building within her.

A soft mewing sound filtered up from the floor beside her.

Claire let go of the button on the side of the water fountain, killing the stream. She raised her head.

The calico. Her head poked out of the partially open door to the basement.

Claire smiled. "Well, well, well. If it isn't *Sweet Pea.*" She wiped her mouth with the back of her hand. "You liked my dinner, did you? The smell get to you?" Claire giggled.

But the cat merely yowled, flicked her inflated tail, and dipped back through the open door, rushing down the stairs.

"Serena," Claire called. She gathered her skirt into her fists, her shoes clicking softly as she followed, slowly inching her way down the dark staircase. This was going to stop, just like she had stopped that boy in Chicago from ruining Rachelle's reputation. She was going to put an end to the craziness. And this time, she was *not going to get hurt.*

"Here, kitty, kitty, kitty," Claire croaked, creeping forward. The basement shadows lengthened. Dripping sounds—like drops of water hitting a metal tub—interrupted the silence.

"I've got something for you," Claire called. She reached into her pocket, pulling out the cameo necklace.

"You want it, don't you? Come get it," Claire teased. "Come get your necklace, Serena." She inched along, looking into every crevice for the old cat, detecting the faint smell of coconut.

Claire stopped and listened, hoping to hear old cat sounds in between the drips of water. She waited.

As she listened, she realized she hadn't been hearing water at all, but high-pitched notes of laughter.

Now a voice—lower. Hushed.

More laughter—as musical as a wind chime in a gentle breeze.

Claire crept past the old gym and several classrooms—searching for the source of the laughter. She finally paused outside a classroom, its door left slightly open.

She watched as a blue suit jacket tumbled to the floor. Images flashed: a body in a red dress, back pressed against the top of an old teacher's desk. Arms stretched to wrap around a back. Long blond locks. A boy's mouth smeared with red lipstick. A woman's head tilted back. The boy lowering his mouth into the woman's neck, working his way down her chest. Even though Claire couldn't see the entirety of his face, he seemed familiar, his blond hair combed smoothly over his head.

White legs emerged as a dress was pushed up toward hips. Mouths pressed together. Hands in hair.

Claire jerked backward, her heel striking an old metal bucket. She cringed as the bucket clanked, tumbling against the floor.

Isles and Owen . . . together . . .

"What was that?" Isles asked, pulling her mouth away from Owen's as she tried to rearrange her dress and push herself off the old teacher's desk.

"I don't know," Owen answered, trying to wipe away Isles's red lipstick, but only smearing it into an odd pink stain. Like the blood Claire had seen on the mouths of the feral cats out in the woods.

Claire's head reeled. She had to process the idea. Owen and Isles, making out. Like a couple. *Owen and Isles?*

She turned, desperate to get away from the classroom. She had just seen something she shouldn't have. Knowing secrets was dangerous—far more dangerous, even, than wayward spirits, ghosts. She needed to get out of the labyrinth of the basement. She raced toward the stairs, rounding a corner, another, her feet too heavy, her hard-soled shoes too noisy against the tile. She was too easy to follow.

As soon as she turned the last corner, Claire smiled. *Finally. The stairs. Freedom.*

But instead of pumping faster, the click of her heels stopped abruptly, less than three feet from the staircase.

The old calico sat on the bottom step, her slender tail swishing happily behind her. This time, though, Claire was not going to stomp her feet and send the cat skittering away—not like she had back at the cemetery. It was time for a confrontation.

"Come out of there, Serena," Claire shouted. She dangled the necklace. "Come *on.* You want your life back? You come get it."

But the cat only raised her front paw, as though in greeting. As though inviting Claire to play.

"I'm tired of your games," Claire shouted. "I'm not going to be your toy!"

She raised her head, glancing about the dim hallway. "Casey!" she shouted. "You come out, too! Come on! Do you hear me?"

Claire's booming voice frightened the old calico; she crouched down closer to the floor, lying flat, elbows hugging her ribs, hissing.

When Casey didn't answer, Claire shook her head angrily.

"Don't tell me you're a coward, Casey," Claire screamed. *"Come out!"*

The intensity of Claire's screech tugged a similar sound from the old calico, who suddenly found it necessary to defend herself. The cat pounced, flying straight for Claire's face.

Claire screamed, lurching out of the way, backing into a nearby room. As her eyes landed on shelves of half-used cleaning supplies, she realized she was in the old janitors' office.

A whole slew of hisses exploded as she moved. Ferals. Clustered on the desk, the floor, their heads dipped into Claire's canned foods. A gray tabby pushed his face through the open ground-level window, dropping to the desktop.

"You brought them all, huh?" Claire shouted at Serena, who had trailed her into the office. "Your gang? You showed them where the food was, didn't you?"

The calico backed up on her haunches. She moved like a fencer waiting for the perfect time to strike.

Claire screamed, waving her arms and sending the cats

skittering. "Out, out, out!" she boomed, stomping and fearlessly reaching forward, pushing the cats out with her hands.

The calico remained.

"You're the one I want, Serena," Claire told the calico. "Come on. I'm here."

Suddenly, the door behind her slammed; when Claire turned, she found herself staring straight into Owen's face.

FORTY-ONE

"Not again," Owen said, grabbing Claire by the shoulders roughly. But his touch, his words, weren't angry. He was afraid, pleading.

"Don't do this to me again," he repeated, his eyes flashing.

"Don't do what?" Claire said. "I've got to—the cat—"

"Don't play dumb!" Owen shouted. "You saw. You saw me. You saw Jennifer."

"Jennifer?"

"Isles! You saw us! You're going to go rat me out. You're going to tell Becca—and everyone else—we're cheating. I know you girls. You blab everything to each other."

"Cheating," she repeated.

"It's not like that," Owen said, still gripping Claire's shoulders, even as Claire took a step back, trying to get out of his way. He took the step with her. Following her. This time, though, Claire was being followed while looking straight into a boy's face. His wild, frenzied face.

"Don't you know how old she is? She's hardly older than me at all. We've got plans, okay? Not like me and Becca. God—Becca's just a girl. She doesn't know *anything*. Neither does Chas. They act like *kids*. We love each other, me and Jennifer. She's going to get out of this stupid place, because of her students' good grades. She's going to get a job someplace like Kansas City or St. Louis, some *real* place, and I'm going to go with her. Don't you get it? She's taking me. We're going to be together. This is my chance, okay? I don't have As. I'm not good enough at football to ever play past high school. I don't have college. I have Jennifer. She's everything. My whole life. If you tell anyone, I lose my *whole life*."

"Casey," Claire called. Her eyes roved about the office, searching for signs of him. "Casey!"

"God, what *is* it with that stupid story? Stop it, Claire, all right? Just stop it. Repeat after me: There's nobody here but you and me. You. And me."

She craned her neck to look behind her. Serena had dipped into the shadows of a corner, unseen. Waiting. Now that Owen was here, would Claire lose control of the situation? What if Serena got away, managing to skitter out the open window before Claire found out what happened to her? Owen was ruining everything, *everything*.

"Casey!" Claire shouted. She needed him to stop Serena, corner her, keep her from running off.

"No!" Owen screamed, now shaking her forcefully, like he could dislodge the idea from her head. "No Casey. Is *that* why you came down here, too? Are you chasing that same lame story? He's not here, Claire. And neither am I. And neither is Jennifer. Okay? Say it with me: There's no ghost. End of story. And there's no *other* story here, either. Say it, Claire. *Damn* it. Just say it!"

He was so desperate, the vibrations of his voice buzzed against the glass in the window above them. He shook her again. His touch wasn't fearful, not anymore—it was threatening.

Claire knew about angry touches. She knew how they could rip skin. She knew that they left a girl close to death, to spend month after month trying to heal. But things never did completely heal, go back to being the way they were before. There were always scars. And scars hurt. Nobody said that. But it was true—scars hurt.

Claire was tired of hurting. She wailed, raising her arms and pushing them outward, wrenching Owen's hands away. She took a giant, forceful step backward. She felt an opening behind her. A way out. An exit.

This is it—I'm going to escape, Claire thought. *I'll do it. I'll get out.*

A door—there was a door, too. Her left arm brushed up

against it. Her fingers wrapped around the edge—it felt funny, it was metal, and it was thinner, too, not like a door to a room.

But a door was safety. She would put it between her and Owen, and she would be safe.

She pushed herself all the way through the opening, and she slammed the door in front of her.

Blackness exploded.

FORTY-TWO

Claire *wasn't* free. She was locked inside something. Not a room. Where was she? The space was smaller than a trunk.

"No!" Owen screamed. "Not again. Don't do this to me, Claire. You have to get out of there!"

Claire's eyes adjusted with the help of thin streams of light slipping through the door in front of her. Metal slats. Like on the front of a locker door.

Claire's heart kicked her ribs. *I'm not free. I'm stuck in a locker. I'm trapped. I'm cornered.*

"Help!" Claire shouted, pounding on the inside of the locker door with her fist. "Help me!" Panic thrashed inside of her. She pressed her eye against the little metal slats. "Please," she begged, her face so close to the vents that her eyelashes brushed against them. "Please help me."

"I'm trying, Claire," Owen said. "The handle's stuck. The door's warped. It's too hot down here. Next to the boiler. The fucking boiler."

Claire's arms were right in front of her face, in the same position they'd been when she'd raised them to protect her face in Chicago. She remembered the way the parking lot lights had looked as they'd shone through the space between her arms—before they'd been snapped like twigs.

"Jesus, Claire!" Owen pleaded. "Why the hell did you *do* that?" He banged on the door from the outside, kicking the locker at the base, wiggling the handle furiously.

"It was an accident," Claire called. It was all she could think of. Why else would she put herself in a locker?

"*Accident*," Owen growled. "Not again."

Claire stared at her hands. In the tightness of the locker, with her shoulders squeezed, curving in toward her chest, she had no way to put her arms down. Her tiny gold satin clutch still dangled from her wrist, just a couple of inches from her nose.

Claire suddenly remembered the phone she'd tossed inside. She fumbled with the drawstring, turning the phone on. The new phone her father'd bought her, and had laid on top of her dresser.

911, she would dial, and the operator at the other end would ask, *What is the nature of your emergency?*

But the moment the phone came to life, her tiny bubble of celebration popped. She recognized the face in the picture being used as the phone's wallpaper—both faces, actually. One girl with light blond hair, the other with thick brown hair, both in Peculiar High uniforms, their faces smashed together as they hugged. Becca and Serena.

Becca and Serena? Claire's mind spun. How did they get on her phone?

Her thumb flew over the screen, as she discovered a folder of pictures labeled Basement Story. Photos of the janitors' office, the vacant classrooms, the gym, the boys' locker room. What the picture taker had seen walking down the deserted downstairs hallways. And what Claire had seen herself only moments ago—Owen and Isles, bodies tangled.

This wasn't Claire's new phone at all. It was Serena's old phone. Claire remembered the pink scarf on top of her dresser, bunched in the middle. Serena always went to her old house. Wasn't that what Becca'd said? Did Serena leave her phone there? Had the phone been beneath the scarf the entire time?

Yes, Claire answered herself. *The whole time. Hidden beneath the bunched-up folds of the scarf. Just waiting to be found.*

"She knew about you," Claire called. "Serena. She knew about you and Isles. She saw you—when she came down to investigate her ghost-hunter piece. Her story about Casey. Didn't she?"

Owen kicked at the locker again, as pieces of the puzzle came together in Claire's head.

"Were you looking for it?" Claire asked. "Her phone? Is that why you said you'd clean out her locker?" But the phone wasn't in her locker. And it wasn't on her body. Because Serena didn't have her phone with her the day she died. She'd already hidden her phone in her old house. Her favorite house. Of course she had. Almost as though she'd known—as though she'd had some sort of *premonition*—the same word Mrs. Sims had used when talking about her daughter.

Claire hurried through Serena's apps, her hands shaking. She pulled up a writing app, found it filled with notes she'd taken for her story. The basement. Casey.

And Owen. *Creep!* read one of Serena's notes. *Chas couldn't get away with cheating on me, and Owen's not going to get away with cheating on Becca. Becca stood up for me. I'm going to stand up for her now.*

Meeting w/ O., read another note. *Basement. After school. CONFRONT HIM ABOUT WHAT I KNOW.*

"You met her here," Claire said, in a tone loud enough for Owen to hear. "You met her in the basement. She told you what she knew. That she had proof. That she saw you while she was researching her story about Casey haunting the basement."

"Oh, shit," Owen moaned, as the boiler cranked into gear. "It's coming on again. The heat."

He banged furiously against the locker. "Not again," he begged.

Not again? Claire thought. The basement meeting. The heat. *Worse in hot weather*, Rich had said about Serena's asthma. And the inhaler that had fallen out of Serena's locker upstairs.

A fight—the locker—*not again*—no inhaler. An ice storm. The boiler. Heat. An asthma attack. Panic. Suffocation.

She touched the door in front of her, finding it full of large, fist-sized indentions. Like someone had beaten the locker, trying to get out. She imagined Serena fighting, the struggle only making the locker hotter, while the boiler came on again and again, the panic making her asthma attack worse. She pictured Serena, fists flying, beating the locker, beating her chest, beating frantically for *something* to open up—the door, her lungs.

Claire shuddered. This was it—this was where Serena died. Claire remembered lying in Serena's grave, how cool it had felt. How it had fit.

This fits you now, too, she heard, as stripes of color began to pour in through the vents on the front of the locker.

The colors swirled, congealed, became the same face Claire had seen smiling at her during Serena's funeral—the face on the blown-up picture propped beside the casket.

Claire squinted and squirmed, fighting her blurring eyes—now too hazy to dial Serena's phone, *911, what is the nature of your emergency?* Claire fought surges of nausea as the boiler kicked on again, and heat swelled—far hotter than it had been in 'Bout Out or Owen's car. This was the heat of an infection, a blistered sore, the heat of fear, of panic. The heat of the moment of death.

"You can feel it, can't you?" Serena asked Claire. "Your lungs are closing. That's just like asthma. Owen pushed me in this locker, and in the heat, I had an asthma attack. The worst of my life."

Claire began to wheeze, clawing at her throat. She had asthma too, it seemed—brought on by fear, by the power of suggestion—and by Serena. Serena had powers that Claire did not even fully understand.

"Would be nice to have an inhaler, wouldn't it?" Serena asked. "But I left mine in my locker. I was only going to talk to Owen for a minute. Just a minute, I said. But once I was in here, the air just kept getting hotter and my lungs kept getting tighter. The ice storm had just started—it was so cold, and the boiler kept coming on. My asthma was always worse in the summer. And in here, it was far hotter than any August afternoon."

Claire kicked at the door, whining.

Waves of hot air surged. She didn't know if her lungs were collapsing or about to burst just like the can in 'Bout Out or the coffeepot in Mrs. Sims' kitchen. Claire gagged, choking on the heat. As her body convulsed, fiery air wrapped its fingers around her throat.

FORTY-THREE

Claire grew physically weak. Her breath became shallow as the space grew hotter, the air thinner.

She beat the metal locker door, begging with her fists to be freed. Trying to suck in a breath had become as easy as trying to move air through hardened mortar. And still, liquid fire from the nearby boiler invaded the locker. She clawed at her own throat, tearing her flimsy cardigan. Exposing her shoulders.

Claire knew how hard it had been for Serena to breathe—such a tight space, the heat, her asthma. *No wonder she died*, Claire thought.

A splash of black and white filtered in through the metal grates on the locker door. A new figure appeared, joining Claire and Serena in the heat. A boy with the same black-and-white face Claire had first discovered in the old Peculiar High yearbook—Casey Andrews. "You're not supposed to be here," Casey growled.

Fog began to filter in through the crack at the bottom of the door. The town dead, the spirits, here in the locker.

"You need to go with them, Serena," Casey said. "Go with the fog."

"No, I don't," Serena sneered. "I'm going to get in Claire, get a new body, a better body."

"You don't have to do this," Claire said. "I know what happened to you now. I'll let everyone know."

"*I'll* let them know," Serena said. "With *your* voice. *I'll* write the story."

Serena's eyes flashed as they scanned Claire's scrunched-up shoulders, her scarred skin. Her surprise melted into a wicked chuckle. "That's okay," she said. "I had a couple of scars, too, and a scar is not the same as being dead. So what if I'll have to put on a brave face and pretend like it doesn't bother me, all those times people will be repulsed by the look of me? I won't be *dead.*"

"Please take her," Claire begged Casey. "She's out of the cat now. She got out—like in the woods. She wants in me. You can do it. *Take her.*"

Proof, Claire thought, her frenzied, frantic mind grasping at anything—any solution. *Get proof.*

"How would you like a *picture*, Serena?" Claire asked.

"You took pictures on your phone to get proof for your own story. What if I had pictures on the phone of *you*?"

Claire snapped a photo, the flash illuminating the inside of the locker.

In the harsh, white burst of light, her own face filled the dusty mirror one of the old janitors had attached to the inside of his locker door. Her terrorized face, iridescent with sweat and tears. Her face and her raised hands and the cameo necklace tangled in her fingers and her gold satin clutch—and the four gray metal walls.

When the blackness returned, so did the rippling fingers of fog—and Casey's black-and-white face—and Serena's soul, curdled with rage.

Claire's stomach lurched. Something startling had happened in that flash. But she couldn't quite explain the revulsion that rippled across her body.

Tears searing her fevered skin, Claire took another picture, again seeing only her own image in the mirror. And in the darkness that returned, the fog swelled—far too thick, it seemed, to have ever really disappeared at all.

"Hey!" Claire shouted. "Don't do that! Stop moving around!"

She took another picture, but Serena, Casey, and the fog disappeared in the flash.

"Don't think I won't get you," she said, taking several rapid-fire shots, and finding only the gray walls on the screen.

"Come on," she said, but her lip was wobbling because the locker looked so *empty* in the photos. As though Claire was the only one inside. But that couldn't be true. Serena was there. Casey was there. The fog was there.

Claire trembled, tears increasing, flowing like tormented rivers. She took still another picture; in the blinding flash, her face was the only image filling the mirror on the locker door.

"No," she sobbed. "No, no, no." She snapped another quick cluster of pictures. And in the mirror, with each repeating flash, she saw only herself—only her own scars.

"Get back!" she heard Rich shout, bursting into the janitors' office. "Get away from the locker!"

Claire made a limp fist, struck the inside of the door to her tiny prison cell. "Rich?" she called, through her tears. "Is that you?"

"I'm coming!" Rich shouted, tugging forcefully against the locker door.

"What's going on in here?" Rhine shouted as he clomped into the room.

"The door!" Owen cried out. "I can't get it to open!"

"Claire?" her own father's panicked voice cried out. "Are you in there?"

"Dad?" she asked. How was it possible for him to be there? Where did he come from?

A steady light streamed into the locker, as though someone was holding a flashlight against the vents in the locker door. "Claire?" her father called again. "Say something if you're in there."

In the steady light, Claire could see everything—her own face in the mirror. And Serena's necklace, dangling from her fingers. No fog. No Casey. No murdered Sims girl. Not in the light. She was alone, in the light and the mirror's reflection.

"Here," she called weakly. "I'm here."

"The door is warped!" Owen shouted. "I can't lift up on the handle."

The light disappeared; feet stomped; metal rattled like hands were sifting through a drawer of wrenches.

In the darkness, Casey and Serena were still with her. In the darkness, Serena fought against Casey, ready to slip inside Claire's body, take it for her own, ravage her in ways that even those boys in the Chicago parking lot never could have dreamed up.

As the search for a tool to free Claire continued, she sifted again through the pictures she had just taken on the phone: Her face. The locker. No Serena. No Casey.

Glancing behind the screen, she saw them all, still there, swirling through the darkness.

But what, exactly, did that mean? Maybe, she thought, they simply had a way to hide. Maybe the flash was so strong that it obliterated them. Maybe spirits just couldn't show up in a picture. Of course that was it, she told herself. They were hiding. Surely they were. She didn't make things up. She didn't see things that weren't there.

"Claire," her father shouted, shining the light back against the grate. "Say something."

In the light, she saw herself in the mirror again. Her terrorized face was the only thing filling the locker. No spirits. No fog. No dead girl.

What was happening to her?

"Please. No. It can't," Claire begged. But the light had illuminated the truth: she was alone in the locker. The fog and Serena and Casey were not there, crowding the tiny space where she was trapped.

Flashes of memory burst in front of her eyes, just as quickly and powerfully as the flash from Serena's camera. In the basement, the reflection of her face in the doorway had erased the vision of the alley—and Casey. After the funeral, the reflection of her face in Serena's temporary marker had erased the fog. Owen had been cleaning out Serena's locker when the reflection of her face in the window had erased the ice in the hallway. Over and over it had happened: her reflection erased the fog—and the ice—and Casey—and now Serena.

She wailed. Because as she struggled to breathe, as she fought for her own life, she knew what she wanted most, what she had always wanted, ever since that night in April: her old life back. She wanted her old body. And if she could not get her old body back, she wished she could trade in her body for a new, better one. A body that did not look as scuffed and battered in her own bathroom mirror as the body of the old calico she'd met outside in the woodpile.

She didn't want to be a half-dead thing lying in a parking lot. She wanted a second chance at that night back in April. She wanted to never leave the library alone. She *wanted her old life back.* The words echoed in her head. Didn't that sound like something Serena had said?

We both want the exact same thing? How is it possible?

But Claire already knew the answer: it was possible because Serena had never existed beyond her death. There was no spirit manipulating Claire's surroundings. The cats in her room really had just been after a place to get warm. Owen's car really had just had an electrical malfunction—and the heat had frightened Owen because he knew how Serena died.

Claire gagged against the blasts from the boiler. Her lungs refused to open. She was suffocating.

Out in the woods, the spirit of Serena had tried to get inside her body. Back in Chicago, that was what the boys had been after. To get inside her. Good God—it was all the same.

Serena and I want the same thing, Claire thought, coughing against the fiery breath of the boiler, wheezing as the remaining oxygen slipped away through the vents in the locker.

Serena wanted her old life back. Serena didn't want to be reduced to a half-dead spirit rattling inside an awful body.

"Neither do I," Claire moaned, hitting the door limply. "We *are* the same." Serena had become the voice of everything

Claire wanted. Everything she was afraid to say.

"Here," Rhine shouted. "Stand back."

He attacked the locker door—it sounded like he was hitting the handle with a hammer. The force of a blow dislodged the mirror; it slid down the door, shattering against the base of the locker. But Claire felt the entire world was shattering—the world as she had built it up in her mind, anyway—a world of ghosts and hauntings. A world in which what had happened in Chicago was over. A loud boom exploded as Rhine knocked the handle off; the broken metal piece clattered against the tile floor below.

Metal claws of a couple of crowbars slipped into the side of the door. After Rhine shouted, "One, two, *three*," both crowbars pulled at the same time, popping the door open.

Claire tumbled out, coughing and wheezing. Rhine and Rich both stood before her, crowbars in their hands. Rich dropped his tool, squatting down beside her. "Claire?" he asked, tilting his head, trying to get her to look in his eyes.

She pressed her palm against the cold tile floor to steady herself. In the harsh fluorescent office light, she glanced back at the locker—just one more look. Just to make sure. *Empty.*

The necklace tumbled from her hand, the cameo clinking against the tile floor.

Claire gasped, filling her lungs with cool air. Owen stared straight ahead, Isles's lipstick still staining his mouth.

"Claire," her father shouted, lunging for her, sprawled

across the basement floor in front of the open locker. "Are you all right? Talk to me. Rachelle sent me about a hundred texts, and I came to the school right away."

"Dr. Cain showed up in the gym right after you'd left," Rich said, obviously still upset. "He told me something was wrong. We had to find you."

Claire glanced up, finding Becca and Chas in the basement, too.

"Phone," Claire coughed, wiping at her tears, her chest lurching as she tried to catch her breath. "It's on Serena's phone—proof—of them—together—in the basement." She pointed first at Isles, who stood in the doorway, then swiveled her hand back toward Owen. A tear building in Owen's left eye rolled off his lower lid, down his face.

"You?" Becca whispered, staring at Isles. "*You?*"

Isles shook her head at Rhine, unaware that her lipstick was smeared into one of her cheeks. "I didn't know what was going on," she tried to tell him, pretending to have only just arrived in the basement herself. "I was just—I was—there were noises. So I came. To check on them."

Owen turned a wounded face toward Isles. "It's out," he shouted. "They know."

"I have no idea what he's talking about," Isles said.

"Are you really going to do that?" Owen wailed, through the lipstick stain on his mouth. "After everything I did? I tried to hide it all for you, but now that it's out, you won't stand up for me? Huh? I love you, and you said you loved me. And now, you won't stand up for me?"

"I don't know what he's talking about," Isles repeated.

"He met with Serena," Claire coughed. "The afternoon of the ice storm."

"You were *here*?" Becca asked. "You didn't tell me that. You said you unloaded groceries for your mom."

"He was," Rhine said. "He came back. Asked me to let him in. I didn't think anything about it, because a few teachers and some students came back, too. Said they'd left their books or papers, in their rush to get out."

"What did *you* leave?" Becca demanded, grabbing Owen's arm.

He only shook his head and looked at the floor.

"*When* did he leave?" Becca asked, turning her angry face toward Rhine.

"I never saw him come back out. Not that I noticed, anyway. I just assumed I must've missed him—that he came out with another student or something, so that it didn't stick out in my head. But I swear, I had no idea Serena was still in the building."

"Serena had proof," Claire said. "On her phone. Proof of Owen and Isles. Cheating."

"Good God, Owen," Ms. Isles whispered, her face blanching. "What did you do?"

Owen screamed, kicked the locker, as though to punish

himself. "I only wanted to scare her!" he shouted. "Scare her into giving up her phone! I met her down here—where we'd have privacy. We fought—I tried to grab her and she fell back into the locker. I figured I'd let her think about it for a while. Then she'd be glad to give up her phone. So I turned the lights out and left her. I slipped upstairs and hid out in a bathroom stall. I was afraid someone would see me. I never would have left her in there if I'd known—if I'd heard—when I came back, maybe an hour later, she was so quiet. And the door was all dented. It took me a while to open it. When I did, she was—how could that *happen*?"

"Asthma," Claire said. "Her asthma."

Owen collapsed onto the floor. Isles covered her mouth, her red dress now blotchy with sweat and fear. With shock etched across his face, Rhine began dialing his phone. Three buttons: 911.

Claire tried to stand, but stopped when her hand brushed against her ankle. She braced herself for searing pain from what had been an oozing black sore only that morning. Now, when she touched it, the wound was merely tender. Peeling her dress back, she found that the scabs had been all but completely absorbed by her healing skin. The infection in those scratches hadn't been real, either—only a way for her mind to play with her, to convince her that Serena had a grip on her, was weakening her.

As her father's face shifted to reflect all the love and

concern he felt for his daughter, Rich reached for Claire's hand, offering to help her to her feet.

Claire glanced about the room; she could feel everyone's eyes rolling over the pink crisscrossing marks on her shoulders, bare now that her gossamer cardigan dangled in tatters from the knot at her waist.

It was a relief, she thought, to let them see her, scars and all.

FORTY-FOUR

Claire's father drove her straight to a Kansas City hospital. He rushed her to the emergency room, where doctors in scrubs began to search for the wound that had brought her to them, the torn-open place, the broken thing that needed mending.

She was talking the entire time, chattering on like a radio with no off switch. At first, the ER doctor who tried to examine her treated her endless yammering like a sleeve that had to be rolled up, hair that had to be pulled aside so that he could find the source of whatever was hurting her.

After a few minutes, though, the doctor squinted at her, began to really pay attention. And he draped his stethoscope around the back of his neck, pulled a chair close, and listened. Because Claire's words weren't something he needed to brush aside so that he could begin to treat her wounds. Claire's words *were* the source of her hurt.

She spoke in a long ramble, about reflections and ghosts and cats. And she began to talk about a gang. About an ice storm. About being hunted.

It poured out of her—every event, every fear. "I wanted it to be over," Claire said. "Last spring, as soon as I woke up in the hospital, I just wanted it all to be over. More than that," she confessed, "I wanted it never to have happened. Any of it. I just wanted—all of it—to be gone. I thought—if I could just get control over everything, it would be different this time. "

The doctor nodded with a sympathetic expression on his face. "PTSD," he said. "With hallucinations. Surely brought on by the second traumatic event—the discovery of the girl's body in the woods."

He stood to assure her. "It's going to be okay. We're going to make sure of that."

He closed the curtain surrounding her to write on her chart.

Claire fell back on the gurney, clutching to his words like they were a life preserver.

Three days later, Dr. Cain leaned over the front desk, where Claire's checkout was being slowed by the need to make arrangements for ongoing sessions with an on-staff psychiatrist at the same hospital. Craning his neck to view the screen on the receptionist's computer, where she was pointing to available times on her calendar, he fumbled his phone. It slid from the counter, threatening to shatter on the floor.

Claire lunged forward, catching it. She grunted happily at her small victory, and glanced up, expecting Dr. Cain to be smiling at her with gratitude. But the calendar had stolen his complete attention. He didn't know he'd nearly broken his phone.

She sighed, staring into the screen. And the world around her—every noise and smell and sight in the hospital—became a hazy-white distant blur. Because a text had just come in. From Rachelle.

Frowning, Claire read, *Pls, Dr. C. How is she?*

Claire's feet started moving, drifting across the tile toward the hospital door as she scrolled through her father's old texts. Outside, in the shade beneath the entrance awning, Claire began to shake. "It was you," she whispered as she read the sea of Rachelle's messages. "You told Dad. I sent you that wild email by accident—the one I wrote the night of the dance. And you instantly started texting him. That's why he came to the school." And the rest had been a domino effect—Rich and Rhine racing to the basement after her father. The three of them freeing her from the locker. Without Rachelle, Claire knew, she might not have been found in time. She could have met the same fate as Serena. Rachelle had saved her.

She threw her head back and gasped, like a near-drowning

victim breaking the surface of the ocean, taking in her first deep clean breath.

Rachelle had just texted her father. That meant she was still there, near her phone. A single tear raced down Claire's cheek as she fought to gain control of her trembling fingers.

She dialed, raised the phone to her ear. It rang once, twice.

"Hello?" Rachelle said, her voice tight with worry. "Dr. Cain? Please, is Claire—is she—"

"Rachelle," Claire said softly. "It's me."

FORTY-FIVE

Mavis sighed a "wow" under her breath, tossing her glasses onto her desktop. "That's quite a brave subject matter," she said, after hearing Claire's pitch for a new series. "It hasn't been long, though—just over a month since the dance. Is it still too soon to write about all of it?"

In truth, the past month had felt a little like a year to Claire. She'd worked from home, yet again, as she'd attended daily virtual visits with her psychiatrist and her father had driven her to Kansas City for in-person sessions three times a week. She'd learned to meditate; she'd taken up yoga; she'd worked hard at opening up to her father and making emails to Rachelle a semi-regular habit.

Rich had brought her daily assignments, and made sure she'd kept up with everything happening at Peculiar High. His visits had, in fact, been the only completely non-tedious part of the past month.

"You know," he'd told her, as they'd shared an afghan on the Simses' old porch swing during a particularly sunny day in February, "no one would have known, without you."

Claire had frowned, not understanding.

"Maybe some of the things you saw weren't real—but you were right about there being more to the way Serena died," Rich reasoned. "Without you, Serena's death would have been listed as accidental—and no one ever would have known the truth."

He'd sat silently beside her, letting her mull it over, before adding, "Never is a bad that's *completely* bad. There's always a speck of good in there somewhere."

Slowly, Claire began to realize that for the first time since her attack the previous April, she wanted to write—*really* wanted to write. Not because she had always written, and clunking around on her keyboard would give her the appearance of being fine. Not because she wanted to convince herself that nothing had changed, that she was still destined for great things. She had that old ache now to really dig into a new project. And she knew exactly what she wanted that new project to be.

"Are you sure you'd be okay with exposing yourself like that to the entire student body?"

"Look behind me, Ms. Mavis."

The instructor's eyes landed on Claire's classmates, the clusters of students working at computers scattered throughout the room.

"A couple of them, I'd bet, are staring right at me," Claire said. "The rest keep sneaking looks, while trying to pretend they're really not eavesdropping. And everyone's avoiding your desk right now—no one's asking for a pass or your approval for a story topic or turning in a paper."

Mavis nodded slowly.

"There's been an empty circle around me the past couple of days, ever since I came back to school," Claire informed her. "If it wasn't for Rich, there wouldn't be a soul here who would look me in the eye or talk to me directly. I've got a few teachers—not you—but a few who try not to look my way when they lecture. No one knows how to act around me. I think it'd be harder for me *not* to address the issue. Writing the series would help."

Mavis tapped her fingers on her desk and cleared her throat. In her best journalism teacher voice—which still cracked here and there—she suggested, "I wouldn't think that recovering from PTSD would happen in a straight line. There are bound to be a few setbacks. Are you prepared to also chronicle those setbacks for your readers as well?"

Claire's eyes grew hazy as she thought of the past few weeks. She remembered a night spent sitting at the kitchen table, wool socks on her feet and a cup of tea steaming beside her. She remembered the sound of rain clicking on the door beside her, the way the taps had crawled up her arms, and the steam from her mug had begun to curl, almost menacingly— like fog. Like a ghostly spirit.

It's just steam, Cain, she'd told herself. *You know that.* She'd rubbed her eyes, stood, and emptied a can of tuna into a small bowl. She'd thrown open the back door and braved the rain for a moment to place the bowl under the tarp, in the woodpile. Sweet Pea was probably hungry, she figured. Hungry for *food.* After all, Sweet Pea was a homeless cat. She was not a creature possessed by a spirit hungry only to get inside another girl's body.

She'd gone back inside to finish her email to Rachelle. To tell her about the fear that had gripped her, for a moment, and the way in which she'd managed to reason it away.

"Ms. Mavis," Claire said, "I kept everything that was going on with me buried inside. So much so that I had to finally see visions of ghosts in order to admit to myself what I wished for the most—that the beating in Chicago never happened. I tried to bury my hurt, to cover it, to pretend it wasn't there. That's how I got in trouble before. You're right—I do have good days and bad days. Before, I tried so hard to get control over everything . . ." Her voice drifted off as she thought of the times she could have told Rich about the visions she'd been having in the basement, the cemetery, but held back—as though she knew somewhere deep down that all of it was imaginary.

"I'm not in control of the world around me," Claire acknowledged. "I have no control of the things that happened in the past. I can't change any of it. But maybe if I own up to it all—get everything that happened out in the open—maybe that gives me all the control I could ever hope for. All I know is, whatever happens in the next few weeks and months, I'm not going to be afraid to look at myself in the mirror. And I think that exposing myself to readers would be the best medicine ever for my own healing process . . . however and wherever that takes me."

As Mavis took a breath, considering what Claire had just said, Claire turned to find Rich standing a foot from the desk. He raised his hand to give her the thumbs-up.

FORTY-SIX

"It should be out today, right?" Rachelle asked, folding her sleep sweats and placing them back in her suitcase.

Claire stared as Rachelle snapped the suitcase shut and placed it neatly in the corner of Claire's bedroom. Rachelle had arrived in Peculiar the day before with the intention of spending spring break with the Cains. But despite their emails and texts and a couple of short phone calls over the past few weeks, the air was still tense—frosty really—between them. So much had happened—so many bad feelings, resentments—sometimes, Claire thought as she watched Rachelle wipe the steam from the window with her fist, friendships got scarred, too. Healed, but not in the way they'd been before.

"What is that out by the cherry tree?" Rachelle asked, pointing.

"A grave," Claire croaked.

"Grave?" Rachelle repeated. Even worry could crinkle her face in a pretty way, Claire thought with still a slight twinge of jealousy.

"Sweet Pea," Claire said simply. "An old barn cat who used to live near the house. Dad and I found her body in the woodpile last week."

Rachelle sucked in a deep breath. "You really think you're going to stay next year?"

"Dad made some discoveries in his cave," Claire explained. "I want him to finish his work."

"It'd be our senior year, though," Rachelle said.

Claire smiled, nodded as she fell into place beside Rachelle, near the window. She felt the bulge of her phone in her pocket—the same phone her father had left on her nightstand the night of the dance, that Claire had never seen, not after discovering Serena's old phone and mistaking it for her own. She thought about trying to say something about being in touch the whole year, but wasn't sure how. Both girls crossed their arms over their chests as the outdoor air seeped in. Spring still had a chill to it.

A honk in the driveway made Rachelle jump. "Is that him?" she asked.

"Should be," Claire said, grabbing a yellow cardigan and throwing it on over her shoulders.

The girls' feet thundered against the stairs and through the front door, where Rich sat in his truck.

"Is it out?" Rachelle shouted at Rich, before Claire could even introduce them.

"Let's go see," he said, motioning for the two girls to climb into the cab.

Spring had only just begun to tug greenery out of its hibernation. As they drove through Peculiar, they passed by the high school, where half of the building was illuminated by sun. The other half had fallen into a gray shadow, reminiscent of the dark days left behind. While a few trees along the streets had sprouted buds, the woods near the school were still filled with naked branches, black crooked fingers that scratched viciously against the blue sky.

Rich turned a corner, slowing to make room for an animal control van. Two workers were putting small crates into the back of the vehicle—cats who had surely just been snatched by the scruffs of their necks. If they were young enough, they'd be sent out for adoption; if not, they'd be sterilized, as part of a town-wide effort to reduce the feral population.

The truck ambled past a streetlight, bearing the faded, tattered remnants of one of the old yellow "Missing" flyers featuring Serena's school picture.

"Who is *that*?" Rachelle blurted, pressing her face against the passenger-side glass.

Claire leaned around Rachelle to find Chas jogging down the sidewalk, his breath shooting out in a long gray stream, his body toned by long hours of exercise. In the weeks since the Winter Formal, Chas had backed away completely from any kind of social interaction. During lunch, he quickly downed wraps and protein shakes before heading straight back to the weight room. He lived in the gym, using all his free time to train, to talk with the coach about his future as an athlete: next year's football season, scholarships. He was even participating in track and field this year, though Rich said he'd never seemed to have interest before. The thrill of competition, Claire had often thought as she watched him push himself—faster, faster, sprinting—would never disappoint him in the same way people could. The game—any game, any sport—offered Chas a level of comfort.

"Quickest crush of all time, apparently," Claire finally responded, trying on a tease with Rachelle for the first time since her arrival.

Rachelle shot her elbow straight into Claire's ribs.

Claire's eyes tingled as she realized she may very well have missed the teasing elbow jabs even more than Rachelle's laughter.

Rich pulled into the lot at 'Bout Out; Rachelle popped her door and raced up the sagging wooden stairs. Claire and Rich followed, their group coming together in a small cluster before the latest editions of the nearby town newspapers.

A few of the headlines still stung, months later. Though Serena's death had been an accident, charges were still pending for Owen: involuntary manslaughter, hiding a corpse, obstruction of justice. Today, the banner across the front page indicated that his family had been granted permission to relocate while awaiting his court date. The Martin house stood empty in one of the pictures, the early spring grass promising to grow wild around the fringes of the drive.

The story, Claire figured, would also go on to rehash some of the other details: that Isles had been fired. She would be referred to as a shamed instructor. As a history teacher who would never teach again, and was facing her own charges for sexual misconduct with a student.

When Claire glanced up, she saw Becca standing near the checkout counter with a fresh-faced freshman cheerleader—a girl apparently idolizing her, hanging on to Becca's every word as though they were rocks on a cliff, keeping her from falling to certain annihilation.

"Good intentions are one thing," Rich whispered into Claire's ear, somehow reading her mind. "But Becca will never give up her love of being adored."

"Look!" Rachelle said, pointing at the *Star*. "It's here."

"Lucky thing you all came for that paper when you did," Maxine called from the front counter, while Becca and her new friend finished paying for their coffees and turned to leave the store. "We're *'bout out*."

Claire chuckled as she carried her copy to the counter, plunked her money down. She tore through the pages, stopping when she finally found what she'd been looking for—her own byline—*Claire Cain*—and her headshot. In the *Kansas City Star.* "The Face of Fear," an ongoing first-person account about living with PTSD. A series that Mavis had felt was far too big for the *Peculiar High Press.*

Rich and Rachelle leaned in close to her, reading over her shoulder. "It's good," Rich said. "Really good. Honest."

Claire smiled up at him. "I hope so," she said. She folded the paper under her arm, planning to take it home to share with her father.

A soft brush against her jeans drew her attention toward a strange cat swirling around her ankles. A calico missing her right ear. Claire gasped, closing her eyes tightly.

Ain't no house cat, Claire heard bouncing through her mind. It was still a struggle to keep a tight rein on wild thoughts that kept trying to invade her reality.

"Claire," Rich called softly. "Claire."

Her heart thundered and sweat began to turn her cheeks shiny as she cracked her eyes, forcing herself to look down at the cat's tricolored face.

"That's Maybelline," Maxine shouted. "Named her that 'cause I found her in an old shipping box of lipstick. Showed up about the same time animal control started roundin' all the ferals up. All those wild cats used to like to shadow me a bit every now and again, mostly when they were hungry or wanted to play a bit, but Maybelline seems to have a special interest. Followin' me around like a human, that one."

Claire flinched. "Human?" she repeated, glancing through the plate-glass window, toward the cemetery.

"Now, don't let that cat's looks scare you, hon'," Maxine insisted, leaning against the barn-wood counter. "She looks rough, but she's the sweetest ol' thing. Gonna have to take that one in for good."

Sweet Pea is dead, Claire reminded herself, *and she was never anything other than a cat. Maybelline is a cat, too, Claire. A cat—nothing more.*

Claire squatted, reached for the calico. Maybelline leaned into her hand, purring the moment Claire started rubbing the back of her neck.

She smiled, letting her fingers dig deeper into the cat's fur. When she hit a sore spot behind the cat's ear, though, Maybelline let out a fierce yowl and swiped at Claire's hand with her claws.

Letting out a yelp of her own, Claire checked her knuckles to find that Maybelline hadn't broken the skin. But when she glanced into the yellow eyes of the adopted and soon-to-be spoiled store cat, she saw it still buried inside: a hint of the wild thing she could have easily become.

Serena

She felt it again—the tug. It started gently, like the first warm ray of sun after a violent spring storm. It came as relief, like the gentle kiss of rain on a drought-cracked earth. It intensified, pulling at her with kindness, like a child begging her to come outside to play. Serena answered the call—as she always did—and found herself hovering above the spot marked with her name.

The tugs occurred regularly—as often as she was remembered. She relished those times when memories brought her back to the world and she got a chance to smell the sweetness of grass that had just been mowed, to feel the silvery smoothness of the moon rippling around her like a whirlpool, to taste the sunshine. Sunlight on the fields where Serena had spent her childhood tasted like the banana Popsicles she'd loved when she was little.

Her father had been the first one to tug her back to the cemetery—shortly after her permanent marker had appeared. "Looks good there, kiddo," he'd said of the marker, in the same awkward way he'd once talked of new dresses she'd put on for church, once she'd filled out and had gotten a more womanly shape. He bent down to pull a few extra-tall strands of grass away from her headstone, the same way he'd once straightened her collar.

"Know what I was just thinking about?" he'd asked. But he didn't need to tell her. Serena *had* already known—her first-day-of-school kindergarten dress. He'd picked it out for her, on a shopping trip they'd taken together. *Blue flowers to go with those big blue eyes*, he'd said, smiling at the little dress he'd plucked off the rack. That was part of being called back—reliving the joy that a memory of her had brought someone else.

Other tugs had been painful, though—especially the one from the girl with the big blue coat and the troubled eyes. The girl who'd told Serena the strange story—about visions and Owen. "It's okay now," she'd assured her. "Everyone knows what really happened."

Serena had wished, then, that she could reach through the murky gray area between being and not being, between the real and imagined, and comfort the poor girl. Wished for some way to thank her.

Serena glanced about the cemetery, eager to find who had tugged her this time.

It was her best friend who paused inside the wrought-iron gate to take a deep breath. So Becca had finally come. She'd had to talk herself into this visit, Serena knew. The permanent marker made the rest of it permanent, too.

Becca'd cut her hair all the way up to her shoulders. It made her look older. Or maybe it was everything that had happened in the last few months that had aged her.

She'd walked halfway to the grave before Serena realized that the woman accompanying Becca was her own mother—not Mrs. Holman.

It seemed so strange to see them together—but it pleased Serena, too. Her mother had come before, but always by herself, and always so sad. Being together, she knew, was helping them both.

Serena studied the two portraits the two women had hung in their minds: Her mother was thinking of the swaddled baby she'd carried into the old house, first day home from the hospital. And Becca was fondly remembering the nights they'd spent in the same old house, after the family had moved out, laughing and getting tipsy on the booze they'd all tried to pretend was not the most vile thing they'd ever tasted.

No one person ever saw another as they really were—it took a variety of images from a cluster of loved ones to finally get the complete picture. To understand who someone had been. Some of the memories were true, and some were distortions, some complete fiction—but that, Serena knew, was all part of getting the full picture. The two portraits Becca and her mother carried were a good start.

Serena watched the two slowly trudge between the white stones to bring handfuls of her favorite lilies to place beside her marker. They squatted, the downward curve of their shoulders showing how heavy a task it was. How much they wished the three of them could all be somewhere else—together.

It was hard to look at the weight they carried—even now, months later. She turned her attention upward, slightly, toward her own tombstone.

Her initials, *SS*, had been engraved at the top. Now, as Serena stared, she swore the matching pair of letters looked like a set of bookends. There wasn't much space between them—just as there weren't many chapters filling the space between the beginning and end of her life.

Serena sent a breeze down to tickle the backs of the women's necks. *It's me, and I love you, and when you remember me, you bring me back. Don't you know that? Don't you feel me here with you? There's not enough space between my bookends for bad stories. Fill it with all the good.*

When the women stood, Serena blew another breeze—a harder one this time, almost like a tap to the shoulder—that made Becca turn her head up. She wiped a couple of silvery tear tracks from her cheeks. "Hey, look at that," she said, pointing. "That cloud looks like two *S*'s."

Serena's mother sniffed as she glanced up at a pure white puff and the patch of blue sky shining out in the midst of the dark gray underbellies of surrounding clouds. "It does," she agreed. Her own tears trailed away as her face spread into an awkward, almost apologetic smile. She draped an arm across Becca's shoulder, and Becca shaded her eyes to get a better look.

After a while, they lowered their heads. Mrs. Sims brushed a stray green leaf from the top of the headstone, and Becca reached down to straighten the bouquet that Serena's breeze had tilted, as though a well-manicured grave showed the depth of how much they had cared—and still cared, even now. Slowly, they headed back for Mrs. Sims's car. Their shoulders, Serena noted with pleasure, were not quite as round as before.

As quickly as the S-shaped cloud had formed, it began to dissipate. It didn't change shape, and it didn't roll away. It simply, quietly, dissolved.

Acknowledgments

As I sat down to draft *Feral*, I had a mental outline of where the story and its main characters would take me. But when Claire and I crossed the city limits of the fictionalized city of Peculiar, neither of us could have anticipated where our journey together would ultimately lead. Writing this book has been a wild, surprising ride.

Thanks to:

My incredible editor, Karen Chaplin, who encouraged me to think about *Feral* in an entirely different light. Thanks for asking the hard questions, for unabashedly honest critiques, and for pushing me to take this book to a new level.

My agent, Deborah Warren, for her enthusiasm and her positive energy.

Copy editors Veronica Ambrose and Bethany Reis for ensuring the tiniest details helped make *Feral* come alive.

The entire talented crew at HarperCollins, for such a great cover, and for giving *Feral* a home.

Team Schindler—my exceptional first reader, photographer, and biggest fans.

My fabulous readers and bloggers, for always making long hours at the computer screen worthwhile.